MW01221715

AMBASSADOR

Assignments

AMBASSADOR
Assignments

CANADIAN DIPLOMATS REFLECT ON
OUR PLACE IN THE WORLD

Edited by
David Chalmer Reece

Fitzhenry & Whiteside

Fitzhenry and Whiteside Limited
195 Allstate Parkway
Markham, Ontario L3R 4T8

www.fitzhenry.ca

In the United States:
311 Washington Street,
Brighton, Massachusetts 02135

godwit@fitzhenry.ca

Fitzhenry & Whiteside acknowledges with thanks the Canada Council for the Arts, and the Ontario Arts Council for their support of our publishing program. We acknowledge the financial support of the Government of Canada through the Book Publishing Industry Development Program (BPIDP) for our publishing activities.

 Canada Council
for the Arts
Conseil des Arts
du Canada

 ONTARIO ARTS COUNCIL
CONSEIL DES ARTS DE L'ONTARIO

Library and Archives Canada Cataloguing in Publication
Ambassador assignments: Canadian diplomats reflect on our place in the world/edited by David C. Reece.

ISBN 1-55041-074-1

1. Diplomatic and consular service, Canadian. 2. Canada—Foreign relations—1945–. 3. Diplomats—Canada. I. Reece, David, 1926-

FC242.A64 2006   327.71'009045   C2006-902907-5

United States Cataloguing-in-Publication Data
Reece, David, 1926-
Ambassador assignments: Canadian diplomats reflect on our place in the world/
David Chalmers Reece.
[256] p.: cm.
Summary: A picture of the Canadian foreign service in the present era. The essays cover a wide sweep of geography and of the duties and achievements of the service to Canadians and the world.
ISBN 1-55041-074-1
1. Diplomatic and consular service, Canadian. 2. Canada—Foreign relations—1945-. 3. Diplomats—Canada. I. Title.
327.71/009/045 dc22   FC242.R44 2006

Cover design by David Drummond
Interior design by Darrell McCalla
Printed and bound in Canada

1 3 5 7 9 10 8 6 4 2

CONTENTS

INTRODUCTION

From Greenland to South Africa, Cuba to Indonesia, and Washington to Beijing, Canadian ambassadors bring influence to bear on our world. While key elements of their duties are to assist Canadians wherever they are and to develop opportunities for Canadian foreign trade and investment, they also promote development in many host countries and thus contribute to the improvement of living conditions for their people. This collection of memoirs offers a window on the part played by Canadian diplomats in Canada's role in world affairs. Diverse and interesting stories of Canadian ambassadors and foreign policy in the present era are recounted. Several include historical background to the diplomatic missions, thus providing a better understanding of how the complicated political arenas work and what role the Canadian ambassador plays.

The theme of constant effort to provide enhanced opportunities for both Canadians and people in the host countries is woven throughout this book. We see ambassadors working trade and politics to apply diplomacy in the effort to lessen human suffering as well as make economic gains. Nineteen different accounts (trois essais sont en français) of dedicated service to Canadians and the world at large are described by the individual ambassadors with clarity, insight, and humour. Faced with interesting challenges, they were successful in dealing with difficult situations, many of which reflect on present international situations.

The authors were heads of mission, meaning they were ambassadors in foreign countries, and high commissioners in Commonwealth countries. Most had more than one posting in that capacity, and had previous experience in diplomatic work abroad and in Ottawa as External Affairs officers. These accounts recall vividly their experience in head of mission assignments in every part of the world, and give specific examples of Canadian relations with other countries and international organizations. The collection covers a wide sweep: Europe, Asia, the United States and the Americas, Africa, the Caribbean, the UN and NATO, and the Vatican. The essays demonstrate the variety of Canadian interests abroad: consular, cultural, political, trade and investment, aid, immigration, security and peacekeeping, and participation in international organizations and conferences. Canadian policy operations and mechanics in the flowing river of foreign policy are fully illustrated, including the important and sometimes difficult relations between Ottawa and the Canadian embassies in their work with their assigned country's governments.

Chief Justice Roy McMurtry recounts his time as high commissioner in London, England in a time when the Canada-United Kingdom relationship had altered dramatically. The Canadian position against apartheid in South Africa strained relations, and Canada's preoccupation with the United States, intensified interest in strengthening relationships with other European countries such as Germany and France, and the importance of Canadian trade with Japan, made representing Canadian interests in Britain a challenging task.

Derek Burney describes his role as our ambassador in Washington in the time of free trade, protectionism, and acid rain. He speaks of the political ploys, relationships, and strategies used to represent Canada's interests with the world's most powerful country.

The influence of the Roman Catholic Church is significant in Canada and many other countries. E.P. Black describes his experiences with the Vatican, and also gives some historical background as to how and why diplomatic relations between Canada and the Holy See were developed.

Assignments in many countries were not only diplomatic challenges but at times involved physical threats and nervous moments. Jack Maybee, present when Communist forces invaded China, tells of the ways and means of carrying on under life-threatening situations. While listening to machine gun and rifle fire, classified documents are burned in the pit normally reserved for cooking meat for socials, and a watch is organized to prevent looters from pillaging their food stores as the usual diplomatic role is suspended.

Efforts to use economic contacts to promote and improve human rights in post-1989 China are narrated with reflective thoughts by Fred Bild. Rampant corruption, human rights abuses, and diplomatic after-shocks of the military oppression demonstrated in Tian'anmen Square made for a complicated working environment.

Ambassadors Lee and Middleton, appointed to South Africa, found themselves called upon to perform the reverse of the traditional ambassador's duties. Their difficult mandate in representing Canada was not strictly to promote friendly relations with the then South African government, other than in a narrow legal sense, but rather to make clear that Canada sympathized with and supported the views of the opposition, both black and white.

One frequent feature of envoy responsibility is dual accreditation. The ambassador and his or her staff are often accredited to one or more countries and governments in addition to the one where the embassy is located. This means regular visits to other countries to meet leaders and senior officials and to further Canadian interests including trade and the shared gains from the often present Canadian aid programme. Another regular function is official entertaining to provide increased opportunities for personal relations with senior government personnel and other diplomats who can be helpful as sources of information and judgment. The ambassador must also perform, sometimes frequently, the very important task of arranging and participating in visits by Canadian ministers, officials and journalists to the embassy country or the dual accreditation. Participation by the spouses of diplomats in many aspects of the posting is not often mentioned but its significance cannot be measured. Derek Burney acknowledges this in his account, and I would like to take this opportunity to recognize the contributions of my wife Nina who received a medal from Pope John Paul II for her efforts in raising funds from abroad for health and education in Zambia (during our posting/accreditation there).

Regrettably, two of the authors who contributed essays to this book have recently died – John Stiles and E.P. Black. They were talented colleagues in the foreign service, and will be sadly missed.

David Chalmer Reece, Wilton, 2007

WASHINGTON YEARS

by Derek Burney

I arrived in Washington in January 1989 believing many of the absolutes that most Canadians hold about the United States and our bilateral relations. I learned very quickly that those absolutes needed adjustment, and that my views had enormous scope for enrichment. I had a lot to learn. But the experience was as enervating as it was satisfying, and here are some of the reasons why.

Four Momentous Years

My four-year tour coincided with the single four-year term of President George Bush. The initial highlight was the opening of our new embassy in May 1989 on Pennsylvania Avenue – a powerful, even majestic, symbol of our presence in Washington and of Canada's significance to the United

Ambassador Burney with Prime Minister Mulroney and Secretary of State James Baker at the opening of the new Canadian Embassy building in Washington

States. The embassy quickly became a magnet for attention in Washington and a showcase for much of the best of Canada in the heart of American democracy. We used it representationally and functionally to bolster all of our diplomatic activity – to feature Canadian artists and artworks, to support medical research and charities, and to attract a network of contacts from all branches of the American government.

If the embassy serves as a symbol of our relationship, the leaders of our respective governments set the tone for the relationship. During my time as ambassador, I was fortunate in that the personal relationship between President Bush and Prime Minister Mulroney was open, direct, and very positive. The frequency, the scope, and the quality of their contact were unprecedented. All of that made the diplomat's principal task – initiating or improving access – more immediately achievable. It allowed more direct and, I believe, more productive access to senior channels in the White House and to major government departments. This political partnership at the top gave Canada special relevance and influence in Washington at a time when the world witnessed the most dramatic changes since the second World War: the collapse of the Berlin Wall, the reunification of Germany, the implosion of the Soviet Union and the Warsaw Pact, in short, the end of the Cold War and the dawn of a new and still evolving era of global diplomacy.

These four short but momentous years were the ones during which I had the privilege of being in a catbird seat – a time when relations between Canada and the United States reached a high point in terms of dialogue and achievement. Intimate deliberations at Kennebunkport immediately followed Iraq's invasion of Kuwait, and more of the same took place in the lead-up to and conduct of the Gulf War. The failed coup in Moscow prompted similar exchanges in Washington and Ottawa. The leaders of our respective governments were grappling with extraordinary events, searching candidly and on highly personal political terms for prescriptions for solidarity and stability. Preparations for the G-7 Summits, in which I served as the prime minister's personal representative from 1990 through 1992, added a broader dimension to the network and the evolving consensus. A wary overture to Moscow from Houston was followed by an explicit invitation – first to Gorbachev, then to Yeltsin – to attend in London and Munich respectively. These meetings, more than any other event, signalled the end of the Cold War and were, for me, the high point of global diplomacy – occasions where the ideals and values we share with Americans helped us both respond to the challenges of the new era.

Ambassador Derek Burney and U.S. President Bush, 1989

Perhaps the most satisfying piece of bilateral business was the conclusion of the Acid Rain accord in March 1991. This accord had been an objective for successive Canadian governments for more than a decade. It was a major theme of our prime minister's speech to Congress in April 1988 and a key part of my own message to President Bush when I presented my credentials in February 1989. Thanks to the president, the congressional leadership, and to Canadian perseverance, we met that objective. What had for too long been a serious irritant in our joint stewardship of the North American continent was resolved ably and successfully. Persistence paid dividends, which went beyond cleaner air for North America. Cooperative efforts were forthcoming on environmental issues generally and invigorated the spirit of one of the oldest agreements between us – the Boundary Waters Act of 1909. Success does breed success in diplomacy and failure can never be considered absolute. It was not always easy. When the government of Canada, through our embassy, opposed oil drilling in the Alaska Wildlife Refuge because it would threaten the calving grounds of North American caribou, the U.S. Department of Energy took umbrage and barred its officials from accepting embassy hospitality. (In short, there was no free lunch!) After an abstemious interval, and to the relief of Canadian oil and gas exporters, the ban was quietly ignored. Meanwhile, Congress voted against the oil drilling.

A major success story was the achievement of full partnership status in NAFTA (North American Free Trade Agreement) and seeing those negotiations through to completion. In such an agreement, our preference was to be part of the central hub, not at one end of a spoke, but few realize to this day that Canada's involvement was anything but assured. The Mexicans wanted quick agreement with the United States. The Bush administration and many powerful congressional leaders – notably from states close to Mexico – wanted the same, and for more reasons than trade. Neither craved Canadian involvement and in Ottawa itself attitudes were divided. The aftermath of the FTA (Free Trade Agreement) and a looming recession did little to whet the government's appetite for "another free trade negotiation." Furthermore, by the time the Canadian government chose to be involved, preparations in Mexico and Washington were already underway. Both capitals feared Canada would simply complicate or delay the process. We made our case for inclusion quietly but firmly at all levels in Washington and to key Mexican officials. The prime minister spoke directly to both presidents. We contended that the most sensible objective for exporters in all three countries, and the most beneficial goal as well, was to extend the Canada-U.S. FTA to Mexico. That argument, and a little Canadian charm – something we seldom trumpet – eventually prevailed. In fact, Canada's role ultimately proved catalytic to such a degree that the successful outcome even managed in 1993 to convert the newly-elected Canadian government which, on the other side of the House, had opposed both the FTA and NAFTA. A side benefit of this negotiating process was the catapulting of Canada-Mexico relations onto a higher level of contact, dialogue, and cooperation. We saw first-hand the advantage of working together, an experience that, I believe, heightened Canada's awareness of and attention to the hemisphere as a whole. Perhaps we had viewed the hemisphere simplistically as an American preserve. Whatever the reason, for too long we had sacrificed significant relations in our own neighbourhood for more distant pursuits. The change was welcome all around.

Those were the high points. There were, however, bumps along the road and moments of sharp discord. How could it be otherwise in a relationship as broad and deep as that between Canada and the United States? Obviously, the sluggish economy in the early 1990s made a major part of the embassy's task tougher and meant some of the actions on trade were less satisfying than they might have been. It was not the best of times to be implementing a free trade agreement, let alone negotiating a new one. As the record will show, the FTA, too, was obliged to carry a lot of baggage and blame in Canada, much of which had little to do with provisions of the agreement. But scapegoats and logic often travel on separate paths in the cut and thrust of democratic politics.

In the United States, the recession of 1990-91 ignited virulent strains of protectionism. In Canada, fears of a recession fuelled free trade phobia. The politics of expediency and the politics of fear were mutually reinforcing. The Bank of Canada's massive assault on inflation, necessitated by the fiscal profligacy of the 1970s and 1980s, only compounded the problem, virtually choking the productive and export capacity of many Canadian enterprises just as they were striving to adjust to the liberalizing features of free trade and the imperatives of globalization. The dispute settlement provisions of the agreement, including the "extraordinary" elements, were pushed to the limit.

In time, however, the dividends, in terms of export growth and productivity gains, exceeded all initial expectations. Exports from Canada to the United States have increased 150 percent since the implementation of the agreement (from $92 billion to $229 billion) and the growth has been particularly significant in sectors where tariffs were reduced and ultimately eliminated. Also notable is the fact that, in the same period, Canadian exports more than doubled to both Japan and the European Union. Significantly, Canada has become less dependent on the export of resources as knowledge-based sectors have dramatically increased sales to the United States and elsewhere. Firms have restructured successfully to capture new global opportunities, to become more specialized within a more global economy, and to be less dependent on the small, domestic market.

The boom in bilateral trade was, for years, the single bright light in Canada's economy. In policy terms, the success of the FTA helped stimulate not only the NAFTA with Mexico but also the evolution of trade remedy rules and disciplines under the aegis of the WTO (World Trade Organization). Perceptions inevitably focus more on disputes than on trade statistics, and, during my time in Washington, we had some nasty ones – on lumber (as always), beer, pork, autos, and fish – some of which were as unnecessary as they were unwelcome. It is obvious that we could never win an all-out slugfest with the United States over trade – or anything else – where sheer power could overwhelm principle. That is why we need rules impartially adjudicated. That is also why, for Canada, the efficacy of the dispute settlement regime was the essential pillar – and the singular achievement – of the FTA. That these provisions were extended to the NAFTA and mirrored in the WTO is Canada's best compliment as well as our best guarantee of unfettered market access on a broader plane. What is even more salutary is that some of the FTA's harshest critics became, in government, among its most fervent champions.

The constitutional uncertainty in Canada, flowing first from the failure of the Meech Lake agreement and then from the defeat of the Charlottetown accord, furnished more unwelcome baggage for Canada's Washington representative. When one is trying to confidently assert or defend Canadian interests, a fractious, inconclusive debate on the home front can be distracting if not disillusioning. Fortunately, the American attention span for issues affecting the Canadian constitution was minimal. If anything, Americans were as puzzled as Canadians seemed exhausted by the ordeal. Fortunately, the scope for mischief-making by would-be sovereigntists was negligible during my time in the most powerful political capital in the world.

Lessons Learned

In all of this the most important lesson I learned was that responsibility centres were more elusive in Washington than anywhere else I had served – including Ottawa! It was not simply because the system of government is different and the branches are indeed separate. That is what we know from textbooks. What is paramount is that "all politics are local" and, for every issue, there is a different constellation of power brokers and decision makers. Whether it is softwood lumber or cross-border garbage, meat inspection or fishing licences, water quality or air pollution, the constituency for each in America is different and the support mechanisms for these constituencies are also different. To make matters more challenging, there is virtually no "Canadian" constituency or coalition in the United States to which we can turn for support. Once you determine who is responsible or who has a stake in a given issue you need to marshall your best explanation as to why and how the result Canada prefers is in their interest as well. Goodwill and a sense of neighbourliness may get you in the door but you need more than a smile and a maple leaf to register your point. It is retail politics every day and, as diplomats, we were both buyers and sellers in the hectic Washington bazaar, with the added handicap of being non-American. A good political chemistry at the very top can help, and it often did, but there are no guarantees that even the White House can prevail over special and local interests. As I was told more than once, "After all, Mr. Ambassador, Canadians don't vote here."

My second lesson flows from the first. What was once taboo in Washington – direct representations to Congress – had become an essential part of the ambassadorial agenda. This was, in fact, a more time-consuming part of my schedule than representations to the administration. Often it was needed to contain or forestall problems, rather than resolve them, thereby following one unwritten rule of Congress: it is always easier to prevent than to undo. I was fortunate to have a highly committed and professional cadre of congressional liaison officers in the embassy who knew exactly whom we needed to meet, when, and with what message. This was the product of careful research and careful nurturing of congressional staff – a feature of diplomacy unique to Washington. Some years ago one of my distinguished predecessors had been instructed by Ottawa to make such a representation to a very influential senator. My predecessor resisted, on grounds of tradition and precedent. He was overruled. (That can happen even to ambassadors!) When he reluctantly, but loyally, called and made his case to the senator, his concern was resolved by a single phone call. The senator was Lyndon Johnson who, it is probably fair to say, could do more with a telephone than most generals can do with an army. It was, nonetheless, the only call on Congress that Canadian ambassador ever made. Times and diplomacy have changed.

Public diplomacy was a key part of doing business in Washington. Calls on Congress, speeches, media interviews, statements, and fact sheets articulating Canadian positions or concerns – all were part of the ambassador's repertoire in Washington used to explain, persuade, rebut. You have to choose your spot, select your target, and make your point clearly and concisely without giving offence but often by stretching the norm in terms of diplomacy and tact. It is Washington, after all. (It also helps immensely when your facts are airtight.) Fundamentally, diplomats are in Washington to put their country on the American radar screen. I experienced a good-news/bad-news moment on that front. During the World Series in Atlanta – one of the years the Blue Jays won, I hasten to add – our flag was flown upside down before a massive television audience. We tried to play it down, but the U.S. Marine Corps was seriously embarrassed. One message from Canada put it in perspective: "Tell 'em stem down, eh!"

If America's richness stems from its people, Washington is a veritable treasure trove. Undoubtedly the most fascinating and stimulating part of my assignment, and probably the element from that life that I miss most, was meeting people – real characters, men and women with views and influence, opinionated and interested people who know how and why decisions are taken, and where the bodies are buried, the citizenry of Powertown, USA. After all, the power of personal relationships is the hallmark of effective diplomacy in Washington or anywhere else. It does not come automatically with the title. With almost two hundred "ambassadors" in Washington, you have to earn your place in the pecking order. Quite literally you have to feed it, water it, and nurture it, and my waistline was a good measure of my total commitment! In my experience, a lot of candour, a little humour, and a tendency to speak directly worked best. I was also fortunate to have the full support of my wife who was a remarkable asset throughout my assignment. She had her own high level network and earned deserved tributes for the friendships she cultivated and for her activities in support of Arena Stage, the Washington Performing Arts Society, and local charities like the Columbia Lighthouse for the Blind. On many occasions, I served simply as a front man for her and for a first class embassy staff who supported Canadian interests and me unstintingly. Knowing that what they did was actually relevant to genuine Canadian interests was the best motivator of all. I was merely the beneficiary.

The Paradox of Proximity

When we began consultations in Canada on trade policy in the early 1980s – a process that led eventually to the free trade negotiations – a constant refrain then was "you have to start by getting relations right with the United States." Those being consulted did not necessarily define what would make things "right," though there was clear agreement that improvement was needed. Getting things right with the United States is a perennial pursuit for Canada even though it is an objective that defies tidy definition. I tend to believe that Canadians generally want good relations with the United States. It can be tricky trying to reconcile this sentiment and others similar to it with the realities of the relationship. It is probably an inevitable by-product of the power imbalance between us as well as the countless ties that link us.

America's presence and power can be a bit overwhelming or intimidating, even if unintended. This is a phenomenon felt most acutely by Canadians. I recall Goldie Hawn's answer in the movie *Protocol* when asked if she had visited many foreign countries. "No," she replied, "I visited Canada but it is not really foreign. It is sort of attached." Being "sort of attached" – and in ways quite different from Mexico – is the paradox of our proximity. We do so many things together, we see, read, and hear so much about America and Americans that we agonize about our own identity. We labour to define or measure ourselves as being different simply to reinforce for ourselves our status as a distinct North American entity. The fact that most Americans are oblivious to all this Canadian angst and somewhat puzzled when we try to explain it doesn't help.

I usually used humour to try to explain it sensibly to Americans. For one thing, I would suggest that Americans think the best compliment they can give is to say "you're just like us" whereas, for Canadians, the highest form of flattery was to be told "you know, you really are different." Similarly, Americans are proud of what they are – "Americans" – while Canadians are proud of what they are not – "Americans." Then, of course, it is said that Americans believe anything worth doing is worth overdoing, whereas Canadians believe anything worth doing is probably worth a government grant! In the end, it seems that Canadians can be unrestrained in the advice they offer Americans but Americans offering advice to Canadians face a double whammy. If they say anything it may be seen as provocative, and if they say nothing, that can be even more offensive.

In a more serious vein, during my four years in Washington I became keenly aware of the enormously disproportionate nature of the political challenge and risk for a Canadian government that openly asserts the premium it places on having good relations with the United States. There is simply no comparable risk for other governments in Washington nor, I suspect, much appreciation of the conundrum facing Canadians expressing this view. Many countries crave a special relationship with the United States. For some, like Israel, it is automatic. For others, like China, Russia, Germany, Japan and Britain it is obligatory. For the most part, Canadians may recognize the need but refrain from seeing it as a desire. It is probably because we are "sort of attached."

It can be difficult for Canadian leaders to reconcile the need with the underlying hesitancy. And there have been periods when Canadian leaders saw more advantage on the home front from determined aloofness or calculated differentiation than from close engagement. It is not hard to play the differentiation game even if the most conspicuous foil for such happens to be Fidel Castro. Mr. Mulroney chose the opposite tack, benefiting the country in the long term but dearly costing himself politically. After election in 1984, he was determined to refurbish the relationship in ways that he was convinced would serve key Canadian interests. In the principal bilateral areas of trade, environment, and security, the initiatives and actions of his government did precisely that. It also gave him and Canada a rare degree of access and involvement on major global issues.

Cravings for greater distance and differentiation are understandable but points of differentiation need to serve distinct interests to be effective. It is easy to denigrate our relationship with the United States as "too close" as if distance were a virtue in itself. It is more challenging, certainly less popular, to try to justify a foreign policy position that parallels or complements that of our southern neighbour. The significance of a given position should be measured by its ultimate results and by the manner in which it serves Canadian interests. To get results you need the respect of your partners. To be relevant you must be prepared to bolster your position with real commitments. Ultimately, your influence depends on your access and your ability to deliver. You do not get either if you confuse posture with position. The Americans, better than most, know the difference, after all, they can be masters at both! But Canadians should have no hesitation in being different or acting differently provided we hold to that fundamental distinction.

I have never understood what value accrued to Canada – our interests, our relevance, or our influence – from minimizing the degree to which we actually agree, from time to time, with the Americans. We do have shared visions for global peace and prosperity, which offer enormous scope for joint effort. We also share a very long and peaceful border and the largest two-way trade account in the world. On the other hand, I have never shied away from an opportunity to advocate or articulate real differences to Americans in a manner as civil or as emphatic as the occasion required. Such plain speaking, incidentally, was usually more effective when done in private, face-to-face, and beyond the reach of media coverage.

There are definitely differences between us but in all my experience representing Canada to Americans, I was reluctant to define Canada's significance simplistically by an arithmetic yardstick of differentiation. I was much more comfortable defending or explaining a substantive policy difference, domestic or international, on its own merits. I was always mindful of the most important difference of all in diplomacy – that between relevance and irrelevance. There is not much point expounding a difference if it doesn't register. Difference without impact is just that. I had no difficulty explaining the difference between our health care system and that of the United States. I took pride in outlining the difference and often used personal experiences to anchor the point. But I never tried to sell our system to Americans. It was and is a matter for Americans to decide. Most Americans have the best health care money can buy and that seems to be what most Americans prefer. All Canadians do not have to be concerned about the cost of their health care and that is what most Canadians prefer. A clear difference, an honest difference, open to much debate and hyperbole on both sides, but a measure of distinction nonetheless.

Canada has the opportunity, indeed, the luxury, of being among the most respected and trusted nations to try to exercise influence on the United States but we are not alone. On any given day Washington attracts a veritable parade of would-be influencers. The real gauge of our influence will be the quality of our position and the value of our commitment. There is a difference between being a player and a kibitzer on the world stage. We have had experience with both roles in Washington and the choice is essentially ours to make.

The management of this highly complex and vital relationship is not a simple either/or proposition between agreement and disagreement. Nor is there a guarantee that logic or reason will prevail, especially over the politics of expediency or the exercise of raw muscle. We have encountered both in our relationship with the United States, and there were certainly days when greater distance might well have provided a welcome sanctuary. But as the much smaller of the two we have to work harder and smarter to temper the power imbalance. The embassy was in the front line in this effort. Our best defence for Canadian interests was and is a full court press of public diplomacy and the negotiation of better agreements, better rules, bilateral and multilateral, and better methods for dispute settlement.

We can speak frankly to Americans about themselves and ourselves, more so, I suspect, than many others. That is an advantage that can serve Canadian interests, both domestic and global, if we choose to use it. With the right political will and a coincidence of interests we can do exceptional things together. We have demonstrated tangibly the power and some of the dividends of our proximity. I believe we can reap even greater advantages from a sense of genuine partnership while maintaining a healthy awareness of being different. I had the privilege of working toward that objective during four years in Washington. Many times I stated publicly, and with obvious bias, that it was "the best job in the Canadian foreign service." On most days, it was exactly that.

REMINISCENCES OF A HIGH COMMISSIONER TO THE UNITED KINGDOM: 1985-1988

by Chief Justice Roy McMurtry

C anada's first high commissioner to the United Kingdom was appointed in 1880 as a result of prolonged pressure by the Canadian Government to establish a more formal relationship with the Mother Country, which would involve independent representation in Britain. There was considerable resistance from the British Government who argued, "that the Queen could not appoint an ambassador to herself." The official Canadian Government position was that while Canada "could not as an integral portion of the Empire maintain relations of a strictly diplomatic character ... [the government] wanted the Canadian representative to have a status in every way worthy of his important function." The title of High Commissioner was reluctantly agreed to by the British Government and evolved into the one given to ambassadors of every Commonwealth country.

The first two Canadian high commissioners in London, Sir Alexander Galt and Sir Charles Tupper, were Fathers of Confederation and members of Sir John A. Macdonald's cabinet. My predecessors also include two former premiers of Ontario, Howard Ferguson and George Drew. The former actually resigned as premier of Ontario to accept the appointment from Prime Minister R.B. Bennett in 1930. My own appointment as Canada's eighteenth high commissioner followed a more unusual route to London than that of my predecessors. When I was appointed high commissioner to the U.K. in February of 1985 by Prime Minister Mulroney, I had been the attorney-general for Ontario for almost ten years. I had also just been an unsuccessful candidate for the leadership of the Progressive Conservative Party in Ontario. Had I won that bid, it would have made me the premier of Ontario at that time. At a dinner in my honour shortly after the appointment, a friend commented upon the circumstances of my appointment by offering a new definition of high commissioner: "A high commissioner is someone who is denied a job by his political colleagues but who is given employment by the prime minister on the condition that he leave the country."

The offer of the appointment by Prime Minister Mulroney came as a complete surprise. I had never even considered living outside of Canada at that particular time in my working life. However, the prime minister thought that my experience in government and my personal relationships with senior members of governments throughout Canada would enable me to effectively carry out my responsibilities in the United Kingdom. In the months that followed, I also became aware of the sensitivity of political appointments to senior diplomatic posts given Canada's highly professional career foreign service. However, the great majority of Canadian high commissioners in London have been from outside the ranks of the public service and, not surprisingly, I personally believe that there are sound policy reasons for this tradition. Nevertheless, I also believe that the tradition of political appointments should continue to be limited, if Canada is to maintain the necessary competence and level of morale in our foreign service which is so highly respected internationally.

My experience as a high commissioner made me conscious of the widespread lack of knowledge regarding the role of ambassadors in the modern age. Indeed, there appears to be very little awareness of the varied and extensive responsibilities of Canada's diplomatic corps. The realities of modern communication and information technology often tend to divert attention from the importance of having representation on the ground, as it were, if Canada's interests are to be adequately served and supported.[*]

In any event, I had a great deal to learn about my new responsibilities before I arrived in London in April 1985. There were a number of days of briefings in Ottawa dealing with the broad parameters of the political and economic relationship with Britain, the central importance of London as an international centre of commerce, our immigration policy, the Commonwealth Secretariat, and the many other activities carried on by our high commission in London in support of Canadian interests. I was, of course, well aware of the very extensive and close relationship between Canada and Britain created by the forces of a shared history, family ties, and our many political, legal, and cultural inheritances from Britain. When one added the many ongoing government, professional, business, military, and educational contacts, Canada's relationship with the United Kingdom was closer than that with any other country, with the exception of the United States. However, I soon became aware that traditional and sentimental ties had to be set against the recognition of considerable changes marked by Britain's rapidly increasing role in Europe. As well, our own preoccupation with the United States, our interest in strengthening our relationship with other European countries, particularly the Federal Republic of Germany and France, and the importance of Canadian trade with Japan, had altered the Canada-U.K. relationship.

My Ottawa briefings reminded me that Canada was now a less significant priority for Britain than many of her lesser European Community partners. It was pointed out to me, for example, that because of Europe's consensual approach to political co-operation, Britain in 1985 needed Greece's "vote" more often than Canada's. Foreign Minister Joe Clark's initial lengthy letter of instructions to Canada's new high commissioner stressed the following aspects of my responsibilities:

> *Under your management and leadership, I expect the post to adapt to these conditions as well as to exploit the longstanding historical, cultural and corporate links between the two countries in order to achieve our objectives. In this effort I cannot stress too strongly the importance of your own contacts with British decision-makers at the highest possible level. Nor can I impress upon you too strongly the importance of your participation in the activities of all post programs.*

My briefings and instructions also stressed that Britain's position as a major economic power and one of our summit powers required that my officers and I take a particular interest in the British approach to the full range of global political and economic issues, as well as promoting Canadian views in these areas. I was also urged to pay particular attention to Commonwealth affairs and to maintain close personal contact with the Commonwealth Secretary-General. Commonwealth affairs did in fact become a personal priority, but at the same time there were very different views as to the importance of the Commonwealth within the senior ranks of Canada's Department of External Affairs. Canada's involvement in the Commonwealth was sometimes described as a 'soft option' as compared with the 'hard options' of Canadian involvement in G7 summits, NATO and the United Nations. The less enthusiastic supporters of the Commonwealth within External Affairs actually mirrored many of the attitudes I came to encounter in the British government.

In 1985 the United Kingdom was Canada's third largest trading partner and by a significant margin Canada's leading market in Europe. Britain was and perhaps still is our second largest source of foreign capital and, after the United States, the most important destination for Canadian investment abroad. As British investment was a major source of investment in Canada it was important for me to emphasize in London that the creation of Investment Canada marked a new attitude to foreign investment in Canada. The new Investment Canada Act, which took the place of the former Foreign Investment Review Agency (FIRA), did create a significant change of perception in Britain in relation to Canada's attitude to foreign investment. When I moved to London I quickly became aware of how negative perceptions are enormously magnified as they cross the Atlantic. Given the long historical and commercial relationship, I was surprised to learn that the majority of the leaders of British business and industry actually knew very little about Canada. The creation of FIRA also created a strong belief in British business circles that foreign investment was very much unwelcome in Canada. One of my priorities as high commissioner was therefore to deliver the message that Canada was truly "open for business." In a report to Joe Clark three months after my arrival in London, however, I wrote:

> The general message that Canada is open for business will now require a greater degree of focusing and specific targeting. The communications strategy will therefore be crucial. As I travel through the "City," the psychology of investment is often of greater importance than the detailed analysis that one could expect from "hard headed" businessmen who are often influenced by simple "gut reactions." We are still regarded by most potential investors as an "afterthought" in relation to the U.S. We will have to deliver a much stronger message as to the advantages which Canada presents, including issues related to "quality of life."

My schedule on arriving in London in April 1985 was to be a very busy one as Prime Minister Mulroney was to arrive two weeks later for his first official visit. It was therefore necessary for me to meet a number of senior British officials before that time. In the view of my fellow ambassadors, I was beginning my diplomatic career at "the deep end," given the visit of my prime minister so soon after my own arrival.

Several days after my arrival, I spent a day at the British Foreign Office preparing for Prime Minister Mulroney's visit. I met first with Baroness Young, deputy to Foreign Minister Sir Geoffrey Howe and the government's foreign affairs spokesperson in the House of Lords. We enjoyed a cordial chat about Canadian-British relations, embracing everything from the twinning of cities to sporting links. Her most interesting observation was that because Canada was such a friendly and close British ally, our country did not get the attention in Whitehall that was afforded much less important but "troublesome" nations in South America and elsewhere. I also met all of the senior civil servants in the Commonwealth and Foreign Office who had any responsibilities that might touch on Canadian interests. All of the British officials professed to be delighted by what they perceived as a strengthened relationship between Canada and the United States, which they believed would benefit Britain. My day of meetings at the F.C.O. (Foreign and Commonwealth Office) ended with a lengthy conversation with the Foreign Minister Sir Geoffrey Howe who was very congenial, relaxed and low key. We agreed that the only significant bilateral irritant at this time appeared to be the European ban related to the Canadian seal hunt. The issues of defence procurement and technology transfer were discussed at some length. Both nations were anxious to maintain a balance between exports and imports in the defence field. Sir Geoffrey was of the view that joint ventures and co-operation in defence research were the wave of the future. He spoke of the concern of British industry regarding the transfer of their technology without something in return. My visit also included a rather special note of welcome and informality. Two women who worked in the Canadian section greeted me, smiling, wearing campaign buttons from my political leadership campaign in Ontario several months earlier.

My first week in London also brought me into contact with the Duke of Edinburgh and Marlborough House, the home of the Commonwealth Secretariat. There was a reception hosted by the Commonwealth Secretary-General, Sir Shridath "Sonny" Ramphal, for the purpose of raising funds for several World War veterans living in poverty, particularly in South Asia. Prince Philip was the principal speaker. After his remarks, he responded to questions from the members of the media who were present. The London Press had been preoccupied for some days with revelations about the Nazi past of the father of Princess Michael who was married to a cousin of the Queen. The first question was directed to that subject which, of course, had nothing to do with the plight of Commonwealth war veterans. Prince Philip was clearly irritated and responded, "Are you kidding, who are you anyway?" The journalist replied simply that he represented an American publication and Prince Philip replied, "Is that the only reason that you came? Your question is totally irrelevant as to why we are here." A senior officer accompanying the Duke of Edinburgh turned to me and stated, "High Commissioner, that fellow took a naval broadside and was never heard of again."

During my second week in London, I had my first official visit with Prime Minister Thatcher. Having followed the "Iron Lady's" career, I was interested to discover that Mrs. Thatcher appeared much younger and more attractive than she appeared in newspaper photos and on television. I soon learned that she was someone who could use both a formidable demeanour and femininity with equal effectiveness. She was clearly pleased that Mr. Trudeau had been replaced by a conservative prime minister, and had obviously followed the recent Canadian election campaign closely. As I reported back to External Affairs, Mrs. Thatcher was optimistic that Canada-U.S. relations would improve under Prime Minister Mulroney and that this would benefit the United Kingdom. "She looked forward," I reported, to "greater like-mindedness among Canada-U.K.-U.S.A. heads of government at summits in place of what she referred to as the Trudeau-Mitterand axis." Our conversation covered a number of political issues with an emphasis on the upcoming Bonn Summit. Notwithstanding a British unemployment rate of approximately 13 percent, Mrs. Thatcher's priority was to keep the Summit leaders focused on the need for continued caution and restraint in macro-economic policy to prevent a resurgence of inflationary pressures. She was also clearly troubled by the American deficit and its impact on British and European interest rates.

During my initial meeting, I learned of certain personal attitudes that characterized her approach to many issues and personal relationships. Firstly, she was clearly skeptical of multilateral institutions, whether they were Summit Seven meetings, the United Nations or the Commonwealth, which she often referred to as "talking shops." She clearly preferred a bilateral approach to many international issues. In relation to the Bonn Summit, which was only two months away, she told me that 90 percent of the final communiqué had already been written, which, she stated, recognized the reality that there would be little in-depth discussion between the leaders of the industrial world. Secondly, while she obviously enjoyed vigorous and "no-holds barred" debates on policy issues, she was very sensitive to any behaviour or conduct which could be interpreted as a personal slight. For example, I learned during our first meeting that her antipathy towards the "Trudeau-Mitterand axis" was as much fuelled by what she regarded as their rudeness in conversing in French in her presence, as by any policy differences between her and "those leftist leaders." In contemplating the Bonn Summit, she obviously was still very irritated by an incident that had occurred at the last summit involving the French translation of the final communiqué. Apparently she had had to rather aggressively persuade Mr. Mitterand and Mr. Trudeau to support President Reagan's wish to include a reference in the communiqué to an American space programme. The reference was included in the English version but, according to Mrs. Thatcher, a Trudeau-Mitterand conspiracy led to its exclusion from the French translation. Throughout much of our conversation, Mrs. Thatcher's pro-U.S. bias was clearly evident, notwithstanding her opposition to the size of the American deficit and her skepticism about President Reagan's Star Wars initiative. Nevertheless, despite her skepticism, she was anxious for British participation because of her concern about the future prospects of young British scientists.

My first very modest diplomatic triumph was also achieved during my initial visit with Prime Minister Thatcher. Her officials had told us that it would be impossible for Mrs. Thatcher to come to Canada House during Prime Minister Mulroney's first official visit. However, much to the dismay of her private secretary, I was able to persuade Mrs. Thatcher to come to a Canada House reception. The visit apparently involved some rescheduling of what the secretary regarded as more important meetings. Her Canada House visit the next week did in fact create a further minor diplomatic incident. Contrary to the instructions of Mrs. Thatcher's security people, Prime Minister Mulroney met her outside of Canada House where a media scrum prevented Mrs. Thatcher from entering the building for a few minutes. In the opinion of her security advisers, the impromptu meeting outside made her more vulnerable to a potential assassin.

On April 30, 1985 Prime Ministers Mulroney and Thatcher had their first official meeting at 10 Downing Street. (They had met informally in Moscow six weeks earlier at the funeral of President Chernyenko.) I reported to Ottawa that the meeting was "characterized by palpable warmth and cordiality." The meeting lasted more than half an hour longer than planned and touched on a wide range of subjects. In relation to the upcoming Bonn Summit, Mrs. Thatcher expressed her concern that the leaders on their arrival would encounter a communiqué that was "all but complete." At the same time, Mrs. Thatcher realized that if there was not extensive prior discussion most of the leaders' time would be spent "haggling over words." Nevertheless, she regarded the process of extensive prior negotiations as inhibiting a spontaneous discussion. (The control of public spending and the reduction of protectionism would be major themes at Bonn and generally the discussions would be quite predictable.) Both prime ministers were clearly sensitive about their own public's perceptions of their relationship with President Reagan. They felt that the domestic media had been excessively unfair, the British media often referring to Mrs. Thatcher as "Reagan's poodle" and the Canadian media to Mr. Mulroney as the "lackey of Reagan." At the same time they agreed that the United States could be a difficult ally, sometimes arrogant, and often failing to adequately consult with their closest allies. Mrs. Thatcher was highly irritated by the embarrassment of not being informed in advance of the Grenada invasion; Prime Minister Mulroney was still upset by Secretary Weinberger's remarks at the Quebec summit, made without prior consultation, that the United States wished to place anti-cruise weapons in Canada. There was agreement that the large American deficit was an obstacle for international economic growth because of the high interest rates it generated, and that American trade barriers were a problem. During discussion about the American SDI (Strategic Defence Initiative) or Star Wars initiative, it was suggested that a number of European countries were concerned by President Reagan's announced intentions to "make the world safe from nuclear weapons," as this ran directly counter to NATO's fundamental position which depended on nuclear weapons to deter the possibility of a conventional Soviet attack on western Europe. The subject of South Africa did not come up in the April 1985 meeting, however within a year it was to become the source of considerable tension between Canada and the United Kingdom.

My first meeting with the Queen took place the same day that the Mulroneys left London. The first meeting between a new high commissioner and the Queen is a much less formal affair than when a non-Commonwealth ambassador presents his or her credentials to Her Majesty. In the latter case, the ambassador travels to Buckingham Palace in a horse-drawn carriage and has a brief, formal encounter, not involving any substantial conversation. High commissioners are denied the horse and carriage transportation to Buckingham Palace but are treated to a more relaxed meeting with the Queen.

The question "What is the difference between a high commissioner and an ambassador?" is often asked of a high commissioner. The simple answer is that there is no difference with respect to their responsibilities. Both are the senior representatives of their countries and both serve their countries' interests in the host country with traditional ambassadorial duties. In Britain, however, high commissioners and ambassadors are segregated at formal diplomatic receptions, sometimes causing confusion in the ranks of visiting heads of state. I overheard the most interesting but perhaps somewhat paternalistic response to the question of distinctions at a reception for the King of Saudi Arabia at Windsor Castle. As the King entered the salon occupied by the high commissioners, he questioned why the ambassadors were in one room and the high commissioners in another. The British official accompanying him replied very simply, "The ambassadors are our friends and the high commissioners are family."

The first official visit of my wife and myself with the Queen was indeed more familial than formal. It was far more personal than the very brief meetings given to non-Commonwealth ambassadors presenting credentials. The Queen chatted about a number of Canadian matters, displaying a considerable knowledge of current Canadian issues. Our conversation ranged from political issues – including her surprise over Bill Davis's retirement as premier of Ontario – to our family. My wife volunteered that as happy as we were to be in London, we would miss our six children. When the Queen learned that our eldest daughter lived in Regina, however, she volunteered that we might as well be in London, given the distance between Toronto and Regina! At this meeting, the Queen made a specific request to her new high commissioner regarding a totem pole displayed in Great Windsor Park. The government and people of British Columbia had given as a gift to the Queen a Haida-carved totem pole to mark the centennial of the province's entry into confederation. It had deteriorated somewhat in recent years, and the Queen thought the damage was a result of acid rain. I enthusiastically volunteered to speak to British Columbia premier Bill Bennett to resolve the problem. A few weeks later, two Haida carvers, one a son of the original carver, arrived at Great Windsor Park. Not long thereafter the totem pole was returned to its original beauty and the Queen attended a little ceremony at the site to thank the carvers. The totem pole problem was a modest example of the huge variety of undertakings for an ambassador. On any given day, they might range from being called to a very early morning visit with Canadian exporters at the London Billingsgate fish market, to a meeting at 10 Downing Street.

I had many other official visits with Her Majesty during my three and a half years in London. Some were very brief where a little small talk was exchanged during formal public events. More serious discussions occurred during which the Queen was often surprisingly frank and did not avoid controversial subjects. It was obvious on a few occasions that she expected me to deliver a message to Prime Minister Mulroney about some issue that was of particular concern to her. While by no means a major part of our years in London, royal occasions were always interesting. The British talent for pomp is world famous, and events at Buckingham Palace or during the Queen's official birthday were magnificently staged. While often reminiscent of a world that no longer exists and viewed as an anachronism by many, the monarchy remains central to British culture. The past decade has, of course, been very challenging for the royal family, and has contained more than one *annus horribilis*. Nevertheless, the institution continues to demonstrate an enormous resilience and adaptability. However, while it is appropriate for the queen to pay taxes and give the public greater access to Buckingham Palace, I don't expect that the Queen or her successor will be seen bicycling around London.

The Queen and her family were always gracious both as hosts and guests. When they visited our residence they were always willing to respond to requests to pay particular attention to one or more of our guests who, for some reason, may have been facing a personal problem or tragedy. They were also generous with their time in attending functions in the United Kingdom that were of importance to Canadians. The Queen Mother was a particularly delightful guest. She had a deep and abiding affection for Canada ever since her 1939 visit, a visit that had a markedly positive impact on Canadian war mobilization. She would often speak of the warmth of the crowds that welcomed her and the King, even though people were allowed to knock on the windows of the royal train late at night. The Queen Mother on occasion reflected on the paternalism of Prime Minister King in his absolute insistence on accompanying Their Majesties to the United States during that same 1939 visit. The Prime Minister's determination to not let the royal couple out of his sight during their American tour appeared to me as a delightful reversal of earlier British insistence on the controlling and shaping of Canadian foreign policy.

It became apparent that the Royal family's advisers actively facilitated its visits to Canada. The Queen, as head of state of Canada and other Commonwealth countries, clearly strengthens Britain's role in the international community. This relationship allows Britain as a middle power to exercise influence in world affairs beyond her economic and military power. While some of this influence is related to the Empire's history, her parliamentary and common law models, and long-term political stability, the monarchy is still an institution that enlarges Britain's international stature. Nevertheless, after three and a half years in Britain, I returned home somewhat ambivalent with respect to the future role of the monarchy in Canada. Certainly the sharing of a queen with Britain does reinforce the colonial attitude towards Canada that still pervades some segments of British society. However, this is probably of little importance so long as the monarchy remains a unifying force in Canada and does not undermine Canada's independent role in world affairs. The general indifference of Canada's francophone citizens to the monarchy and its lack of relevance to many of our fellow citizens from other nations is a matter of concern. These issues may be the subject of more vigorous discussion in the years to come, as is now the case in Australia.

I had assumed that for practical reasons my responsibilities in Britain would focus almost entirely on Canada-U.K. relations and that there would be little time for significant meetings with other ambassadors. I soon learned, however, that London provided a special listening post within the international community and that most countries were represented by senior individuals who were very knowledgeable about important issues related to their own countries. Formal calls on or by other ambassadors were therefore arranged in order to obtain their views on matters of interest to Canada. I found that ambassadors in London were likely to be more candid in their views to a fellow ambassador than in official communications between governments. Ottawa was very interested in these meetings and always provided me with a specific list of topics to discuss.

During the summer of 1985, anti-apartheid protests in South Africa escalated and the South African government's response was brutal. Before a policy of news blackouts was initiated, much of the violence was reported on international television. Prime Minister Mulroney became increasingly disturbed by what he witnessed, and the battle against the apartheid regime soon became one of his government's foreign policy priorities. The Canadian response towards South Africa not only became a significant irritant in our relations with the United Kingdom but also threatened the future of the Commonwealth. The British public appeared to be quite ambivalent at best and was often even openly hostile towards the Commonwealth as an institution. Regrettably, every society harbours the virus of racism and Britain is certainly no exception. Since the Second World War, significant racial tensions have been exposed in the presence of a growing non-white population in the United Kingdom. The conflict has occasionally escalated into serious violence such as the Brixton riots which occurred shortly before my London posting. The changing face of Britain has not been well received in many segments of society, and the changes have often been blamed on Britain's role in the Commonwealth. The generous immigration policy that for many years applied to member nations became very controversial, evidenced in Enoch Powell's infamous "rivers of blood" speech in 1968.

During my years in London the most racist institution I observed was the tabloid press. Indeed, the former leader of the Labour Party, Neil Kinnock, advised me that, unfortunately, any real understanding of British society required a familiarity with the tabloid newspapers. The obvious racist tone of the tabloids invariably turned negatively towards the Commonwealth. At the same time the tabloids generally supported politically the Conservative Party. This combination of factors weakened in my view the government's commitment to pursue initiatives related to racial harmony.

The anti-Commonwealth stance, however, was by no means confined to the tabloid press. The editorial policy of the so-called reputable broad sheet presses, with the exception of *The Guardian*, was also generally anti-Commonwealth. I recall a particularly scurrilous piece written about the Commonwealth Secretary-General Sir Shridath "Sonny" Ramphal which appeared in the *Sunday Telegraph*. I wrote a letter to the editors criticizing the article and this led to a rude exchange between the Canadian high commissioner and a *Sunday Telegraph* editor several weeks later at a dinner party.

The British business establishment generally favoured the apartheid *status quo* in South Africa. In fairness, the leaders of the business community generally recognized the despicable nature of the apartheid regime, but they did not appear to believe that any meaningful change could be made short of a violent revolution. In view of the significant British investment in South Africa and the fact that a million white South Africans held British passports, the prospect of a bloody civil war was clearly unacceptable.

An apocalyptic vision of the ending of apartheid was shared by both the British and American governments. Sir Geoffrey Howe, the British foreign secretary, advised me "in confidence" of these views, as this assessment was never expressed publicly by either government. Nevertheless, this so-called "realistic assessment" clearly influenced their rather timid response to apartheid.

Chief Justice Roy McMurtry

Canada's leadership within the Commonwealth during the early Mulroney years was a major factor in strengthening the resolve in the fight against apartheid. At the same time, Britain became more and more isolated within the Commonwealth. This did not particularly disturb Mrs. Thatcher as Britain's isolation within a generally unpopular Commonwealth probably strengthened her political position. To many Britons, the Commonwealth's aggressive stance towards South Africa was hypocritical given the lamentable human rights records of some Commonwealth countries. A common refrain in the United Kingdom was that the blacks in South Africa were better off than the majority of blacks elsewhere in Africa. It was appalling to me that the collective conscience of Britain would not be more shocked in view of the fact that the "mad scientists" of apartheid were members of a white minority whose roots were largely in Europe.

Mrs. Thatcher often spoke of the ANC "terrorists" and would refuse to meet with any representative of the African National Congress. She opposed sanctions against South Africa on the grounds that she was not going to "create black unemployment in South Africa which in turn would create unemployment in Britain." While there have always been persuasive arguments for and against the effectiveness of economic sanctions, there nevertheless appeared to me to be a disturbing level of insensitivity within the ranks of the British government in relation to this issue.

The Commonwealth Heads of Government established a committee, made up of the high commissioners in London, to monitor the evolving situation in South Africa. Shortly after my arrival in London, I was invited to chair the committee. My role as chair did not endear me to Prime Minister Thatcher as the committee frequently issued statements critical of the British government, with only the British Foreign Office representatives on the Committee dissenting.

The most imaginative Commonwealth initiative during my London years was the creation of the so-called Eminent Persons Group (EPG) at the Commonwealth Heads of Government Meeting (CHOGM) in Nassau in 1985. The EPG, representing Britain, Canada, Australia, India, Nigeria, Zambia, Zimbabwe and Barbados, was created with a mandate to visit South Africa and report on their findings to the Commonwealth Secretary-General. Somewhat surprisingly, the South African government agreed to the visit, which led to direct discussions between the EPG and the South African cabinet as well as many other organizations and individuals. Prime Minister Mulroney provided a Canadian aircraft to facilitate the group's travel in Southern Africa.

Mrs. Thatcher appointed a former Conservative Chancellor of the Exchequer, Lord Barber, as the British EPG member. She clearly intended Lord Barber to keep the process "on the rails" in the sense of "not rocking the boat," insofar as the British government was concerned. Lord Barber was to become a major disappointment to her, as he signed the EPG's scathing report, which recommended stronger international initiatives against South Africa. He later told me that the EPG report had made him a "non-person" in the eyes of Mrs. Thatcher.

The EPG visited many leaders of the South African black community; one visit with Nelson Mandela in prison was particularly impressive. During a subsequent meeting with the South African cabinet Lord Barber told President de Botha and his colleagues that he had met "the true man of peace ... Nelson Mandela and that it was most unfortunate that the South African government was continuing to keep him in prison." Lord Barber also recounted to me the almost surreal scene of Canada's EPG representative, Archbishop Ted Scott, lecturing the purportedly religiously devout Dutch Reform cabinet ministers on the proper interpretation of biblical texts that had been distorted by apartheid's many religious adherents. The South African cabinet had agreed to a second meeting with the EPG. However, President de Botha apparently became very apprehensive about the international coverage being given the visit and the nature of the evolving dialogue between the EPG and his cabinet. The result was that the South African Air Force was ordered to bomb the areas in Lusaka, Zambia where the ANC were believed to be headquartered. The dialogue between the EPG and the South African cabinet was thereby effectively ended.

The unanimous report issued by the EPG recommended an increase in the level of international sanctions against South Africa. The British government refused to accept the recommendation and Britain became further isolated within the Commonwealth. Several high commissioners in London spoke to me about the possibility of moving the Commonwealth secretariat from London to Ottawa to protest the intransigence of the British government in the fight against apartheid. This was not encouraged in any manner by the Canadian government, given the historical role of Britain in the Commonwealth and the crucial leadership of the Queen as its head. In any event, the pressure placed upon Her Majesty's government by her Commonwealth partners was clearly resented by the supporters of the Thatcher government. I recall attending the foreign policy debate at the autumn 1986 annual conference of the Conservative Party, together with the other invited members of the diplomatic corps. My Commonwealth

Chief Justice Roy McMurtry

*High Commissioner Roy McMurtry chairing a meeting in London
of the Commonwealth Committee on South Africa*

colleagues and I were somewhat shocked by the boos and catcalls that echoed around the meeting hall every time the Commonwealth was mentioned. It was also apparent that the Party faithful attending the meeting only included a handful of non-white faces.

The unpopularity of the Commonwealth at the 1986 Conservative conference was also fuelled by the boycott of the 1986 Edinburgh Commonwealth Games by a number of African and Caribbean countries earlier in the summer. Organizers of the Games had spoken to me earlier in the year, hoping that the assistance of the prime minister of Canada could be obtained in averting the threatened boycott. Prime Minister Mulroney enjoyed a high level of credibility throughout the Commonwealth by reason of his leadership in the fight against apartheid. I had several conversations with him in relation to the development of a strategy. Prime Minister Mulroney and Prime Minister Gandhi of India almost succeeded in averting the boycott. They developed a statement for Mrs. Thatcher that would have emphasized her opposition to the apartheid regime in South Africa without committing her to any additional specific initiatives. The statement by her would probably have averted the boycott, but Prime Minister Thatcher refused to co-operate. Her intransigence did not enhance her declining political popularity in Scotland where many thousands of people had served as volunteers before and during the Commonwealth Games. The role of the Commonwealth in the ultimately successful struggle against apartheid was perhaps "its finest hour." The importance of Canada's role was recognized by Nelson Mandela when he visited Canada shortly after his release from prison. The challenge, however, remains to ensure that the Commonwealth continues to be a relevant institution as we prepare for the millennium. Given the degree of ambivalence towards the Commonwealth in Britain, Canada, Australia and New Zealand, the leadership role of Canada will become increasingly important if the institution is to survive in a meaningful form.

A high commissioner in London is always faced with a number of irritants related to trade that have to be suitably managed. In my experience, they ranged from Canadian import taxes on English tea bags to defence procurements. During my tenure, Canada's announced intention to acquire nuclear-powered submarines became a very sensitive issue as Britain was competing with France for this very major defence contract. In such circumstances the British government expected the Canadian high commissioner to assist the local submarine industry by ensuring a fair hearing by the decision-makers in Ottawa.

During this period, Lucien Bouchard was Canada's ambassador to France. Lucien and I exchanged visits and I soon became aware of his passionate commitment to the Canada-France relationship. In fact, he made it clear to Ottawa that if Canada were to choose the British Trident submarine over the French product, that France-Canada relations would be irreparably damaged. Prime Minister Thatcher, not surprisingly, also conveyed her own very strong views to Prime Minister Mulroney. Despite the many millions of dollars that were spent by the British and French competitors, the Canadian government, faced with ferocious competition between two close allies and growing domestic opposition, decided to abandon the project.

During my years as high commissioner, Northern Ireland was also a priority for me. My own Irish ancestry and the many family links between Ulster and Ontario undoubtedly contributed to my interest in searching for Canadian initiatives that might contribute to the process of reconciliation between the two communities in Northern Ireland. Queen's University in Belfast was a centre for Canadian Studies in Britain, and therefore closely linked to the Canadian Studies program of the High Commission.

The development of Canadian Studies courses at various British universities was an important undertaking of the High Commission in London. The program does much to strengthen the relationship between the two countries by promoting academic partnerships, teaching, research, and publications about Canada in the United Kingdom. It has also long been recognized that international Canadian Studies initiatives can have an important economic spin-off as knowledge of Canada expands.

My first official visit to Northern Ireland took place shortly after Prime Minister Thatcher endorsed the Anglo-Irish agreement of 1985. The agreement provided a formal mechanism for a consultative role for the government of the Republic of Ireland in the governing of Northern Ireland. The object of the agreement was to provide a forum for discussion and, hopefully, the means for resolving a host of issues important to both Catholic and Protestant communities in Ulster. It emphasized greater police cooperation between the Irish Republic and Northern Ireland in the fight against terrorism, and the monitoring of human rights issues in relation to the Catholic minority in Ulster. A principal goal of the agreement was to quieten the traditionally strident Irish political lobby in the United States. The activities of the Irish-American lobby also produced substantial funding for the IRA and their terrorist activities. President Reagan persuaded Mrs. Thatcher that the funding would decline significantly if the mainly Catholic Irish-American citizens were satisfied that there was a process to respond to the concerns of the Northern Ireland Catholic minority.

The Ulster Unionist politicians were not consulted on the terms of the Anglo-Irish agreement and not surprisingly the Protestant majority became apoplectic when the agreement was announced. In my view, prior consultation would only have served to undermine the negotiations between Britain, the Republic of Ireland, and the United States. The Canadian government strongly supported the agreement and I had a role to play in making its support more generally known in Northern Ireland. Upon my arrival in Ulster, a dinner was held in my honour at Hillsboro Castle, an elegant stately home outside of Belfast where members of the Royal Family, senior government ministers, and ambassadors are lodged. For security reasons, the identity of an official guest was never revealed in advance, even to the other guests who were carefully chosen from the Protestant and Catholic communities. In any event, a false rumour circulated that the official guest was a dignitary from Dublin. An angry mob gathered outside the gates before the dinner, and several automobiles of guests were damaged, although fortunately no one was injured. (The angry protesters were identified as supporters of the Reverend Ian Paisley.) My dinner speech emphasized the support of the Canadian government for the Anglo-Irish agreement, and the Protestants present clearly did not greet my remarks with any enthusiasm. As a Protestant of Irish descent, it would not be the only time that I would be disappointed by many Protestant political, professional, and business leaders in Northern Ireland. They simply failed to provide the leadership towards the social and political reconciliation that the challenge demanded. The sad reality has been that too many successful professional and business persons in both communities have avoided becoming involved in such processes, allowing the political and public forums to be dominated by the reactionaries, bigots, and demagogues on both sides. One hopes that the Good Friday Agreement of 1998, followed by the horrific tragedy of Omagh, will serve to remind all the citizens of Northern Ireland of their individual responsibilities.

My interest in Northern Ireland led me to consider many proposals for a continuing Canadian contribution to the peace process. One proposal brought about the involvement of the Canadian Labour Congress under the leadership of Shirley Carr who was prepared to engage in a dialogue with the Irish Trade Unions Congress in Dublin. The latter group curiously represented the labour union movement in both the Republic and Northern Ireland. This initiative took me to Dublin where the Canadian Ambassador, Dennis McDermott, was Shirley Carr's predecessor as President of the Canadian Labour Congress. McDermott arranged a meeting between the Irish Trade Unions leaders and me. Dennis was somewhat bemused by the fact that a former Conservative politician would be anxious to work with the union movement. Unfortunately the Irish union leaders were reluctant to associate themselves with any reconciliation initiatives in Northern Ireland. For them it was challenging enough to maintain the trade union headquarters in Dublin without taking any initiatives that might fracture the sensitive and fragile relationship between Protestant and Catholic unionists in Northern Ireland. In another proposal, I recommended to Minister Joe Clark that Canada open a commercial office in Belfast in order to strengthen the positive ties between Canada and Northern Ireland and enhance economic partnerships on both sides of the Atlantic. Unfortunately the timing here too was inappropriate as External Affairs was being asked by the Treasury Board to close existing embassies and consulates in Europe and elsewhere.

One of my visits to Northern Ireland took place two days after the IRA bombing atrocity in Enniskillen, Northern Ireland in November 1987. Eleven people were killed, including a young nurse by the name of Marie Wilson. A day after the bombing her father Gordon gave a most courageous

Chief Justice Roy McMurtry

and remarkable media interview where he described holding his daughter's hand in the wreckage and talking to her before she died shortly after the bomb blast. Notwithstanding the emotional trauma and horror that he had experienced, Gordon Wilson pleaded for forgiveness and reconciliation. His remarks had a strong emotional impact in Northern Ireland and appeared to provide some real momentum for reconciliation in both communities. The day after Mr. Wilson's media conference, I had breakfast with Tom King, the secretary of state for Northern Ireland in Mrs. Thatcher's government. We discussed how Canada and other countries might perpetuate the spirit of Gordon Wilson's plea for reconciliation. Later that day I announced that several young people, both Catholic and Protestant, would be brought to Canada every year in memory of Marie Wilson to work together in the spirit of reconciliation. In May 1988, I traveled with King to Enniskillen to announce the young people who had been chosen to come to Canada that summer. The choices had been made after many applicants had been extensively interviewed. The summer of 1998 was the eleventh anniversary of the Marie Wilson Voyage for Hope. Each year, three young people from each community in Enniskillen, committed to the principle of reconciliation, have come to work together with disadvantaged children in Ontario. Sadly, all of the participants to date have told me that there would be little opportunity for them to become friends in Enniskillen. The Marie Wilson Voyage for Hope is a very modest initiative but we are hopeful that it has made at least a tiny contribution to the process of reconciliation in Enniskillen. As I stated at the formal inauguration of the programme in May 1988, "I hope that the experience these young people will have in Canada will provide them with something that will be useful in their participation in cross-community relations when they return." My own experiences in Northern Ireland were simply illustrative of the many, often unexpected, roles that can be performed by those who are privileged to be official representatives of Canada in the international community.

A sequel to my activities in Northern Ireland was a request by the governments of Britain and the Republic of Ireland in the spring of 1991 that I chair the political discussions in Northern Ireland scheduled that summer. I had just become the associate chief justice of the High Court in Ontario, but readily agreed to what I knew could be a most challenging assignment. However, the Reverend Ian Paisley stated that his political party would boycott the discussions if I were the Chair. Some fifteen years earlier, as attorney-general for Ontario, I had made an uncomplimentary reference to Mr. Paisley which had received considerable media attention in Ulster. Once again I was reminded of the long memories that are very much a part of the Irish culture. In any event, the Reverend Mr. Paisley was able to continue to frustrate the process in 1991 after a former Australian governor-general agreed to act as the chair.

One of my final social engagements before returning to Canada at the end of the summer of 1988 was to act as the honorary chair for the first time at a dinner of the Canada Club. This Club is essentially a British institution that was founded more than 175 years ago by British businessmen who had commercial relations with pre-Confederation Canada. It was a memorable event as up to the summer of 1988 I had boycotted the dinners because of the club's refusal to admit women as members, or even allow women to attend its events. (My only female predecessor as Canadian high commissioner in London had chaired the dinner as an "honorary male.") I had also instructed members of the high commission staff that they should not attend any Canada Club dinners until the policy changed. Needless to say my stance was much criticized in certain circles, but three years after my arrival in London the constitution of the Canada Club was changed and women have been made welcome as members and guests ever since.

This brief overview of some of the highlights of my role as a high commissioner cannot adequately recognize the dedication and commitment of the many men and women who assisted me in London, but it is because of them and people like them that Canada has been well served by her diplomats. The contribution of our Foreign Service has always made Canada a respected participant in international forums. I am grateful for the opportunity to have been involved in this service, however briefly.

REVOLUTION IN CHINA; TROUBLES IN LEBANON

by Jack Maybee

D iplomacy can be practiced under many different circumstances, including the state of war. The breakdown of law and order – or the threat of
it – in the capital city can compel a shift in an embassy's priorities. The
focus narrows to the safety of Canadian citizens, including mission staff
members and their families. I experienced this situation twice in my diplomatic life abroad – first, as a junior officer in Nanking, China in 1949, and
again as ambassador to Lebanon in 1967. I was posted to Nanking in the
fall of 1947, not long after the transfer of the capital from Chungking.
Some apprehension of the troubles to come began in November 1948, and
had an immediate and fairly drastic effect on the embassy's operations. Law
and order did not disappear until April 1949, and then only over a course
of three days. An extended period followed when there was a diminishing
risk of bodily harm, but during this time, the Nanking embassy's functions
were severely limited.

Hostilities between Chiang Kai-shek's Nationalist government and the
Communists began in 1927 and continued intermittently from that time.
The Japanese invasion of China in 1937 interrupted the conflict. Following
the defeat of the Japanese, the American government in 1946 sent General
Marshall to China to mediate between the two groups, but the effort failed
and hostilities resumed. The Nationalist efforts to regain control in
Manchuria and north China in 1948 failed, and the Communists began
moving south on a wide front. I wrote to a friend on October 16, 1948:

> *It's certainly a very peculiar civil war. What takes a lot of getting
> used to out here is that the logic of events is not the same as any-
> where else in the world. Given a certain set of circumstances, you
> can draw conclusions that seem almost foolproof, only to find that
> you have completely missed the mark. Climaxes seem to approach
> with relentless certainty, only somehow to dissolve into nothingness.*

Tension mounts, disaster threatens, and then suddenly everything begins to relax and the firecracker fizzles out. If there is anything mysterious about the East, that's it.

In November 1948, the Communist forces closed in on the critical centre Xuzhou (Suchou), about three hundred kilometres northwest of Nanking. Clearly, if that Nationalist stronghold fell, Communist forces would be in a position to move south to the north shore of the Yangtze River near Nanking. On November 10, 1948, the Canadian embassy reported to Ottawa that there were 843 Canadian citizens in China – 150 in North China, 358 in the Nanking-Shanghai area (the great majority in Shanghai), 201 in West China and 134 in South China. Those in West China – mostly missionaries – had been advised to withdraw in January 1948; few decided to do so. On November 11 further warnings were given to Canadians in the Peiping-Tientsin area and in the Nanking-Shanghai area.

At a meeting of the diplomatic corps in early November, heads of mission were informed that the Chinese foreign ministry was requesting all foreign missions to move their dependents out as soon as possible. Food was scarce and likely to become scarcer, and the coal situation was becoming acute. Our own ambassador, the Honourable T.C. Davis, acted promptly on this recommendation. In mid-November his own wife, the military attaché's wife (who was one of the Canadian secretaries) and my wife and son departed promptly for Shanghai, en route to Canada, and the second Canadian female staff member was ordered home. The wife and daughters of the counsellor, Chester Ronning, left very shortly afterward.

The departure for Canada of the ambassador's secretary and the counsellor's secretary – both experienced members of the Department of External Affairs – had an immediate and rather drastic effect on the work of the embassy. Very few support staff remained. The military attaché's sergeant, Warren Smith, was still with us, but he was fully occupied in work for the colonel. The administrative officer had left some weeks before the crisis and his replacement had not yet arrived. Ambassador Davis was a reasonably able hunt-and-peck typist, so he typed first drafts of his reports and I, a touch typist since my student days, usually produced final versions. We had a very able Chinese secretary, Tessie Wong, who could handle the unclassified material but there was no one to do the classified secretarial work or – more importantly – the filing of classified material. I worked at that rather fitfully but could not keep up with the accumulation.

The Chinese government's call to foreign residents to leave China was clearly based on its expectation of soon losing the battle for Xuzhou. The Communist armies would be able to move down to the north shore of the Yangtze River. The Nationalist government was preparing to move its seat south to Canton. In mid-January the Chinese ambassador in Ottawa requested the Canadian government to instruct its ambassador to accompany the Nationalist government to Canton if it was compelled to leave Nanking. The authorities in Ottawa, like most other governments with diplomatic missions in China, did not decide immediately to comply with this request, owing to the possibility that the Nationalist government might simply fall apart. In case the move did turn out to be desirable, the government decided to maintain a consular office in Nanking. Counsellor Chester Ronning and I were given consular status as consul and vice-consul respectively. As a further measure to afford protection for Canadians remaining in the Nanking-Shanghai area, the Canadian government ordered the frigate HMCS *Crescent* to proceed to the Far East.

Radio news reports in late November indicated that the Communists had broken through south of Xuzhou and were advancing rapidly towards Pengpu, a town about 280 kilometres north-west of Nanking. Rumours flashed around the city with amazing rapidity. What was told to me in strictest confidence one evening was repeated to me as the talk of the town by my Chinese teacher the following morning. By November 23 the peace rumours of the previous week had gone into limbo; they were followed by further indications that the capital was going to move to Canton. This was vigorously denied, and the latest report was that Nanking would be declared an open city.

The general uneasiness in the city was aggravated by some practical problems. The city's electrical supply was becoming increasingly unreliable. Power was available in middle of the day when electric lighting was not required, but about 4:00 p.m. when the light was failing, the power went off. It came on again about 7:30 or 8:00 p.m. and went out again shortly after midnight. In addition we had a local heating problem: every now and then the hot air vents in the chancery emitted great clouds of coal gas. We had to open the doors and windows, making the place pretty chilly. The repair team was having difficulty tracking the cause of this trouble.

On December 3, 1948 the Nationalist government gave all civil servants in Nanking two months' pay and certificates to their families for free transportation to their homes, though the civil servants themselves could not leave the city on pain of death. One of the main streets leading out of the city was packed with escaping dependents, all of whom for some reason were being searched at the North Gate as they left. In early January, an American press correspondent managed to spend a week or so in Communist-held territory north of Pengpu, about two hundred kilometres from Nanking. Although his movements were restricted he was well treated. He reported that the morale of the Communist forces was very high, though they did not expect to be in Nanking for some time yet. A couple of weeks later – January 20 – the government line was reported to be no more than about 50 kilometres north of Nanking. On January 20 the Nationalist government requested that the Canadian ambassador accompany the government when it expected to move to Canton in the near future.

In the absence of the normal embassy support staff, we had rather unusual procedures for turning out reports to Ottawa about the situation in China generally and Nanking in particular. Instead of having the first draft of a communication prepared at a junior level, and then amended by more senior and experienced hands prior to the ambassador's signature, Mr. Davis would hammer out a draft and then pass it down the line for comments and corrections. I often had the first go at the ambassadorial draft, and after I had made my amendments, it was passed on to the military attaché and the counsellor. A conference session often completed the job.

In December 1948 the foreign ministry informed us that the Nationalists had captured a Canadian by the name of Elliott. He had been trying to cross into Communist territory up in Ninghsia where he was suspected of espionage. We were told that he was in Lanchow and would be brought down to Nanking in due course, when we would be notified of his arrival. (Dealing with the problems of individual Canadians was an occasional rather than a regular activity in Nanking.) Early in January the embassy received a letter from Elliott – delivered by an unknown hand – saying that he was jailed in Nanking and please would we help to get him out. We telephoned the Foreign Ministry who promised faithfully to look into the matter and see about his possible release. When we visited the Ministry later the same day they had done nothing. They weren't even sure what jail Elliot was in. Chester Ronning began looking for the most likely jail. He finally found it and got to see Elliot, who seemed to be in fairly good shape. He had no complaints about his food. Although he reported the prison fare lousy, he was incarcerated with some former government employees who shared the good food brought daily by their families. We persuaded the authorities to parole him to the embassy.

In late January the Communist armies were reported to be within about 25 kilometres of Pukou, the town just across the Yangtze River from Nanking. The Ambassador said that when he was visiting the British naval ship in harbour he saw dozens of *sampan* (small boats) ferrying soldiers from Pukou across the river to Nanking. He said that later the streets were filled with these soldiers, evidently being evacuated from the other side of the river. This was a good sign in the sense that if, as seemed likely, the Communist forces were to cross the river soon, there would not be a long interval between the departure of the Nationalists and the arrival of the Communist troops. Working conditions at this point were not ideal. In a letter dated January 25 I wrote:

> *The routine has been particularly heavy the last few days, or perhaps I might say the last three weeks. Since the beginning of the month we have averaged a telegram a day, most of them cyphers which involve my work from the earliest stages, sometimes down to delivering the thing to the telegraph office. I enjoy the early stages, when we sit around and discuss and argue, but it sometimes get a bit grim when you find yourself still working or cyphering at ten at night.*

Though resolution of the military standoff seemed imminent in January 1949, the state of suspense was to continue for nearly three more months. Government units continued to move to Canton. The ambassador received instructions to remain in Nanking and most of the other ambassadors also stayed on. British and Australian naval ships began to come regularly up the Yangtze River to Nanking, to give encouragement to Commonwealth residents. This placed a certain obligation on the embassies to provide some entertainment for the ship's company, and the Canadian embassy was regularly involved in this.

Every few weeks there was a scare, with rumours circulating that invasion by Communist forces was in the offing. Expectations of artillery sent thousands of people streaming out of the city, and cases of looting were reported. Then everything would calm down for a while. The local food market was rather limited in these uncertain times and the ambassador arranged for additional supplies to be brought in. An RAF plane came in from Shanghai on February 17; I was assigned to meet it and pick up the embassy's supplies which consisted of 200 lbs. of flour, 200 lbs. of sugar, 50 lbs. of tea, a case of olives, cans of salad oil and a side of bacon.

Our revised pattern of working arrangements in the embassy office had a beneficial effect on my particular situation, which I recorded in a letter of February 20, 1949:

I have found out one trick of adjusting to TC's [the ambassador's] ways that has made a considerable difference to the amount I have been able to contribute to the political reporting that goes home from here. The trick is simply to be around at the right time. When all the girls were here I used to work busily away in my own office; I never got assigned a dispatch by TC, and not very often got a finger in the political reporting, except in the monthly report. Since the girls went away I have been doing quite a bit more of my work in the main office, with beneficial results. Whenever Mr. Davis comes in from seeing Dr. Stuart [US ambassador] or Sir Ralph Stevenson [British ambassador] or one of the Chinese top dogs, if I'm on the spot, I'm able to find out what transpired. It's a great advantage to be in the know that way, and can only be gained by happening to be there at the right time. Then again, TC writes a great many of his dispatches in the main office, and for some time has been in the habit of passing them on for me and Chester to look at. For a long time I was very diffident about making comments or corrections, until one time the hash was so bad I couldn't resist the temptation to really do the job all over. To my surprise the ambassador liked it, and he has now got in the habit of just pouring forth his ideas in a rough draft and then passing it to me, saying "Here, fix this up for the bag." I don't fool when I fix now, and he doesn't seem to mind, even when I insert liberal portions of my own invention. I usually check the thing with Chester, and then if there are points where we don't agree with TC we take the thing in to him and argue it out. I think it's a good system, as we all have a chance to contribute our notions, and TC is wonderful in the way he will listen to and often accept ideas which he doesn't have much truck with at the start.

There was another unusual feature to office work in the chancery, which I recorded in a letter of February 22, 1949:

After a late dinner I came back to the office to work on a dispatch for today's bag. When I switched on my light, there, sitting on my shelves in the cupboard was a rat. We gazed solemnly at one another for a few minutes, while I began wondering what instrument in the room would be best for dispatching the creature. I knew if I left the room my quarry would disappear and I would lose him. I finally decided on the steel bar that locks my filing cabinet. As I was getting it, the rat made a run, got himself cornered behind the cabinet, and then began a merry chase. I found his hole was through the cold air intake under the window and I reckoned if I could keep him away from that I should be able to get him sooner or later. I bounded around the room after him for quite a time, sometimes losing track of him for a few minutes, but managing to prevent him from escaping. I then called the Sikh guard who was in the building to give me a hand. We worked out several stratagems, but the creature was usually just too fast for us. One time he jumped accidentally into the wastebasket, and I nearly had him, but he managed to leap out again. Finally after the hunt got pretty hot, he made a dash for his hole, and in doing so had to pass behind the wastebasket, which I had placed in front of it. I was well positioned and was able with a swift kick to pin him with the basket, and thus brought his career to an end. I felt pleased, as the beast had been gnawing the backs off a number of books in my office. It was certainly a merry chase, and I was amazed to discover afterwards that I had been at it for nearly half an hour.

At the end of February 1949 I endeavoured to assess dispassionately the possibility of my family returning to China. I summed up my forecast of what would happen:

Some time between tomorrow and next October or November the control of Nanking may pass from the government to the Communists; then, from the time when this begins until the new lot get control, there will be a period of great uncertainty, including possible rioting, looting, disease and food shortage; and that following such a period, and the takeover, there will be a fairly long period when life in Nanking will be relatively safe, but hedged about with a number of inconveniences which may arise out of the shortage of supplies which normally come from abroad.

A few days later all of us at the embassy became heavily involved in preparations for the visit of HMCS *Crescent* which had arrived in Shanghai on February 23 and was due to take its turn after the British and Australian ships to go up to Nanking for a ten days' visit. I went down to Shanghai by train and came back on board the *Crescent* – a pleasant adventure for me as an ex-naval officer. We stopped at anchor overnight on March 10 and arrived after an uneventful trip on March 11 late in the afternoon. The embassy staff then began twelve days of strenuous activity to ensure that the ship's companies were well entertained during their stay in Nanking. I was involved daily in taking groups of sailors on sightseeing expeditions and feeding them lunch or accompanying them to lunches elsewhere. The relief ship, HMS *Consort*, arrived on March 23, and the *Crescent* left an hour later, taking the ambassador and Mrs. Davis with them to Shanghai. The ambassador returned on April 8 bringing with him, to my delight, Jim Staines, the new administrative officer. There were strong rumours that day that the Communists had delivered to the Nationalist government an ultimatum, laying down the terms of a peace settlement. Failure to accept it would bring the Red armies across the river within a very short space of time.

Each Sunday morning about a dozen members of various embassies used to go on a hiking expedition outside the city, driving some distance by car, and then walking for a couple of hours. On April 18 the group went to the Temple of the Thousand Buddhas. From the top of the mountain behind the temple we had a fine view of the Yangtze River as it flows down from Nanking, turns around close to the bottom of the hill where we stood, and runs on towards Shanghai. As we stood on the top we could hear occasional bursts of machine gun fire from the far side of the river. The river was rising steadily and in a few more weeks would be swift and dangerous. It was clear that the Communist forces would probably cross the river soon.

On April 20 we learned that the British frigate *Amethyst* which had been coming up to Nanking to relieve HMS *Consort* had been grounded and badly damaged in a gun battle with the Communists. About twenty crew members had been killed and a number of others injured. There were reports that Communist forces had crossed the river some 130 kilometers above Nanking. Two days later it appeared that the Nationalist government was leaving the city. We could hear planes going through the night and on into the day. Colonel Clifford and I spent an hour or so destroying classified documents at an outdoor barbecue pit in the area between the office and the residences in the embassy compound. We could hear the sounds of battle across the river as we worked, and later that night we could see gun flashes.

The next morning, April 23, I learned when I got up that the Nationalist troops and police were leaving the city and that looting had started. Apparently it was good-natured looting, carried out in something of a carnival spirit and not at all what it might have been had the city been surrounded for a few weeks as we had expected. Before nightfall our servants told us that the small colony of hut-dwellers just across the street from our compound were planning to raid the embassy storehouse where some of our food supplies were kept. When it began to get dark we parked two of the embassy cars at the top of the hill, facing downwards so that we could switch on the car lights and illuminate the gate at the bottom of the hill and the approaches to the storehouse. We established a duty watch roster for Ronning, Clifford, Staines, and myself to turn up the car radios and switch on the car lights from time to time. The precautions worked, and we were not raided. During the night, someone put a torch to the railway station, which produced a spectacular fire and inspired a Canadian newspaper to run the headline, "Nanking in Flames" – a disturbing sight to our families back home. We had some anxious moments ourselves during the day on April 23. From our hill we could see looters pulling other places apart and hear the crack of rifle fire as a hastily organized people's protective corps tried to stop the looting. For three days this sort of thing went on, though Saturday was by all odds the worst. We just steered clear of the looting areas and hoped the looters and the people shooting at them would stay away from us. Luckily they did.

On Sunday morning, April 24, the Communist troops entered the city. They were tough-looking, well-equipped troops; it was not hard to see why they won the battles. In the course of the day we drove into the city to deliver some telegrams to the telegraph office and had a fairly good look at the soldiery. They seemed to have good discipline and went directly about their business without troubling the populace. Freddie Clifford and I both sent off messages to our wives –"Takeover complete all well"– which we later learned got through all right in advance of the official report. My wife had the pleasure of informing Arthur Menzies on the China desk in the Department that all was well, before the embassy telegram reached Ottawa.

In the course of the next week we had two visits from Communist Army squads, for both of which I happened to be on duty. One group wanted to get a view from the top of our hill; after their surveillance of the neighbourhood they left with no further requests. The second lot came to ask if we had any arms. We registered Colonel Clifford's pistol, and all was well. They explained that they were here to protect foreigners and Chinese alike and that they were pleased to have us in Nanking as long as we cooperated with them. They said it was all right for us to walk about our immediate district, but if we wished to go any farther, we should go to the police school around the corner and get a chit that we could show to any patrols that stopped us in other parts of the city.

The Communist troops did a number of rather simple things that quickly won them popular support. I was told how a squad of soldiers was halted at a traffic circle where there were a number of food shops. Nationalist troops in that situation would stroll around from shop to shop, helping themselves to anything they wanted without paying. The Communist soldiers just squatted by the curbside and rested, and did not raid any shops – to the astonishment and delight of the shopkeepers. The Communist army units which arrived a few days after the initial invasion often had an entertainment squad – uniformed women who waved colourful banners, athletes who performed stunts, and soldiers who led a simple little dance and invited the spectators to join in. These elementary tactics quickly generated a positive attitude towards the Communist military.

The Communists' takeover of Nanking cut off communication with the outside world and left us isolated from our families, whether they were at home in Canada or just staying in Shanghai. Our work patterns were considerably affected since we could no longer communicate regularly with Ottawa. There was a big backlog of office chores; in particular, the filing system badly needed reorganizing, so we did not stop work by any means.

Although none of us in Nanking doubted that the takeover by the Communists was permanent, we did not have any sense that the war was over. Nanking was targeted for air raids for some weeks: a single plane would fly over the city, not very low, and drop two or three bombs before disappearing. Usually the port area was targeted. We never heard whether much damage was done, but these aerial visits reminded us that the war was not very far away.

The Communist authorities were careful not to treat the embassies as embassies: mail addressed to the Canadian embassy was not delivered. They did, however, treat embassies with reasonable courtesy in the first five months of their occupation. Most of the Canadian staff members left China in the summer and early fall of 1949; on September 30 I left by ship from Shanghai for Hong Kong, and from there got a flight back to Canada.

The People's Republic of China was proclaimed on October 1, 1949. Chester Ronning stayed as chargé d'affaires until 1951. The latter part of his time there was not very agreeable. Canada, among other nations, did not recognize the legitimacy of the People's Republic soon after its proclamation in October 1949. The Korean War in 1950 also found Canada contributing to the UN force defending South Korea from Northern armies, and the latter were strongly supported by Chinese military units. As a consequence, it was not until 1969 that Canada recognized the People's Republic as the government of China and exchanged diplomatic representatives.

The onset of troubles in Beirut in 1967 was more sudden and much briefer than had been the case in Nanking. War fears in the Middle East mounted quickly when Syria, which had been involved in a number of border incidents with Israel, appealed for Egypt's help. The Egyptian government moved troops to its borders with Israel, demanded the withdrawal of a UN peacekeeping force which had been stationed on the Egyptian side of the border since 1956, and on May 22 ordered the closing of the Gulf of Aqaba to Israeli shipping. Other Arab states rallied to Egypt's support and international efforts to defuse the situation were of no avail.

Although Lebanon, an Arab state, shared a border with Israel it was not an active ally. This circumstance exasperated the substantial number of Palestinian refugees in Lebanon – over 186,000 – and many of the Muslim Lebanese as well. Certainly there was apprehension that if war broke out, Lebanon might become involved in one way or another. This concern was further aggravated by reports of a dynamite explosion near the American embassy late on Saturday May 27, causing some damage but no casualties. As a result, guards were placed at the Canadian embassy, the official residence, and some other buildings.

Monday, June 5 started as a normal day. Radio broadcasts late in the morning, however, reported massive Israeli air attacks on Egypt, Syria, and Jordan. We learned later that Israeli troops and tanks had moved into the Sinai Peninsula where in due course they met the advancing UAR forces; also that fighting had broken out around Jerusalem and the Syrian border. These developments posed a host of questions as to how Lebanon might be affected.

On Tuesday morning, June 6 we saw smoke from what appeared to be a spectacular fire to the north of the city. We learned later that it was the Shell Oil refinery. Shortly afterwards my driver arrived at the embassy residence to report that a big demonstration was forming in west Beirut and that it would be unwise to drive to the office. A little later a diplomatic colleague telephoned me. He lived not far from the Canadian chancery in west Beirut and regularly passed it in his car on the way to his own office. That morning he saw a knot of people standing around on the street and he asked his driver to enquire what was happening. The crowd answered that they were waiting to watch the attack on the Canadian embassy. He said to me, "I thought you might like to know."

I called a couple of other people in west Beirut to ask whether they had seen or heard anything of the demonstration. One reported that he had heard there was a parade, which seemed to be heading north towards the Avenue de Paris, the road that ran along the seashore in north-west Beirut. I called the chargé d'affaires at the British embassy, located on that same road just west of the American University of Beirut, and asked him if he had seen anything of a demonstration parade. "Yes," he said, "they're just forming up in front of the chancery now." I got quickly off the line.

I learned later that the demonstration had started that morning at the Makassad School in south central Beirut, with a large group of men from the nearby settlement of Palestinian refugees. The group marched first to the Palestine Liberation Organization Centre and then worked its way toward the American University of Beirut in the north-west corner of the city, where they hurled stones at the buildings, demanding the destruction of the university as an "imperialist institution". Police confronting the mob fired rifles in the air and gradually dispersed the crowd. The demonstrators moved out of the university compound and proceeded east to the American embassy. A further stone-throwing attack broke many windows on the ground floor. The police again fired rifles in the air and forced the mob back into the university compound. The demonstrators, reinforced by students, then made their way towards the British embassy just outside the north-west corner of the campus. Again there was a stone-throwing attack. At this point Lebanese army tanks appeared and fired in the air, gradually driving the demonstrators away eastwards, back to the vicinity of the American embassy. This time the crowd attacked cars parked nearby belonging to embassy personnel, setting several of them on fire.

There were also large demonstrations in the streets of Tripoli in north Lebanon and in Saida in the south. These events gave a new dimension to the question of the evacuation of Canadian citizens from Lebanon. On May 29 the secretary of state for External Affairs had made a statement in the House of Commons indicating that a warning had been issued to Canadian residents in several centres of the Middle East, suggesting that they leave those countries unless they had essential reasons for remaining. The minister went on to say that heads of mission in the area had been given discretion concerning the temporary removal to adjacent centres in Europe of dependents of members of their staffs and members whose services were not deemed essential in the present circumstances. We had also been informed that an aircraft was being sent to Nicosia to evacuate Canadians from the area to Cyprus. A telephone team in the embassy tried to contact the 371 Canadians believed to be in Lebanon. Part of the first message read as follows:

> We recommend that single women and all dependents pack a bag and be prepared to leave Lebanon on short notice, unless they definitely intend to remain. We understand that the airport has been temporarily closed and that commercial flight schedules have been interrupted. Until means of departure become available, it may not be feasible to leave Lebanon by air. Passengers on an evacuation plane will be expected to reimburse the cost of their passage to a nearby safe haven (probably Cyprus) and would be on their own from that point. Persons evacuated must go on their own responsibility.

A couple of days later a second call was made to those who had expressed an interest in going on an evacuation aircraft to Cyprus, asking them to confirm their continued interest, and instructing them how to proceed. The evacuation aircraft did not arrive, and it became necessary for the embassy to organize other procedures. Initially I enquired of the American embassy whether there was any space on their evacuation aircraft. They indicated that that was quite possible, but Canadians would have to wait until the last American who wanted to leave was on board. This did not sound very promising. We contacted the Lebanese airline, which had suspended scheduled flights, and ascertained that they were ready to provide charter aircraft. Ottawa approved this arrangement but when I contacted the Lebanese airline to make firm arrangements, they insisted they could not fly to Cyprus (a distance of 250 km) but only to Athens (1,100 km). The airline wanted an immediate confirmation, and there was no time to consult Ottawa, so I confirmed and hoped for the best. To my relief, the decision was approved.

We discovered, on arrival at the airport at about 2:00 p.m. on June 7, that while there was a regular crew available to fly the aircraft, it was our responsibility to line up the passengers, collect fares, and ensure that they had ready at hand their passports. With just one embassy staff member to help with these tasks, I drafted my wife and two older children. We also had to ensure that passengers boarded: they had so much to talk about that some of them did not hear the summons to board! My family had come to the airport ready to go if there was room for all of them, but to stay behind if there was not. There was room, and they boarded with the rest of the group.

Canada's Israel-Arab policy was intended to be more or less neutral but various events in Beirut – such as the group of people who had been waiting to watch the attack on the Canadian embassy – indicated that many Arabs regarded Canada as pro-Israel. Another indication was hearing a man shout "Canada to Hell!" as our official car with flag flying drove through west Beirut. A third event was a bit more disturbing. One evening after my family had gone to Greece I worked through the evening at the chancery, which was in west Beirut. I had told my driver to take the evening off, intending to hail a taxi to take me to the residence in the heart of Christian east Beirut. I hopped into the first cab that came along and didn't notice until we were under way that the driver was a Muslim. One could always tell: Christian drivers always dangled a small cross over the dashboard; Muslim drivers spread artificial flowers on the ledge under the rear window. A few minutes after we were under way, the driver drew my attention to a very large, long knife resting on his dashboard. I wondered whether he intended to blackmail me into surrendering all my money when we reached the residence. I remembered that the foreign ministry had assigned guards to diplomatic residences since the war began, but I also remembered that they weren't always in evidence. I would not know – nor would the driver – whether the guard was visibly on duty until we were just a few yards from the door to the apartment building, since the route to the embassy involved a sharp left turn from a street where tall buildings restricted one's vision. Happily, as we turned the corner, I spotted the armed guard where he was supposed to be and I was able to hop out and pay my fare without worrying whether the driver would threaten me with his knife.

On June 10 – the day the war ended – there were demonstrations favouring Nasser's continued leadership. Muslim, Druze, and Christian political leaders, and the UAR ambassador addressed the crowds gathering at the United Arab Republic embassy. Afterwards the crowd broke into smaller groups. One of them destroyed property: various business establishments dealing in British and American goods such as Ford, Coca-Cola and Shell were badly damaged. Official cars of the Danish and Mexican ambassadors were wrecked and the residence of the Mexican ambassador was nearly invaded by the mob; fortunately, the chain on his front door did not give way. The rioters did not have any particular animosity against Mexico; the ambassador's apartment was simply situated above the Ford automobile agency. Realizing that the Internal Security Forces were not able to prevent these unfortunate events, we were left with feelings of continuing anxiety.

On Monday, June 12, however, we reported to External Affairs in Ottawa:

> *We are cautiously optimistic that an uneasy peace that has reigned in Beirut since Saturday afternoon (10 June) will continue. Principal political groups both Christian and Muslim united in declaring support for Nasser's continuance in power. Government's story in Sunday's newspapers that property destruction was carried out by gangs of troublemakers after the main demonstration was over seems to be substantially true.*

Following the riots of June 10, the Internal Security forces transferred authority to the army, which maintained order in Beirut. Four thousand troops moved into the city from South Lebanon. The security forces had been working under heavy strain for the previous two to three weeks. No further demonstrations were attempted after noon prayers at mosques on June 16.

Happily, we survived the Six Day War and the disturbances and uncertainties it caused in Beirut without any disasters, but not without some anxiety. Our families returned from Greece on June 28. Our only real concerns arose from the demonstrations of June 6 and 10, which suggested some uncertainty about the ability of the government to maintain law and order. Otherwise our only misfortune was the necessary cancellation of our July 1 centennial reception.

THE CANADIAN EMBASSY TO THE HOLY SEE

by E.P. Black

Why does Canada have an Embassy at the Vatican? First, some facts and history are necessary to answer the question. The Roman Catholic Church is the oldest and largest religious institution in the world with approximately one billion baptized members, of which over half are in the Third World. The Church came to North America with the settlers from France; it has played an important role throughout Canadian history and about 46 percent of all Canadians are baptized Roman Catholics. They worship in the Latin rite, in English, French, their mother tongue, or in one of the eastern rites. Among the latter, the Ukrainian Catholic Church has the largest number of adherents.

Unofficial relations between Ottawa and the Vatican were first investigated over a hundred years ago when Prime Minister Alexander MacKenzie requested that Rome send a representative to examine the state of the Church in Canada and its relations with the civil authority. An Irish priest, Monsignor Conroy, wrote a report but died before his return to Rome and there was no follow-up. In the 1890s Sir Wilfred Laurier, reacting to the Manitoba Schools Question, sent one of his ministers to Rome to encourage a further visit. The papal envoy, Monsignor Merry del Val, recommended that the Vatican should have an apostolic delegate (unofficial papal representative) in Ottawa. The first incumbent, Monsignor Falconio, took up his post in 1899. Representation by a line of apostolic delegates remained unbroken until Canada and the Holy See established diplomatic relations in 1969. At that time the apostolic delegate became pro-nuncio and Canada named an ambassador to the Holy See.

Diplomatic relations were established for a number of reasons. The dramatic humanity of Pope John XXIII and the results of the Second Vatican Council turned the Church away from a certain besieged mentality toward a greater openness to the world. The pope and his successors were established as unique spokesmen for the moral and ethical points of view in foreign relations. Canada found that in its foreign policy there was a convergence with Vatican views on questions relating to aid and development, refugees, human rights, social justice, religious freedom, and reunification of families. They also shared similar perspectives on the European Conference for Security and Co-operation which was designed to lower barriers between Eastern and Western Europe. In addition, there was a belief in Ottawa that the Vatican could provide "a unique listening post" to gather information on international developments of interest to Canada.

Against this background the Embassy undertakes four types of activity. The classic diplomatic task is to inform the Holy See of areas of mutual interest or reasons for differences of approach in Canadian policy. For example, both Ottawa and Rome abhorred apartheid, but unlike Canadian policy makers, the Vatican did not believe in the usefulness of economic sanctions. The second aspect is building bilateral relations, generally well established with state visits. There have been two papal voyages to Canada in 1984 and 1987, a state visit by the governor general in 1986, and subsequent visits by prime ministers and ministers of Foreign Affairs. One important new development involving the Pope, the Federal government, and the provincial governments is the increasing tendency of Native Peoples representatives to appeal to His Holiness to further their objectives in Canada. The embassy assists Native Peoples representatives during visits to Rome, informs the Holy See of Canadian policy, and reports on the results of the visits. A third aspect is the analysis of Vatican policy as it affects the Pope's message on minorities. For example, in my time we examined the Pope's message on minorities, his Encyclical on the Third World, and the Church's studies on racism and Third World debt. The final dimension of diplomatic responsibility in Rome is to report on Vatican analysis of developing international situations. The Church's position provides a unique view, evidenced in the examination of the role of religion in the changes in Eastern Europe and the former Soviet Union, and discussions regarding the future of the Holy Land and the difficult peace process there.

A colleague has described the diplomatic task at the Vatican as a lay observer reporting to a secular government the activities of a major international player whose actions, taken for religious reasons, often have political consequences. Another describes it as the duty to report on the analysis of political events by diplomatic professionals whose assessments are naturally affected by their being priests of a particular religious institution. These descriptions may be clearer if I outline some of the matters which the embassy follows each week in order to complete three to four telegrams of analysis on approximately twenty-five countries and international agencies. John Paul II was an indefatigable traveller and his voyages to his Catholic parishioners around the world often had political fall-out, as in the Philippines, Haiti, and Chile. More dramatic effects were seen in his home-land of Poland. From 1985 to 1989, the embassy evaluated the negotiations leading to diplomatic relations between Poland and the Vatican, the revival of religious belief and protest in Czechoslovakia – a precursor to its new-found freedom, the gradual return to relations with Hungary and, on the occasion of the Christian Millennium in Russia in 1988, the first official contact between a representative of the pope and the head of state of the Soviet Union. The latter led to the unique visit of Gorbachev to the pope in Rome. Of particular interest to Canada had been the fate of the Ukrainian Catholic Church, declared illegal by Stalin after World War II, which has approximately four to five million adherents in the Ukraine and over 200,000 in Canada.

Throughout the slow rapprochement between Moscow and Rome it should be kept in mind that, for the pope, improved relations with the sec-ular states in Eastern Europe and greater religious freedom for all churches may eventually lead to a healing of the oldest major schism in Christianity (1054 AD) between the Roman Catholic Church and the Orthodox Churches of the former Byzantine Empire. The Vatican's relations with the secular states of Western Europe are good but Rome believes that, after cen-turies of anti-clericalism and humanistic ideologies, Western Europe has become largely de-Christianized. The church has supported the movement towards European unity and the breaking of barriers between East and West as the only way to a stable and peaceful continent. It hopes that in these conditions the European's loss of spiritual memory can be revived through an interest in their common culture of which Christianity was a central part.

The way that Latin America resolves its contemporary problems will have its effect on the evolution of the Church itself. Soon, half the world's baptized Catholics will live on that continent where social and economic disparities are vast. Conditions certainly exist for the practice of the tradi-tional church mission to the poor and deprived. In carrying out this mis-sion, however, Rome faces many difficulties – its own past, opposition from local oligarchies, rich fundamentalist sects, and division within the Church itself on social policy. Is its policy to be based on economic determinism, as many Latin American theologians have argued, or must it not flow, as the Pope has said, from faith and not ideology? The embassy's role is to take all

The Pope and Ambassador Pat Black.

these various elements into account in analyzing the attitudes of the Vatican to specific economic and political developments in such places as Brazil, Chile, and Central America.

The issues facing the continent of Africa are of tragic proportions: famines, ecological disasters, wars, refugees, and extreme poverty. The Vatican and Canada have similar views on how to meet these problems through humanitarian aid and international development. The contributions of Canada's aid programmes, the work of Canadian missionaries and Canadian NGO's are well recognized in Rome. The very gravity of the situation of the continent is likely to ensure that we shall be working towards many of the same ends in the years ahead, and the Canadian embassy will doubtless continue to provide useful analysis of the Vatican's activity in Africa in order to facilitate that cooperation.

ACCREDITED TO A NORTHERN KINGDOM – DENMARK AND GREENLAND: 1986-1991

by D. Armstrong

D enmark was once a considerable empire, at its height consisting of Norway, Iceland, southern Sweden, and in the middle ages, Baltic lands. Although a casual observer might assume that the modern version included only the "core" islands of Zealand (with Copenhagen), Funen, and the Jutland peninsula, they would be overlooking the far-flung kingdom of today that encompasses the Faroes, north-west of the Shetlands, the island of Bornholm, which lies in the Baltic north of Poland, and most importantly, Greenland. These additions make Denmark and its territories larger than the largest country in Europe as well as Canada's closest European neighbour.

Canada and Denmark are like-minded about much in international life and cooperate closely, and not only because the alphabet throws us together in many multilateral settings. This state of affairs might presage a pleasant if uneventful posting for a Canadian diplomat in Copenhagen. In fact, beyond the normal day-to-day work of reporting on, promoting and representing our interests, and involvement in perhaps an unusual number of engagements by Canadian performing artists and naval port visits – a tribute to the city's special allure, I found it to be full of surprises and unexpectedly moving experiences. When a crisis over polar bears only days after my arrival threatened our bilateral relations, I realized that the "northern dimension" was no theoretical concept, but a lively element of our foreign policy.

The "Core" Group

One of the Canadian envoy's regular duties is participation in memorial services on November 11 at the Commonwealth war graves site near Copenhagen. This requirement led me to explore further, and I discovered that 180 young Canadian airmen lost their lives flying over Denmark with the RAF from 1940 to 1945. They are buried in forty-seven official cemeteries throughout the country. Many of the losses were sustained over occupied territory as their aircraft flew to and from bombing raids in Germany. Beginning in 1943, more were lost at night supplying ammunition to the Danish underground resistance forces. This sorrowful connection between our two countries, which is nevertheless an inspiring one, was brought home to me during my visits to these memorial places, and at the ceremonial unveiling of a monument in Jutland by the Crown Prince in 1990. It honours especially those allied airmen, including Canadians, who lost their lives helping the Danes fight back against the occupation.

Military cooperation continued in my time, though in a more contemporary sense. There were bi-annual NATO exercises of the Ace Mobile Force that included Canadian troops. On several occasions our military attaché and I moved by helicopter in all kinds of weather to various staging points to greet and presumably cheer our soldiers in their improvised dug-outs. (Queen Margrethe was doing the same, more grandly.) We would usually complete our tour at the mess tent where there was a choice of three surprisingly edible menus, all in plastic bags – "We just add hot water."

Perhaps even more significant during this time was the cooperation of the Canadian and Danish military in pilot projects testing the potential of women in combat roles including, specifically, the first training of female jet fighter pilots. This was the front line of institutional change for both countries and the whole question was hotly debated at cabinet level in Copenhagen, leading to regular and close consultations on our part with the defence minister and his staff. In the end, Denmark opted for naval exercises and it was left to Canada to graduate a class of female (CF-18) fighter pilots in 1989, the first country in the world to do so, and no small achievement. It was several years before the United States, for example, followed suit.

In peace, war, or revolution, there is a tradition of mutual help between Canada and Denmark. The world heard a great deal about the hostage taking in Iran in 1979, when revolutionaries seized the American embassy and held its large staff prisoner for months. It also later became public knowledge that the Canadian ambassador and counsellor sheltered, at considerable risk, six Americans who had been outside their chancery compound at the time, eventually spiriting them out of the country in what was a dangerous undertaking. Few know, however, of the work of the Danish ambassador in Teheran, Troels Munk, and his successors. They showed courage by volunteering to manage Canada's affairs, in the face of retaliatory threats to

Canadian diplomats and presumably their friends, fending for the remaining Canadian business people, and keeping an eye on our properties through eight troubled years of ferment in that country until Canada reopened its embassy in 1988. In Libya also, it was, and is, the Danes who represent our interests. It was therefore gratifying to me to be able to show our appreciation at a special evening during which we honoured Ambassador Munk.

Predictably, there were a few blips on our bilateral screen here and there. Because of the role of Banting and Best in our medical history, it took some time for Canada to recover from the shock of losing the insulin monopoly to an enterprising Danish firm in the early 1980s. And our long-running dispute over the sovereignty of Hans Island, a barren arctic rock in the Nares Strait, regularly planted with rival flags by passing mariners, only half in jest, periodically emerged as a real point of contention.

The Outer Reaches - The Faroe Islands and Bornholm

The autonomous Faroe Islands (there are eighteen) lie in lonely, windswept isolation in the North Atlantic beyond the Hebrides. One spring, wishing to make contact with another part of the Danish realm, I joined a group of twenty ambassadors for an official tour. The Faroes, however, are not for the faint of heart. The weather is invariably and euphemistically termed inclement and our first taste of it was landing on a fog-bound airstrip, situated uncomfortably near a cliff's edge. Although we were regaled with tales of near misses, we arrived intact to find a dramatic, mountainous landscape, a complete contrast to the serene flatlands of Denmark itself.

The economy of the Faroes is almost entirely fish-based and we saw a number of processing plants and other aspects of the industry. We also saw evidence of the Faroese straightforward, independent cast of thought (they are actually of ancient Norse stock and have their own language) and lifestyle, inured as they have been over the centuries to hardship and the rough elements. Along with this goes the habit of plain speaking. At one plant, our host suddenly turned and severely berated me before all my surprised colleagues for a recent moratorium on Atlantic cod fishing imposed by NAFO, the North Atlantic Fisheries Organization. Canada was perceived as having played a leading role in this policy that deprived the islands of some of their traditional fishing rights and I understood his anger. The local economy was in stagnation with high unemployment and young people were forced to leave. I tried to explain the need for the action taken, but there is rarely enough time when emotions are high. Fortunately, the contretemps was quickly set aside as we moved about enjoying the wild beauty of the islands. The farewell banquet at Torshavn featured a classic Faroese menu, whale meat and boiled potatoes. Since that visit there have been high hopes about possible oil discoveries offshore, something that could play a major part in their survival against the odds.

Bornholm

Bornholm lies in the Baltic off the coast of Poland. It has a unique postwar history because it happened to be east of the region for which the Western powers were deemed responsible, making it the only west European territory to be liberated by the Red Army in 1945. This occurred after a short bombardment of the occupying Nazis. My journey to Bornholm, which took several hours by hydrofoil, ended in the discovery of an oasis. Verdant and flower-filled, it is blessed with one of Denmark's largest forests and has extremely good bicycling conditions. Because of its strategic position throughout the Cold War period, it also featured an important Danish military base and operations centre for tracking Warsaw Pact naval and shipping movements. It is still an attractive venue for NATO seminars. Though ostensibly on holiday, I paid a formal call on the base commander and spent many hours in the local museum which is full of photos and artifacts illustrating the Russians' extended stay. The Russian forces refused to leave for a full year, departing only in April 1946. Compared to the rigours they had recently experienced, Bornholm must have seemed a paradise to them. While cycling along sun dappled forest paths, I reflected that in their place I, too, would not have wished to leave it for Novosibirsk or worse.

Greenland – Early Days

Canada's first official link with Greenland was forged through strategic necessity in World War II. In spite of our close geographical proximity in the far north (only a few kilometres of water or ice separate the tip of Ellesmere Island and the Thule area) Greenland was, until the outbreak of war, an unknown quantity to most. It was only following the Nazi invasion of Denmark in 1940 that Canada made official and urgent contact. As a colony of Denmark, Greenland was now (strictly speaking) enemy territory on Canada's doorstep. Greenland was also the only known source of cryolite, an essential component of the aluminum vitally needed for wartime aircraft production. Three priorities quickly became apparent: firstly, to prevent the establishment of enemy bases along its coastal areas; secondly, to safeguard the Danish cryolite mine at Ivigtut against sabotage; and, thirdly, to see that the scattered communities of Greenland had basic supplies now that they were cut off from Denmark.

From the day of occupation on April 9, 1940 a flurry of consultations began among officials in the Department of External Affairs and with their equally concerned Washington counterparts. Hugh Keenleyside, the official responsible (strongly supported by the Aluminum Company of Canada which had obvious vested interests) urged the establishment of "a small defence force" in Greenland. The still neutral Americans, though, feared that Japan might use this to justify its expansionist activities in South East Asia.

Intense activity resulted in the agreement reached on April 23 between President Roosevelt and Prime Minister King that Canada should take the initiative to ensure that food, clothing, medicines and other necessities were delivered in return for a guaranteed cryolite supply. Canada was also to appoint a consular official to oversee the proceedings. Meanwhile, the Danish minister in Washington, like most of his colleagues elsewhere, had cut himself off from Copenhagen, refusing further instructions from that source, and had formally taken responsibility for Greenland's affairs in cooperation with both American and Canadian governments. Only four weeks later in May 1940, the fully laden Hudson Bay Company supply ship *Nascopie* sailed for Ivigtut with Mines and Resources officials, military representatives, agents for Alcan, and the RCMP on board. Unfortunately, the Danish governor, suspecting some kind of military takeover at the mine, refused to allow them to unload the cargo of much needed commodities. They were stalled for some time until the arrival of a European ship bearing the newly appointed Canadian consul, Kenneth Kirkwood.

A scholar and aesthete, Kirkwood, whose last post had been The Hague, may have seemed an unlikely choice. "I left behind me suddenly a beautiful home with a personal library of nearly 3,000 books," he later wrote. "Within a few days on shortest notice, I was steaming my way through bleak and fog-swept northern seas to an Arctic outpost where I was to put in two winters and a summer. The Arctic winter is very long, with a four-month season of almost complete black-out." To make matters even more trying, the consulate set up at Godthaab was a small and unprepossessing wooden structure (destined to be the first of Canada's international network of consulates), and daily life there a far cry from Kirkwood's worldly existence in Europe. He likely experienced no small measure of culture shock. However, good professional that he was, he set to work immediately. By all accounts, he performed excellently from the first moment. His diplomatic skills calmed the passions at Ivigtut and allowed the *Nascopie* to complete its mission. Throughout his posting he conducted business with efficiency and common sense. His successors, among them arctic experts Trevor Lloyd and Maxwell Dunbar, maintained these high standards.

The relief supplies from the *Nascopie* were duly unloaded and replaced with 1500 tons of cryolite. This was the beginning of regular runs. Some of these mine shipments were subcontracted to the British, while the Americans, who established military bases there in 1941, made their own arrangements. But it was Canada, with Alcan as chief purchasing agent, that continued to be a lifeline for Greenland's communities, supplying them with basic necessities throughout the war – along with items as diverse as Christmas trees and hunting ammunition. By the 1950s, however, the mine at Ivigtut had been depleted and the industry had begun to rely on artificial cryolite. In 1946 our consul withdrew, our humble headquarters closed down and Canada's relations with Greenland faded.

Modern Times

We fast-forward now to 1987, when Ottawa, after an extended interval of several decades, decided that our bilateral interests merited the renewing of official ties with Greenland and the reopening of our consulate. The Hockin-Simard Report of that year recommended more emphasis on arctic affairs, though its authors had probably not known about the polar bear crisis. For generations, Greenlanders in the Thule area had walked across the pack ice to hunting grounds in Ellesmere, oblivious of boundaries. Recently they had come face to face instead with NWT (Northwest Territories) law enforcement officers: Canada had declared the animal an endangered species. The real cause of the uproar that ensued, as we later discovered, was that polar bear trousers are not only good insulation – they are a badge of manhood for the Thule people. Matters became so politically tense over this that our Foreign Ministers were meeting at the U.N. to try to defuse the issue. The Canadian solution, a time-honoured one, was to set up a task force to develop a management policy for a "sustainable harvest," which cooled things down for the time being.

By this time there were also joint fishery and environmental questions in the north that needed closer coordination. But much had changed and it was a new Greenland that Canada would be approaching. The wartime influx of outsiders had led Greenlanders to chafe against their colonial status.

A local political movement eventually resulted in Home Rule in 1979, providing a wide measure of autonomy and their own parliament. By the late 1980s an all-Greenlandic government was in place, though Denmark retained ultimate responsibility for justice, defence, and foreign affairs, provided regular financial grants, and held some senior positions in the bureaucracy. All of this was attractive to northern Canadians and many from the NWT went to Nuuk (the former Godthaab) to have a closer look. There seems little doubt that this may have provided some of the impetus for today's Nunavut, and the interplay between the two areas is likely to continue. In any case, both northern peoples were meeting regularly in the I.C.C. (Inuit Circumpolar Conference) the pan-Arctic association which began life in the late 1970s.

There were other, more delicate issues that needed to be addressed. Even though a moderate Gorbachev was newly on the scene, the Cold War had not yet disappeared and Greenland was strategically situated from a NATO point of view. The Soviets were still active along Greenland's coasts and regularly promoted cultural events and exchanges with Greenlanders. Members of a small separatist wing on the political left, in particular, were invited to visit the USSR. For a number of reasons, then, it was decided in Ottawa that the time was right for an official Canadian presence to provide a modest counterweight. Several Nordic countries had preceded us, but we were assured that Canada was in a special category and would be particularly welcome.

My first visit to Greenland in the spring of 1987 was undertaken to announce officially the opening of our new consulate some weeks hence and to make the necessary administrative arrangements. The visit vividly reminded me of my country's great distance from Denmark and yet how close Greenland is. One lands first at the Sondre Stromfjord airport, then transfers to a much smaller aircraft offering a more adventurous experience north to Nuuk via Greenlandair. All told, the journey takes over five hours. It is my recollection over the years that the weather on that last lap tended to be stormy, whatever the season. On these unsettling flights, over undeniably beautiful landscapes, I had the satisfaction of noting that the Green-landers, who presumably made the trip often to undertake studies or attend meetings, were as white-knuckled as I. Safely on the ground, one of my first discoveries at Nuuk's main hotel was an unexpected and agreeable example of history repeating itself. Surprised to see a well-stocked salad bar, as well as fresh flowers and potted plants in such an arctic setting, I made inquiries and learned that First Air, a small private airline based near Ottawa had, since 1981, been flying in fresh fruit, vegetables, and other foodstuffs from Canada along with miscellaneous supplies weekly via Frobisher Bay – now Iqaluit – to several communities. It still does in 1999. No longer is this service the only lifeline, as in the days of *Nascopie*, but it nevertheless provided, and provides, a welcome addition to the quality of life and, from the Canadian point of view, a striking continuum.

The lunch given for me jointly by the Danish High Commissioner and Premier Motzfeld illustrated subtly the fact that Denmark was still responsible for foreign affairs. Any diplomatic envoy dealing with Greenland needed to keep Copenhagen informed, a situation with which Canadians are familiar, and to which we are sensitive. That occasion also reminded me that I was in a different culture, as the menu moved from smoked salmon and shrimp to dried caribou and blubber in small, shimmering cubes. Our discussions that day centered on the logistics of our new consulate, the naming of a local citizen as our honorary consul, and ways in which our bilateral relations could be enriched. Diplomatically missing from our agenda was any mention of the "Black Angel" lead and zinc mine at Marmorilik that a Canadian mining firm had recently closed, leaving behind some environmental problems. In spite of this the Greenlanders continued to need, and were encouraging, more Canadian mineral exploration.

A highlight of that first visit was an opportunity for me to witness an opening session of the Landsting (Parliament), preceded by the procession of members in their characteristic white anoraks against a memorable backdrop of majestic icebergs floating in the harbour. Indeed, one of the greatest rewards of my responsibilities during that posting was the experience of dealing on a regular basis with Greenlandic politicians. Greenlanders are essentially an Inuit people, though some have part-European ancestry. Their informality makes contacts easy, as I discovered that day when I was introduced in the Landsting to the leaders of the three political parties and the founding fathers of the Home Rule movement, one of whom was the premier himself.

Canada Week

With the consulate duly opened, we undertook to put our best foot forward as a country and good neighbour in a "Canada Week," designated in September 1989. Originally planned as a trade fair it was agreed along the way that it should have a considerably broader appeal. This would be, after all, the first time Canada had been presented to the wider Greenland public. Given the distances involved, and with a three-sided Ottawa/

Copenhagen/Nuuk operations centre, it proved to be a considerable feat of organization. Nevertheless, it began on schedule at the end of the caribou hunting season. Nuuk was festooned with Canadian flags and posters, and the two major hotels and restaurants had been persuaded to feature Canadian culinary specialties that week. The Canadian icebreaker *Henry Larsen* (named for the first European navigator of the Northwest Passage from west to east) was on hand for ship visits and social events. Embassy staff members and enthusiastically received RCMP officers participated in programs for high school students, and a book and grant presentation was made to the fledgling University of Greenland.

The main action took place in the university gymnasium, which doubled as an exhibition hall. Forty Canadian firms, provinces, and associations had set up display booths which were visited by most of Nuuk's population of 11,000 persons. They included businesses from eastern Canada, tourist agencies, and education groups like the World University Service. A Canadian Inuit carver demonstrated his art during the week and presented the impressive result to the premier. On opening night, a major commercial and social event of the season, I assisted Premier Motzfeld in officially inaugurating the week, venturing a bit of Danish and some rather feeble Greenlandic. This was followed by a northern program that included local talent as well as Canadian Inuit dancers and throat singers juxtaposed with, from the south, Liona Boyd, whose ethereal presence and Bach partitas were the source of wonderment and admiration. During the reception that followed, an RCMP honour guard escorted the premier to meet each exhibitor and to discuss their products. At the end of the week all the goods were auctioned to raise funds for Green-landic students to study in Canada, a popular and unusual postscript to an exhibition.

Results from such ventures are rarely immediate, even with such an auspicious start. However, Canada Week renewed our long-dormant ties, gave us a modern basis for joint activities, placed Canada firmly in the Greenlandic orbit, and directly stimulated the movement of peoples. In December 1989, in the early stages of a closer relationship, I had the privilege of co-signing with Kai Egede, the Greenlandic Fisheries Minister, the Beluga/Narwhal Protection Agreement, the first international agreement signed by the Greenlanders on their own. Later there were cooperative arrangements in fisheries, environmental and wildlife management, educational and archeological exchanges, and tourism.

Ambassador Armstrong with Premier Motzfeld at the opening of Canada week in Greenland, October 1989

We urged more shipping links to stimulate trade, while Greenlanders on their side hoped for and needed more mining exploration to ease their dependence on the fragile fishery. At one point it looked as though Canadian mining companies had made a gold strike, but these hopes were not to be fulfilled, at least in the short run. Efforts continue, however. Today, in the era of the eight-nation Arctic Council, Greenland is no longer an unknown quantity. It is an integral part of the circumpolar community, and a familiar partner for Canada.

CORRESPONDANT: LAGOS 1966

by André Couvrette

"C'est un géant qui dort: sur-veillez son sommeil," me dit un jour M. Jules Léger. C'est vrai, l'Afrique est encore le royaume onirique, des nuits étoilées du Sahel aux mille rumeurs de la forêt guinéenne. J'ai fait croisière sur le Niger à bord du "Général-Soumaire" en 1974, avec trois compagnons d'ambassade, de Mopti à Gao en passant par Tombouctou. Ville de rêves des siècles passés, d'où un cortège fastueux était apparu au Caire en plein milieu du Moyen Age, et dont le roi Kankan Moussa avait déversé une pluie d'or sur la ville des Pharaons: l'or du Bambouck et de la mystérieuse Tombouctou. J'ai aussi traversé le pont d'Onitscha sur le

André Couvrette

Niger et la forêt biafraise en 1966, six mois avant que tout le Nigeria sombre dans la guerre civile la plus sanglante depuis les massacres du Congo belge de 1960, préfigure des horreurs de l'Ouganda et d'Éthiopie. C'était le sommeil d'un géant noir peuplé de rêves d'or et de cauchemars de sang.

Un jour, quelques six mois après mon arrivee, un petit curé, mission-naire canadien-français, est arrivé à la chancellerie de Lagos pour faire renou-veler son passeport. À vrai dire, il venait simplement voir un consul, mais à mon habitude, je lui ai demandé de venir dans mon bureau, au moment de la signature, pour prendre de ses nouvelles et lui poser quelques questions.

Les missionnaires, occupés des choses d'En-Haut et aussi à enseigner l'hygiène de base et la vie de famille, ne s'intéressaient aucunement à la politique. Mais on ne vit pas dans un village ou une petite ville de province sans voir des choses que ni les correspondants, ni les diplomates ne verront jamais. Il y aurait beaucoup à dire sur "Bishop Delisle" et cette cohorte de missionnaires que notre peuple sage mais aventurier a déversés pendant cinquante ans en Afrique du Commonwealth: du Basutoland à la Rhodésie – c'était alors leurs noms – de l'Éthiopie d'Hailé Selassie aussi, au Ghana et au Nigeria. Il m'est apparu un moment que le Nigeria, déchiré entre ses musulmans, ses chrétiens et tous ses animismes, n'avait que des évêques canadien-français pour tenir les bouts. Une religion par village, une culture par cité-État, dans la forêt où la mouche tuait tout bétail: pas de traction animale, donc pas de roue, sauf peut-être celle de l'Éternel retour – et ces croyances diverses le plus souvent superposées dans un syncrétisme étonnant – c'est l'Afrique, ses rêves métaphysiques et ses cauchemars.

J'interroge donc mon client: "D'où venez-vous et comment va la vie, simple et tranquille?"

"Pensez-vous! La fin de semaine dernière, un pauvre type est entré chez moi comme dans un sanctuaire, pour sortir par la porte d'en arrière. Il était poursuivi par une meute qui en voulait à sa vie."

"Qu'avait-il fait? Un petit bandit?"

"Pas du tout, un brave garçon comme tant d'autres. Non, c'était la politique."

"Ah tiens, combien se font tuer pour la politique?"

"Une soixantaine par semaine."

Ça se passait l'automne 1965, six mois avant que n'éclatent les coups d'État, et la guerre du Biafra allait suivre dans un an et demie. Mais c'était déjà la guerre civile.

Au même moment, Dakar, avec une population égale à celle de Lagos, avait connu deux meurtres en un an, dont l'un (c'est un grand port de mer) entre marins étrangers.

Il en mourait plus que ça tous les jours à Oyo – alors, pensez Lagos et Ibadan! Depuis ce temps, j'ai toujours jeté un coup d'œil intéressé sur la criminalité du pays où je vivais. "L'homme ne vit pas que de pain"; il ne meurt pas que pour du pain non plus.

"Et vient toujours un moment où la quantité change la qualité," comme disait mon vieux professeur allemand de Georgetown ... Les "politologues" qui fondent leurs études sur la sociologie, pour faire scientifique et donc moderne, ont tendance à oublier le moment où la quantité devient la qualité ou par exemple, la quantité des crimes modifie "la qualité de vie," expression abstraite qui se traduit en images par des coups d'État sanglants, des rébellions et les guerres ouvertes. La guerre fédérale du Nigeria a-t-elle tué soixante pauvres types par semaine dans la ville d'Oyo?

Au mois d'août 1966, à Lagos, j'étais le principal agent politique canadien car le haut-commissaire était en congé en Nouvelle-Écosse. (Pourquoi les coups d'État trouvent-ils toujours les hommes politiques et les diplomates en congé? Réponse: parce que si ceux-ci les voyaient venir, ils n'auraient pas lieu. Les diplomates les annonceraient, et les politiques les empêcheraient ... bien sur?) Je me préparais moi-même une gentille petite excursion au Sénégal, où j'allais de temps à autre comme chargé d'affaires. Avant de prendre la voiture pour l'aéroport d'Ikeia – déjà deux heures de voiture de la Marina où étaient nos bureaux, à travers un trafic infernal – je demande au communicateur de vérifier le départ de l'avion de Dakar. Il me revient au bout de cinq minutes. "Pas de réponse, la ligne est coupée." "Donnez-moi du papier et un crayon." Je regarde par la fenêtre: défilé de camions militaires. J'écris: "Un coup d'État est en cours. Trois possibilités: ou bien le numéro 2 a décidé de faire au numéro 1 (Ironsi) ce que Nasser a fait à Neguib, et alors rien de changé, sauf que la Junte sera un peu plus intelligente; ou bien les types du sud ont remis ça pour assurer leur révolution, et alors nous aurons un régime "progressiste"; ou bien enfin se sont ceux du nord qui se vengent, et alors, c'est la guerre civile."

C'était la troisième hypothèse, et six mois plus tard la guerre du Biafra allait commencer. Quelle dépêche, le "scoop" diplomatique, différent en cela du "scoop" de journaliste, en ce qu'il ne raconte pas, mais prédit. Une heure plus tôt et j'aurais été pris en l'air loin du poste, comme un imbécile. Quiconque s'attribue le mérite de ses bons coups ne sait pas ce qu'est la chance.

Le hasard, l'accident, ont un rôle inquantifiable et sont ignorés de la science politique, des analyses historiques, où pourtant comme à la guerre, tout est affaire de moment. Et comme on sait, la guerre est la moitié de l'Histoire, même en Afrique où nous ne voyons que des "problèmes de développement."

Les professeurs et les intellectuels jouent, ou rejouent, aux échecs des parties déjà perdues qui étaient toutes logiquement gagnées d'avance, tandis que les États et les gouvernements jouent au poker la partie d'aujourd'hui. Selon les règles, certes, mais avec le hasard pour partenaire. "La guerre est un art simple et tout d'exécution," disait Napoléon. La diplomatie non plus. Et comme on sait, la victoire change les règles du jeu.

A IS FOR ARISTIDE

by John W. Graham

I groped for the phone. It was about 1:30 in the morning.

"John, can you meet me at the Palace in an hour?" It was Beatrice Rangel, Minister of the Venezuelan Presidency and President Carlos Andres Perez's principal advisor on major foreign policy issues.

"In an hour's time? What's up?" And then a few cobwebs parted. I asked "It's Aristide?"

"Yes," she said. "General Cedras has taken charge of the coup d'état. The president spoke to him a few hours ago and persuaded him to release Aristide to exile in Venezuela. The president has sent his personal aircraft to Port-au-Prince. It should be back at Maiquetia airport about 4:00." She promised to tell me more on the way to the airport. I was to meet her at the entrance to the car park at Miraflores Palace. The guards would expect me.

It was Wednesday, October 1, 1991. The previous day had been a disaster. The Reverend Jean Bertrand Aristide, who at 37 had won the presidency of Haiti in elections supervised by the UN and the OAS on December 16, 1990, had crashed to the bottom of a roller coaster week. On September 25 he had made his debut at the United Nations General Assembly. He spoke of the usual things – "dignity" and "democracy" – and impressed the UN with his intelligence and compassion. In Port-au-Prince two days later, he gave a very different speech. Fuelling a lethal eloquence was mounting apprehension that the election he had won nine months earlier was threatened on three fronts: by the wealthy bourgeoisie, by hard line Duvalierists, and by the Haitian army. In the preceding weeks, a number of Aristide's opponents had been "necklaced" by street crowds, a procedure in which a gasoline soaked tire is slung on the shoulders of the victim and ignited. Another local term for this grisly form of execution is "père Lebrun," after the owner of a tire store. In this speech the President referred directly to "la supplice du collier" (the torment of the necklace) and urged the crowd of militant supporters not to forget to give the enemy "what he deserves." He also spoke of the value of the Constitution and then intoned ambiguously but with unmistakable menace:

"Quel bel outil! (what a beautiful tool!) Quel bel instrument! (what a beautiful instrument!) Quel bel appareil! (what a beautiful machine!)"

Four months earlier and soon after Father Aristide had won the first authentically free and fair elections in Haitian history, the President of the Dominican Republic, the country next door, predicted a bloody conclusion to this experiment in democracy.

There were other similarly sanguinary forecasts. And so they came to be. About midnight, September 29, a group of soldiers surrounded the private residence of President Aristide. Alerted apparently by telephone, the French ambassador extricated Aristide from his home and left him in the Presidential Palace under the protection of the president's bodyguard. By 8:00 a.m. rebel troops encircled the palace. Aristide attempted to broadcast a message exhorting the Haitian people to "go out into the streets to save democracy." Through the morning there were reports of widening disturbances and revolt, including the news, subsequently confirmed, that Sylvio Claude, a former presidential candidate, had been burned to death and that Dr. Roger Lafontant, a Duvalieriste, who had been arrested for instigating an abortive coup against Aristide in January, had been shot in his jail cell.

In New York, the Haitian ambassador to the United Nations sought an emergency meeting of the Security Council to "consider the situation and its consequences for regional stability." A majority of the members, led by India and China, opposed action by the Security Council on the grounds that what was happening in Haiti was an internal matter. Perez de Cuellar, the secretary general, issued a communiqué October 1 noting the role undertaken by the United Nations in helping to establish the democratic process in Haiti and "deeply regretting" the coup. The Organization of American States responded with greater vigour. Its Permanent Council met October 1 and scheduled a meeting of OAS foreign ministers for the following afternoon.

I was in Caracas, where there was rising concern, but little hard information. Bernard Dussault, the Canadian ambassador in Port-au-Prince, was unable to send a telegram. Shooting in the streets kept him from his chancery. I was anxious to find out how President Perez was reacting. Venezuelan relations with the Haitian Government were close and the President's office probably knew as much as anyone outside of Port-au-Prince, with the possible exception of the Americans. There is a special bond between Venezuela and Haiti dating from the timely support given by General Pétion of the independent black republic to Simon Bolivar in his war of independence with Spain. Despite initial concern that Aristide might be a rudderless populist, the relationship had flowered anew between Presidents Perez and Aristide. I knew that Perez and Rangel would be alarmed and called for an appointment with Rangel. She would see me at two that afternoon, but cautioned that it would be brief.

Beatrice Rangel had a long rectangular office in the north wing of Miraflores Palace, facing Avenida Pastor, the main roadway outside the palace. I recall the juxtaposition because eight months later a rebel tank moving along Pastor raked the windows with heavy machine gun fire. On that occasion President Perez used cunning and audacity to turn the tables on incompetently led rebel troops (led by Lt. Col. Hugo Chavez, who was subsequently imprisoned). In the early afternoon of September 30 it seemed unlikely that I would learn anything. The office was bedlam. Senior military officers and civilian aides rushed in and out with paper and verbal messages. Worse, a phalanx of six telephones on Rangel's credenza pealed like an electric xylophone. Four were handled by two secretaries in the outer office. The fifth was a direct line to President Perez. The sixth seemed to be a direct line to military intelligence. I sat on her sofa, sipping chamomile tea, waiting for a break in the storm. When it came, the situation she described was bleak. Rebel soldiers surrounded the Haitian Palace. No units of regular soldiers had emerged to defend Aristide.

I asked Rangel if I could tell her a story. "Just listen, I'll compress it." I did compress it, but what follows is a fuller version of what became known as the Dominican parable.

Just before November 16, 1961 a well organized military coup was being launched in Ciudad Trujillo, soon to be returned to its original name of Santo Domingo. Six months previously the dictator, Generalissimo Trujillo, had been assassinated (with a little help from the CIA) and now his less bright but equally villainous brothers were attempting to restore the family dictatorship with the wholehearted support of the Dominican army. I knew about this because I was there. Ciudad Trujillo was my first post.

As the soldiers set out to occupy key points in the capital and as lists were being made up of people to be seized and shot, success appeared well within the brothers' grasp. However, when dawn broke, the profile of a small U.S. naval force could be seen on the horizon. Two frigates and a destroyer were steaming three miles off shore.

Another unexpected complication faced the Trujillo family. The military attaché in the U.S. consulate general had uncovered the plot. The consulate informed Washington and the military attaché, a Marine lieutenant colonel, opened clandestine negotiations with the general commanding the country's only more or less functional attack aircraft, two squadrons of World War II P51 Mustangs. One squadron was based near the capital and the other at Santiago de los Cabelleros in the North. The previous night the General had deployed the squadron in the capital to join the other in Santiago.

At first light on November 16 he launched both squadrons in a bombing raid on army bases in the capital. The aircraft were unconventionally armed. Without any brackets for bombs and with inoperative machine guns, each pilot was given a sack of hand grenades. Meanwhile on the ground, the anti-aircraft defences were not so much unconventional as impractical. Alerted to the attack by the roar of propeller engines and the crunch of hand grenades bursting harmlessly around the perimeter, soldiers at the army headquarters in the city raced to the roof. Headquarters was the Fortaleza Ozama, a crenellated fortress of the Beau Geste style much favoured by the late dictator. On the roof were Krupp water cooled machine guns, purchased some years before by the Generalissimo's Puerto Rican financial advisor, Hector Benitez Rexach. What Rexach may or may not have known and the soldiers belatedly discovered was that the machine guns had been manufactured about 1905. These pre-Wright brothers weapons were capable of only minimum elevation. As a result, a sort of Three Stooges historical tableau unfolded with troops wrestling hopelessly with their ancient weapons while overhead pilots in antique aircraft lobbed grenades with uniform inaccuracy.

More serious developments were visible out to sea. From the embassy roof I could see that the three warships had been joined by four more, including the aircraft carrier *Boxer*. My secretary and I completed the arcane chore of converting my report in book cypher. I delivered the telegram for External Affairs to the All America Cable and Wireless Office and set off home for lunch. As I turned onto Avenida George Washington, a broad thoroughfare that ran along the edge of the Caribbean, I saw a group of American officers from the consulate standing by the sea wall, looking out to sea. I recognized them all: a vice consul, the information officer, a CIA officer, and the Marine lieutenant colonel. I stopped the car, walked over and was making a facetious remark about gunboat diplomacy when the colonel looked at his watch and said: "Damn! They're late." At this moment there was a gathering, thunderous roar from the west and three squadrons of Sabre jets from the Guantanamo naval base in Cuba swept low across the waterfront. They passed six times, backwards and forwards the full length of the city. By the time they had returned to Guantanamo, the coup was over and incredibly, no blood had been shed.

"What was that?" I said disingenuously.

"President Perez ordered his F-16s to scramble and buzz Port-au-Prince." Skol paused. That would have put the wind up. At that speed, rocketing over the city, everyone on the ground, especially the army, would have thought they were American. But, too bad ... it didn't happen. The palace surrendered and Aristide was taken before they could get airborne."

Aristide landed at about 5 a.m. accompanied by two secretaries, the chief of police of Port-au-Prince and five members of his bodyguard. I wrote at the time that he "looked terrible, torn between gratitude that his life had been spared and feeling that martyrdom with his people might have been preferable." As he emerged from the aircraft the worst of the ordeal was over. But there was one surprise still waiting for him and most of the small reception party. Within minutes of landing Ambassador Libourel informed Aristide that on instructions from his government, he wished to invite the president to stay at his residence and then, when sufficiently rested, to proceed to France. Libourel then withdrew to his residence and prepared for his guest. The infuriated personal representative of the president of Venezuela, the U.S. ambassador, Aristide, and I followed in a separate vehicle. En route we suggested to Aristide that the image of following Jean Claude Duvalier (Baby Doc) to France might not be popular with his supporters. Rangel also indicated delicately that it would be appropriate for him to move to the presidential suite at the Hilton that had been prepared for him.

In the course of the drive, and over coffee and defrosted canapés provided by Libourel's dyspeptic majordomo, Aristide gave us his account. It was heavily punctuated with the emotion of the previous three days. We sat in the main floor gallery of Libourel's large italianate residence. The windows looked out on the fairway of the 6th hole of the Valie Valle Arriba Golf and Country Club, from where I had once hooked a ball onto Libourel's roof tiles. Aristide looked crumpled, a condition magnified by his short, frail stature. An expressive face, which usually telegraphed his feelings, showed misery and flashes of anger. The extraordinary charm that I was later to enjoy was not visible.

Aristide told us that he first learned of the plot on Saturday, the 28th. Given reassurance by General Cedras and other officers, he dismissed the rumours as a joke. Only on Sunday did he recognize the seriousness of the situation. He said that it was not until the coup was well under way that he realized that his handpicked army chief, Raoul Cedras, had become the coup leader.

On the basis of his account, Aristide was fortunate to be alive. He repeatedly emphasized that Dufour, the French ambassador in Port-au-Prince, had saved his life. Alerted that the president was in danger, Dufour drove to Aristide's home to find that rebel soldiers surrounded it. Weapons were fired sporadically and one of Aristide's bodyguards was killed. The ambassador managed to get Aristide into his car and set off for the presidential palace despite bursts of sub-machine gun fire directed at the ground in front of the car. Dufour deposited Aristide within the walls of the palace in the centre of town on the Champs du Mars. At this time bodyguards protected the palace, but the situation deteriorated as the morning wore on. Soldiers isolated the palace and opened fire on the defenders.

However, as we later learned, the phone link had not been cut and Aristide and his staff were able to appeal to some Haitians, Americans, and Venezuelans for help. By late afternoon, with no sign of loyal soldiers, Aristide walked out of the palace and surrendered. The soldiers who seized him argued about who should shoot him. Aristide's hands were tied with his own necktie and he was led off to the Dessalines army barracks that adjoined the palace. In the barracks he was forced to lie face down on the floor. Again, he thought that he was about to be shot. Soldiers mocked him, shouting, "To hell with democracy ... thank God the army is in charge."

At this point, two things happened: Cedras appeared and announced that he was in charge, and Ambassador Dufour reached the Dessalines barracks by telephone. According to Aristide, this call lowered temperatures and negotiations soon began for Aristide's exile. These discussions were undertaken primarily with the Americans and the Venezuelans. Late that evening Aristide was taken to the airport. Inevitably there were delays. President Perez's aircraft was en route from Caracas when it was found that the Haitian air traffic controllers had fled. A dozen military trucks were requisitioned to illuminate the runway with their headlights. Aristide told us that the control tower was operated by the American air attaché. I learned much later that Aristide had decorated Ambassador Boccachiampe for the protection she gave to him. A petite woman, only slightly smaller than Aristide, she stood beside him and insisted on the observance of the Perez/Cedras agreement during another tense and vulnerable period while they waited for the Venezuelan aircraft.

Several times Aristide brought the conversation back to Cedras. Deeply offended by Cedras's treachery, he referred to a list of people to be shot that was being compiled by the army. There had been a lot of killing that day, perhaps as many as twelve hundred had died. Most had been targeted and then murdered during the night and morning of September 30 and October 1. Aristide accused Cedras of greed and power madness. He did not know what was happening to members of his own family, his friends and his cabinet. Fatigued, disoriented and depressed, he broke into tears.

At last, Libourel led Aristide off to bed and Skol, Rangel, and I tried to piece together what we thought had ignited the coup. There is a multitude of versions still circulating in Haiti about what really happened. On one point everyone agrees. It was a coup waiting to happen. The long-standing antagonism of the elite became reinforced by Aristide's charismatic populism. René Préval, the prime minister, also had enemies. More serious was Aristide's provocation of the army. Mutual distrust had grown since the election and had been inflamed by Aristide's decision to establish a militia group, independent of the army and loyal to the president. Aristide had taken this step for reasons of self preservation. To the army it resembled a sort of remodelled Tonton Macoute. It did not take a long memory in the Haitian army to recall that the regular forces had been outmaneuvered by François Duvalier (Papa Doc), who had formed his own militia, the original Tonton Macoute, and emasculated the army. The Tontons had been *déchouké* or "torn apart" – in many cases literally – after the flight of Baby Doc. The army had been attempting to reassert its position as the nation's principal political arbiter.

Neither General Cedras nor his senior colleagues would have been enthusiastic about a well-armed competitor. Nevertheless, the coup was not well orchestrated and did not have the committed support of all officers. But soldiers and NCOs, already menaced by Aristide's popular justice, felt especially targeted by his extraordinarily provocative and maladroit speech of September 27. The attack on his residence the following night may have been undertaken by a small group of soldiers from the elite Leopard Battalion, within which an anti-Aristide group had formed. Cedras, senior officers, and other units of the army waited through the night and early morning to see who and how many would defend Aristide. And, of course, they waited to see what response there would be to Aristide's appeal to the people to come out into the streets. When it was clear that no significant defence was emerging, that the American Embassy was doing nothing to discourage the coup and in the absence of F-16s, Cedras and the others moved off the fence and joined the coup. In Cedras's case, the rebels had appealed to him to join, presumably to give greater depth and "legitimacy" to their cause.

Cedras had betrayed his president. Aristide loathed him with a scorching intensity. Over the next three years, as de facto leader of an increasingly brutal, corrupt and chaotic government, Cedras was demonized by much of the international community and by the international press. Evil is not a label lightly fastened on all the crooks and conspirators in this macabre and dolorous episode. Cedras was probably not evil, but he was unable or perhaps unwilling to curb the appetites of those around him who were. Principal among these was Colonel Michel François. François was ruthless, increasingly prosperous and already openly accused of being a key man in a narcotics transhipment enterprise. Drug trafficking was one of the issues about which the new Aristide government was becoming energetic. According to some accounts François chafed under the new policy and set about securing a free hand by actively plotting against Aristide.

In September 1994, Jimmy Carter, Colin Powell, and Sam Nunn negotiated with Cedras and found a man driven not so much by greed or power but by a swollen vision of himself as a patriot. He saw himself in the tradition of the founders of the first black republic – Dessalines, Christophe, and Pétion – prepared to fight to the end defending his country from foreign invasion and domination. The Carter team found in this noble fantasy an opening through which they could appeal to his patriotism and offer comfortable exile and immunity from persecution. The exile of Cedras and his family and that of his principal confederates was negotiated, and the following morning U.S. forces came ashore unopposed and without loss of life. To my knowledge, neither Cedras, who may have regretted it, nor Aristide the beneficiary, ever referred to Cedras as one of those who saved the president's life. However, from Aristide's own account of the events of September 30 it seems clear that Cedras's intervention with his soldiers, whatever his motives or outside pressures, kept Aristide alive after his capture until lifted away by President Perez's aircraft.

Neither Cedras nor Aristide had warm feelings about the United States. Cedras was a graduate of the Fort Benning Army School of the Americas in Georgia, then notorious as a "staff college" for future military dictators. His disenchantment with the United States appears to date from the international isolation of Haiti following the coup. Aristide's antipathy ran deeper and for a much longer period. In varying degrees, Haitians had not forgiven the United States for the painful and humiliating occupation by American Marines from 1915 to 1934. In Aristide's case, the list of grievances was long. The Reagan Administration had supported a succession of corrupt and brutal governments. Para-military support services had frequently tried to assassinate him for stirring the poor with his courageous and increasingly popular liberation theology. It was no secret that several American ambassadors regarded Aristide as a "destabilizing" presence. Later, as a presidential candidate and president in exile, he was the subject of apparently fabricated and leaked CIA allegations that he was mentally unstable. Aristide was further grieved by his perception of the ambiguous role of U.S. embassy staff during the critical period when Cedras and other senior officers were deciding which way the wind was blowing. There was also relentless U.S. pressure to have Aristide agree to work with Cedras in Haiti, pressures to which he capitulated in the abortive Governor's Island (New York) Accord of July 1993.

Aristide's strong feelings about the United States surfaced from time to time in our conversations, but never so sharply as during our meeting on Boxing Day, 1991. Aristide was extremely concerned about his life expectancy following his return from exile to Port-au-Prince. He spoke of enemies and "other interests ... other forces" which, in his view, controlled many politicians and army officers.

"Other interests ... the bourgeoisie?" I asked.

"Non, plus haut que ça," More specifically, he remarked that the United States was in control of these "forces" and would determine his life and more probably his death soon after his return. I tried to soften this image, reminding him of the support he had received from President Bush and Bush's own condemnation of the coup. The conversation was interrupted by the telephone. Madame Mitterand was calling to convey encouragement and Christmas greetings. The discussion resumed and fell quickly back into the old grooves. On the role of the Organization of American States, he was skeptical. He felt that time was running out for him and that both OAS solidarity and the embargo were showing wear and tear. Apart from the United States, most OAS members meant well, but what could they do beyond sanctions that weren't backed up by the UN at that time? He had confidence in only a few members of the Haitian legislature. He referred to one senior member as an "ex-Macoute" who attended meetings of the chamber with a revolver in one pocket and a grenade in the other.

Two threads kept reappearing: his feeling that he had no control over events and fatalism about "the forces" opposing him. He repeated his foreboding that upon return to Haiti, "I will not last long before I am assassinated." For someone who spent long periods in hiding, lay flat on the floor of the jeep when changing hiding places, and who had escaped an assassin's bullet or the blade of a machete at least half a dozen times, this was a reasonable anxiety.

The setting of this conversation and the absence of family at Christmas time probably contributed to his gloom. For better security and privacy, President Perez had moved him from the Hilton Hotel to a presidential mansion within the "Círculo Militar" on the outer edge of Caracas. Well inside the perimeter of Venezuela's largest military base, Aristide had both security and privacy – and for his taste, too much of the latter. He had few friends in Caracas and in any event was not encouraged to leave the protection of the Venezuelan army. The house was vast, modern, and impressive from the outside. Inside, it was sparsely furnished, cold and impersonal. Aristide's loneliness in this house no doubt contributed to the warm welcome which he gave to me and a few of my colleagues and to the alacrity with which he took up the opportunity to move. Over the course of his stay in Venezuela, roughly five months, I visited Aristide fairly often. Haiti had become a special focus of Canadian foreign policy, and a particular interest of Prime Minister Mulroney.

A strong relationship between the prime minister and President Perez had developed over the issue. Perez paid his first visit to Canada at the prime minister's invitation only eight days before the coup. I had flown in Perez's plane and attended the lunch at Sussex Drive where the president and the prime minister agreed that it would be useful to form a Haiti support group comprised of France, the United States, Venezuela, and Canada. Despite differences, particularly with France, this support group sprang into active engagement immediately after the coup. Assessing the group in order of enthusiastic, constructive involvement, Perez was well ahead of the pack, followed by Mulroney. Bush soon became lukewarm and Madame Mitterand was much more personally committed to Aristide and Haiti than her husband.

When I saw Aristide off at the airport on October 2, bound for an OAS ministerial meeting in Washington twenty-eight hours after his arrival in Caracas, he singled out for their prompt solidarity this support group, and included Prime Minister Manley of Jamaica. He was delighted that

Prime Minister Mulroney had spoken to him the previous evening, and felt it was the beginning of another warm relationship. I had last seen Aristide at the French ambassador's residence and the change was astonishing. International endorsement, rest, and President Perez's well-organized and high profile treatment had transformed Aristide from a dejected, scruffy, emotionally drained figure into "a calm, purposeful leader." The new wardrobe provided by President Perez certainly helped and perhaps also the move, the evening before, to the Hilton hotel.

These conversations invariably focused on two issues. The first was the search for a suitable candidate for Prime Minister of Haiti who could serve as a bridge between the de facto government (including the military and the legislature) and Aristide. The second was the means by which both sides could be persuaded to accept or accommodate each other. While a number of candidates were nominated, including the former head of the Haitian Communist Party, neither the sanctions nor the leverage of this powerful group of leaders were able to achieve a negotiated solution. In the end it was the threat of force and the actual visibility of an American invasion fleet that brought down the regime and opened the way for Aristide's return. Eight months previously Beatrice Rangel had forecast this imbroglio in the event that Aristide won the presidency. She doubted his willingness to develop a modus vivendi with the army and with the entrenched brigands – the Duvalieristes and Macoutes. The popular wisdom of the time was that without an accommodation with these groups Haiti would be ungovernable.

Within days of the coup, mutual intransigence and many institutional interests slammed doors to Aristide's return. Important elements of the two main currents of Haitian religious life opposed Aristide. One was a group of powerful Voudu priests and Ligonde, the Duvalieriste Archbishop of Port-au-Prince, whose anti-Aristide views were shared by the Vatican. Aristide's rising prominence as a liberation theology priest had made relations with Rome uncomfortable. Relations deteriorated further when Aristide entered politics. The Vatican emphasized its distinctive view of the Haitian political scene by becoming the only sovereign entity to formally recognize the Cedras regime.

Moderate Haitians considered that any viable solution would require Cedras's presence. On this issue more than any other, Aristide was inflexible for the first year. Messages from many of his supporters reinforced his stubbornness. And then there was the French factor. The support group was not all of one mind. On October 17 I advised the Department that "concern

John Graham with a colleague in Haiti

remains that the already difficult task of restoring constitutionality and Aristide ... is becoming unnecessarily more difficult as a result of conflicting advice that Aristide is receiving from the French and others." The French line was that Cedras's departure must be a condition of Aristide's return.

It can be argued in retrospect – and Aristide undoubtedly would agree – that his situation would have been politically untenable and physically dangerous if he had worked in harness with Cedras and a largely uncleansed army. However, Haiti paid a heavy price for three years of truculence on both sides. Early compromise was blocked and the sanctions failed to achieve their purpose. They had been disastrous. Ian Martin, the former deputy head of the OAS/UN monitoring team in Haiti described the turmoil of haphazard and inadequately targeted applications of sanctions as "mangled multilateralism." The sanctions were biting.

It is difficult to exaggerate the impact of three years of sanctions on almost every segment of Haitian society. In October 1994, when President Aristide returned in triumph, the normally formidable task of governing had become many times more difficult because of economic, social, political, and agricultural devastation. Several thousands had been killed or had "disappeared," roughly fifty thousand fled by sea, many of them drowning when their flimsy, overcrowded fishing boats sank. Many more thousands were displaced from their homes. So appalling were the economic consequences and the rising toll of human rights abuses that by early 1994 many observers, including persons in the human rights community, had concluded that the only humanitarian option was military intervention.

Through the spring and summer of that year Somalia cast a debilitating shadow and kept the Clinton government tied to the sanctions policy. However, by midsummer, President Clinton also concluded that there was no alternative to invasion. On July 31 the United Nations Security Council authorized the United States to take military action on behalf of the UN. Clinton urged Mr. Chrétien to join him and commit elements of the Canadian forces to the invasion. The Canadian government was expected to agree given the narrowing of options, reinforced by the special responsibility that Canada had assumed for Haiti. However, the government turned down Mr. Clinton, saying that it would support the post invasion phase – the policing of Haiti.

My last conversation with Aristide took place in April 1995 in the presidential palace in Port-au-Prince. I had left the Department and was running a NGO (non-governmental organization) programme in Haiti in support of the elections that would choose a successor to Aristide. The occasion was the investiture of Mr. Mulroney with Haiti's most exalted decoration. After our many sessions in Caracas and one in Washington, it was extraordinary to see Aristide presiding over his government in his own country. He radiated self-assurance and the joy of long-denied power. In our short discussion he repeated that his best and staunchest friends in the international community were Brian Mulroney and Carlos Andres Perez. Outside, on the edge of the Champs de Mars, demonstrators chanted in creole "*Tidid, Prezidan pou vie!*" (Aristide – President for Life!).

AN INTERVIEW WITH AMBASSADOR ARTHUR MENZIES

by Tom Earle

Mr. Menzies: When I was head of the Far Eastern section, from 1946 to 1948, and then head of the American and Far Eastern division from 1948 to 1950, we were preoccupied with purging Japanese militarism and establishing a more democratic form of government in Japan. In this we were greatly helped by Dr. Herbert Norman, who was the Head of the Canadian Liaison Mission in Tokyo. Herbert Norman had been born of Canadian missionary parents in Japan and grew up speaking Japanese. He had studied Japanese after his university work in Canada and had written a very impressive book called Japan's Emergence as a Modern State. It described the transformation of Japan from the 1868 military feudal Tokugawa government to the Meiji restoration and Japanese modernization with a Westminster style of government. Norman had excellent contacts with parliamentarians and academics in Japan, and he sent us a good deal of advice, some of it, of course, exchanged with British, Australian, New Zealand and other colleagues there. It was of great assistance to us in the work of the Far Eastern Commission in Washington.

Mr. Earle: In 1950, at the age of 33, you were the youngest person ever to hold a position comparable to Head of the Canadian Liaison Mission, succeeding Herbert Norman. If at the time Canada and Japan had been formally at peace, it was said, the mission would have been an embassy and your title would have been ambassador.

Mr. Menzies: My wife and I and our two little children went off by ship from San Francisco to Tokyo in late November 1950. We were met at the dock in Yokohama by Dubs Dritton, the commercial counsellor, and Charles Eustace McGaughey and their wives. We were driven in a little cavalcade up to the Canadian embassy in Tokyo. There we were left at the front door, to be confronted with thirty-two Japanese servants, who all bowed. Their spokesman wished us well on our entry to this great Marler mansion that had survived the bombings of Tokyo.

It was a great reinforced concrete building, without a doubt Canada's largest legation or embassy building abroad. I remember one little Japanese-American lad who was invited to my son's birthday party saying to his mother, "That room is so big. It starts here"– and he stretched out his arms like a man giving an account of the size of a fish he caught – "and it just keeps on going from there to there to there." It was so big, in fact, that the living room was 60 by 40 feet and the dining room could seat 46 people at the table.

Circumstances in Japan changed remarkably between Herbert Norman's time and my own. He was involved very much in the effort to democratize Japan, and for that purpose, personal knowledge of Japanese society was invaluable. However, in June 1950 the Korean conflict broke out and Canada took part in the United Nations' response, first by sending three destroyers out to Far Eastern waters, and then a special brigade of troops. Probably my greatest preoccupation during my three and a half years in Japan was the war in Korea. We ended up with about 5,000 troops in Korea and another 3,000 in Japan during this period. Troops in Korea came back to Japan for rest and relaxation on their holidays. I went over to visit the troops in Korea quite a number of times, and on several occasions I had an opportunity to interview Chinese prisoners of war. That, for me, was quite an interesting experience.

At the beginning of my time in Tokyo, one of my early tasks was to present a letter of introduction to General Douglas MacArthur. In his very busy program I was given a slot at the end of a long afternoon; I think I went for a six o'clock appointment. I sat, and I sat, and I sat, and finally I was ushered into a darkened room, probably 30 feet long by 20 feet wide. General Macarthur sat behind his great desk at one end of the room. American and United Nations flags hung behind him, and a light was focused on him. I more or less crept in the door and stood there quietly until the general finally arose from his desk. He came along and grabbed me by the hand, tore open the envelope with a letter from Mike Pearson, whom he had met before, and slouched down on a heavy leather covered sofa with me sitting beside him. He smoothed a few bits of hair he had over the top of his head and he said, "My, it's tough to be a defeated general." This, of course, was a play for sympathy. He gave me an account of the current situation, in which Chinese volunteers had entered North Korea and had started to drive back the U.S. forces, which had moved up close to the Yalu River. This was what he referred to as being a defeated general. MacArthur had great abilities in showmanship and knew how to deal with American senators and other visitors. He was adept at getting their sympathy for his position.

General MacArthur was very highly regarded by the Japanese for the relatively sympathetic if firm position he had taken, and the Japanese generally regarded the occupation of Japan as an American phenomenon. They didn't give credit to any of the other countries that were represented there, even those with troops. In this connection, I should mention that while Canada had been prepared to send a sixth division to enter the war against Japan, only a few of the advanced units had reached Okinawa by the time the atomic bomb was dropped on Hiroshima in August 1945. The British, Australian, New Zealand, and Indian governments all sent troops for the occupation of Japan. The Canadians, however, decided they had not been sufficiently directly involved in the war against Japan to warrant sending troops for the occupation. As a result, the Canadian role in Japan was limited more to a diplomatic one. In some ways, that role gave us easier access to the Japanese foreign ministry, which didn't treat us as an occupying power but, rather, as a potential trading partner across the Pacific.

Mr. Earle: *What about the aspect of the mission dealing with the actual Japanese peace treaty?*

Mr. Menzies: Canada had a general interest in western policy toward Japan. We had participated in the trials process and specifically in the trials of Japanese officers who had abused Canadian prisoners of war, principally those who had been taken prisoner with the fall of Hong Kong in December 1941. We had particular interests in the Japanese peace treaty relating to Japanese pre-war trading practices, which we did not think were very honourable, and we were very much concerned about Japanese fishing boats.

Mr. Earle: *With regard to fishing, what about the clause that Canada expected and wanted a firm binder on Japan to observe all international fishing agreements in the Pacific? Japanese fishermen had consistently broken the prewar agreements prior to 1941.*

Mr. Menzies: You have put it very well. We were concerned about Japanese fishing practices, particularly Japanese boats fishing off the west coast of British Columbia. We wanted a clause put into the Japanese peace treaty to cover this. Our American friends, however, finally took the position that if Canada were to insist on a clause protecting its fisheries and American fisheries, then the Philippines would want a clause protecting their fisheries, the Australians theirs, the New Zealanders theirs, and so it would go. So they suggested that instead of having a clause in the peace treaty, we should negotiate a North Pacific fisheries agreement among Japan, the United States, and Canada. The nub of the matter was a clause in the agreement that said a country would have exclusive rights, or full rights at least, to the fish that spawned in its waters, provided that it managed the fisheries in a scientific way and used the fishery to the maximum sustainable yield. That was a principle that was introduced for the first time in international fisheries law and has served us well. I don't think that Canada could have got such an agreement from Japan if the United States hadn't been the occupying power and able to put a good deal of pressure on the Japanese, who accepted the concept. They agreed not to fish east of the International Date Line for pelagic fish, such as salmon, that moved into Canadian or American waters to spawn and then out to sea for three or four years.

In November 1956 I accompanied the Honourable Paul Martin, who was then the Minister of National Health and Welfare, on a trip out to the Far East. We had a stop in Vietnam where Mr. Martin met President Ngo Dinh Diem, who was a devout Roman Catholic, and his foreign minister, Mr. Vu Van Mau, and reported fairly favourably on the impression they had made. From Vietnam we went on to visit Australia for the Olympic Games, then to New Zealand for a Colombo Plan conference, and on around the world and back to Canada. On that trip, Martin seized every opportunity to get a good press release, and he maintained excellent relations with half a dozen newspapermen who accompanied us. It was a liberal education to work with Mr. Martin. He was up early, read his papers, got into his briefing book, and was ready to go by 8:15 every morning. By evening he'd be pretty well pooped out, but would go to bed and be ready again the next day for whatever encounter awaited him.

[Mr. Menzies then turned to the topic of Malaysia]

During the time when I was high commissioner (1958 to 1961) in what was called at that time Malaya, now Malaysia, communist terrorists under Chin Peng – these were people of Chinese origin – were very active in the jungle areas of the country. A curfew was on, and you couldn't go out of Kuala Lumpur at night without military escort. Certain areas of the country were sealed off from time to time as drives were made by British, Australian, New Zealand, Malay and Gurkha troops.

Despite the communist terrorist uprising, Malaya's economy continued to improve. We wanted to take some part in this, so we began to investigate aid projects. Some of these simply involved the sending of officials of Malay or other ethnic origin to Canada to take further training. We sent quite a few fisheries officers to study fisheries cooperatives and fisheries methods at St. Francis Xavier University. We provided a good deal of training there under the Colombo Plan. We brought people over to Ottawa and attached them to different government departments or sent them to a university for a period of time for refresher courses. We also supplied quite a bit of flour to supplement the rice which is the mainstay of the Burmese diet, and we built or started to build what was called the Thaketa Bridge. It connected the downtown area of Rangoon with a suburb across the Thaketa River, which joined the Rangoon River. This was a swing bridge, and the great central support pylon rested on a very muddy bottom, because the whole structure of lower Burma is really a great alluvial plain. Mud has been brought down the Irrawaddy River for millennia, piling yard on yard. The pylon was poured and in the middle of a local storm it fell over into the mud. That was after I left Burma. While I was in Malaya, I went up to Rangoon two or three times a year. There was a direct flight from Kuala Lumpur to Rangoon, I think it was on a Friday. I could spend a week in Rangoon on business and perhaps another week travelling throughout the country to get some impressions. I have very warm recollections of my visits to Rangoon.

One of the projects from which I derived the most satisfaction established a three-way agreement among the University of British Columbia, Malaya, and Singapore to introduce business management courses. British training up to that time either taught you to be an economist, which was a sort of hands-off intellectual effort to analyze economic trends in the world, or an accountant. Malaya had no university training in business management, and Canada, like the United States, was far ahead. So we made an important contribution through a five-year contract among the universities to introduce business management. Teachers' college technical training was the other program I helped get started. Under the British, the Malaysian school system had been mainly designed to train clerks to fill positions in the civil service. There was a need for technical training in shipbuilding and outboard motor management in the fisheries villages along the coast, woodworking, carpentry work, plumbing, electrical trades, and so on. We brought teachers from training schools right across Canada and offered technical subjects to teachers at a centre in Kuala Lumpur. We worked with the Malayan Department of Education to expand and extend the technical system right down to the elementary level, because quite a lot of the students left at age of eleven or twelve in order to work in their fathers' enterprises.

Mr. Earle: *From 1965 until 1972 you served as High Commissioner to Australia, the sister dominion, as it was once called. Were there any areas of bilateral interest in which Canada was particularly involved during the period in which you held that post?*

Mr. Menzies: In many ways the posting to Australia was one of the most agreeable ones I had. Altogether we were there for seven years. I went out when Sir Robert Menzies was still prime minister, and having the same name as the prime minister of Australia gave me a certain little cachet to begin with on the post.

When we arrived there, I got a lesson in Australian agriculture. The day we arrived in Canberra the agricultural authorities swooped down on a farm in northern New South Wales, burned all the cattle, and used flame-throwers to burn a large part of the bush around the homestead. The reason for this was that an Australian pastoralist, or farmer, had stopped in Canada and filled a thermos flask with Charolais semen which he took back to try to improve the quality of his cattle herd. The Australian authorities argued that this semen could have contained a disease called blue tongue. In fact we have never had any blue tongue in Canada, but there is an open border between Canada and the United States, and some blue tongue, a rather virulent cattle disease, had occurred in Texas, quite a few miles from the Canadian border. So the Australian authorities wanted to set an example. Their people must rigidly avoid all kind of actions that might introduce disease that would adversely affect their cattle or sheep.

During the years we were there, 1965 to 1972, I found that Australia, under a Conservative-Liberal-Country Party Alliance, was making many of the same strides in economic development as we were in Canada. There were huge mineral developments in Western Australia, Queensland, and in the Northern Territory, discoveries of large copper-zinc deposits, iron on the west side, and coal. And to some extent Canada and Australia needed to exchange views about export markets for their minerals. The Japanese, providing one of the principal markets, were quite willing to play one off against the other. We also had a common interest in wheat and other grains on the world market. Australia shares with Canada the same type of federal government. We both inherited the British parliamentary system of government, so legislation in the two countries was quite comparable. We were, I think, ahead of Australia in the introduction of social legislation both at the federal and provincial levels, and there was a good deal of Australian interest in finding out what we were doing in that area.

We were also, of course, closely associated with the Australians in looking at many of the world's problems, whether at the United Nations, in the Commonwealth, or in the Asia-Pacific area.

One of the most difficult issues I had to face was the Australian commitment of troops to Vietnam. Canada, as a member of the International Commission for Supervision and Control, did not commit any troops to fight alongside the Americans in defence of South Vietnam. I went quite often to speak to groups at the Returned Services League, which is like the Canadian Legion, and the men there would say, "Well, you were with us in the First World War, you were with us in the Second World War, you were with us in Korea; but where are you now that we need more support in Vietnam?" I tried to explain that we were engaged in the International Commission's work of supervision and control but it didn't wash with them. It was only toward the end of my time, with Gough Whitlam's Labour government coming in, that the Australians began to change their attitudes toward Vietnam and realized that this was a no-win situation.

Mr. Earle: *While you were serving as high commissioner to Australia, you also held the post of high commissioner to the government of Fiji. Did you*

*have to go there often on official business? And what kind of bilateral
activity took place during your tenure?*

Mr. Menzies: On our trips to Australia from Canada, the Canadian
Pacific Airlines touched down at Nandi in Fiji so we had seen the Fiji
Islands en route. As Fiji moved towards independence in 1970, I took
two or three days off as a bit of a holiday to write some reports on conditions there for the Department of External Affairs. Canada had a
number of missionaries in Fiji, and the B.C. Sugar Company imported
a lot of sugar from Fijian cane fields, so I was invited to take on the high
commissioner posting when it became independent in 1970. I enjoyed
visiting there for a week, perhaps three times a year.

I take some satisfaction from having gotten the Canadian
International Development Agency (CIDA) interested in projects there,
particularly those involving marine biology, assisting the Fijians to learn
more scientifically about the seas around their islands and how they
might best be exploited on a sustainable basis. I also started the ball
rolling on CIDA's construction of a science building for the University
of the South Pacific in Fiji. We had, and have, several Canadians on the
staff of the University of the South Pacific.

*Mr. Earle: Your next ambassadorial post was to NATO as permanent
representative to the North Atlantic Council from 1972 until 1976.
I can remember calling on you in NATO headquarters and being given
a briefing on the position of the Canadian government on various NATO
issues of that day.*

Mr. Menzies: When I arrived in Brussels in September 1972, Dr. Joseph
Luns, the Secretary General of NATO, gave me a very hard time about
the reduction of Canadian forces in Europe. That certainly coloured the
first couple of years I was there, because we had cut our troops from
10,000 to 5,000. That reduction had been announced, I guess, about
1969. But it had just taken effect and the troops had actually been
removed immediately prior to my arrival in Brussels. It wasn't a very
popular position because the military leaders of the alliance, the
Military Committee and the Supreme Headquarters of the Allied
Powers, were constantly calling for additional forces to balance what
appeared to be the continued buildup of Russian forces on the other
side of the Iron Curtain.

In fact, I arrived there during a period bristling with confrontation. The Conference on Security and Cooperation in Europe was being discussed, questions were being asked as to how to initiate discussions, and the conference was eventually held in two parts. The Conference on Security and Cooperation in Europe met as a series of committees in Geneva, and at times in Helsinki. Another set of more purely military discussions took place in Austria. They focused on trying to achieve a balance of forces in central Europe between the Warsaw Pact and NATO countries. NATO and Warsaw Pact members had delegations in Austria for those discussions which were called, and aimed at, Mutual Balanced Force Reductions.

When I went to Brussels I had a good deal to learn about Europe in general. I had never before had a posting there so I didn't have quite the same background as most of my colleagues. I found it of great interest to visit the different NATO European capitals, and also to visit the Canadian forces at Lahr and the nearby Canadian air contingent and get their military view of the east-west confrontation. Unfortunately there was a certain rivalry between the European countries, which at that time were trying to pull together economically, and the United States. I think there was jealousy on both sides with respect to the production of military equipment. The Americans did not wish to become dependent on any one country. They wanted to have a complete range of equipment produced in the United States.

Mr. Earle: *A few moments ago you mentioned Canada being somewhat of a pariah in the alliance as a result of slashing its NATO contribution. I think Mitchell Sharp was the foreign minister at the time and Mr. Cadieux was the Defence Minister. Another man who was a defence minister told me that the British were very upset about it. Denis Healey gave Canada a very rough time. This lingered, obviously, when you were the ambassador to NATO. But what was your opinion of the United States? A moment ago you touched on the United States in the NATO alliance when you were NATO ambassador. Was Henry Kissinger the Foreign Secretary and Nixon the President?*

Mr. Menzies: Yes.

Mr. Earle: *What did you think of them?*

Mr. Menzies: Dr. Kissinger was a very impressive performer at the foreign ministers' meetings. He had an ability to articulate the issues relating to east-west confrontation, and in his deep, guttural, Germanic voice he commanded attention. He sought to have private meetings of the foreign ministers where he could exercise his persuasive powers.

Several of the foreign ministers resisted this type of meeting because they didn't have enough command of French or English to engage in the interchange without reading out prepared notes. This was a constant feature of the meetings of foreign ministers in particular, that those who felt at ease in a free-swinging debate were put off by the Turks and others who didn't have the same command of the language.

One of the issues we faced was the introduction of a left-leaning government in Portugal. This government included a couple of Communist Party members, who were to be excluded by the Portuguese Socialist Party from positions where they might gain information about NATO military plans. But it was a very awkward situation for perhaps a year and a half or two years. Another issue that arose while we were there was the fisheries struggle between Iceland and Britain, the cod war. That created considerable tension. Then there was the continuing tension between Greece and Turkey, especially over the situation in Cyprus. The Greeks and Turks were not prepared to go into joint military manoeuvres in the eastern Mediterranean. There were claims to waters off the Greek islands near the Turkish coast, and the question of whether there might be oil in the seabed there. This was a constant source of irritation, and because we had forces committed to UNFICYP, the United Nations Force in Cyprus, our foreign ministers all took time at the foreign ministers' meetings to talk with the Greeks and Turks in an effort to make some progress toward the reunification of Cyprus.

Mr. Earle: Who were the Canadian foreign and defence ministers during the period when you were ambassador, and how did you get along with them? I think Don Jamieson was the foreign minister ...

Mr. Menzies: Yes.

Mr. Earle: How did you get on with the cabinet ministers?

Mr. Menzies: During most of my time there Mr. Richardson was the minister of defence. He was not an easily briefed man but he certainly supported Canada's military role in NATO. During my time we also had a visit from Prime Minister Trudeau.

Mr. Earle: At first he was skeptical of NATO, wasn't he?

Mr. Menzies: Yes, I think that would be an understatement. He certainly had deep questions about the advisability of Canada having troops in Europe. He thought that the Europeans themselves could muster the troops they needed, and he felt that our small contribution would probably be better if it was made air portable.

When Mr. Trudeau visited NATO, I made a special effort with my colleagues, briefing each of them in turn, in order to promote a good discussion on east-west relations. Several of them made rattling good speeches and Mr. Trudeau enjoyed his meetings with the permanent representatives very much. He felt that the council was more worthwhile as a place to exchange views on international affairs than he had thought. His only previous experience of this type of thing was with the Commonwealth Prime Ministers' Meetings, which are a more staid sort of session.

During the time when I was there, the Trudeau government was trying to establish a special relationship with the European Community – a contractual link. Negotiations took place with special representatives sent from Canada; Michel Dupuy came over for talks, for example. Talks at the ministerial level sought a special contractual link between Canada and the European Community as an organization. It didn't really work, but I was involved with General Dextraze, the Chief of the Defence Staff, in a little operation by which we got Helmut Schmidt, the chancellor of Germany, to have a talk with Mr. Trudeau and say to him that Germany would give its support to the contractual link, provided that Mr. Trudeau would guarantee that Canadian forces would be left in Germany. The way that it should be done was to get new tanks, which would anchor them to a land role and not the air-portable role that Mr. Trudeau had been thinking about. Mr. Trudeau said he had no money to buy the Leopard 2 tanks, splendid German tanks that were then being produced. Mr. Schmidt said that he would rent them to us. So we got the Leopard 2 tanks rented until we were in a position to pay cash for them. I think that kept the Canadian role there pretty steady until such time as the Cold War came to an end.

During Dr. Kissinger's time, he was anxious to ensure that there would be informal discussion of foreign policy questions between the United States and members of the European Community prior to the

Community taking a formal position. There had been tension during the Middle East crisis.

Mr. Earle: *The oil crisis?*

Mr. Menzies: Yes. The Americans had put troops in Germany on alert, backing up their position in the Middle East. And on another occasion the European foreign ministers had come out with a declaration on a Middle East settlement about which they had not consulted informally with the Americans. So there was a long, drawn out, informal discussion among council members about how to ensure that there would be suitable consultation before public positions were taken.

The upshot of this was an Atlantic Declaration, issued in 1974 at the meeting in Ottawa when the foreign ministers met there. We had hoped it would be called the Ottawa Declaration, but it was in fact called the Atlantic Declaration. It was to demonstrate the continuing solidarity of the bridge across the Atlantic between Europe and North America. In the initial drafting of the declaration, the references were to the United States and Europe and the bridge between the United States and Europe. My job, in the back room, was to ensure that every time the United States was mentioned in the declaration that, "and Canada" would be added so that there would be a constant recognition of Canada's contribution to the Atlantic alliance and the bridge across the Atlantic.

Mr. Trudeau had serious doubts about the NATO alliance until he got educated about it, well on in his term of office as Prime Minister. At least that is the impression I have: that he had reservations about Canada's place in that alliance, but he was eventually brought around to see that it did some good. You will recall that at the end of his second tour as prime minister he made an impassioned plea for disarmament and made visits to all significant world leaders in the effort to bring about a reduction of the bristling confrontation that existed at that time. But certainly nothing came of it because the President of the United States at that time, Reagan, felt that the United States had to build up its capability to confront the USSR with its military might and industrial capability. It is probable that that had a good deal to do with the eventual approach of Mr. Gorbachev to abandon confrontation and the Cold War and move toward a settlement with the western democracies.

Mr. Earle: What was your assessment of Mitchell Sharp as a foreign minister? That's the last foreign minister I can think of or that I'll ask you to assess. He was in the post for quite a while and obviously he liked it very much.

Mr. Menzies: I was always very impressed with Mr. Sharp's professionalism in the job. Having been a civil servant in the past and having had the exacting role of finance minister for a period of time, as well as having been deputy minister of Trade and Commerce, he knew the workings of the government inside out. He had a remarkable ability to absorb briefs and a very clear memory going back through a long period of time. Also he spoke quite well, just casting his eye on the notes that were put before him. I felt he was a very professional foreign minister.

Mr. Earle: Your next posting was a very important one, ambassador to China from 1976 to 1980. You were born in China and grew up there as what they called a "mish kid," a child of missionary parents. Tell me first how you felt about the posting and the challenges you were going to face when you took it.

Mr. Menzies: Having been born in China and having lived there off and on until I was 18, and then having studied Far Eastern history at Harvard University in the postgraduate school there, and having dealt with the Far East two times during my tours in Ottawa, I was quite keen to go to China before the end of my career. Therefore I was pleased that, at age 59, I was finally able to go back to that country. I realized with the communist government installed there, that this wasn't going to be a piece of cake at all. But as luck would have it, Chairman Mao Zedong died after I was appointed but before I was able to get to my post.

During the four years I was in China, there was a change of outlook on the part of the Chinese Communist Party leadership as Deng Xiaoping took up the reins of government and decided that China would have an "opening to the world," as he expressed it, in order to improve the Chinese standard of living, and at the same time increase China's own economic strength as a potentially great power.

Mr. Earle: What were some of the main issues of Sino-Canadian foreign policy that occupied your time ? What, for example, was the state of Chinese-Canadian relations? Did Canada's delayed recognition of the *government of Red China, as it used to be called, make things a wee bit difficult for you as ambassador?*

Mr. Menzies: No, I wouldn't say that it made things difficult. What we were anxious to do was to take advantage of any opportunities for commercial and investment arrangements in China before the United States, with all its strength in the economic area …

Mr. Earle: Saw the light of day and recognized China.

Mr. Menzies: Yes.

Mr. Earle: What was the state of Canada's relations with China when you took up your post in Peking? Had the great Cultural Revolution spent itself by then? What was the Trudeau government's policy toward China when you went to Peking?

Mr. Menzies: I had been appointed ambassador to China in September 1976. On the night that the Chinese ambassador in Ottawa was to give a farewell dinner for us, word came through about the death of Chairman Mao Zedong, that great figure of the Chinese revolution, so the dinner was cancelled. I postponed my trip to China by a week and arrived in early October, after the arrest of Chairman Mao's widow, Jianq Qing, and the so-called Gang of Four, a radical element that had seized effective power during the final days of Chairman Mao's life.

Mr. Earle: Was this part of the Cultural Revolution?

Mr. Menzies: Yes, it was in effect a resurrection of the Cultural Revolution after the death of Premier Zhou Enlai in 1975.

I had left China in 1935 to return to Canada to attend the University of Toronto, and although I had studied Chinese history at Harvard University and dealt with China during two periods in the Department of External Affairs, I'd never returned to mainland China, although I had been through Hong Kong a number of times in the intervening period. So I was fascinated to go back to China in 1976. That was 41 years after I had left China as a boy.

As we went by train from Hong Kong to Canton, I was greatly impressed by the rice fields laid out in good order and of good size, whereas before the war there had been just inefficient, pocket-handkerchief-sized fields. There was now rural electrification and water was being pumped mechanically instead of being drawn from wells by hand, waterwheels, or oxen. The roads were reasonably good. Bicycles were everywhere. The people looked relatively well fed and well dressed. It made quite an impression on me. Part of the railway track between Hong Kong and Canton was under repair when we went there, and the train slowed down. At one point it went clunk-clunk-clunk and we were off the rails and sitting on the ties. Of course, we all rushed to get out and have a look to see what was going on, but the attendants on the foreigners' cars, which were at the end of the train, quickly locked the doors and kept us in. It was something of a sight for me, though, to see some of the local militia people arresting one poor labourer, who apparently was going to be made the scapegoat for this break in the tracks. We watched from perhaps a hundred metres away as he was beaten to a pulp with the butts of the militia men's rifles. This presented a rather different side of China and it came as a great shock to my wife.

Because of that initial experience, I recalled something of my boyhood in China. At that time where we lived in the interior of China in particular, the peasantry lived a very difficult life – malnourished, wracked with various contagious diseases, put upon by bandits and by unruly soldiers, and generally living what the Chinese call a rather bitter life. The cities were much more lively. There was commerce, light industry, schools and so on. One could say that in this period prior to 1935, under the Nationalist Government, China was making some slow progress in these areas, and in education, transportation, and so on. Unfortunately, there was a good deal of corruption as well, but it didn't take quite the form it did in the later years before the big civil war with the communists.

Then the Japanese invasion brought all of this possible progress to an end. The Japanese invaded Manchuria in 1931, when I was a boy in China, and they invaded north China in 1937. From then on, until the Second World War, there was really very little change in China.

So when the communists took over in 1949 it was they who introduced a great number of reforms. They unified the whole country, they introduced socialization, reformed and nationalized land policy, and they introduced basic education and basic medicine throughout the country. These achievements were of no little importance. They were really significant and I appreciated them during the four years I spent in China from 1976 to 1980.

However, the other side of the coin was that the Communist Party insisted on holding all power in its own hands. It exercised this through the installation of party secretaries in the universities, in factories. Every institution had its party committee, and these sometimes were a source of jealousy, inefficiency, and so on. Much of the Communist Party leadership, made up largely of military men who had been engaged in the Long March and the civil war, did not sufficiently appreciate the need to make use of the perhaps two million intellectuals, people who had had something more than secondary education, to run the country. Many of the intellectuals, because they had been associated with the bourgeois class, had been liquidated, either in the initial revolutionary period, running up to the communist takeover in 1949, or during the Cultural Revolution from 1966 to 1976.

When we got to China, of course, the era of Mao Zedong was over, but during the long period of his rule everyone had learned to be very discreet. We lived on the eighth floor of an apartment building, and I would travel down on an elevator with a lady conductor. Shortly after I arrived, I asked her in my reasonable Chinese what the weather was like. She said, "Oh, I couldn't tell you. I haven't heard the morning's official weather forecast." She wasn't going to stick her neck out and tell me what the weather was going to be like. We found that all the Chinese contacts we had were very discreet. This didn't change until 1978 when Deng Xiaoping, a former vice-premier and associate of Premier Zhou Enlai, returned to power in the Communist Party and then as vice-premier, and finally premier, of the country.

Mr. Earle: What were the Trudeau government's policy and instructions to you when you were sent to China? How important to Canada was our embassy there when you held the post?

Mr. Menzies: Before I went out to China I had an opportunity to visit several of the provincial capitals and meet with provincial ministers in Canada and with senior officials and businessmen. I found that the businessmen were pretty discouraged about the prospects for trade. Some of them had spent quite a bit of money working up proposals for investment in China and joint ventures, but these had been discouraged at the end of Mao Zedong's period by the so-called radical Gang of Four. As far as the political relationship with China was concerned, Mr. Trudeau's views were certainly quite clear that we should do everything we could to open up friendly relations with China, to end China's isolation and to bring it into the community of nations. That was the position he had taken in his public speeches in Canada and during his visit to China in 1973.

Mr. Earle: *How did the Chinese regard you, a "mish kid", as you were called, who had lots of friends among the Chinese from your youth, many no doubt still around, when you went as ambassador?*

Mr. Menzies: I think that like my predecessor, John Small, the fact that we could speak Chinese was an advantage. Even though the official position of the Chinese Communist Party was to regard missionaries as having been the running dogs of the imperialists, I found a friendly attitude on the part of the Chinese. But their rules were very rigid and one was that they were not allowed to fraternize with foreigners. We could invite Chinese in groups of two or more to our residence or to a restaurant for a meal, especially when visitors were coming, but we could not establish a personal relationship with them. We couldn't say, "Let's get together on the weekend or go for a picnic out to the Ming tombs or to the Great Wall," and have an opportunity to get acquainted with them in that way.

Similarly, I made no effort during my initial period to get in touch with friends of my father and people I had known, because I didn't want to embarrass them. That situation changed during the time I was there. In 1978 Deng Xiaoping made a statement that indicated that he wished to open China to the world in terms of science and technology and also to strengthen China's position as a potential great power. That did lead to a number of quite interesting initiatives. The Chinese announced that they were going to send 10,000 junior academics and professional people abroad to various countries to get caught up in science and technology. Because over 90 percent of those who had a second language spoke English, the United States, Britain, Canada, and Australia were the favoured countries. As the United States had not yet established diplomatic relations with China, the emphasis was on Britain, Canada, and Australia.

At that time – I guess it was late in 1978 – we had a delegation made up of a number of provincial ministers of education visiting China. One of the more prominent ones was Bette Stephenson, who was quite a dynamic person as minister of education in the province of

Ontario. They came and talked with the Chinese about the facilities that existed in Canadian colleges and universities for advanced work in science, mathematics, engineering, forestry, aeronautics, and what have you. This was followed by another mission, made up of senior officials, deputy ministers, again from the provinces, who got down to greater detail. Then in early 1979, Ottawa put together a delegation made up of federal and provincial officials who came out to China to negotiate an agreement to provide a basis for Chinese students to come to Canada for advanced educational work, and, in apparent reciprocity, to facilitate visits to China of Canadian scholars who wished to do field work and research there.

At the time the federal government had no program of financial assistance for China in any way. There was in the Department of Trade and Commerce a section that facilitated education in Canada for people from countries that could pay their own way. Initially the Chinese talked about paying their own way but then they found that it was possible to get funds to help with their expenses from the UN Development Program, UNESCO, and other specialized agencies of the United Nations, which they had joined in 1971-72. So when we proposed that the Chinese should pay all their costs in Canada, they replied that they were prepared to pay for travel and a per diem for living costs but they hoped the Canadian side would provide office accommodation, instruction, lab equipment and so on for free. This presented the Canadian federal representatives with a real problem, and it was only when two or three of the deputy ministers phoned their ministers in Canada to ask for the promise of some money that an amount of $500,000 was put together to fund the program. So we can say that indeed the provincial governments were ahead of the federal government in recognizing the value not only to China but also to Canada of the exchange of scholars, and in promoting its steady development.

Mr. Earle: *What about Canadian trade and cultural missions to China when you were ambassador? Were there many of those?*

Mr. Menzies: I would say that during the last three years I was in China we had annually about a hundred delegations. Most of these were greeted from the Chinese side by a welcoming banquet. At the end of their three- or four-day stay, the delegates were expected to give a thank-you banquet. Sheila and I were stuffed to the ears by Chinese banquets during that time.

I'd like to say something about the cultural side. During the Cultural Revolution Madame Jiang Qing, Mao's wife, sought to eliminate all western influences from China. So the symphony orchestras of Peking, Shanghai, and Canton were simply disbanded in 1966 and had not been resurrected when we arrived in 1976. Musical scores from western composers were not permitted to be played in China, so one got both old Chinese classical music and more modern socialist versions that were of the hortatory type.

The first breakthrough on the Canadian side was when the Canadian Brass visited China for a tour of three different cities. Their melodies quite charmed the Chinese, and before you knew it they had been recorded and were being played over the loudspeakers on the railway trains and in other public places. Following that we had a visit of the Toronto Symphony Orchestra in 1978 with Maureen Forrester and Louis Lortie, a concert pianist. The meetings between the orchestra members and the resurrected members of the Peking Symphony, the Shanghai Symphony, and the Canton Symphony were quite emotional events. The Chinese spoke of ten years during which they were unable to play their instruments in public and were branded as people who aped the foreign imperialists. It was a great tour, and I was very pleased indeed that the CBC sent a television team to tape the program.

In 1978 there was a period of excessive optimism in China. Deng Xiaoping announced that 120 major projects would be launched and foreign companies were invited to come out and make proposals for all sorts of industries, mines, and infrastructure. The trouble was that China didn't have the infrastructure, energy supplies, and trained manpower to make 120 major projects work. Nor did it have the foreign exchange to pay for them. Quite a few Canadian companies felt that the embassy had been too encouraging in the spring of 1978 to get them to spend money to prepare proposals for China's development that were never taken up.

Mr. Earle: *What were some of the more difficult areas, or projects, that you had when dealing with the Chinese Foreign Office? Were you baffled much by the Chinese bureaucracy?*

Mr. Menzies: I always found the Chinese bureaucracy to be very courteous but my meetings were obviously limited by the briefs that had been prepared in advance. Government representatives followed the notes they had before them very carefully. If we introduced any new points into the discussions they would have to take note of these proposals and come back to us in another meeting.

Mr. Earle: You once defined the function of the Canadian embassy in Peking under five categories. To which areas did you give the most importance?

Mr. Menzies: I would come back, I think, to the sheer importance of China as one of the great countries of the world, representing one-fifth of the world's population. So I would say that the strategic significance was perhaps the most important thing.

Canada couldn't do very much about the balance of power except as a member of the NATO alliance and in collaboration with other countries, but it was my interest to encourage the Canadian National Defence College to visit Beijing and to have exchanges of views with their opposite numbers and to encourage Chinese military visitors to come to Canada simply to get them out of their own very narrowly restricted area.

I suppose our second interest, and one that is also all enveloping, is the trade relationship. China offers an important outlet not only for agricultural products like wheat and canola and so on, but also for minerals, for timber products and things of that kind. Increasingly, it offers markets for our areas of engineering know-how and industrial production, which Canada has developed and specialized in simply to make our great country work. Through trade of all kinds there is the possibility of establishing interpersonal relations between our Chinese-Canadian traders and their old families back in China. One can in this way have a very considerable influence. China will gradually open up more and more to the world as we go along.

Mr. Earle: What did you think of China's potential when you were ambassador and what do you think of its potential today, in 1994, as we're doing this interview?

Mr. Menzies: Certainly in the thirteen and a half years since I was there, China has made another great leap forward through privatization of industry. There are many people in China who have not benefited from the new industries that have been set up. There's been much exploitation of cheap labour, sometimes even of prison labour. But there's no doubt that as the country's standard of living has risen there is a wash-off to the benefit of a very large number of Chinese, and I think China's potential for growth as an industrial and agricultural force in the western Pacific and in the world generally is going to continue.

You know that Dr. Bethune was a Canadian surgeon who practised during the Spanish Civil War and then went out to China in 1938 to assist the Chinese Eighth Route Army in the fight against the Japanese occupying North China. He died of septicemia, I think, in March 1939. When I went to China, it occurred to me that we might mark the 40th anniversary of his arrival in China in 1938. I made a bit of an argument for this and presented it to the President of the China Society for Friendship with Foreign Countries. He said, "Oh, we have no such tradition of marking the arrival of foreigners in our country; we only mark the anniversaries of deaths, and we only mark the 50th anniversary." So I felt this had been an unfortunate initiative on my part into which I had put quite a bit of preparatory work. About twelve months later I was summoned to see the President of the Friendship Association. He said, "We have to organize quickly, Mr. Menzies, an anniversary to mark the 40th anniversary of the death of Dr. Norman Bethune, that great friend of the Chinese people." So we got together and organized a visit by some members of the Bethune family and four eminent Canadian doctors, who gave lectures at Chinese universities on medicine in Canada, which I thought would be more constructive than just having banquets. Trying to figure out the reason for this, it appeared from the Chinese speeches made during this visit that the Chinese, who set up figures to emulate, wanted to emulate someone who was not a Russian, who was a scientist, who represented the opening to the world, and encouraged young Chinese to learn from western science and technology.

As you know, there has been a constant expansion of Canadian exports to China since I made a statement on the subject on a visit to Canada in 1979. As the Chinese have strengthened their infrastructure, building more railways and high speed roads, and proceeded with electrification and the training of more and more people with engineering and scientific backgrounds and management know-how, they have been capable of more development-orientated projects. Canada has gone in on several mining projects. In aviation, it has sold aircraft to China and constructed some aircraft parts in China.

There has been, of course, very substantial investment through Hong Kong, quite often by Chinese-Canadians, in the new economic zones in Guangtong province, especially Shenzhen. I believe that today Canadian exports run well over $1 billion a year.

[Mr. Menzies then turned to the topic of Vietnam]

An interesting second string to my bow was to be accredited as ambassador to the Socialist Republic of Vietnam from 1976 to 1979.

Having been responsible for the setting up of the Canadian Delegations for Supervision and Control in Vietnam, Cambodia, and Laos after the Geneva conference of 1954, and having visited Vietnam in the old days, it was very interesting to see the country again after the long period of war between North and South Vietnam and the heavy bombing by the Americans of North Vietnam, which came to an end only in 1975.

The destruction of infrastructure, of houses, roads, bridges and railways throughout North Vietnam was really quite impressive. If you were driving on the highway, you would see railway engines and freight cars turned over and abandoned at the side of the railway tracks. Railway bridges had been bombed to smithereens. Sometimes a flimsy wooden trellis arrangement enabled small loads to get through.

I of course availed myself of opportunities to call on different diplomatic missions and get their views on Vietnam – including the French, British, Australian, and Scandinavian representatives. I also called on the Chinese, who were not on terribly good terms with the Vietnamese, and on the Russians, who were. I made several calls on Premier Pham Van Dong, a very impressive man who had been the foreign minister at the time of the Geneva conferences. Pham Van Dong reminded me that he had met Mr. Trudeau in Cuba and that Mr. Trudeau had expressed interest in the development of offshore oil in Vietnam and had suggested that Canada might be able to provide some technical assistance. This had been followed up by a visit by Maurice Strong, who I think at that time was the president of CIDA and who had gone to Vietnam and talked about putting money into offshore drillings and into a processing plant onshore, if my memory is correct.

However, I think the question of who was going to finance these substantial investments had not been spelled out as clearly in the discussions as might have been desirable, which simply meant that I was pressed by Pham Van Dong on two or three occasions to try to persuade the Canadian government to invest money, when I think there was no early intention of doing so. At a later stage in my stay there Ranger Oil of Calgary and Bow Valley were interested and had rented a Danish oil-drilling platform. It drilled, I think, five holes about thirty miles off the mouth of the Mekong River in South Vietnam without striking any pay dirt at all.

Mr. Earle: So relationships were mostly on a trading basis, bilateral relationships between Canada and Vietnam?

Mr. Menzies: There was the prospect of doing some oil development, with assistance from the government side and private investment. In addition to that, we had assistance being given by the Mennonite Central Committee in hospital work. Non-governmental organizations were providing quite a bit of assistance in Vietnam.

I recommended to the Government of Canada that CIDA should provide some food grain assistance to the Vietnamese because of the shortage of rice due to the dilapidation of the irrigation canals during the war period. I was lucky enough to strike a responsive chord in this respect, and a shipload of Canadian flour was delivered to Ho Chi Minh City, the new name of Saigon. I went with the CIDA officer to inspect the delivery of sacks of flour with the Canadian maple leaf flag on them to make sure that the flour wasn't being diverted to military groups. I think that was an honest and helpful gesture on the part of Canada.

I thought – mistakenly, I found – that the Vietnamese had had a pretty rough time during the war and that they were anxious to start post-war reconstruction and open up trade and better relations with the western countries and with Japan. Then, all of a sudden, early in 1979 Vietnam invaded Cambodia, and I got messages from Ottawa saying, "We are cutting off all government assistance to Vietnam. You were wrong in your messages that suggested that it was time Canada should give aid to Vietnam."

In a sense, Vietnam, which had been teased a bit by the Cambodians on its southern border, decided not just to strike back across the border but to go all the way to Phnom Penh and to occupy the country, saying at the same time that they were doing this to oust the bloodthirsty government of Pol Pot and the Khmer Rouge.

Mr. Earle: They stopped eventually, didn't they?

Mr. Menzies: Well, they occupied all of Cambodia. One other thing about Vietnam. You will of course be aware that many Vietnamese boat people moved to Canada during the years when I was ambassador to Vietnam, and many others were incarcerated in camps in Thailand, Malaysia, and Indonesia. These Vietnamese families gradually put pressure on foreign governments to receive their relatives. Those who had reached Canada in the initial migration of about 50,000 to 60,000 wanted their families, who were in the detention camps or refugee camps, to join them. So we had immigration officers from Bangkok fly into Ho Chi Minh City to interview them and make arrangements for some of those who could get passports from the Vietnamese government to exit the country and move to Canada. That involved quite a lot of negotiation with the Vietnamese government to get their cooperation to interview relatives who were in Vietnam as well as those who were in the refugee camps in Southeast Asia.

Mr. Earle: The general role of being an ambassador has undergone major changes over the last eighty years or so, when powerful people once served in posts, before the advent of high-speed communications, which enabled leaders to speak with leaders. You've said yourself that no decision by an ambassador is now made on his or her own, adding that you and others as ambassadors were too tied to machines. I wondered if you would elaborate on this because despite the restrictions, I'm sure you had an input into government policies toward China when you were ambassador there.

Mr. Menzies: Yes, I think that what you have quoted me as saying there is quite true. But I would argue that in the opening of posts and in a period of change very often it is the Canadian embassy in a certain country, as a team organization headed by the ambassador, which makes proposals to the government back in Ottawa. This is a very important role that embassies abroad perform: that is, to report factual information about developments in the country, to analyze the situation, and to put forward several options that can be incorporated in a submission to ministers in Ottawa.

The competent foreign service officer sufficiently understands the mechanisms of government in Ottawa that he's going to put forward his proposals in a way that has the best chance of being accepted by the government or by the bureaucrats back home. But because of instant communication, one does quickly get a go-ahead or a modified go-ahead from Ottawa. I don't think that's a bad thing at all, provided that one is given a certain amount of leeway to interpret instructions in the light of the local circumstances where the negotiation may be done, as in Beijing.

[Mr. Menzies then discussed his role in contributing to international disarmament]

The Throne Speech in April 1980 spoke about Canada playing its part, through the regional alliances of NATO and NORAD (North American Air Defence), in the maintenance of international stability and security, but at the same time wishing to play a role to contain the arms race that was going on between the Soviet Union and the western countries. In this statement, Mr. Trudeau, through the mouth of the then Governor General, announced that the government was appointing an ambassador for disarmament in the Department of External Affairs to coordinate the role. I was appointed to the position. My job was to coordinate the representation of Canada at the United Nations, both at the General Assembly and in the Disarmament Commission, to visit our delegation at the Committee for Disarmament in Geneva, to liaise with various groups in Canada that were interested in disarmament – academic groups, veterans groups, and others – and to manage a modest disarmament fund. I had to learn all of this on the job.

Mr. Earle: *Were there difficulties in attempting to coordinate government policies from all the different government departments, not just in the nuclear weapons field but I imagine in other areas too, in the disarmament? Coordinating all of this must have been a nightmare.*

Mr. Menzies: Yes, but that was not the most difficult part of my job, quite frankly. I found that I had lived a relatively sheltered life as a diplomat both in Ottawa as head of an operating division and as a diplomat abroad. When I came back to Canada and took on this job as Ambassador for Disarmament, I found that I had a great deal to learn about relations with the Canadian community and more particularly, the rather avid advocacy groups, the so-called peace groups, who of course criticized Canada's cruise missile testing, our relationships with the Americans in NORAD, our position in NATO, and so on.

There had been a conference in 1978, at which Mr. Trudeau had made an important speech in which he talked about the suffocation of the arms race. This meant the cessation of the production of fissionable material, the cessation of the production of new vehicles for carrying nuclear weapons, such as missiles and aircraft, and the gradual reduction, with verification, of defense budgets so that the arms race would gradually decline. A new session of the UN Special Session on Disarmament was scheduled for 1982, and one of my principal responsibilities was to prepare the Canadian position. So I put two papers to cabinet. One was the initial paper suggesting the positions that Canada should continue to take. And I might say in this connection that I was able to get an increase in the budget, the so-called disarmament fund, from $100,000 to $500,000, which enabled us to commission quite a number of special studies to be done in Canada on ways of verifying disarmament. For instance, if there is to be a ban on nuclear underground tests, then seismic systems that can detect the size and location of underground tests can be established in different places in the world. Canada has been a leader in seismic testing or verification of underground tests because of the "ping" that we get out of the Laurentian Shield; the great stone base of the shield gets a good echo from any explosion, even in a distant part of the world. So a good deal of my work at that time was preparation for how Canada could contribute to this special session on disarmament, and the preparation of a speech for the prime minister at this further session.

Mr. Earle: You referred earlier to disarmament views from such quarters as the peace movement, but you also once said that in disarmament there was not much the Canadian government could do except to work behind the scenes to try to influence the two superpowers – the Soviet Union, as it was then known, and the United States of America – to get back to the bargaining table and to have some confidence in each other. Did any Canadian disarmament efforts meet with much success, in your view, or were they mostly behind the scenes?

Mr. Menzies: I would say that Canada was able to make significant technical contributions in the area of verification, verification in terms of seismic testing for underground explosions.

I think we also brought forward quite a few ideas in the area of chemical weapons. One of the big subjects for discussion in Geneva at the Disarmament Committee was an agreement to stop the production of chemical weapons. These terrible weapons had found use in the gas attacks of the First World War, in Iran and a little bit in other places. There were tremendous stockpiles of chemical weapons on the Warsaw Pact side. They were held by the United States, Britain, France, and in western Europe. One had to put up technically valid schemes to verify the holdings of chemical weapons and to say how one was going to observe their destruction.

In many fields of that kind, through the exchange of technical information on verification, Canada and other middle powers who had considerable scientific know-how were able to make a contribution, and to strengthen the environment in which discussions took place. But I wouldn't say we had a profound effect at all on negotiations such as the strategic arms limitation agreement, the discussions between the United States and the Soviet Union on their negotiations to limit strategic weapons.

[Discussion then turned to other matters]

Mr. Earle: *You have referred many times during the course of this oral history to Herbert Norman, the Canadian senior diplomat who took his life in Cairo in the early 1950's. What did you think of that, and the House Un-American Activities Committee and so forth?*

Mr. Menzies: Herbert Norman had a Canadian missionary parentage somewhat similar to my own, but he was nine years older than I was, I think, so we didn't overlap at high school in Japan, where we both attended the Canadian Academy, or the University of Toronto or Harvard University, since he was finished and out before I was entering these institutions. But I developed, while I was at Harvard in particular, a great admiration for his grasp of the Japanese language, Japanese history, and particularly his book *Japan's Emergence as a Modern State*, which described the change-over from the military feudalism of the nineteenth century to the Meiji restoration and modernization in Japan.

I worked fairly closely with Dr. Norman for a year in Ottawa in an intelligence unit where I had an opportunity to become acquainted with him as a man and as a great scholar. He was best man at our wedding in June of 1943, so you can see that I had established quite a close relationship with him.

Mr. Earle: *You were 63 when you were made ambassador for Disarmament in 1980. Two years later, at 65, you became the longest-serving diplomat in the history of the Canadian foreign service – 42 years. You got an extension of your time beyond the normal retirement age of 65 years. What was the reason?*

Mr. Menzies: I had been asked, you might say, to quarterback the Canadian team going to the Second UN Special Session on Disarmament. We had a delegation made up of civil servants who did a lot of the back room work. We had members of parliament and senators. We had academic advisers and representatives of various disarmament groups taking part in the delegation. So we had quite a large symphony orchestra and it needed a baton wielder. My job was more that of a coordinator, because the minister for External Affairs came down to lead the delegation and he had others from the government who spoke in important sessions, including Prime Minister Trudeau himself.

The session was on in the summer on 1982. And as you say, I had passed my 65th birthday. I stayed on until August of 1982 to write the final report on the session.

Mr. Earle: *You said in May 1982 that confidence between the NATO alliance and the Warsaw Pact – this of course was in the Cold War – was the key to negotiation between the two camps. Did the collapse of the Soviet empire and the Warsaw Pact in general astonish you, after all the years during which you were involved in every aspect of the Cold War?*

Mr. Menzies: Yes. This surprised me, because during the ten years that preceded the dramatic events in which Mr. Gorbachev came forward with proposals for real détente with the western powers, the Soviet Union had been increasing its construction of long-range missiles. It had built up its naval equipment so it could challenge the western fleets in the North Atlantic, in the Mediterranean, and in the Far East. There didn't seem to be any sign that the place was falling apart. This was perhaps the fault of some of our diplomats who didn't smell out enough of what was going on in the country, and also in terms of some of the journalists, who might also have predicted what was going to happen.

Mr. Earle: *This is a philosophical question. The External Affairs department, as I've hinted at previously, was very strong in the 1940s, 1950s and 1960s, a very prestigious department. What has happened to the once* *proud department? What has happened to the important part it played in the government scheme of things? Perhaps there hasn't been any change at all, and it's all in my imagination. Was the slippage in the Trudeau era? It certainly didn't have the influence it once had when you started off with it in 1940 and in the 1950s when Canada played a much bigger role in international foreign policy, perhaps because of the war ...*

Mr. Menzies: I think you've put your finger on it. Canada's relative position in the world has altered considerably. We had exaggerated influence handed to us on a platter in World War II. Canada wasn't invaded like the countries of western Europe or even the United States, where the Japanese demolished the Pearl Harbor facilities. We in Canada built up quite an industrial capability and farm productivity during that time. At one time we had a million men and women under arms. With other economies depressed, we were in an advantageous position. Certainly Canada has moved forward, grown a great deal, but in relation to other countries it hasn't moved fast enough to maintain that privileged position.

I think at that time also the other government departments in Ottawa had not built up professional staffs of the size they have now. The senior personnel of all government departments, professionally speaking, are much better qualified today than they were back in the 1950s. External Affairs was one of the departments people wanted to go to because it was a company of gentlemen, you might say, who treated each other as colleagues and friends. One had the opportunity to put forward ideas. There were very capable people in the early days and some of us less capable were given opportunities far beyond our real capabilities. We were stretched, but we responded the best we could.

Mr. Earle: Did the power and prestige of External Affairs change for the worse when the department was merged with International Trade and other changes were made in the last while?

Mr. Menzies: Mr. Trudeau was probably determined to exercise his own influence in the Department of External Affairs when he came in 1968. He had to do something fairly dramatic to alter the vision of the Pearson years that preceded him. He set about, I think, to bring more authority to the Privy Council Office and use that as a coordinating position, a sort of central agency in the government.

On the latter bringing together of the Department of Trade and Commerce and External Affairs, now called Foreign Affairs, arguments can be made both ways. In most countries of the world, trade and the promotion of commercial interests have become a very large part of foreign policy and foreign diplomacy.

Mr. Earle: *What about the policy of tying foreign policy to domestic issues?*

Mr. Menzies: That is certainly an area, especially after the end of the confrontation of the Cold War, in which one can expect that the dynamics of our domestic economy will project itself overseas. But countries other than the superpowers – the United States and to some continuing extent Russia, powers greater than Canada, are such large players on the world stage that in my opinion much of Canadian diplomacy has to be reactive. We're not in a position to influence many events in those parts of the world which affect the 25 percent of our income that comes from our foreign trade. We're definitely interested in the world community as a whole and contributing to stability in all parts of the world in which we have trading interests, or even if we don't have them. I think our diplomacy must be 80 percent reactive to events that are generated outside our borders and perhaps 20 percent to what has been going on inside our borders.

Mr. Earle: *Thank you, Arthur Menzies.*

L'AUBE DU TRANSPORT HYPERSONIQUE

Charles Bédard

Il en est des sentiers de la carrière comme de ceux de la vie. D'aucuns sont attrayants et s'ouvrent plus largement devant nous, mais ne conduisent pas nécessairement vers des objectifs valables. D'autres sont au contraire plus laborieux, voire inhospitaliers – on les aborde avec réticence – mais ils débouchent parfois heureusement sur des découvertes, des joies insoupçonnées.

À mon retour de Belgique, c'était, je le crois, au printemps de 1972, j'avais été tout naturellement intégré au secteur culturel que dirigeait à l'époque notre collègue Freeman Tovell dont on disait la santé très fragile. Tout semblait indiquer un parcours facile et agréable, aux contours familiers. Je n'ai jamais vraiment compris pourquoi – peut-être était-ce l'absence de véritable défi – mais, plus les semaines et les mois passaient, plus mon désintérêt, plus mon ennui grandissait, à tel point que, privé de la perspective de succéder au directeur dans un avenir rapproché, j'avais demandé d'être muté dans un autre service, le juridique, si je me souviens. Entretemps et comme si c'était pour combler mon vide au plan professionnel, mon épouse et moi avions acquis un joli lot dans le Parc Champlain (Hull) et nous étions lancés à fond de train dans la construction d'une petite villa de briques roses, laquelle, vers la fin de l'année, devenait "Villa Rose" où nous avions aménagé et vivions heureux et sans histoire.

Voilà que, de la façon la plus inattendue, un nouveau virage se présentait à l'horizon. Un jour de février 1973, je crois, alors que je terminais mon repas habituel à la cafétéria du rez-de-chaussée de l'Édifice L.B. Pearson, voilà qu'un regard me cherche. C'était nul autre que celui du sous-secrétaire d'État, Ed Ritchie, un aigle, chez nous, que je connaissais peu. Je m'approchais un peu hésitant et il me fit aussitôt part de son désir de me rencontrer à son bureau le jour même, ce qui fut fait.

Il m'expliqua de façon très aimable que le ministère avait l'intention – si j'acceptais, bien sûr – de soumettre mon nom pour le poste de Représentant du Canada auprès du Conseil de l'OACI (Organisation de l'aviation civile internationale, Montréal) et ceci dans les prochains jours. Ce poste stratégique, expliquait-il, avait depuis de nombreuses années – étant donné son aspect technique – été laissé entre les mains du ministère des Transports qui l'avait depuis meublé, parfois tant bien que mal, avec des techniciens de l'aviation. Le Ministère était convaincu qu'il fallait faire un effort particulier pour récupérer au moins sur une base permutante avec le ministère des Transports, sinon sur une base permanente, ce poste dont l'intérêt politique, économique et diplomatique était devenu plus évident. Transport Canada – qui tenait beaucoup à préserver l'acquis technique – avait déjà en tête un candidat. Il fallait donc faire vite et présenter nous-même une alternative crédible. J'avais été choisi par le Ministère parce que, agent de carrière, juriste et, précisait-il, parce que détenteur d'un doctorat en droit "des Transports." "Transports *fluviaux*!" répliquais-je. "C'est quand même du transport," ajouta-t-il, et "ça fera le poids" au ministère des Transports. Il espérait vivement que je rendrais volontiers au Ministère "ce service." Il avait, encore une fois, vu juste!

C'est l'angoisse dans l'âme que je quittais son bureau, angoisse d'annoncer à ma famille que, après à peine quelques mois d'installation, il fallait quitter "Villa Rose" et chercher gîte à Montréal qui connaissait à l'époque une sévère crise de logement. De plus, tout ce secteur de l'aviation, hautement technique, m'était tout à fait étranger et pourrait fort bien s'avérer hostile. J'avais déjà connu à Hanoi une cohabitation difficile avec une composante militaire ("military component") omniprésente. Comment m'accueillerait la composante technique de notre délégation qui avait pris l'habitude d'être aux commandes? Enfin, je décidais de relever le défi et me retrouvais à Montréal au beau milieu de l'hiver avec "Villa Rose" à louer, la famille à déménager et des montagnes de documents techniques (l'OACI ressemble de ce côté à une véritable usine) à dépouiller et à digérer. Le défi était, en effet, de taille!

Et voilà que, pendant quatre années, j'allais oeuvrer en milieu nouveau et connaître les années les plus fascinantes et peut-être les plus fructueuses de ma carrière. Les occupations ne manquaient pas: j'avais tout à apprendre dans le milieu technique où j'allais vivre, et aussi tout à faire pour amener mes collègues du Conseil à mieux comprendre et à aimer notre pays. N'était-ce pas Talleyrand lui-même qui disait du diplomate que sa véritable fonction était de faire aimer son pays? Les membres du Conseil vivaient littéralement coupés du monde extérieur, comme en vase clos. Il fallait ouvrir tous grands fenêtres et coeurs; il fallait faire connaître ce pays, cette province. Et c'est ainsi que, avec la collaboration de nos deux transporteurs aériens nationaux d'alors (Air Canada et CP Air) ainsi que de l'aviation militaire canadienne, j'organisais une série de tournées dans l'Ouest (visites à Abbotsford Airshow), à la Baie James et dans l'Arctique. Au Conseil, nos interventions étaient fréquentes, que ce soit pour faire connaître les points de vue du pays sur des problèmes techniques débattus ou pour informer mes collègues sur le Canada et le Québec, voire redresser certains préjugés et montrer de ce pays, et du Québec, l'image accueillante, ouverte qui est vraiment la leur.

Il fallait, en phase Conseil principalement, ingurgiter des masses de documents; être disposé à aider tel ou tel collègue à mieux comprendre le sens et la portée des nouvelles exigences linguistiques au Québec; collaborer au déménagement du siège de l'organisation (de Beaver Hall Hill au 1000, rue Sherbrooke), y compris contrer les critiques malveillantes; diriger le Comité sur les conditions de service; prendre, afin d'encore mieux comprendre le milieu où j'œuvrais, des cours de pilotage (vol à vue, seulement!); enseigner à l'Institut de formation en aéronautique civile; donner des cours à McGill (Institut de Droit Aérien et Spatial) sur "La responsabilité du Transporteur aérien sous le système de Varsovie"; assister aux assemblées générales ainsi qu'aux nombreuses réunions du Conseil – phase Conseil et phase Comité – et même participer à quelques conférences régionales de l'aviation civile internationale. Bref, les années ont volé et j'ai constamment eu l'impression d'être un représentant, un interprète utile de mon pays.

Au cours d'un déplacement personnel en France au début de mon mandat, j'avais eu l'occasion de connaître le président de la SOCATA (aile aviation légère du groupe de l'Aérospatiale), Pierre Gautier, avec qui je me suis lié. Il était lui-même l'un des grands apôtres français du transport supersonique et promoteur acharné du projet Concorde depuis le début des années soixante. On sait que ce premier avion supersonique de ligne, avait, après bien des difficultés, effectué le 20 mai 1976 la première liaison Paris-Washington. L'intérêt pour le nouveau-né était tout naturellement très grand au sein de l'OACI où l'ensemble du dossier – y compris l'affaire désormais célèbre de New York – était bien connu. C'est pourquoi, confiant que ce dossier pourra vous intéresser, je me permettrai, dans les paragraphes qui vont suivre, d'en retracer pour vous les grandes lignes, grandes lignes que Pierre Gautier et moi avions déjà dégagées dans un article publié en 1979 dans les Annales de Droit Aérien et Spatial de McGill, sous titre "L'aube du transport supersonique" et dont je citerai ici quelques extraits.

Lorsqu'en 1962, la France et la Grande-Bretagne signaient un accord de coopération pour la mise en chantier d'un avion de transport supersonique, ils prenaient, en quelque sorte, un pari aussi aléatoire que celui que prenait Kennedy lorsqu'il proposa publiquement à l'Amérique la conquête de la lune. Tout semblait s'y opposer: hausse brutale en 1975 du coût du carburant; évolution tarifaire défavorable; exacerbation de la sensibilité écologique qui avait conduit à une réglementation américaine très sévère pour les supersoniques.[1]

Devant un progrès technique évident et dont, pour la première fois, elle n'occupait pas l'avant-garde, l'Amérique dut s'incliner, mais non sans de nombreuses réticences. En effet, alors que le "ministre" des Transport des États-Unis accordait le 4 février 1976 aux compagnies Air France et British Airways l'autorisation d'exploiter, pour une période d'essai fixée à 16 mois, Concorde de et vers Washington et New York, (le premier vol commercial fut Paris-Washington le 20 mai de la même année), New York multipliait les mesures dilatoires pour empêcher le Concorde de se poser chez elle. Il fallut une ordonnance du tribunal compétent[2] pour permettre l'ouverture simultanée, 18 mois plus tard (soit le 22 novembre 1977), des lignes Paris/New York et Londres/New York.

On peut, je le crois, dire de Concorde qu'il a été un succès technique, en particulier sur le plan de son acceptabilité aux aéroports et sa grande régularité, sans parler de sa sûreté.

"Mais on ne peut parler d'une technique sans penser à toutes celles qui lui sont liées. Il faut en effet s'assurer d'une base pyramidale de plus en plus large pour être à la pointe de la technique.

La réussite de Concorde a donc exigé non seulement l'aérodynamique la plus élaborée, mais aussi la métallurgie la plus moderne, une électronique perfectionnée, des systèmes évolués et cela a profité évidemment à l'ensemble des techniques nationales de pointe.

Une des vérités premières de la technologie moderne s'est trouvée vérifiée, qu'il existe un haut degré de probabilité pour que les problèmes aient une solution, même si on ne possède pas encore toutes les connaissances permettant de les résoudre.

Quand on ignorait, par exemple, au départ les propriétés exactes de l'alliage qu'il fallait utiliser pour le revêtement extérieur d'un avion de transport supersonique, il en résultait à fortiori une incertitude quant aux moyens de traiter ou de façonner ce métal d'où incertitude sur les outillages pour le travailler. Bref, autant de motifs qui pouvaient augmenter dans des proportions considérables le délai de réalisation de la machine."[3]

Peut-on parler, comme on l'a fait parfois, d'échec commercial dans le cas du Concorde. C'est essentiellement, à mon avis, une question d'optique.[4] Était-il raisonnable, alors que la certitude de l'atterrissage aux U.S.A. n'était pas acquise à l'époque, d'engager en 1976 le découvert considérable qui aurait résulté de la poursuite au-delà du nombre 16 (atteint en 1978) de la chaîne Concorde?

"Pour nous pencher de façon plus spécifique sur l'avenir du supersonique commercial, on peut faire appel à un excellent document préparé par R.D. Fitzsimmons, pour Douglas Aircraft et présenté au 14e congrès annuel de l'AIAA.[5] L'auteur indique, sur le plan technologique du moins, la marche à suivre pour la mise en opération d'un avion supersonique rentable, capable de satisfaire à la fois les normes acoustiques et celles de l'environnement.

En résumé, l'auteur préconise, en se basant sur une longue étude de la NASA, un supersonique de deuxième génération, à technologie améliorée, dont le rayon d'action serait de 50% supérieur à l'actuel Concorde et dont la capacité serait de 250 passagers. Un tel type de supersonique, par une efficacité de croisière globale accrue de 35%, atteindrait à une économie de carburant de 50% par passager transporté, tout en rencontrant les normes acoustiques actuelles.

Ceci ouvre toute une gamme de possibilités pour une catégorie de passagers spécialement négligés ces dernières années, les hommes d'affaires payant plein tarif. Bien sûr, les marchés traditionnellement dominés par un tourisme toujours en quête de tarifs réduits, iraient aux subsoniques de plus grande capacité, cependant qu'un marché important, peut-être de l'ordre de 20 à 35%, s'ouvrirait pour le supersonique plus rapide mais de moindre capacité, dont le tarif se situerait entre la première classe actuelle et la classe économique. Quel acquis pour l'homme d'affaires qui voyage souvent et qui cherche, sans frais excessifs, à économiser de précieuses heures (voir note de base de page no. 3)."

Qu'adviendra-t-il le jour où les quelques Concordes encore en service seront complètement déphasés et ils ne manqueront pas de l'être bientôt? Il n'y a toujours pas de successeur crédible à l'horizon. Peut-être l'avion supersonique lui-même est-il déjà sur le point d'être dépassé et verra-t-on l'avènement au début des années 2000 d'une nouvelle génération d'avions, plus rapides et de capacité plus grande (les "hypersoniques" géants, Jules Verne en a peut-être rêvé) qu'on utiliserait, d'abord pour le transport des marchandises – ce qui appellerait la mise sur pied de grandes gares de triage aériennes régionales; puis pour des vols nolisés long courriers pour passagers en quête de villégiature lointaine. Ici, je ne puis m'empêcher de penser que notre bel, notre grand aéroport – maintenant, hélas, en sommeil – Mirabel, pourrait bien un jour prochain retrouver ses lettres de créance, ses ailes, en même temps que la destination pour laquelle, dit-on, il avait été conçu, celle d'une grande gare aérienne de triage d'avant garde, capable d'accueillir tous les types d'avions: subsoniques, supersoniques, hypersoniques, en particulier les cargos géants, et de desservir tout l'est du continent nord-américain. À condition, bien sûr, qu'un réseau ferroviaire et routier adéquat soit mis en place pour assurer des liaisons rapides et sures avec les grandes villes de la région.

L'OACI qu'on dit être l'organisation la plus efficace de la famille des Nations Unies est peut-être aussi celle où l'on retrouve les plus grandes continuités: continuité de la technique et continuité des hommes chez qui perdurent de façon admirable, tradition et souvenir.

Aujourd'hui encore, alors que j'ai quitté l'Organisation depuis 22 ans et exerce ma profession d'avocat à Montréal, je fréquente toujours les cercles de l'aviation civile internationale. J'y retrouve avec plaisir une grande fraternité ainsi que de nombreuses connaissances d'alors et, en particulier, ce pilier de l'Organisation, le Dr. Assad Kotaite. Secrétaire général de l'organisation depuis déjà plusieurs années à l'époque de ma nomination (1973), Kotaite était en 1977, alors que j'étais président par intérim, élu à la présidence du Conseil. Il a été depuis, à l'unanimité, reconduit dans ses fonctions à chaque élection – et pourrait bien l'être encore. Ici, continuité devient synonyme de sûreté et prudence, deux mots qui laissent à tous les niveaux de l'organisation leur empreinte comme à toute l'aviation civile elle-même.[6]

---

1 Voir à ce sujet le document de la U.S. Federal Aviation Authority FAA 4910-13, titre 14, "Aeronautics and Space," chapitre I "Civil supersonic Airplanes – Noise and Sonic Boom Requirements," – pages 28406 à 28407.

Les pages 28412 à 28417, en particulier les titres H) – "Economic and Technical Considerations," I) – "Non-Discriminatory Treatment of Concorde" et J) – "International Fairness," valent la peine d'être lues in-extenso, parce qu'elles montrent à quel point la FAA, tout en appliquant à Concorde des normes acoustiques strictes et jusqu'à un certain point dépassées, était soucieuse de ne rien faire qui puisse contrevenir aux règles sacro-saintes du fairplay ou qui puisse avoir des incidences fâcheuses sur le développement de l'aviation civile internationale, ce qui aurait pu alarmer dûment l'OACI. À cet égard, le passage suivant est révélateur: "It is noted that these rules will allow the operation into the United States of the first 16 *Concordes*. Inasmuch as this is the total number of *Concordes* which the British and French are estimating they will manufacture, these rules do not harm the development of international civil aviation."

2 Dans son jugement en date du 17 août 1977, le juge Milton Pollack considère que le délai imposé aux deux compagnies en cause a été "excessif" et "injustifié", et que l'interdiction dont est frappé Concorde à New York est "discriminatoire, arbitraire et déraisonnable".

3 Annales de Droit Aérien et Spatial, Vol. 4, 1979, p. 75092, "L'aube du transport supersonique," Pierre Gautier et Charles Bédard.

4 Pour Gordon Davidson de British Airways ce premier vol supersonique aurait amélioré la position financière de sa compagnie. Voir à ce sujet la revue *Flight* No. 1712 du 17/2/79.

5 Voir Douglas Paper No. 6678 "Technology Readiness for an SST."

6 L'OACI a sans doute agi comme une sorte de catalyseur pour Montréal dans le domaine de l'aviation civile. On retrouve, en effet, regroupés ici une foule d'organismes liés à l'aviation civile internationale. Pour n'en mentionner que deux des mieux connus: l'IATA (International Air Transport Association - dirigée par un Canadien) dont la haute direction demeure, il est vrai, à Genève, mais dont tous les avions techniques sont à Montréal; et la SITA (Société Internationale de Télécommunications Aéronautiques) dont l'ensemble des importants services technologiques sont regroupés ici. Tant et si bien qu'on peut, sans exagération aucune, dire que Montréal est depuis plusieurs années la capitale incontestée de l'aviation civile internationale.

FIGHTING APARTHEID: SOUTH AFRICA 1982-1986

by Edward G. Lee, Q.C.

I n 1995 the Canadian International Development Agency (CIDA) com-
missioned a study entitled "Choosing the Right Policy Levers: Drawing
Lessons from Canada's Interventions in South Africa." The report concluded, inter alia, that "in South Africa diplomacy was a tool that was uti-
lized to the fullest extent. While multilateral diplomacy was instrumental
in the build-up of external pressure, bilateral diplomacy helped facilitate
the process of change from within ... The case of South Africa has shown
that there is space for activism in diplomacy. The challenge is to determine
how far it can go, and how much political risk is warranted. In South
Africa, transparency and legality guided the political activities of the diplomatic staff."

As Canadian ambassador to South Africa from 1982 to 1986 I was intimately involved in the diplomatic fight against apartheid, a horrific system
that was probably at its height (or perhaps we should say depths) during that
period of time.

My prior assignment as ambassador to Israel was a good apprenticeship
for the diplomatic activism required in South Africa. The Israeli government
had to be continually but subtly pressured to slow down its establishment of
settlements in the occupied territories of the West Bank and Gaza. At the same
time careful contact had to be maintained with the Palestinian leadership in
those territories and with Israeli Arab mayors. The Canadian government had
to be informed in detail of developments in Israel and the occupied territories
and viable policy recommendations had to be put forward to Ottawa.

In South Africa, in order to be active and influential, we had to keep
lines of communication open not only to the Afrikaans and English speaking communities, but also to their designated "black," "coloured," and
"Indian" communities. The only people we did not talk to were the leaders
of the independent homelands which we did not recognize.

The "White" Community

When I first arrived in Pretoria, I paid calls on the prime minister and foreign minister, as well as visiting all the other cabinet ministers, to emphasize Canadian concerns about apartheid and to ascertain which ministers might be regarded as "hawks" or "doves." Contact was also maintained with senior military and police officers, civilian ministry officials, and members of the so-called parliament to remove doubt about Canada's firm opposition to the racial policies of the government. Along with the embassy's political officers, I also made a priority of developing relations with both the pro- and anti-government journalists and academic and business leaders in the white community. I either lobbied or encouraged them, whilst seeking information which might prove useful in formulating Canadian reactions to apartheid policies.

The foregoing activities involved several rather acrimonious meetings with P.W. Botha, first as Prime Minister, and later as President. He was nicknamed "the old crocodile" for good reason, and he was utterly convinced that apartheid was good for South Africa and was not the business of any other country. Foreign Minister Pik Botha was a better actor, but he certainly never gave any impression that he had any doubts at all about the many South African intrusions into the neighbouring countries of Botswana, Mozambique, Angola and Namibia. I particularly cultivated dialogue with some of the younger Nationalist Party MPs such as Roelf Myer, Leon Wessels and Barend du Plessis, often at one-on-one luncheons. It appeared that they were not in sympathy with at least the harsher aspects of government policies. Some of these persons later became cabinet ministers when apartheid began to unravel. At the same time, I maintained close relations and gave whatever assistance we could to the official opposition Democratic Party leaders such as Helen Suzman, Colin Eglin, and Alex Boraine (who later became deputy chairman of the Truth and Reconciliation Commission).

The "Black" Communities

A major reason for maintaining an embassy in South Africa was to use it as a means of assisting all those struggling against apartheid. By 1985 there were only nineteen ambassadors in Pretoria of which fifteen were from western countries. Upon my arrival in 1982, I established an informal group of ambassadors from like-minded countries which met regularly to exchange views and information and coordinate support to the black community. A similar group that I had founded in Israel had been very useful. The group in South Africa was composed of the ambassadors of Australia, Austria, Belgium, Canada, Germany, Italy, Netherlands, Sweden, and Switzerland. We also kept in close touch with the American and British embassies but they were not included in the informal group because of their somewhat more lenient approach to the South African Government. This informal coordination of diplomatic and aid activities provided a flexible way to collaborate while responding to our respective domestic constituencies. It was this group, for example, which decided to boycott the opening of the new parliament in September 1984 because there was no black representation.

When I was recalled to Ottawa in August 1985 after the imposition by the South African Government of particularly harsh measures against the black communities, I had to argue against closing the embassy in Pretoria at a special cabinet meeting held at the Meech Lake government retreat. Prime Minister Brian Mulroney was under considerable domestic pressure to do so and many cabinet ministers saw no reason to continue Canadian representation in South Africa. The Secretary of State for External Affairs Joe Clark and I argued that to close the embassy would have a devastating effect on the black community. I described some of the specific ways the embassy supported the struggle against apartheid.

On the political front, highly visible attendance by embassy officers at funerals of activists in the townships demonstrated to that community that they were not alone in their struggle but had the support of much of the international community. Since political meetings were banned in the townships, these funerals were the only legal way that blacks could meet in large numbers and deliver and hear speeches. (At one funeral the South African police tear gassed one of the Canadian embassy officers along with other participants.) With the same purpose in mind, I attended periodically (often with my wife) trials of blacks who had been accused of breaching various racial laws. We would arrive at the courthouse in the official vehicle with the Canadian flag flying and sit in the front row of the public section of the court wearing maple leaf pins. Inevitably the judge would take more care in assessing the guilt or innocence of the accused and on one occasion we even had the judge suddenly address us from the bench to explain what he was attempting to do. On another occasion in Johannesburg we attended the trial of the wife of the *Maclean's* correspondent Alistair Sparks. She had been accused of obstructing justice when she telephoned her husband at his office and warned him that their home was being searched by the police. It was generally believed that our attendance had helped her avoid punishment.

On the economic front, Canadian support of micro aid projects in the black townships promoted political objectives. The Dialogue Fund and the South African Education Trust Fund assisted churches, schools, kindergartens, and health clinics at a critical time. The embassy officers and I developed close contacts with influential individuals in the black community and demonstrated to the public generally that we were with them in their struggle against the South African government. In doing this we had to be very careful because we were violating diplomatic protocol in order to adopt a political stance, but the circumstances were exceptional. We even went so far as to give funds to Winnie Mandela to establish a health clinic at Brandfort in the Orange Free State where she had been banished and put under village confinement. This enabled her to keep in contact with the black community and to continue some of her African National Congress (ANC) activities. While we normally did not give aid to the so-called Bantustans or Homelands, we did make an exception for Chief Mangosuthu Buthelezi in Kwazulu, which did not claim the status of an independent state. The embassy officers and I kept in close touch with him and gave some funds for his Inkatha-operated schools, and clinics.

The following excerpt from a letter written by my wife in 1983 gives an idea of the contact we had with some of the black community:

> *The human rights position in this country is appalling. This last week we went with a Roman Catholic priest (Australian) and a black social worker to three of the black ghettos near Capetown. Guguletu is an area of makeshift and cement "houses" with 4 walls and corrugated iron roofs; Crossroads is all tents and black plastic over wooden frames and KTC is an open field where the blacks bury their night shelter materials every morning and hope the police will not find them. Tens of thousands of people live in the most dreadful conditions because they are evading the police pass laws. They do not have permits to live and work in Capetown but they leave their "homelands" because there is no work and no food and they do not wish to starve. We went to a low inconspicuous building beside the highway where the blacks unlucky enough to get caught were being sentenced. The sentences averaged about one*

Edward G. Lee, Q.C.

month's salary in fines and eviction rides back to their homelands.
The magistrate processed one accused every 4 to 5 minutes and they
call that justice. On Friday we went to Langa and Elsie's River
which are "coloured" townships. They are a little better off than the
blacks. We visited schools, day care centres, and clinics and talked
to the teachers, doctors, and ministers. It was a real insight into
how the majority of the people in this country live.

I also maintained, through visits and luncheon meetings, close relations with Archbishop Desmond Tutu and ANC leaders such as the Reverend Alan Boesak and Trevor Manuel (later to become President Mandela's Trade and Finance Minister). Some of these meetings had to be held clandestinely because of the interest of the South African police and intelligence services in our activities. Indeed, I was once called in by the director-general of the foreign ministry to receive a formal complaint about the activities of the Canadian embassy, but we knew that the South African Government would not expel us because they were careful not to cut any of the tenuous links that existed with the outside world.

Sanctions

By 1982, the UN had imposed an arms embargo, sporting contacts with the outside world had been restricted, and preferential tariff treatment had been terminated. Our trade officers had been recalled. As the apartheid regime became ever more harsh in the face of rising opposition in the black communities, I became convinced that the only way to get some relaxation of the worst aspects of apartheid was by squeezing the pocketbooks of the white community and increasing their isolation in the sports and cultural areas so that they would conclude that apartheid was an untenable system. Although it made our relations with the South African government and the white community very difficult (even Helen Suzman and the famous liberal novelist Alan Paton opposed sanctions), I was pleased that the Canadian government, in concert with other Commonwealth governments, fought hard to impose further sanctions. When I was recalled in August 1985 for six weeks, I visited editorial boards, business groups, and religious leaders across Canada to explain to them the utility of further sanctions and the necessity of maintaining an embassy in South Africa to support the black community.

In 1985 Canadian sanctions imposed a ban on direct air links. Insurance provided to Canadian exporters to South Africa by the Export

Development Corporation was terminated. Other measures included a voluntary ban on the sale of Krugerrands, a voluntary ban on the sale of petroleum and refined products, the abrogation of the double taxation agreement, a voluntary ban on new bank loans and sales of sensitive technology to the South African Government, and the restriction of Canada's contact with the military. We were aware that some of these sanctions would negatively affect the black community, but our soundings of the ANC leadership indicated that the blacks would be willing to accept the short term pain for the long term gain of overthrowing the apartheid system. Consequently by 1986 both bilaterally and sometimes through Commonwealth agreement the following additional sanctions were imposed: a Canadian import ban on all agricultural products (including wine), uranium, coal, iron and steel, a halt on government purchases of all South African products, a ban on promotion of South African tourism in Canada, the closure of the visa office in the Canadian embassy in Pretoria, and a voluntary ban on new bank loans extended to the private sector. All of these sanctions certainly helped to energize the process of dismantling apartheid that culminated in the release of Nelson Mandela from prison and the ensuing historic 1994 election in South Africa.

The South African Government was extremely unhappy with Canada for taking a leading part in the imposition of the Commonwealth sanctions in August 1986. As a consequence, my scheduled August departure for a new assignment in Canada was postponed for 3 months because Canadian officials were fearful that the South Africans would not approve the appointment of my successor. Given the tense diplomatic relations that existed, it was considered that the embassy should not be left without an ambassador in place.

Commonwealth Eminent Persons Group

When the Commonwealth Eminent Persons Group (EPG) visited South Africa in May 1986 the Canadian ambassador was designated to be their chief political advisor. The EPG Co-Chairman was Malcolm Fraser, a former Australian prime minister who belonged to a political party that was then the official opposition in Australia. Consequently the Australian ambassador was placed in a difficult position and did not play an active role with the Group. Likewise the British ambassador was sidelined. More than other Commonwealth governments, the United Kingdom, with an enormous trade relationship at stake, maintained a more sympathetic attitude toward the policies of the South African Government. The EPG had made great headway in brokering a deal to initiate serious negotiations between Nelson Mandela, the African National Congress leadership located in Lusaka and South Africa, and the South African government. Unfortunately, the day before they were due to meet with the full cabinet, the defense minister Magnus Malan ordered his forces to launch air raids and commando attacks on alleged ANC bases in the neighbouring Commonwealth capitals of Botswana, Zambia and Zimbabwe, with a view to sabotaging the Group's work.

At a tense meeting immediately after the attacks I advised the EPG to leave South Africa as soon as possible. I argued that Malan would have obtained President P.W. Botha's permission before mounting the raids and that the government obviously did not want to seriously negotiate. Malcolm Fraser strongly favoured proceeding with the meeting the following day with the Cabinet, undoubtedly for his own personal political reasons. Surprisingly, he accused me of being a traitor and indicated he would be reporting to Prime Minister Brian Mulroney that I had ill advisedly recommended the termination of the Group's work. Fortunately other members of the EPG such as Archbishop Ted Scott of Canada, the other Co-Chairman General Obasanjo of Nigeria, Dame Rita Barrow of Barbados, and the former Tanzanian foreign minister agreed with me and castigated Fraser for his unfounded criticism. Some of them even wrote to Mulroney and Clark to defend me. The EPG left before meeting the cabinet. In 1997 former Foreign Minister Pik Botha told the South African Truth and Reconciliation Commission that the Group had come uncomfortably close to reaching an agreement to begin serious negotiations to release Mandela and give political power to the black majority. President Botha had not in fact been willing to accept Mandela's release at that time. This episode was certainly a strange situation for an ambassador to be placed in, and ended when the Canadian Government temporarily recalled me to Ottawa once again to protest the South African raids.

Lesotho, Swaziland, and Namibia

I was accredited not only to South Africa but also concurrently to Lesotho, Swaziland, and Namibia. The first two are Commonwealth countries heavily influenced by the situation in South Africa. Namibia was a UN trusteeship with an administration appointed by the South African government. Lesotho is totally land-locked by South Africa and a huge segment of its male

High Commissioner Lee opening a village water project in Lesotho in 1954

population worked in the South African gold mines. Swaziland is surrounded on three sides by South Africa and was heavily dependent on the South African economy. Canada had large aid programmes in both countries and I put considerable effort into consulting with their respective cabinet ministers and officials on how best to counteract the effects on them of South African policies. I routinely visited the numerous Canadian aid projects in both countries to ensure that they were tailored to the maintenance of economic and social independence from South Africa. During each visit to Lesotho I exchanged views with their king, who was not only wary about South Africa but was also worried about factions in the Lesotho political arena who seemed sympathetic to South Africa.

In Namibia we supported the rebel South West Africa People's Organization in their struggle for independence through consultations and the funding of their small technical assistance projects. During each visit to Namibia I also met with the South African administrator-general in order to ascertain conditions in areas under his jurisdiction. When UN Secretary-General Perez de Cuellar flew to Capetown in August 1983 for consultations on Namibia with Pik Botha and the "Namibia Contact Group," including Canada, I was able to brief him personally and make recommendations on the situation in Namibia because of our previous friendship when he was UN Special Representative to Cyprus.

Conclusion

On the basis of the various diplomatic activities described in this essay I believe we could honestly say, "We made a difference." The following excerpts from a telegram in 1986 to the Department of External Affairs in Ottawa upon my final departure from South Africa demonstrate the context in which I had to work. Although the seeds had been planted, I expected it would take a much longer time to overthrow apartheid than fortunately turned out to be the case.

> *The last three years in particular have been marked by a steady deterioration in both the domestic situation and South Africa's relations with the outside world. A number of false dawns during the period have only served to deepen pessimism about prospects for the future. Widespread belief in black political circles that the government will soon be forced to negotiate a transfer of power to the black majority seem no more realistic than government expectations that the silent majority of blacks will support the ruling National Party's own cautious limited plans for reform. The current pattern of continuing unrest contained by government repression of increasing scope and ruthlessness seems set to continue for a prolonged period. Violent revolution is the prospect, with ever-increasing division and polarizations within and between communities. It is unrealistic to expect significant changes in the current depressing situation in the foreseeable future. All evidence suggests that things are going to get much worse in southern Africa before they get any better – if they ever will.*

GETTING STARTED IN KOREA, 1973-1977

by John A. Stiles

Although there had been important personal ties between Canada and Korea since late in the nineteenth century when Canadian missionaries first arrived in Korea, Canada's official relations with the Republic of Korea (South Korea) date only from 1963, when agreement was reached by the two countries to exchange diplomatic representatives. To date, Canada has not officially recognized the Democratic Peoples Republic of Korea (North Korea).

In 1964 South Korea opened an embassy in Ottawa and their first ambassador took up his appointment in 1965. Canada, in the beginning, tried to cover Korea through double accreditation of our ambassador resident in Tokyo. As relations between the two countries began to show increasing possibilities for expansion, particularly in the fields of commerce and immigration, and as the Canadian government was desirous of showing Canada's growing interest in the countries of the Pacific Rim, it was decided to open a separate embassy in Seoul in 1973. This essay describes conditions in South Korea in the period 1973-77 and reviews how our bilateral relations developed during that time.

The appreciation of the South Korean Government for the opening of a Canadian post in Seoul was shown by the warm welcome extended to the advance party which arrived in Seoul in late August 1973. Every assistance was offered to facilitate our getting established. The general impression left was that the Koreans were as keen as we were to establish mutually beneficial relations. On our side, in order to get off to a fast start, the officers who had been handling the different aspects of relations with Korea, either from headquarters in Ottawa or from our embassy in Tokyo, were posted to Seoul, which meant that an experienced team was in place from the beginning and it was possible to declare the post "open for business" in mid-September. We were also able to thank the British Embassy in Seoul for their past help and to advise them that we were able in the future to look after any Canadian consular problems that might arise.

As the official residence in Seoul was undergoing substantial repairs, I was asked to delay my arrival until early January 1974. This made it possible for my wife and me to undertake an intensive course in Korean language, history, and culture at the Center for Korean Studies in Hawaii. At the time, this center was headed by Professor Suh Dae-Sook whose father had been a Korean interpreter for one of the early Canadian missionaries, the Reverend Duncan MacRae. Professor Suh was most helpful in arranging an appropriate course for us with access to many specialists in various aspects of Korean culture, in addition to Korean language training. When we left for Korea I was given a wide range of most helpful letters of introduction to members of the Korean academic community.

Following our arrival in Seoul on January 11, 1974, I presented my credentials to President Park Chung-Hee on January 17. In conversation with him after the ceremony it was clear that he had been well briefed on the details of our relationship, even knowing that the Korea Electric Company had recently given a Letter of Intent for the purchase of a Canadian nuclear reactor. He urged me to do everything possible to facilitate the successful conclusion of this transaction which he said had a high priority in Korea's future plans. Then came the many courtesy calls normal in diplomatic life. These were made to other foreign ambassadors, appropriate Korean cabinet ministers, local and regional officials, as well as Korean business firms interested in Canada. One could not fail to be impressed with the prominent position occupied by the American embassy in Seoul. This was readily understandable considering the tremendous contribution made by the United States to the support of Korea in the 1950-53 war and the subsequent period of reconstruction. The Japanese embassy was also very active, as were the British, French, and German diplomatic missions. Koreans appeared to reserve a special place in their feelings for the sixteen countries that came to their aid in the Korean War (Canada contributed 26,000 troops of whom 516 were killed) and appreciated that since 1953 Canada had continued to cooperate closely with the United Nations Command in Korea through a Canadian Liaison Officer.

Strong Military Leadership

South Korea was run by a strong military leadership. It had fully mobilized for armed confrontation at the Demilitarized Zone thirty-five miles from Seoul. There, South Korea's 600,000 member defence force, aided by

40,000 Americans, faced over 1,000,000 North Korean troops. The nightly curfew, plus air raid alerts in Seoul on the fifteenth of each month, all provided a continuing reminder of the North Korean threat. I had commented on the need for Korea's tight security controls during an official call on Prime Minister Kim Jong-Pil. He asked how I would feel if an enemy bent on destroying Canada was as close to Ottawa as Smith Falls, Ontario?

General Park Chung-Hee had come to power on May 16, 1961 after leading a coup d'état and setting up a military regime in Seoul. After ruling for two years as a military junta, a new constitution was drawn up and in October 1963 elections returned Park, who ran as a civilian candidate, as president. Under the constitution, the president's term was four years and restricted to two consecutive terms of office. During his second term, in 1969, Park asked the National Assembly to allow a constitutional change to permit him to run for a third term. Despite nation-wide protest, bitter debate in the National Assembly, and much delay, the proposal was finally approved. The popular displeasure was reflected in the elections of 1971 when Park was returned by a greatly reduced majority, narrowly defeating the opposition leader Kim Dae-Jung.

From the beginning of his third term in office President Park set out to make radical changes. Regulations were passed designed to crush student demonstrations and freedom of the press. Laws forbidding criticism of the government were passed which imposed heavy sentences on those arrested on charges of communist conspiracy to overthrow the government. Finally, in October 1972, martial law was proclaimed and the new Yushin or "Revitalization Constitution" was publicly announced. A national referendum on November 21, 1972 approved the new constitution by twelve of thirteen million votes. On December 23, 1972, the newly formed electoral college, the National Unification Conference, re-elected Park for another six-year term. Besides providing for indirect presidential elections the National Unification Conference was authorized to appoint one-third of the elected National Assembly, on recommendations made by the president. Thus, the executive had powerful control over the budget and the ability to declare emergency powers when thought necessary.

Following the breakdown of the North/South Korean talks in August 1973, North Korea built up its military and tunnelling programme along the Demilitarized Zone. The government decided that any internal instability, no matter how slight, would play into the hands of North Korea's Kim

Il Sung. Accordingly, a series of emergency decrees was passed beginning in January 1974, which forbade criticism of the Yushin Constitution or of the South Korean president. The opposition New Democratic Party broadly supported these measures on national security grounds. They gained additional support following the attempted assassination of President Park at the National Theater in Seoul on August 15, 1974. The North Korean gunman from Japan missed the president but killed Mrs. Park, the First Lady. This brought a period of very strained relations between Korea and Japan before a suitable apology was worked out.

There was little doubt of President Park's firm control of the political situation at the time of the opening of our embassy in the fall of 1973. The vast majority of Koreans seemed to be quite satisfied with the continuing trend towards a strong executive. This was undoubtedly related to South Korea's Confucian past, but also, the many crises their country had experienced encouraged Koreans to yearn for a strong authoritative leader. The economic success to date, too, had been attributed to Park's leadership. Opposition to the government appeared to be confined to academics, church leaders, and certain labour groups, all of whom were closely monitored by the government's security forces. This monitoring from time to time resulted in protests of alleged human rights violations being brought to the embassy's attention, usually via Canadian church groups having close affiliation with Korean Christian churches.

Korea's Economic Miracle

President Park Chung-Hee, who had graduated as a Japanese officer from the Japanese military academy and had studied closely the Japanese development system, was a strong supporter of centralized economic planning. He had been responsible for the implementation in 1962 of the first Five Year Economic Development Plan. It was by all accounts a success and in the period 1962-66 the South Korean economy recorded an average annual growth rate of 8.3 per cent. In the second Five Year Economic Development Plan, 1967-71, South Korea achieved an average annual growth of 11.4 per cent, with almost all major economic goals achieved ahead of schedule.

The establishment of the Canadian embassy in Seoul coincided with the implementation of South Korea's third Five Year Plan, 1972-76, under which it was intended that the economy would achieve an annual average growth of over 11 per cent. The highly centralized government of South Korea (all state governors and senior state officials were appointed by the government in Seoul) greatly facilitated the preparation and carrying out of government plans. A feature of the system was the personal annual review by President Park of each government department's activities at the beginning of the year. In essence, Park operated a straight "Management by Objectives" system, aided by six presidential agencies – Special Presidential Assistant, the Presidential Secretariat, the National Security Council, the Economic and Scientific Council, the Board of Audit and Inspection, and the Korean Central Intelligence Agency. Through his situation room in the Blue House (the presidential residence) Park personally followed the progress of all development projects, both public and private.

South Korea's military regime had been strong enough to implement programmes, however unpopular, that might promote development. A case in point was the normalization treaty with Japan signed in 1965, despite public opposition, that promised to provide economic support at a time when American aid was diminishing. There was only one important public issue – how to improve the economic situation. Economic growth was the government's main domestic goal and the Five Year Plans were the principal economic policies adopted to implement the political strategy.

Canada-Korea Relations: Trade

The favourable publicity surrounding the opening of our embassy in 1973 brought numerous enquiries from Korean firms wishing to do business with Canada and confirmed the value of having a local Canadian mission. Many of the areas of development outlined in Korea's Third Five Year Development Plan proved to be of interest to Canadian suppliers. This was the case not only in the industrial raw material field (e.g., wood pulp, aluminum, and copper) but also in certain fully manufactured products (microwave telecommunication equipment) and in agriculture (cattle, hides, tallow, potash, sulphur).

In January 1973 President Park had announced an ambitious plan to establish six strategic heavy industries: iron and steel, shipbuilding, chemicals, electronics, non-ferrous metals, and machinery. His thinking was undoubtedly influenced by a perceived need to confront the build-up in North Korea. There, most of the heavy industry on the Korean peninsula had been established by the Japanese prior to World War II. Park was particularly anxious to establish a modern steel industry which he considered essential to the creation of an industrial base in South Korea. After American and World Bank sources turned down requests for help with the necessary financing, he approached his contacts in Japan, who agreed to assist. The proposed steel mill (which eventually became one of the world's leading producers) required large quantities of imported coking coal. Our embassy was able to help find a suitable Canadian company to supply it.

South Korea's rapid economic development was paralleled by its increased need for electric power. The very limited domestic power resources available were soon fully tapped and the country became heavily reliant on imported oil. The increased cost of this oil, particularly following the OPEC oil shock, forced Koreans to rely increasingly on thermal units fired by imported bituminous coal, as well as on nuclear power plants. We were able to help Korea procure supplies of Canadian bituminous coal and, as indicated above, we had a commitment from Korea to purchase a 678 MW CANDU nuclear power unit.

Into this picture came the Indian nuclear explosion of May 1974 which caused the Canadian government to review its entire nuclear export programme, including the proposed sale to the Korea Electric Company. After months of deliberations, which included an assessment of South Korea's rumoured desire to develop nuclear weapons capability, the Canadian cabinet decided in January 1975 to proceed with the Korean sale, provided South Korea agreed to join and abide by the NPT (Nuclear Non-Proliferation Treaty). In addition, Canada and South Korea were to sign a Nuclear Cooperation Agreement that spelled out additional safeguards. The Koreans eventually agreed that it was in their interests to accede to the NPT and on January 26, 1976, following strenuous negotiations, they signed the bilateral agreement with Canada permitting the sale to proceed. Construction of the plant began soon afterwards and it came "on stream" in 1982. (Korea's satisfactory experience with this unit eventually led to additional purchases).

In the field of agricultural products we had hoped to sell Canadian wheat and barley to South Korea. Unfortunately, in the period 1973-77 we were not successful due to U.S. Public Law 480. Under this law, Korea was able to obtain these commodities from the United States under very favourable terms, sometimes with 40 years to pay. Our Canadian Wheat Board could not match such conditions. We pointed out to the Korean authorities that Canada had signed a most-favoured-nation agreement with Korea in 1965 under which we were supposed to be treated equally with other suppliers, but to no avail. Years later Korea opened this market to Canadian competition on an equal footing and substantial sales developed.

Mention has been made of Korea's strong efforts to develop her own export trade. Canada became one of the countries where attractively priced Korean products found a ready market. At the time, Korea's sales included a whole range of textile products, footwear, canned mushrooms, television receivers and radio-phonograph sets. The vast increase in textile sales to our market, when combined with similarly large increases in textile shipments from other low-cost countries, resulted in the penetration of the Canadian market of upwards to 50 per cent in some areas. Following bilateral consultations between Korea and Canada, voluntary quotas were agreed to which, in turn, led to a system of multilateral import quotas. These brought criticism in Korea of Canada's action in restricting textile imports. Canadian officials responded by pointing out that Canada's record as a liberal importer of textiles and clothing was considerably better than most other industrialized countries.

In 1972 our total trade with South Korea amounted to $76.6 million with Canadian sales amounting to $32.9 million and our imports totalling $43.7 million. By 1977 the total had risen six-fold to $466.1 million. This included Canadian exports of $143.4 million and imports from Korea of $322.7 million. Prospects for additional Canadian sales in the future appeared excellent, particularly in the agricultural field, as well as in capital equipment (for power generation) and larger supplies of industrial raw materials. One of the principal factors accounting for Canada's growing export sales in this period was the increasing confidence in Korea's future shown by Canadian banks and by the Canadian Export Development Corporation. In 1977, two Canadian banks were given permission to open branches in Seoul, while a third opened a representative office. A Korean bank was also expecting to open a branch office in Toronto within a year.

Immigration

One of Canada's broad objectives in establishing a diplomatic mission in Seoul was "to promote Canada's economic growth and cultural enrichment through immigration and other programmes related to human resource development, founded upon principles of non-discrimination and universality." From the beginning, many Koreans showed a keen interest in emigrating to Canada. No efforts were made by our embassy staff to persuade Koreans to consider Canada as their future homeland. Despite this, during the period 1973-77, several thousand families elected to make the move. Most of them eventually became successful and productive

Canadian citizens. The record shows their excellent ability to adapt to Canadian conditions. The vast majority appear to have opted for Toronto as their new home. Others have settled in such cities as Vancouver, Edmonton, Calgary, Montreal, and Ottawa. Some limited Canadian adoption of Korean orphans also occurred during this time.

Development Assistance

Following the Korean War Canada contributed development assistance to Korea through the United Nations Korean Reconstruction Agency, the Asian Development Bank, and the Colombo Plan, as well as through a number of private agencies such Care Canada, Save the Children Fund, and the Unitarian Service Committee. In 1967 a one million dollar soft loan was granted for the purchase of Canadian dairy cattle and equipment. In 1970 a further commitment of three million dollars was made, mostly in the form of food aid. By the time our embassy was established in 1973 these programmes were decreasing as the Korean economy continued its rapid recovery. One of the embassy's tasks was to explain to the Koreans that it was time to wind the private programmes down. This proved not to be easy as many of the projects had been very successful. It was explained that future assistance would more likely be in the form of favourable export credit terms.

Political Relations

During the period 1973-77 political contacts between Canada and South Korea began to increase steadily. In addition to exchanges of parliamentary delegations, a growing number of ministerial and official visits took place. Contacts between Canadian and Korean representatives at the United Nations in New York grew more frequent. South Korean delegates to the UN appeared pleasantly surprised by and appreciated Canada's interest in the security aspect of the relationship. Much of the political aspect of our bilateral relationship was concerned with supporting the position of the Republic of Korea in international forums, particularly the United Nations, in concert with Korea's other allies. While welcoming proposals that could help reduce tension on the Korean peninsula Canada remained committed to the principle that the Republic of Korea must play a leading part in any settlement of the Korean problem.

Summing Up

On completing my assignment in July 1977, I had the impression that while our bilateral relations with Korea had developed satisfactorily since 1973, much remained to be done. Important contributions by succeeding colleagues were the extensive public relations programmes designed to make Canada and Canadians better known throughout Korea. These were particularly effective at the time of the very successful 1988 Seoul Summer Olympic Games.

It was a privilege to have had the opportunity of getting to know beautiful Korea and something of its culture and its more than five thousand years of recorded history. I also greatly enjoyed meeting and getting to know a wide variety of its hospitable, talented, and courageous people, who through an accident of geography, have on many occasions had to cope with the multitude of problems associated with foreign invasions.

WATCHING THE POLISH ROLLER COASTER, 1980-1983

by John M. Fraser

M y wife and I flew into Warsaw from London in the middle of September 1980. The "Gdansk Agreements," ending a summer of widespread strikes and growing turmoil, had been reached a little more than two weeks earlier. For the first time in the Soviet-dominated world a communist government had been forced to recognize an independent trade union (*Solidarnosc* or "Solidarity") and the right to strike. Moscow was clearly unhappy with this turn of events.

The process of preparing newly appointed heads of post for their impending responsibilities was a good deal shorter and less elaborate than it has since become. I remember some useful tips on financial management (always something of a mystery to me), and a film on "defensive driving" to foil aspiring hostage-takers, which I was happy to know was likely to be irrelevant in Poland. I also remember a senior officer telling us that we should forget everything we had previously been doing in our careers. We would now be managers, and it was on the quality of our management that we would be judged. The Department of External Affairs was then in the grip of its decades-long obsession with management – often, it seemed to me, for its own sake.

Once in Warsaw, I soon concluded that managing the embassy (which did, of course, have to be done) was simply part of the background noise. What I was really there for, or so it seemed to me, was to try and keep track of the dramatic twists and turns of the Polish situation, and give my assessment to Ottawa of what was going on and what might be expected in the near future. This does not mean that I was always right. Like many others, I was taken by surprise by the imposition of martial law when it actually happened.

What had been more of a preoccupation for most of the three years we were in Poland was whether, and in exactly what circumstances, Moscow would lose patience and send in the Red Army as they had done in Czechoslovakia in 1968 and Hungary (and almost in Poland) in 1956.

Many of the things that the Poles were now doing or not doing, the Hungarians and Czechoslovaks had done or failed to do before them. It was universally assumed that there was a line, the crossing of which would precipitate a Soviet invasion if things in Poland got too far out of hand.

The embassy had a thriving Immigration section, as thousands of Poles flocked to Canada to visit relatives. The job of our visa officers was to try to screen out those who might seek to work illegally in Canada or who seemed to have no compelling reason ever to return to Poland. I explained this to the chief of protocol when he said that we should speed up our procedures and not interview so many visa seekers. "But Mr. Ambassador," he protested, "don't you know that *all* of them are going to work illegally?"

Our commercial counsellor and his staff were also busy – not so much in generating new Canadian exports to Poland, as in trying to get Polish enterprises to pay Canadian suppliers for goods already sold. The extravagances of the 1970s had left Poland with a very large hard currency debt and few means of paying it. Debt collection rather than trade promotion was the order of the day.

The West had a tradition of being more favourably disposed to Poland than to any of Moscow's other satellites. This had been the case ever since Wladyslaw Gomulka managed to persuade Nikita Khrushchev in 1956 that the former's brand of "national" communism need not be a threat to the Soviet empire. Strikes and riots by workers in Gdansk in December 1970 precipitated the fall of Gomulka (who, it turned out, might have been a Polish nationalist but was no liberal). His successor, Edward Gierek, was considered to be a technocrat with the ability to make things work, and Poland was viewed even more favourably by the West. Allan Gotlieb, our undersecretary thought of making it one of the "countries of concentration" for Canadian foreign policy, and I was warned early in the summer that my arrival might have to be accelerated if plans materialized for a visit to Poland by Prime Minister Trudeau. The visit did not take place, no doubt because of the upheaval and labour unrest that had raged throughout the summer. When we arrived, Gierek was gone. The official explanation was heart trouble. A Polish joke at the time claimed that it was really leukemia – "30 million white cells and only a few hundred Red!"

Just because the Gdansk Agreements had been signed and Solidarnosc recognized as an independent trade union did not mean that the crisis was over. "The Polish Crisis" was a generic title for embassy telegrams for much of the next three years. I conveyed to Ottawa in a telegram a month after my arrival my first impressions of the situation:

John M. Fraser

Although life goes on normally and without any sense of immediate crisis, there is underlying uneasiness and apprehension. Everyone agrees that Poland's troubles are far from over; no one pretends with any confidence to know how they can be resolved or how the situation will develop.

I was struck by the massive lack of confidence on the part of the population in the government and in the Polish United Workers Party. Even the government and Party lacked confidence in themselves. It also seemed to me that, while both Solidarnosc and the authorities were showing remarkable restraint, many in the union leadership had understandable doubts about the government's good faith. While there was certainly some apprehension about possible Soviet intervention, there was probably also a feeling, particularly among those too young to remember 1968, much less 1956, that the Soviet Union "wouldn't dare" move against Poland in 1980. It was not only young people who felt this way. The widow of a Polish ambassador used the same words two years later to quash my suggestion that if General Jaruzelski had not imposed martial law in December 1981 Soviet troops might have been in Warsaw in fairly short order. In general, Polish history has been marked more by heroic gallantry than well-calculated realism. Most observers believed that the Soviets would intervene, the consequences for détente notwithstanding, if the Polish leadership were not able to restore stability on an ideologically tolerable basis. The concept of stability would certainly include continued avoidance – by restraint or (perhaps preferably, from Moscow's point of view) by suppression – of popular anti-Russian feelings that lay just beneath the surface in Poland.

The first "crisis," in late October, related to the formal registration of Solidarnosc, when a Warsaw court tried to insert language into the union's statutes committing it to respect the "leading role" of the Communist party and not threaten Poland's alliances. This was widely seen as an attempt by the government to dilute or even negate what it had agreed to at Gdansk. Solidarnosc reacted with the threat of a general strike. After intensive late-night talks, Solidarnosc and the government agreed to refer the question to the Supreme Court. The Court's "compromise" ruling on November 10 seemed to remove the immediate threat.

The tension subsided only briefly, and returned many times in the months to follow. Solidarnosc challenged the authorities, usually accusing them of bad faith; union demands encroached more and more upon "political" and security questions. Union activists threatened major strike action, with a nation-wide general strike held as the ultimate weapon, and then an eleventh-hour compromise would be negotiated, usually involving government concessions, averting strike action. The union activists, who believed that no concessions would be made or honoured unless the authorities were pushed to the brink, would work on some future challenge while Party activists (often at the local level) would try to think of ways to reverse the heresy of recognizing an independent (i.e., free of Party control) trade union.

The first of these confrontations arose hardly ten days after the settling of the registration dispute. A police raid on the Warsaw headquarters of Solidarnosc found in the union print shop a confidential document from the office of the prosecutor-general setting out tactics to be used towards dissidents (presumably including union activists). The person suspected of having leaked the document to Solidarnosc and the printer (apparently preparing it for widespread dissemination) were arrested, then "conditionally released" in the face of a threatened general strike in the Warsaw area. Some Poles thought the document a fake, its prose style being much too literary for a communist government memorandum.

The union then proceeded to demand such things as a reduction in the police budget and a public inquiry into the role and activities of the security services. Acceptance of such demands, I wrote, in a report to Ottawa, "would be an important step towards the revolutionary transformation of Polish society. This is not what the regime wants, and it is scarcely conceivable that Moscow would tolerate it. Acceptance by the government of any demands in the security area could be taken by Moscow as proof certain that the Polish authorities had lost control." I went on to suggest that

> *Walesa and other moderates in the Solidarnosc national leadership (who have spent much time with Government leaders in the past few weeks) probably recognize this. They must surely also realize that national security policy is the most delicate possible area on which to challenge the Government, and one on which the authorities can least afford to give way. There are other forces in Solidarnosc, however, that combine intense distrust of the authorities' good faith (of which many have unhappy previous experience) with the conviction that they can push the Government harder and further without significant risk ...*
>
> *This cannot go on forever. On the other hand, it is hard to see what line the Government could hold successfully in a confrontation with the workers. Developments overnight suggest that Walesa*

and even dissident leader (and Solidarnosc adviser) Kuron recognize the dangers of such confrontation and have dropped the air of insouciance with which they used to greet suggestions that there was a risk of Soviet military intervention. In talks with striking Warsaw steel workers last night Kuron apparently urged the avoidance of confrontation, and Walesa argued that the workers might lose everything if they pushed too far ...

I have always thought that that statement attributed to Walesa was a prescient forecast of coming events. I also thought, as did all Western observers in Warsaw at the time, that the risk of Soviet intervention was real and imminent, and that the only way to avoid it was for dissidents to show restraint and let the communist authorities at least seem to be in control. That dissidents would ultimately triumph without any effort on Moscow's part to prevent them was impossible for us to imagine in 1980-81. The "Brezhnev Doctrine," declared in 1968 to justify intervention in Czechoslovakia as necessary to preserve socialism there (not unlike Jacques Parizeau's "lobster doctrine"), was still very much alive although Solidarnosc activists and other dissidents in Poland chose to ignore it and tended to be rather scornful of us for urging them to moderation.

A Soviet invasion seemed very close on the first weekend in December 1980 when my wife and I were en route for Berlin for my presentation of credentials (the Canadian embassy to Poland was also accredited to the German Democratic Republic). Having stopped in Poznan for the night, we were somewhat surprised to come down to breakfast and find two embassy employees who had driven through the night to convey a message from Ottawa that I should return to Warsaw immediately. There was, although I did not know it at the time, intelligence to the effect that Soviet troops were massing at the border. Ironically, as I reported on December 8, this was happening "when domestic tranquility seemed to have been restored in Poland itself, with fairly good prospects for restraint and calm over the next few months ..."

I took the message from Moscow to be "You are getting very close to the limits of what can be tolerated." It seemed that Soviet forces were so deployed that a move into Poland could be made at any time, and could serve as a "semi-permanent reminder to the Polish Government and people that recent trends simply cannot be allowed to go further ..." A more disturbing possibility, I added, was that "Moscow may have decided that Poland has already broken through tolerable limits and must pull back. Except in very small ways this is probably not possible ..."

The Polish roller coaster continued to soar and swoop during the next twelve months. The possibility of Soviet intervention was never far from our minds (and probably not far from minds in the Kremlin). In many ways a Soviet invasion wouldn't make sense, but, as I pointed out in one telegram, "that does not always guarantee that it won't happen anyway."

In April 1981 I wrote,

> *Clearly Moscow fears and detests what is happening in Poland and the inability (often mixed with unwillingness) of Polish leaders to do whatever might be necessary to return Poland to the ways of orthodoxy. Equally clearly, Moscow very much does not want to intervene. If they were not so reluctant they would probably be here already.*

The reasons for Soviet reluctance, as I saw them, were not only the risks to détente and their global interests but also considerations of a much more practical nature. An invasion of Poland might be accomplished fairly quickly, but the occupation necessary to keep the Poles down would have to continue indefinitely. Moscow would also have to use Soviet troops to take over the Warsaw Pact tasks assigned to what would now be considered unreliable Polish forces.

On May 28, 1981, Cardinal Wyszynski, primate of Poland, died. The funeral mass on Victory Square (since renamed Pilsudski Square) in the centre of Warsaw was made a state occasion, with every co-operation from the authorities. Foreign delegations attended the service alongside various senior figures in the regime who looked only slightly uncomfortable. As ambassador I was made head of the Canadian delegation which consisted of two members of parliament and three heads of Canadian Polish organizations. Since I had taken up my post in Warsaw a few days earlier than the American ambassador, we were placed ahead of the American delegation – to the visible irritation of the visiting dignitaries from the United States. The organization and crowd control were impeccable as was consistently the case when masses of Poles gathered in potentially explosive circumstances. Church and Solidarnosc marshals were in charge; there was not a uniformed policeman in sight.

The summer of 1981 offered two dramatic events: the Emergency Congress of the Polish United Workers' Party in July and the first Solidarnosc Congress in August and September. The Emergency Party Congress had been gathering steam since early in the year with the selection of delegates genuinely by Party rank and file. This was unprecedented, not only for

Poland but for the entire Soviet Bloc, and it can be imagined that Moscow was less than enthusiastic – particularly since, at one point, it seemed that few if any of Moscow's hard-line supporters would be elected. The new Central Committee chosen by the delegates and the new Politburo chosen by the Central Committee had few members who had been members of the outgoing bodies, although in the end, this didn't seem to make a great deal of difference. More openly dramatic was the Solidarnosc Congress, held in Gdansk, which featured a serious challenge to Lech Walesa's leadership and a notorious "Appeal to the Workers of Eastern Europe," which urged the creation of independent trade unions in the other Warsaw Pact states. As the Congress opened, the Soviet Union showed its uneasiness by staging naval manoeuvres just over the horizon.

The autumn brought more confrontations, usually ending with concessions by the authorities. Solidarnosc demands were becoming increasingly "political," although the union continued to insist that it was not a political movement and that it could not be expected to make proposals for solving Poland's economic problems. It was said that was the government's job. Solidarnosc did, however, take the view that the government had no right to make policy decisions without consulting the union. Like many who demand consultation, Solidarnosc really wanted the power of veto. The government, to the extent that it was willing to engage in consultations at all, saw the process as one in which it would listen to the union's point of view and then make its decisions.

On September 19, an official Soviet démarche to Polish leaders was published in Moscow. It accused them of failing to act against anti-Sovietism in Poland. In fact, there had been very little overt expression of the almost universal detestation in which the Poles had always held the Russians, although some of the more exuberant delegates at the Solidarnosc Congress did query the need for Poland to be an ally of the Soviet Union.

Observers generally believed that there were two things that Poland must do if Soviet intervention were to be avoided: to respect its alliances (i.e. with the Soviet Union and other Warsaw Pact members) and to retain some kind of recognizably "socialist" system. The latter would have to preserve a "leading role" for the Communist party, which by then was almost totally discredited – even among its own members. Many of them were also members of Solidarnosc, and whenever Party instructions conflicted with the union's views it was the Party line that was usually ignored.

Soon after taking over, Jaruzelski tried to set up a structure for co-operation with Solidarnosc and the Church. This so-called "troika" framework seemed to offer real hope for a peaceful solution to the Polish crisis. Perhaps not surprisingly, these efforts broke down. The authorities may never have been sincere; certainly Solidarnosc showed little trust in them. Walesa himself was quoted at a secret Solidarnosc meeting in Radom, shortly before martial law, saying that he hadn't trusted any of them since the 1970 shooting of workers in Gdansk.

Confrontations and events likely to lead to them became more frequent in December than in previous months. A major point of contention became the introduction of anti-strike legislation. Solidarnosc threatened a twenty-four hour protest strike if the Sejm (Polish parliament) voted to give the government special powers, and then a general strike, presumably of indefinite duration, if the government were to use them. Cardinal Glemp, primate of Poland, wrote an open letter to the Sejm opposing the proposed legislation. The Sejm was due to meet on December 15 and 21. The Warsaw branch of Solidarnosc called for a protest strike on December 17, the eleventh anniversary of the shooting of the Gdansk strikers. Other regions were urged to join the protest and it was widely believed that a massive nationwide demonstration was in the making.

Poland had slid past so many crises in the fifteen months since the Gdansk Agreements that diplomatic observers were inclined to think that a way would be found to slide past this one too – but probably not many more. One factor in our thinking was the assumption that if the authorities did try to assert their authority with some kind of state of emergency it would misfire and the country would explode. The authorities, we reasoned, knew this even better than we did.

Solidarnosc leaders were caught napping when martial law was accomplished with exemplary skill on the night of December 12. It was probably not so much fear of Soviet intervention that drove Jaruzelski to take this step; it was more that Poland was becoming ungovernable. He had apparently been assured that the Soviet Politburo had decided not to take such action – although he might reasonably have lacked total faith in such assurances. It had become almost impossible to imagine circumstances in which the government could prevail in any difference of opinion with Solidarnosc.

My wife and I were in Paris at the time. I was taking part in a meeting of all the Canadian heads of post in Europe – indeed I was due to lead a discussion of the Polish situation on Sunday morning, December 13. Fortunately we had heard the BBC World Service news broadcast before I left the hotel so that I could tear up the notes I had prepared and try hastily to scribble out some new ones. My wife, from our hotel window, had a grandstand view of the demonstrations that went on across the street outside the Polish embassy for most of the day.

I wrote a telegram for Ottawa with my absentee analysis of these unexpected developments, which, I conceded, was necessarily speculative. I suggested that we avoid "the facile conclusion about Prime Minister Jaruzelski's action: Moscow put him up to it. While this tough line is obviously one that Moscow thinks long overdue, there are more than enough Polish reasons for such action."

I went on:

> *It is not necessary to defend the measures taken ... to conclude that Jaruzelski acted as he did in the understandable apprehension that events were about to get totally out of control. He may have had the possibility of Soviet intervention more in mind than [did] Solidarnosc, [which appears to have] dismissed it totally from [its] calculations. As head of government he must certainly have been overwhelmed by a sense of looming disaster and the need to do something (almost anything) to get Poland back on the rails.*
>
> *What was done must (because it was done so efficiently, for which we ought to be thankful) have been planned very much in advance. I do not think it follows that Jaruzelski intended to do this from the beginning. Contingency planning is not proof of intention. Particularly disturbing is the suggestion in some Western media that the declaration might be part of some package that includes Soviet invasion, or makes it more likely.*

It took us a couple of days to find out the most promising route back to Warsaw because all air connections with Poland had been suspended An overnight train from Vienna finally delivered us on December 17. I discovered that rumor (always a lively Polish industry) would have it that every step in the martial law process had been and was being stage-managed by the Russians. I asked the primate, when I called on him later, whether information available to the church bore this out. "Oh no," he said. "If the Russians were really that much in charge things would be much worse!"

The embassy reported on December 13 that all our staff were safe and well. While telephones and telex had been cut off and travel out of Warsaw forbidden, movement within the city was unhindered and it was not difficult to get in touch with everyone. The lack of telex communication did mean that we had to rely on generously given help from the British and American embassies to send messages to Ottawa, although we quickly organized a weekly courier run to Vienna by train for less urgent traffic.

The evening of our return to Warsaw the Polish foreign ministry rounded up all the Western ambassadors it could find (a task complicated by the lack of telephone service) to tell them, before it was officially announced, of tragic news from Katowice and Gdansk. In Katowice a sit-in by miners had been broken up by police and troops. Six miners had been killed. In Gdansk rioting had left many rioters injured along with almost as many police. The Vice-Minister went on to stress the unhelpful exaggeration in the Western media (which claimed, for instance, that 45,000 people had been interned, while the real figure was less than 4,000).

The Austrian ambassador, dean of the diplomatic corps, responded with protest at the suspension of our communications, which was a breach of the Vienna Convention. The vice-minister promised to see what could be done, but it was obvious that the Foreign Ministry had little clout with those who were now running Poland.

It continued to be difficult for us to get an accurate picture of the number of detainees or of the conditions in which they were being held. We could not verify the frequent reports of clashes and casualties in various Polish cities. What information we did have, however, led me to report on December 21 that "the martial law regime, while strict, has hardly been surprisingly so. Public reaction, while hostile, has been more muted than it might have been." The freezing weather may have had something to do with this. "Warsaw," I went on, "is not a city in terror: comparisons with Budapest in 1956 are fatuous." I argued that the West should wait to see how the Polish authorities handled the situation before flinging too many thunderbolts. The question of how we should react was very much at the top of NATO's agenda. Sanctions were eventually agreed upon. My concern, from first to last, was that our sanctions policy had not been thought through. Did we really want to take the position that it would have been better to let anarchy overwhelm the regime and have a Soviet invasion?

I was also concerned that the "criteria" we established for ending sanctions (which seemed almost to amount to the restoration of the December 11 status quo ante) were simply unrealizable. How could we ever end sanctions if conditions such as the restoration of Solidarnosc were never met? It is easier to climb out on a limb than to scramble back. I noted in one report that Western leverage was limited. "The Polish government will not act at our behest in ways they consider suicidal."

The embassy's consular responsibilities were obviously not easy to carry out during the first days of martial law when communications and travel were so restricted. We had, however, been in touch with all Canadians registered with the embassy before martial law, when we had in mind possible Soviet intervention. Most Canadians living in Poland were retired Polish-Canadians who had returned to their home villages, where Canadian pension cheques went further. Almost all of them replied with thanks for our interest, but told us that they were not going to leave Poland again, no matter what happened. There was a small group of Canadians at Rzeszow, working in a joint venture with a Polish aircraft factory. Two embassy officers were able to travel by car to Rzeszow and Lublin (where there were Canadians at the Catholic University) on December 29 and 30. It was the first time any of us had been able to observe conditions outside Warsaw.

In the next months we followed the twists and turns of martial law – on the whole being relaxed, but at a painfully slow pace. Phone communication within towns was restored within about a month, with the very Polish addition of a lady who told you when you made your connection that your conversation was being monitored – foreigners, especially diplomats, had always assumed this to be so. The curfew was relaxed, as was the ban on travel within Poland. Detainees were being released in gradual stages, and I had frequent occasion to suggest (usually without instructions from Ottawa) to Polish officials that international reactions to the martial law situation might be more understanding if more detainees were freed more quickly.

The minister of the interior announced further relaxation measures on February 28. I described them as a "relaxation by halves, or even quarters." I found the régime's timid approach puzzling and concluded that it was "probably indicative of Jaruzelski's determination to take no chances, not even small ones." In early April I described the state of Poland as "rather like that of an airliner in a holding pattern but still losing altitude. There is a general air of nervousness among the passengers, who have noticed that all is not well and are far from sure that the pilot knows where he is going, much less how to get there. The pilot himself is probably confident, but unseemly squabbles keep breaking out on the flight deck none the less."

Popular protests against martial law were amazingly persistent. They ranged from mass demonstrations to the setting up of floral crosses in public places. People gathered around the crosses singing hymns or Polish patriotic songs (often, a Polish official once told us, with rather hair-raising new lyrics). The police would occasionally hose down the crowds with water cannon, and more often simply at night remove the crosses. They never failed to reappear.

The demonstrations were more alarming, occasionally violent, but always kept under control by the authorities without the use of lethal force. To some extent, these were trials of strength between the regime and its opponents, which the regime seemed gradually to be winning as Poles lost energy and hope. "Underground" Solidarnosc rhetoric rarely translated into activity that constituted any real threat. One slogan, "Winter is yours; Spring will be ours" inspired some apprehension that the dissidents might take to the woods in emulation of the World War II partisans. It never happened (and may never have been intended). Spring was cold and miserable, and the anonymous but prolific makers of political jokes claimed that the authorities knew the slogan and had cancelled spring.

Major demonstrations continued to erupt on significant anniversaries, despite the authorities' best efforts to frighten people off. One of the largest was on May 3, 1982, the anniversary of the 1791 Polish constitution. This was after a relatively tranquil May 1, the International Workers Day, used in all communist countries to organize workers into shows of loyalty to the regime. It was the night of a farewell party for members of the embassy staff leaving that summer. The consular officers had to leave early, to rescue a Canadian television crew that had become embroiled in the mêlée.

The spring ministerial meeting of NATO was imminent, with Poland and NATO sanctions sure to be on the agenda. Polish officials were now taking the line that Poland had given enough "signals" in the form of relaxation in martial law measures to earn them some relaxation of sanctions. "Just what did we want to achieve?" a vice-minister of Foreign Affairs asked, "Did we want Poland to be isolated? Did we want living standards to fall yet further? Did we want Poland thrust into associations solely 'in one direction'"?

My own analysis, sent May 10, suggested that we should be clear in our own minds just what our objectives were. Did we insist upon a return to the December 12 status quo ante? Did we identify ourselves totally with the Solidarnosc agenda, however unrealistic? Were we really seeking, in effect, the government's overthrow in Poland, which had been established without popular consent and unable to win it? I suggested that our answer should be a resounding "Yes, but ..." We were clearly not going to support the dissidents to the point that we might become involved in a military confrontation with the Soviet Union. I have no way of knowing what impression such arguments made in Ottawa – or, indeed, who read them. It was, at least, comforting to know that Prime Minister Trudeau, for his own reasons, had said that martial law was not necessarily the worst thing that could happen to Poland.

There were more demonstrations on August 31, the anniversary of the Gdansk Agreements, generally less violent than those held May 3. On October 9, a new trade union law was passed, which, inter alia, banned Solidarnosc. The popular reaction was spontaneous, hostile, and brought quickly under control. No doubt the regime was mildly embarrassed. A call for a general strike on November 10, the anniversary of the legal registration of Solidarnosc, did not get much response. Demonstrations on November 11 (Poland's pre-war independence day) were sufficiently mild to be greeted with restraint on the part of the police. Determinedly non-provocative demonstrations, some of them impressively large, continued for some months. But Poles were less willing to risk injury and possibly other sanctions to show their ineffectual opposition to the regime.

After the second visit of Pope John Paul II to Poland was safely over, martial law was "suspended" on December 31 and formally brought to an end on July 22, Poland's national day. At the same time, legislation was passed giving the government all necessary tools for keeping the population under control. I observed:

> *Our enthusiasm for Solidarnosc (whose populist urgings would not be well received in our own countries outside far Left circles) owed much to our hope that the union's success might open the way for ... more fundamental changes that would at once meet the aspirations of most Poles and provide maximum discomfiture to our Soviet antagonist. This is not now going to happen. If we insist that it must be allowed to happen before we are prepared to return to normal relations with Poland, we are in fact deciding not to have normal relations with Poland. This, in my opinion would serve neither our own interests nor those of the Polish people.*

With the end of martial law, an extraordinary period in Polish history was over. Not the least extraordinary feature of the revolution and counter-revolution of 1980-81 and 1981-83 was that so little blood was shed.

SOUVENIRS D'AMBASSADE: LA CONFÉRENCE DES MINISTRES AFRICAINS FRANCOPHONES DE L'ÉDUCATION: LIBREVILLE, GABON, 1968

Elmo Thibault

Pour bien situer cette affaire, il est bon de se rappeler que, alors que la Révolution tranquille battait son plein au Québec, le Premier ministre québécois du temps, Jean Lesage, avait exigé "la reconnaissance du droit inaliénable du Québec d'exercer sa pleine souveraineté dans les domaines de sa compétence." Le général De Gaulle, en lançant son 'Vive le Québec libre' du haut du balcon de l'Hôtel de Ville de Montréal ne pouvait pas ignorer cette déclaration de M. Lesage. Encouragé dans ses vues sur le Canada d'une façon éhontée par Daniel Johnson, le successeur de Lesage, (qui ne demandait rien de mieux pour ses propres fins politiques que d'embêter le fédéral dans quelque domaine que ce soit), le Général était allé jusqu'à confier le 6 janvier 1968 au nouveau consul général de France à Québec[1], que "les petites gens (mais non pas les élites, trop compromis avec le régime fédéral) souhaitaient l'indépendance sous une forme ou l'autre ..."

Ce sont là les prodromes de ce qui suivrait à Libreville, comme plus tard à Niamey et à Kinshasa, et dont, en fait, on continue d'en vivre les séquelles.

Il serait aussi bon de se rappeler que le Gabon d'alors ne connaissait de l'indépendance que le nom. La France, par le truchement de son Haut représentant, comme de ses conseillers techniques installés à demeure dans tous les ministères, y faisait la pluie et le beau temps.[2]

À Québec, le Premier ministre Johnson pouvait s'en remettre pour sa politique vis-à-vis du fédéral, aux avis et conseils de ses plus proches collaborateurs, entre autres: Marcel Masse, Jean-Noel Tremblay, Claude Morin, Louis Bernard, Paul Gros d'Aillon et André Patry, que secondait à merveille à Paris le délégué général du Québec auprès de la République française, Jean Chapdelaine.

Et, enfin, à l'opposé de Churchill, qui dès 1945 a compris que la fin de l'ère coloniale approchait, De Gaulle a tout fait pour rétablir l'Empire français dans son intégrité.[3]

Il y a de cela un peu plus de vingt-neuf ans, je m'absentais de mon poste à Yaoundé pour assister à Libreville, au Gabon, aux obsèques du 'Père de la Patrie', Léon M'ba. En temps ordinaire, je m'y serais rendu tout comme mes prédécesseurs, dûment accrédité auprès des autorités locales. Hélas, le hasard voulut que mon arrivée en Afrique équatoriale coïncide avec la dernière maladie du vieux Président. Force me fut donc d'y représenter le pays à titre d'ambassadeur extraordinaire *pro tempore*. Débarqué à Libreville la veille avec deux de mes collègues du Cameroun qui, eux, avaient déjà présenté leurs lettres de créance, je fus reçu, comme eux, au nom du gouvernement gabonais, par un tout jeune ministre frais émoulu de l'ENA[4] et titulaire, si j'ai bonne mémoire, du Ministère de l'Environnement du temps. Présentations faites, notre jeune ministre voulut bien ouvrir la conversation en nous informant que Libreville serait, dans un avenir rapproché, l'hôte d'une Conférence des Ministres africains francophones de l'Éducation. Et d'ajouter, pour mon bénéfice, qu'il lui paraissait souhaitable que le Québec y soit représenté, d'autant plus que l'éducation, s'il avait bonne souvenance, était de son ressort exclusif. Par respect pour mes collègues de Yaoundé toujours présents, il eut été malséant que je m'engage dans un débat où ils n'avaient strictement rien à voir. Je m'en tins donc à rappeler au ministre que la constitution canadienne prévoyait la répartition, entre le fédéral et les provinces, des pouvoirs de gouvernement, mais que seul le fédéral était habilité à représenter le pays aux instances internationales.

Abstraction faite de ce bref échange de vues avec le jeune ministre qui, soit dit en passant, ne siégea que très brièvement sur la banquette ministérielle, il ne me revient de cette première visite à Libreville que le souvenir, lors de la mise en terre du Père de la Patrie, de cette nuée de chauve-souris qui jusqu'alors, paisiblement suspendues aux branches des cotonniers dont s'ornait le vieux cimetière, eurent tôt fait de s'abattre en criant sur nos têtes, dès que se mit à tonner le canon de l'aviso français amarré en rade pour l'occasion.

Encore faudrait-il que je rappelle ici la consécration officielle comme président de la République gabonaise, que valut au jeune successeur de Léon

Elmo Thibault

M'ba, Bernard Albert Bongo, jusqu'alors secrétaire général à la Présidence, et la présence, au déjeuner qui suivit les funérailles, de l'ensemble des chefs d'État de l'Afrique francophone, y compris les vieux routiers Léopold Senghor, Houphouët-Boigny et Hamani Diori. Quoi qu'il en soit, personne ne se trompa quant à ce qui s'était passé depuis le décès du disparu: le ci-devant secrétaire-général à la Présidence avait réussi à s'affirmer sur place envers et contre tous.

On épiloguera longuement sur le rôle de l'ancienne métropole et de son haut représentant à Libreville dans cette affaire. On saura, en passant, qu'exception faite de la Guinée, l'ambassadeur de France dans chacune des anciennes colonies africaines était, outre haut représentant de la France, doyen *ipso facto* du Corps diplomatique local.[5] Maurice de Launay, titulaire du poste à Libreville, était un de ces ex-gouverneurs coloniaux pour qui les nouveaux détenteurs du pouvoir demeuraient à toutes fins utiles ce qu'ils avaient été pour lui dans le passé: des administrés. Qui sait, dans les circonstances si, sur instructions reçues de la métropole, il n'était pas à l'origine du vœu à peine voilé que m'exprimait, à la veille des funérailles de Léon M'ba, le jeune ministre, de voir le Québec participer de plein pied à la Conférence des Ministres africains francophones de l'Éducation.

Cette fameuse Conférence me valut, presque coup sur coup, pas moins de trois visites "officielles" à Libreville.[6] J'y rencontrai, en effet, la première fois, le ministre de la Coordination. Lors de ma deuxième visite, il me fallut presque forcer la porte du vice-président du gouvernement, M. Stanislas Migolet, dans mes efforts à trouver quelqu'un qui voulût bien m'entendre. Ce dernier geste de ma part me valut, à mon troisième voyage, d'être ouvertement tancé par un jeune fonctionnaire du Protocole local. Il s'en donna avec d'autant plus de satisfaction que, n'ayant moi-même aucun statut officiel vis-à-vis des autorités gabonaises, la Centrale avait cru bon m'y dépêcher à titre de 'chargé d'affaires intérimaire,'[7] nonobstant les instructions qu'avait alors adressées Libreville à mon collègue gabonais de Yaoundé selon lesquelles "le personnage en question veuille bien surseoir à sa visite."

Ma première visite avait pour but de bien faire comprendre aux autorités locales qu'il importait que toute invitation ayant trait à la participation du Québec à ladite Conférence soit adressée au ministère des Affaires extérieures du Canada comme c'était d'ailleurs la coutume, quel que soit le sujet qu'on se proposât de soulever en instance internationale. D'autre part, on m'avait autorisé à dire, le cas étant, qu'il y avait tout lieu de croire que le Québec serait dûment représenté au sein de la délégation canadienne.

Le Ministre, bien sûr, m'assura qu'il n'était pas question pour le Gabon d'agir autrement et que, de toute façon, aucune invitation quelle qu'elle soit n'avait, à ce jour, été faite. J'en fis donc rapport à Ottawa dès mon retour à Yaoundé. Comme on semblait alors croire le contraire à la Centrale, on me chargea de retourner sans tarder à Libreville pour bien insister auprès des autorités sur la gravité qu'il y aurait de déroger à la pratique ayant cours aux États fédéraux concernant toute invitation à quelque instance internationale que ce soit. Et, bien sûr, je devais m'assurer qu'aucune invitation à la Conférence n'avait été adressée directement au Québec.

Après avoir essuyé une fin de non-recevoir de tous les ministres intéressés (Affaires étrangères, Coordination, Éducation), il ne me restait plus que de tenter ma chance auprès du vice-président du gouvernement, M. Stanislas Migolet, ce que je fis sur l'heure en entrant dans son bureau sans m'y être fait d'abord annoncer. Tout en m'excusant d'avoir ainsi forcé sa porte, je lui expliquai brièvement ce dont il était ici question en insistant tout particulièrement sur la gravité de la situation, sur l'impossibilité pour moi d'obtenir des intéressés quelque renseignement que ce soit, ainsi que sur le fait, patent pour tous, qu'il ne restait que peu de jours avant le début de la Conférence.

Bien qu'il m'avoua ne s'être pas penché sur le dossier, M. Migolet voulut bien m'assurer qu'il s'en informerait auprès des autorités compétentes, quitte à m'en faire rapport en fin de journée. Comme bien l'on pense, il ne découvrit rien qui puisse lui faire croire qu'une invitation avait été adressée au Québec. Il ne me restait plus qu'à rentrer à Yaoundé pour en informer la Centrale, ce que je fis *illico*.

On comprendra aisément qu'après avoir brusqué un tant soit peu le vice-président du gouvernement ainsi qu'il m'arriva de le faire lors cette dernière quête aux renseignements, on ne me rendrait pas la vie facile s'il m'arrivait de me présenter de nouveau à Libreville. Je m'y rendis pourtant avec les résultats que l'on sait. Et comme les portes des ministères m'étaient dorénavant fermées, il ne me restait plus qu'à rentrer par le premier vol à Yaoundé. Or, tout en regagnant ma chambre d'hôtel, il m'arriva de traverser le square faisant face à l'Hôtel de Ville où la Conférence devait tenir ses assises, et en prévisions desquelles on avait pavoisé le site de tous les drapeaux des États participants y compris le Québec. Nous en étions donc là: le Québec serait représenté sans que le fédéral y trouva place!

On connaît la suite de cette ténébreuse et bien regrettable affaire. Le Canada suspendit ses relations avec le Gabon et ne devait les reprendre qu'en août 1968. L'affaire ne fit rien pour améliorer nos relations, déjà ten-

Elmo Thibault

dues, avec la France. Elle empoisonna pour longtemps ce qui restait, dans le domaine constitutionnel, de contacts personnels entre Ottawa et Québec.

Heureusement, le gouvernement fédéral ne s'en tint pas là. Il fallait à tout prix contrer l'effet que pourrait avoir dans les pays de l'Afrique francophone le geste posé par le Québec à Libreville, visant à s'affirmer seul dans les domaines de sa compétence. Pour se faire, Ottawa mit sur pied une mission (dirigée par l'honorable E.R.E. Chevrier qu'appuyaient Henri Gaudefroy du Bureau de l'Aide extérieure et Jacques Dupuis de l'ambassade canadienne à Paris) laquelle était chargée d'offrir à ce qui avait été jusqu'alors chasse-gardée de la France (exception faite, bien sûr, du Gabon), aide et développement se chiffrant au total à environ 40,000,000$. Le succès de l'entreprise et les recommandations que fit la Mission à sa rentrée furent à l'origine du programme d'aide à la fois varié et bien étoffé que gère actuellement l'ACDI à l'endroit des pays de l'Afrique francophone.

Muté au pas de charge de l'Argentine à l'Afrique équatoriale en pleine année du Centenaire, j'eus à peine l'occasion de me familiariser avec la situation prévalant dans ce qui serait mes quatre pays d'accréditation. On me prévint tout de même qu'en pratique, l'aide extérieure qu'offrait notre pays à ladite région représenterait l'essentiel de mon boulot. Et voilà! En pareille circonstance, il m'eut été particulièrement difficile, voire même impossible, de hasarder quelque commentaire que ce soit sur les instructions qui me parvenaient de la Centrale concernant l'attitude que semblaient devoir prendre les autorités gabonaises vis-à-vis d'une représentation canadienne à la Conférence. Il m'eut été utile alors de savoir (ce que j'appris par la suite, d'expérience) qu'il n'était guère, dans les pays d'accréditation (Cameroun, Centrafrique, Gabon, Tchad, dont l'indépendance était toute récente), un seul ministère qui n'eut son conseiller technique français répondant directement à ses matières de la Coopération à Paris, ou encore au conseiller chargé des questions africaines auprès du général De Gaulle, Jacques Foccart; et que, enfin, pratiquement rien de valable ne s'accomplissait dans la région (pour ne m'en tenir qu'à celle-là) sans l'aval de la France. Sachant tout cela (ce que j'ignorais alors), on aurait pu, ce me semble, s'en prendre avec un peu moins de sévérité envers les hôtes de la Conférence et taper un peu plus fort sur les véritables fauteurs de troubles.

En somme, tous ces efforts que nous avions déployés de part et d'autre ces derniers temps, se soulevaient par un lamentable échec. Certes, le Ministère voulut bien me faire savoir en temps utile combien on avait apprécié à la Centrale tout le trouble que je m'étais donné dans cette affaire. Le fait n'en demeurait pas moins pour l'instant, que de toute évidence, le Québec, seul, participerait à la Conférence des Ministres de l'Éducation de l'Afrique francophone.

On sait maintenant, de ceux qui se sont penchés sur l'histoire des relations France-Québec-Canada du temps, pour nous en avoir raconté les péripéties, que cette participation du Québec à Libreville avait été orchestrée dès septembre 1967 alors que le porte-parole du général De Gaulle, Alain Peyrefitte, était l'hôte du Premier ministre Daniel Johnson. D'après Godin, Johnson aurait, quelque temps plus tard, fait savoir à François Leduc, l'ambassadeur de France du temps, que le Québec irait à Libreville si on l'invitait, et ce, sans passer par Ottawa. Et de fait, le 17 janvier 1968, une lettre du ministre de la Coordination du Gabon parvenait au Québec, adressée au "Ministère des Affaires étrangères du Québec," et invitant à titre personnel le ministre de l'Éducation, Jean-Guy Cardinal, à représenter "le Canada français" à la Conférence. Ainsi que le fait remarquer Godin, les instructions de Johnson à son ministre ne prêtaient guère à équivoque: "Allez-y fort. Je vous envoie au Gabon pour faire l'agent provocateur!"

A Libreville, Cardinal fut évidemment de toutes les fêtes et le président Bongo le décora de l'Ordre national gabonais. Était-ce pour donner suite aux instructions qu'il avait reçues de Johnson que l'idée, pour le moins saugrenue, lui vint (de son propre chef ou de ses conseillers?) de profiter, au cours de l'escale à Douala en direction de Paris, pour inviter les coopérants canadiens d'origine québécoise, à l'accompagner dans leurs voitures jusqu'à Yaoundé où il se proposait, semble-t-il, de rencontrer le ministre camerounais de l'Éducation et de l'instruire quant aux buts de sa présence à Libreville. Comme je pouvais d'avance répondre de l'attitude du Ministre comme de celle de son gouvernement en la matière, je m'en tins à faire rappeler aux coopérants enclins à se prêter au jeu de Cardinal qu'ils détenaient leur contrat de l'ACDI, agence du gouvernement fédéral, et qu'ils n'avaient qu'à bien se tenir s'ils n'entendaient pas, en cas contraire, se retrouver dans les plus brefs délais au Canada, et sans emploi. Inutile d'insister: Cardinal et sa suite ne vinrent pas à Yaoundé.

Quant aux visites à Libreville que m'occasionna la Conférence des Ministres de l'Éducation de l'Afrique francophone, la première eut lieu du 8 au 10 janvier 1968; la deuxième, du 16 au 21 janvier 1968, et la dernière, les 1er et 2 février1968. À noter en passant que pour se rendre à Libreville à partir de Yaoundé, il fallait agencer son départ avec l'horaire des vols à long cours en partance de Paris pour les mers du sud (UTA) et faire obligatoirement escale d'une nuit à Douala, aboutissement des lignes aériennes camerounaises du temps.

Au cas où on l'aurait oublié, en aucune occasion durant mon séjour en Afrique équatoriale n'ai-je pu présenter les lettres m'accréditant comme ambassadeur du Canada auprès de la République gabonaise. A mon arrivée à Yaoundé, on m'apprit que le 'Père de la Patrie', Léon M'ba, était mourant. Notre démêlé avec les autorités gabonaises s'engagea alors que l'on traversait la période de deuil prévue pour le grand disparu. D'ailleurs, son successeur à la Présidence, Bernard Albert Bongo, avait déjà quitté le pays pour la France en vue de présenter ses devoirs à qui de droit. De toute façon, l'imbroglio de la Conférence et ses séquelles devait mettre fin à toute possibilité pour moi de le faire.

J'eus pourtant à me rendre une quatrième fois à Libreville, cette fois-ci du 1er au 5 août 1969, à la demande expresse des autorités gabonaises qui ne désiraient rien de mieux que reprendre nos relations "interrompues de façon si regrettable" (sic) suite à la tenue de ladite Conférence. On me parla de méprise, de malentendu et que sais-je encore, tout en débouchant du champagne, sans doute pour se donner bonne conscience et, évidemment, dans l'espoir que, ce faisant, je m'empresserais de dire à mes supérieurs jusqu'à quel point on se sentait, localement, contrit d'avoir par pure mégarde offensé un si bon ami! Ottawa se montra bon prince. Les relations usuelles d'amitié reprirent en temps et lieu. Pour ma part, je devais quitter Yaoundé le 23 septembre 1969 pour réintégrer la Centrale où j'étais appelé à prendre la direction des services de l'Inspectorat jusqu'en février 1971.

(Le présent article a été rédigé à partir de souvenirs personnels, de lectures, et sans recourir aux archives du ministère des Affaires extérieures.)

1 Pierre de Menthon, qui aurait dorénavant le rang et tous les privilèges d'un ministre plénipotentiaire et adresserait ses rapports à Paris non pas par l'intermédiaire de l'ambassadeur de France à Ottawa mais directement à son ministre des Affaires étrangères, Couve de Murville.

2 Au cas où l'on croirait que j'exagère quant au degré d'indépendance dont jouissait le Gabon lors de mon affectation en Afrique équatoriale, voici ce qu'en dit *Jean-François Revel* dans ses Mémoires intitulées *Le Voleur dans la maison vide* et que cite *Louis-Bernard Robitaille* dans un récent entretien avec l'auteur lui-même (cf. *Jeu de massacre: l'Actualité*, 1er mai 1997, pp. 50-56).

3 Les citations attribuées plus tôt au Premier ministre Jean Lesage et au général de Gaulle sont tirées textuellement de la biographie de Daniel Johnson, publiée aux Éditions de l'Homme en 1980, dont l'auteur est Jean Godin.

4 l'École nationale d'Administration, à Paris.

5 En vertu d'accords intervenus avec l'ancienne métropole lors de l'indépendance. Ces accords couvrirent la Défense, l'Aide et la Coopération (conseillers techniques, etc...).

6 Je mets ce mot entre guillemets puisque, bien que Libreville ait accepté de me recevoir comme ambassadeur, la maladie puis le décès du président Léon M'ba obligea les autorités en place de reporter à plus tard la présentation de mes lettres de créance. Je n'avais donc, à toutes fins utiles, aucun statut officiel au pays, ce que les Gabonais se firent évidemment fort d'exploiter.

7 Cette vieille astuce du métier qui ne trompe jamais personne. En consultant mon vieux passeport diplomatique du temps, je constate que je mis pied au Gabon pour la première fois le 3 décembre 1967. Ma présence à Libreville avait pour but de représenter notre pays aux funérailles de Léon M'ba. Je rentrai à Yaoundé le surlendemain, soit le 5 décembre 1967.

DIPLOMATIC REFLECTIONS OF INDONESIA: 1974-1977

by Peter Johnston

In a little clearing in the South Sulawesi forest, at the spot where the cornerstone of our cement plant was to be placed, the head of a water buffalo had just been buried, and incantations had been uttered over the site. I wondered what the prayers had asked. My own silent prayer was that these worthies could be held to their commitment to buy the necessary machinery, gas turbines, boilers, and whatnots from Canada and not from the French who seemed to have written the book on cement plants. In the pause that followed our prayers, I was gently nudged from behind and pushed towards a microphone standing before some fifty or sixty ladies and gentlemen dressed in their Sunday best and seated on tiered planks.

I should explain why this exotic scene sticks so in my memory and must go back to the previous day when my wife and I arrived in Ujung Pandang, the capital of the Province of South Sulawesi, part of one of the most beautiful of the many lovely islands of the Indonesian archipelago. As ambassador, I had been asked by the Indonesian minister of industry to take part in the ceremony of inauguration, as guest of the governor of South Sulawesi, because the Canadian government had provided much of the financing for its construction. I had also been briefed by my staff about what to expect in the way of protocol, and reminded that when my predecessor had paid his first official visit to Ujung Pandang he had found the governor, an army general, to be a generous and thoughtful host, and the General's wife to be someone I was unlikely to forget. She was quite a character, they said: when a colleague and his wife were met at the airport and hands duly shaken, she announced to him that she was the mother of eleven children and how many did he have? "None," he replied. "Oh," she said, "so sorry, is there something the matter with you?" Nobody seemed able to remember what came next.

We passed a restful night at the governor's residence, disturbed only by my efforts to compose and commit to memory the speech which I expected I would have to make in the Indonesian language at the next day's ceremony.

We dutifully struggled over breakfast with durian, an evil-smelling fruit native to South-East Asia which tastes, they say, like heaven and stinks, I say, like a ripe Muskoka septic tank. We drove through the forest to the factory site where I delivered my sugary little speech about the many fine things that Canadians and Indonesia can do together. There followed sweetmeats and small talk with our new Indonesian friends (in the course of which no one showed interest in the size of my family). The governor returned us to his residence, fed us, presented me with a key to the city of Ujung Pandang, drove us to the airport and gave us a cordial send-off. Apart from the novelty of speechifying over a decomposing part of a water buffalo, this was, on the whole, a working day like any other. Whether it comes under the heading of "Diplomatic Practice," which is what this essay is meant to be about, is perhaps a moot point.

I had received notice of my appointment as ambassador to Indonesia in the spring of 1974 when I was serving as minister/counsellor at our Tokyo embassy. On the face of it, neither appointment made much sense; I had had no training in the Japanese language which was essential for the job I was asked to do. My predecessor and my successor in Tokyo were both, I was given to understand, accomplished Japanese speakers. I had no previous experience in East Asian affairs. Indonesia and its language were a closed book.

My entry into the Department of External Affairs, as it was then called, was unorthodox. In 1957 I had been working for some nine years in the Russian language in another part of the government, cannon fodder in the Cold War, when I saw a public service announcement of a vacancy in the Department for someone familiar with Russian affairs. I applied for the job and was accepted, partly because I had Russian and claimed to know something of the working of the Soviet economy, partly because I demonstrated to a pretty dim board of examiners that I had, at one time or another, spoken comprehensible Italian, Spanish, Russian and German and held a not terribly practical first class Honours degree in French literature from the University of Toronto, and partly because there seemed to be no one else about. The intervening years were passed either at headquarters or in postings to London, Dar es Salaam and Tokyo. As my colleague Arthur Blanchette has observed in his most interesting memoir on Indochina (*Special Trust and Confidence*, published by Carleton University Press), the two paramount personnel requirements of the Department are adaptability and flexibility. Indeed.

Pre-posting briefings for Indonesia in External Affairs were excellent. On the political side, I detected no great enthusiasm for improvements in our relations with the Indonesian government. Evidently our Far Eastern division had enough on its plate with the problems of staffing and dealing with the Truce Supervisory Commission in Indochina and our relations with Japan and China. I was a small potato. I was, however, authorized to remind President Suharto of our government's standing invitation to him to visit Canada. There was unease in the Department of Trade and Commerce about our export figures and I was urged to give priority to our trade relationship. Officials in the Canadian International Development Agency (CIDA) noted that Indonesia was the second or third largest recipient of Canadian aid and saw no likelihood of any change. Generous arrangements were made for me to call on provincial officials and companies actively interested in trade with Indonesia, notably in Quebec, Montreal, Toronto, Winnipeg, Regina, Edmonton, Calgary, Vancouver and Victoria. There was optimistic talk of aircraft sales, opportunities in the oil and gas industries, potash sales, and genuine interest in the fields of electronics and railway technology. British Colombia alone seemed unsure of what to do with me. The rosy vistas of Pacific Rim markets seemed not to have yet captured the imagination of BC politicians as they did in the 1990s. However I did respond to a mysterious invitation to call at the Vancouver head office of the forest company, MacMillan-Bloedel. It seemed a waste of time for both sides. I was left with the impression that the company did not have much more than a casual interest in Indonesia as a source of tropical hardwoods. I learned later that MacBlo may have been more actively interested than I thought at the time.

These were all interesting and valuable visits because I was a firm, if naive, believer in the Third Option policy. This had been devised a couple of years earlier by Prime Minister Trudeau and our Secretary of State for External Affairs, the Honourable Mitchell Sharp, whose objective was to diversify our trade relations away from undue dependence on the American economy.

My introduction to the External Affairs Information and Cultural Division's offices was a pleasant surprise. Rooms usually kept tightly locked away (from marauders) contained a treasure trove of Canadian art objects – Inuit carvings, pottery, prints, coffee table books and even some delectable Glenn Gould albums. When I was conducted through these rooms, I was told that I could pick, with discretion, whatever I thought I might need for presentation to Indonesian VIPs (but please not the "Goldberg Variations").

These were all impressive signs of a fine, new, enlightened policy of encouraging the arts in Canada and projecting a civilized picture of us abroad. I wonder if it has survived.

The Indonesia to which I was sent in September 1974 was an extremely complex society which would take rather more than a two or three year posting to understand. A population of close to 200 million (mostly Muslim) inhabits a chain of islands extending over three thousand miles in length. It is held together by a common language, Bahasa Indonesia, and by a sometimes tenuous sense of national identity. It was impossible for a short-term visitor to gain more than just a broad picture. It was rich in a wide range of natural resources: tropical forests, tin, nickel, copper, coal, and gold, including, as numerous Calgary investors would attest, a plentiful supply of Fool's Gold, plus ample oil and gas reserves. It was a member of the Organization of Petroleum Exporting Countries and not anxious to be seen to exploit its membership for political purposes. Its Islamic traditions were also moderate in comparison with the fire and brimstone ways of some Muslim nations over the western horizon. The country's leaders, notably in the armed forces and the friends and relatives of the president had, however, an eyebrow-raising reputation for venality.

This was a politically stable country. (In 1974, however, stories of the horrors of the Indonesian riots of 1965 in which more than a hundred thousand were slaughtered were, unfortunately, still fresh in my mind.) In "Cold War" terms, Indonesia's leaders were pro-Western. President Suharto wished it to be understood that the Chinese and the Russians were behind the abortive "communist" coup attempt of 1965 whose events took General Suharto to the presidency in the following year. And, of course, pro-Western attitudes were seen to be necessary if the country was to continue to attract the foreign aid and investment it needed. These attitudes were understandably encouraged by the United States whose president might have said of Suharto – as one of his predecessors once said of President Somoza, the late lamented tyrant of Nicaragua – "Sure he's a sonofabitch but he's our sonofabitch." Indonesia's human rights record was pretty unsavoury. Dissidents were not tolerated. The news media were tightly controlled and the prison island of Buru, over a thousand miles north east of Jakarta, was commonly believed to have held at least thirty thousand political prisoners.

For a number of reasons, the country's leaders regarded Canada favourably. We were a member of NATO and therefore on the side of the angels. We were a member of the Intergovernmental Group on Indonesia comprising of the United States, some West European countries, Australia, and Japan. The group consulted periodically on development aid under the watchful eye of the World Bank and the IMF. The Canadian aid and investment profile was relatively high. Our de Havilland Twin Otter aircraft were used widely in the outlying islands where runways were primitive, and our multi-million dollar INCO nickel mining and smelter project on Sulawesi was well known.

When an ambassador presents his credentials to a head of state, it can be great theatre. I may be biased, but I think my ceremony certainly was. I had previously attended two such affairs in Tanzania and Japan when I accompanied my head of mission up the steps and into the dwellings of President Nyerere and Emperor Hirohito. As a bit player, I found both episodes vastly amusing, each entailing an intimidating grand mise en scène and an elaborate set of movements carefully choreographed and monitored by the presidential chief of protocol. But my case was different. When playing the lead, detached amusement was out of the question. A couple of weeks after my arrival in Jakarta I was warned of the event only the day before. Shortly after daybreak I was alerted by the throaty rumble of half a dozen Harley-Davidson motorcycles in the driveway of the residence and met at the door by the Chief of protocol who ushered me into a magnificent limousine. My wife thrust my forgotten credentials to me through the car window. Five members of my embassy staff were piled into cars behind, and we were driven hell-bent, sirens screaming and Harleys roaring, to the palace courtyard. Here, I was deposited in front of a fierce uniformed gentleman carrying a long sharp weapon, possibly a sabre. Behind him was a company of granite-faced soldiery. The sabre, or whatever it was, flourished perilously close to my nose in a graceful salute. A brass band, stage left, provided some rousing music as I was invited to inspect the troops. As the sabre-rattler and I trotted in step past these guys, I had a piquant flashback. One day long ago, in 1941, as a scruffy infantryman in Aldershot, I was required to stand stiffly to attention during a similar inspection by an equally self-conscious minor Royal.

This marked the end of Act One. I was then invited to do an about-turn and mount the palace steps, with dignity. The bemused members of my staff followed at a respectful distance. I bowed to the president and party waiting for us in the first anteroom, extracted the letters from my document case, handed them to the protocol man, pulled out my little speech, and read it – dry-mouthed. I went on a bit about my government's desire to foster Indonesian/Canadian relations and reiterated my predecessor's invitation to the president to visit Canada. All this was standard boilerplate but I put some emphasis on trade. That done, handshakes followed, and my staff were introduced to the president while soft drinks were sipped and banalities exchanged until protocol reminded me that that they were "doing" the Hungarian too that morning and would I please get a move on.

The Third Act thus began with a relieved and hasty descent of the steps to find my own car waiting at the bottom. But first some saluting had to be done to the strains of O Canada in the background. Into the car and away we drove, Canadian flag adorning the bonnet for the first time. Behind us was the roar of our impatient motorcyclists. Once at the residence, all the Indonesian actors, including the bikers, indeed particularly them because I once rode Harleys while defending England against Hitler's hordes in 1942, and all embassy staff were offered a *vin d'honneur*, which in these circumstances might best be translated as a stiff drink. And that was that.

The next few months were passed in learning that I had a wonderful staff at the embassy who knew their jobs and enjoyed doing them well. Our regular weekly staff meetings were sensible and even-tempered, though I well recall one fractious occasion when it was impossible to please everybody in reaching a decision on how to devise a satisfactory bilingual designation on the doors of our public lavatories. In addition to the External Affairs, political, consular, and administration people, I had three officers from the Department of Trade and Commerce and three from the Canadian International Development Agency (CIDA). All made it plain that they saw themselves as members of the embassy and not as extensions of their parent departments, which, after Tokyo, was a refreshing novelty. Learning something of the language was also important. I learned to make myself understood, and frequently misunderstood, thanks to regular one-hour morning sessions with a teacher before going to the office. And, finally, of course, it was essential to be out meeting people, calling on diplomatic colleagues, paying calls on government ministers and officials, on regional governors and, when appropriate, the odd mayor. On these occasions, small gifts were sometimes exchanged, and I had cause to remember thankfully my visit to the treasure house of Canadian art objects in Ottawa. The most taxing experience was the requirement to be seen in attendance at a seemingly endless series of meetings, military parades and cultural functions. These were arranged by dignitaries to whom one could never say no. Sometimes they had the kindest of motives, but sometimes they requested our presence only to exploit the diplomatic corps for decorative purposes.

Things – things worth recording, that is – began to happen in 1975. That was the year the Portuguese overseas empire fell apart. Their colony, East Timor, was left to fend for itself, and the inhabitants elected to govern themselves. The Indonesian attempt, in December of that year, to fill the vacuum was brutal and bloody, and allegations of the killing of as many as a hundred thousand East Timorese were widely reported. When the fighting appeared to have stopped and the Indonesian Government offered to show foreign representatives how peaceable their new colony had become, I reported their invitation to Ottawa and was told to have nothing to do with it. This was reasonable enough because the presence of foreign diplomats would be seen internationally as recognition of the Indonesian takeover. But what stung a little was the fact that I was not instructed to do any "deploring" at the Indonesian foreign ministry, and External Affairs in Ottawa, as far as I knew, had made no fuss about the matter either publicly or through diplomatic channels. To me, personally, the incident was a good illustration of Talleyrand's advice to his ambassador "Surtout point de zèle," or, more to the point, "Keep your head down and shut up."

I had the impression that my American colleague was being told much the same. I have since learned that both President Ford and President Bush were advised by Brent Scowcroft, the National Security advisor, not to make an issue of East Timor on the grounds that "it makes no sense to antagonize the Indonesians."

It was also in 1975 that I was given notice of President Suharto's wish to visit Canada; an agreement was quickly reached for July. I had very much in mind that we should use the occasion to put a bit of substance into our trade relationship. I was therefore disappointed to receive a telegram from the department in May reporting that it was the government's intention to exchange views with the president and his ministers on questions of peace and security in the Pacific, or words to that effect. Consequently, I asked Reg Dorrett, my commercial counsellor, if he thought we could inject something more purposeful into this pretty mushy statement of objectives. He agreed that something had to be done and suggested we propose to Ottawa that the president and his party be offered a mixed credit for the purchase of Canadian goods, the credit consisting partly of Export Development Corporation credits and partly of CIDA grant or soft loan money. This was what we put up to Ottawa, suggesting something in the order of about $300 million in total. This idea was accepted in principle and I took part in a meeting in a House of Commons committee room during the president's visit where it was agreed by all parties (Finance, Trade and Commerce, EDC, CIDA and External) and put into concrete. As far as I was concerned, this was the centerpiece of the visit that was to mark the remaining two years of my posting to Jakarta.

There were two other events during that visit which still stand out, one pleasantly memorable and one which left a sour taste in my mouth. The first was a magnificent state dinner for the president and his party on July 3 given by the governor general and Mme Léger with over fifty guests. I was able to have a word with the prime minister and his ministers and had an opportunity to have a good talk with former Prime Minister Diefenbaker about his, and my father's, school days together. Now for the sour bit: earlier that day, according to the schedule of events, President Suharto was to meet with Prime Minister Trudeau for "private discussions" in Mr. Trudeau's office. I had expected that, as Mr. Trudeau's ambassador, I would be expected to attend as a matter of course. But it was not to be. Instead, the prime minister was accompanied by his "Foreign Affairs Advisor" Ivan Head, and neither I nor my colleagues in External ever learned, as far as I was aware, what was discussed at the meeting. I was subsequently assured by my colleagues that this was not to be taken as a personal slight and reminded that from the beginning of his tenure the prime minister's confidence in the Department and its officers had never been all that apparent.

The president's visit to Canada did much to generate a new sense of goodwill towards Canada among Indonesian ministers and officials. The little incident I have just recounted notwithstanding, the visit helped to improve my chances of gaining access to ministers when I needed to. I don't doubt that it opened doors for the seemingly endless stream of Canadian visitors which followed. When our Secretary of State for External Affairs, Don Jamieson, arrived with a staggeringly large retinue of businessmen, journalists, and officials, he was given excellent access to ministers. He seemed genuinely convinced, as the visit progressed, that there was much useful work to be done at home to spread the word of the growing importance of Indonesia to Canada both in general political terms and as a market. Though the animal had not yet entered our vocabulary, he saw the country as a potential Asian "tiger." He set the tone for his visit by asking for a very informal evening, upon his arrival, with his entire group. I was requested to review our relations with Indonesia and lead a discussion of the opportunities, and the problems, of interest to our visitors. Thanks to Reg Dorrett, who over the past two years had nurtured a wide-ranging and active Canadian Club for businessmen, we were able to fill the biggest available banqueting room with a resoundingly appreciative lunch-time audience for a post-prandial speech by Minister Jamieson. This gentleman was in a class by himself as an after-dinner speaker.

It was not long after the installment of Allan MacEachen as our new secretary of state for External Affairs that he descended upon us with a slightly smaller and perhaps more subdued, group but similar in composition to Jamieson's. On meeting him, I proposed another briefing meeting like the previous one but was told that he preferred a private meeting with me in his hotel room, accompanied by the Under-Secretary, Basil Robinson. The minister asked me to speak about Indonesia and where we fitted in, which I did for about thirty or forty exhausting minutes, pausing occasionally, expecting questions, but getting none. I finally sensed that it was time to stop and asked if that was enough. It was, and I was left unsure where his interests lay. And so it was for the remainder of the visit. We arranged a relatively small lunch meeting for him with the Canadian Club which failed to attract as many Indonesians as we had hoped. I judged that the most important feature of the visit was a good, solid encounter with Professor Widjojo, the very able Minister for Economy, Finance and Industry and chairman of the National Planning Board. Thus, I found, retrospectively, where Mr. MacEachen's interests lay. Mr. Trudeau wrote in his memoirs of Mr. MacEachen that he was "a very private person, not someone you could get to know very well." As indeed I discovered.

Paul Gérin-Lajoie, President of the Canadian International Development Agency (CIDA) since 1970, was a different kettle of fish. On taking up my embassy, I was surprised to learn that there was no record in the files of him ever having visited Indonesia, which seemed strange given the size of the Indonesian aid budget. So I urged a visit and struggled over a very carefully worded letter to him about the pros and cons of administering aid in this country. In it, I stressed the need for a painstaking selection of sectors of society: where we should put our resources, and where we should be wary of corrupt officials plundering our treasure. I remember quoting extensively from Alexander Herzen's memoirs in which he spoke of the incredible venality of Tsarist officialdom. I argued that things were not much different here.

Paul Gérin-Lajoie came not long after. We had useful discussions with my CIDA staff about the conduct of various programmes, notably agricultural assistance in the eastern islands, bridge-building in Sulawesi, technical advice to the railways, and paper supplies. I have said "my CIDA staff" advisedly because there was some talk among them at that time, prompted, I suspect, by officials at home, of establishing a CIDA office elsewhere in Jakarta, independent of the embassy. I raised this with M. Gérin-Lajoie and he readily agreed that such a step made no sense. I asked him if he had given thought to the possibility of our aid programme facing serious criticism in Canada in the event there should be publicity suggesting that it might be getting into the wrong hands. I mentioned my letter on the problem. He said that he had not seen it and gave the impression that he had not been briefed on the question or at least had no wish to talk about it.

I seem to remember that, at some point, we reviewed the mixed success of a project aimed at providing the Indonesians with an inventory of their vast tropical forest resources based on Canadian airborne mapping techniques. This project worked well until our people prepared to start work in Kalimantan, in the island of Borneo, when they were firmly told that most, if not all, forested land here was out of bounds as it was the property of various generals and admirals who had no desire to have prying outsiders counting their trees. This last incident, taken together with a report I had heard from an Indonesian that MacMillan Bloedel had at about that time put down some heavy money in advance on a large tract of forest in Kalimantan, throws a little light, if it is true, on the mystery of my invitation to call on MacBlo in Vancouver in 1974. I had heard that, after a considerable delay, MacBlo had been told to take their money back because the trees belonged to an admiral who had his own plans for them. I could find no record in my embassy files of the company ever having sought our advice about investing in Kalimantan. If they had, and assuming the report to be true, we could perhaps have saved them some time, money, and embarrassment.

In the days that followed, Gérin-Lajoie proved to be a delightful person, but a bit of a handful. After doing the rounds in Jakarta, I gave him a reception at the Residence to meet the people I wanted him to meet. I got a bit of a jolt when halfway through the proceedings he called out that he wished to talk to us all. There was utter consternation among my guests, including Foreign Minister Adam Malik, who were not used to this sort of thing. But it proved to be a well-prepared and impassioned speech about Canadian aid to the developing countries. The morning after, we set out to drive across the island Java, the islands of Bali and Lombok as our destinations. The seating arrangement in my car became an unexpected problem. As was my wont, I sat in the back opposite the flag and when I went to fetch Gérin-Lajoie and held the door open for him. He chose not to sit where I indicated and inched over to my place. Conscious of the absurdity of the situation, and hoping nobody was watching, I tactfully suggested to him that, as ambassador, I ought to be sitting opposite the flag, and placed my bottom solidly next to his and endeavoured to bunt him sideways. He stood his ground, so to speak, smiled sweetly and murmured, "Non, Monsieur l'ambassadeur, moi, je suis l'empereur." There were now people watching us, so I surrendered.

The next morning, after an uncomfortable night in central Java which slowed Gérin-Lajoie somewhat, I sat in my rightful place in the car and rode in state until we reached Bali. Here, I unaccountably got trapped into giving my friend, the "Emperor," yet another reception for the local dignitaries which entailed my taking over one of the two most expensive suites of the priciest hotel in Denpasar while he, imperial style, took over the other. Some Canadian bank chairmen, from the Big Five, also happened to be there, with wives. They, of course, had to be invited too. This all seemed unspeakably extravagant and I worried a bit about appearances as, I gathered, did my distinguished guest upon our return from Lombok the following day.

We flew to Lombok in one of the Twin Otter aircraft supplied by CIDA to the Ministry of Transport, our objective being to see at first hand the island's water shortage problems and to meet with the governor to discuss a CIDA-sponsored irrigation project. The meeting went well until I stupidly forgot that I was supposed to be acting as interpreter and became absorbed in a longish conversation with the governor in Bahasa about overpopulation and was brought up short by my friend asking irritably if he might be told what the hell we were talking about. The last day, at our wrapup meeting in his Balinese hotel suite with embassy officials, we were interrupted by a telephone call to Gérin-Lajoie from a CBC correspondent in Hong Kong. The journalist asked how the visit went in this evidently prearranged call. When the interview was concluded, I was reminded of the importance attached by our "Top People" to public relations when the CBC man was asked to dateline his story, if there was to be one, as Lombok, please, and not Bali.

There were many other visitors, all a pleasant distraction from routine embassy work. There was Premier Blakeney from Saskatchewan, Minister Bennett from Ontario, and the chairman of International Nickel who kindly invited me to the new smelter's inauguration ceremony with President Suharto; Tom Bata, whose shoe factory in Tanzania was nationalized in 1967 some six months after I had personally assured him that this was most unlikely to happen, Dick Thomson of the Toronto Dominion Bank, Minister Bud Cullen of National Revenue (to attend an Asian Bank meeting), and a gratifyingly large number of businessmen, the most conspicuous being the oil and gas tribe from Alberta.

Two other frequent visitors who had nothing to do with business and who will not soon be forgotten were Lotta Hitschmanova of the Unitarian Services Committee and Douglas Roche, then a member of parliament from Alberta. Both had an abiding and active interest in the welfare of the people in the villages. We tried to help them as much as possible. Lotta was a stickler for cutting down on her administrative costs and on her first visit to Jakarta my wife found her living in a squalid rooming house with no conveniences to speak of. We insisted on putting her up at the residence and she stayed with us regularly on her subsequent visits.

One visit by the Commandant with staff and students of the National Defence College, Kingston, was memorable for the manner of his departure (as was the visit of Minister Cullen). The NDC crowd trooped up the gangway to their plane in Bali. I watched from the background, as, last up the ladder, four sweating men lugged on their shoulders a huge, beautifully carved, Balinese door, evidently the recently acquired property of the Commandant. At the top of the gangplank, the bearers were met by a grim-faced captain who announced loudly and firmly that he was not having that goddamned thing on his plane. The ensuing conversation between captain and Commandant was sotto voce, between clenched teeth, but its meaning was plain. The door came slowly down the steps and I was stuck with it. I also found myself stuck with a very large bamboo organ in similar circumstances as I was saying goodbye to Minister Cullen at the Jakarta departure lounge and he confessed to me that this ceiling-high object was unlikely to qualify as accompanied baggage and would I please deal with it. Both encumbrances were duly shipped home at the owner's expense.

Embassy routine, as opposed to escorting VIPs, entailed numerous jobs. I negotiated with hard-nosed officials about aid projects. I lobbied ministers on behalf of businessmen. I advised distraught parents whose children had been found carrying pot in their backpacks. They often claimed that someone else must have put the drugs in there, and they were anxious to know whom they had to pay to get their child out of jail? There were also openings of Canadian film and art shows, and lectures to the Indonesian Defence College and Rotary Clubs about Canada. I enjoyed the role of guest of honour at the St. Andrew's Day and ANZAC gala balls where speeches had to be made to bibulous and receptive celebrants who were not too fussy about what I said as long as I got it over with quickly. I had a good friend in the Russian ambassador, Spedko, who had been ambassador to Canada. After I had spoken to him about a film of an NHL hockey game, he invited me to screen it in his embassy auditorium for his staff. He also challenged me to speak to his staff in Russian about Canadian hockey, no doubt as comic background. I twitch at the memory of it. I don't feel too badly about my Russian. But I do about my foolhardy boasting about the superior quality of our hockey when I recall what they did to us in subsequent years. These last few extracurricular activities may have not done much to advance the Canadian interest. But they were not to be avoided, and were part of the job of representing Canada.

Throughout the period of my posting, it was plain to me that the main Canadian interest had to be trade promotion. Thanks to Reg Dorrett and his staff, we managed pretty well. In my three years, our export figures went up from about $30 million per annum to something like $300 million and our EDC line of credit was just about used up. This was peanuts, perhaps, in 1990s terms but these sort of statistics made it seem at the time as if the Third Option was feasible. There were setbacks. We failed to get a contract for the sale of locomotives for which we had worked hard until we learned at the last minute that the buyer expected a bit too much off the top. We went to great pains to demonstrate the latest de Havilland Dash aircraft; but the German Messerschmidt Boelkow firm was working closely, unknown to us, with an old friend of President Suharto, Jusuf Habibie, with a proposal to assemble their aircraft, tinkertoy fashion, in Indonesia. The Indonesians put out a bid for a cargo ship, Liberty ship size. We worked for months with an agent of Marine Industries Ltd. of Quebec to interest them in one of ours. But eventually we discovered that the Norwegians, no doubt for good domestic economic reasons, had decided to give them a ship, gratis. We tried to get the Indonesians to look on Canada as a reliable wheat supplier, but the key Indonesian official happened to be hooked on horse racing and was unable to resist a standing Australian invitation to the annual Melbourne Cup. So he bought Australian wheat.

From all this, it might be thought that I would be relieved to make my escape from Jakarta when the Department – in yet another fit of bureaucratic whimsy – advised me that my name was being put up for the Prague embassy. Not at all. The pervasive influence of the military was, of course, oppressive, as was the problem of nepotism and cronyism in the upper levels. Obviously, much of the country's wealth was being siphoned off by the president's family and the "trickle down" theory remained only a theory. But the integrity and professionalism of the officials I had to work with in the economic ministries and the foreign ministry were of a very high order. I made some Indonesian friends and learned to appreciate something of the country's rich history and culture, and its landscape. Most gratifying of all, when I paid my farewell call on President Suharto, he waved away his interpreter and we exchanged compliments in his language.

On our last day, as we were seen off at the airport by the chief of protocol and our colleagues and friends, we enjoyed the unaccustomed luxury of being led to first class seats in the plane. Economy class for ambassadors and all staff, as a general rule, was demanded by the number crunchers who ran the department in those days. But the department permitted the purchase of First Class tickets on official occasions of this sort because it would be unseemly to be seen escorted by protocol to economy seats. This nice little gesture was good for the Jakarta/Singapore leg of our flight home only. After that it was steerage all the way.

A MISSION TO ALGERIA: THE AMBASSADOR AS TRADE COMMISSIONER

by Louis A. Delvoie,
Senior Fellow Centre for
International Relations Queen's University

I n the summer of 1971, I was posted to Algiers as first secretary to open the new Canadian embassy there. When I left Algeria two years later I little expected to return. But fate and the will of my lords and masters in the Department of External Affairs intervened and I was re-assigned to Algeria as ambassador in 1980.

I greeted news of my new assignment with distinctly mixed feelings. I was of course delighted to have been given my first appointment as a head of mission at a relatively early age. I had found Algeria not only a truly beautiful country but also a professionally interesting and rewarding one. It was a leader among Third World and non-aligned countries, its oil and gas resources gave it the means to pursue a highly ambitious programme of economic development, and the groundwork had already been laid for the pursuit of a substantive and productive relationship with Canada.

On the other hand, I had found the working and living environment in Algeria to be anything but congenial. As a whole, the population of Algeria still bore the scars of over a century of harsh French colonial rule and of a brutal and bloody war of independence of eight years' duration. By and large Algerians were dour people, not inclined to either openness or friendliness. These tendencies were reinforced by an authoritarian and secretive government which inundated the population with a steady stream of anti-Western propaganda and which frowned on Algerians fraternizing with foreigners. And running an office or a household in Algeria was often a nightmare. The country's highly centralized economy was operated by an inefficient and frequently uncooperative bureaucracy which resulted not only in constant delays in getting anything done but also in a perpetual series of shortages of everything from potatoes and cement to water and phone lines. Indeed, one

Ambassador Louis Delvoie presenting his credentials to President Benjedid in November, 1980

of the most common refrains to be heard in government ministries, department stores and corner shops was "*Ça manque ... On attend un arrivage.*"

At first sight, not much had changed by the time I reached Algeria for the second time in 1980. The avuncular Chadli Benjedid had replaced the grim and steely-eyed Houari Boumedienne as head of state. But the regime over which he presided was still a one-man, one-party dictatorship bolstered by the army and the security services. Despite a few feeble experiments in liberalization, the government still controlled virtually all significant aspects of the country's economic life, including agriculture, industry, banking, foreign trade and tourism. But what was notably different was that the government's efforts to re-create an Algerian culture after years of French domination were beginning to bear fruit. The Arabic language was steadily displacing French in the classroom, in the media, and in the street, and there was now far more evidence of Muslim religious practice at all levels of society. Another difference, however, which struck me at the time as being of far greater import, was the new pace of Algeria's programme of economic development. It had speeded up considerably, fuelled by rising world prices for Algeria's oil exports. With this acceleration came an ever-expanding market for imported goods and services; if methodically exploited, this could provide new opportunities for Canadian business and industry.

The Evolving Canadian Interest

Algeria had first attracted the attention of the Canadian government in the mid-1960s.[1] In response to the Quiet Revolution in Quebec and to the findings of the Royal Commission on Bilingualism and Biculturalism the government embarked on a systematic effort to better reflect Canada's dual linguistic and cultural realities in its foreign policy and international relations. This meant, among other things, developing Canada's relations with the newly independent countries of francophone Africa, including Algeria, to counterbalance its existing relations with the Commonwealth countries of Africa. This thrust in Canadian foreign policy was given further impetus somewhat later in the decade as a result of three phenomena: (a) the ever more assertive claims of the Quebec government to the right to play an autonomous role in international affairs, (b) the encouragement given some of those claims by the French government, and (c) the development of new international institutions bringing together the francophone countries of the world.

It was in this context that the Canadian government initiated a modest programme of economic and technical assistance to Algeria in 1968. While this programme did serve to launch the bilateral relationship, it did little to meet the government's national unity objectives. Whereas many former French colonies in Africa wanted to preserve and promote the French language and culture and to give expression to *la Francophonie* in new international institutions, Algeria categorically rejected both of these ideas. On the one hand, the Algerian government was committed to the complete Arabization of the country as a means of restoring an authentic Algerian culture. On the other hand, the Algerian government saw in the internationalization of *la Francophonie* little more than a device of the French government to retain its influence over its former colonies. Algeria was thus a non-participant, at least officially, in the affairs of the Francophone community of nations and hence of no help to the Canadian government in bolstering its positions in the Ottawa-Quebec-Paris imbroglios which occurred within the framework of that community.

Algeria did, however, play into the national unity concerns of the Canadian government, but in a totally different way. Algeria's traditional support for liberation movements and its granting of asylum to exiled members of these movements (usually under the auspices of the FLN party rather than the Algerian government itself) came to the fore during and after Canada's FLQ crisis of October 1970. Among the first demands of the FLQ kidnappers of British diplomat James Cross was the release of twenty-three so-called political prisoners and their transportation to Algeria or Cuba. While the Canadian government never considered the release of any prisoners, it did envisage Algeria as one possible destination for the abductors themselves if they released Cross safe and sound. It was in this context that the Canadian government entered into its first sustained political contacts with the Algerian government, in order to discuss possible safe conduct arrangements for the abductors. In the event and for various practical reasons (geographical distance, presence of a Cuban consulate in Montreal and a resident Canadian mission in Havana) it was decided that these arrangements should be made with Cuba. A few FLQ exiles did, however, manage to make their way independently to Algeria. They set up there a "Délégation extérieure du FLQ" which had a short-lived existence from December 1970 to the spring of 1972. In response to démarches by the Canadian government, the Algerian government gave unequivocal assurances that it did not recognize the FLQ as a "liberation movement" and that members of the FLQ living in Algiers would not be allowed to undertake any political or other activities inimical to the interests of Canada. It fully lived up to its word.

The FLQ crisis of October 1970 did underline for the Canadian authorities the lack of an adequate mechanism to deal with the Algerian authorities on sensitive issues. This, together with the conclusion of the first of a series of long-term agreements for the sale of Canadian wheat to Algeria, prompted the Canadian government to open a resident embassy in Algiers in the summer of 1971. It was perhaps a sign of things to come that the new embassy was officially inaugurated during a visit to Algiers of the Minister of Industry, Trade and Commerce, Jean-Luc Pépin, in November 1971. For it became more evident with the passage of every year thereafter that Canada's main interest in Algeria lay not in the fields of national unity or development assistance but rather in the cultivation of a growing and promising market for the export of Canadian goods and services.

Pursuing the Canadian Interest

The pursuit of these interests involved a steady increase in the engagement of Canadian government agencies. After its first export contract in 1970, the Canadian Wheat Board systematically developed a close and productive partnership with its Algerian counterpart, the Office Algérien interprofessionnel des céréales (OAIC), which over the years ensured a reliable and predictable market for Canadian wheat. The CIDA programme was also instrumental in the development of Canada's commercial relations with Algeria by introducing a number of Canadian engineering and management firms to the Algerian market, and by allowing those firms to demonstrate their capabilities and expertise to the Algerian government. Of no less importance was the vision displayed by the Export Development Corporation (EDC) which very early on saw the potential of the Algerian market for Canada. Starting modestly with an export credit of $10 million in 1971, the EDC moved rapidly to broaden its support to Canadian exporters by putting in place a $100 million line of credit in 1973. And as Canada's exports to Algeria grew through the 1970s, so too did the involvement of the EDC. In 1978 the EDC extended a $1.2 billion line of credit to Algeria through the Algerian Development Bank, the EDC's largest single commitment abroad outside of China.

The embassy was also a key actor in the pursuit of our commercial interests. It naturally performed all of the functions normally associated with trade promotion: securing market intelligence, establishing contacts between Canadian and Algerian firms, organizing business missions, and arranging for Canadian participation in trade fairs. But there was far more to its work in the case of Algeria. The extent of the Algerian government's control over the economy meant that the key decision makers in commercial matters were usually ministers, deputy ministers or the heads of state corporations. All the latter were reluctant to become involved in contacts with the representatives of foreign business enterprises for fear of being accused of impropriety. The ambassador therefore became the premier high level lobbyist on behalf of Canadian firms seeking contracts. Building on the very solid foundations laid by two of my predecessors, Christian Hardy and Robert Elliott, I very soon found myself spending over forty per cent of my time on trade files and enjoying it for the very concrete results it produced. And given the Algerian government's strong preference for doing business on a government-to-government basis, I also found myself negotiating and signing multi-million dollar contracts for the export of milk and canola oil, and for the building and equipping of schools and transport maintenance depots. In so doing, I was acting as the representative of the Canadian Commercial Corporation which in turn was acting as the contracting agent for Canadian private sector firms. Making headway in the Algerian marketplace often required a fair amount of imagination, flexibility, and ingenuity.

The Policy of Bilateralism

My efforts on the commercial front were greatly aided by an initiative announced by the Canadian government a few months after my arrival in Algeria. The government decided that the time had come to give more focus to its international relations and to attach greater importance to the development of bilateral relations with a small number of countries as a means of making the best possible use of the limited resources available to our government to pursue its foreign policy objectives. The thrust of what came to be known as the "policy of bilateralism" was explained in the following terms by the Secretary of State for External Affairs, Mark MacGuigan:

> *As a basic instrument of its global, differentiated foreign policy, the government has therefore decided to give concentrated attention to a select number of countries of concentration. The purpose is generally to strengthen long-term relationships with these countries because of their relevance to our long-term domestic development objectives. But the importance of the countries in question would also devolve from their relevance to our overall objectives and interests.*[2]

The countries identified for concerted action and attention included not only Canada's traditional major partners (United States, United Kingdom, Germany, France, and Japan), but also a small number of oil producing, newly-industrializing countries. Mexico, Venezuela, Algeria, Indonesia, and Nigeria were described as having "emerged as new centres of strength and influence. They are now where a lot of the action is in matters of commerce and economic development."[3]

In the case of Algeria the "policy of bilateralism" translated itself into a steady increase in bilateral contacts at the political level. A Canada-Algeria joint commission on economic and technical cooperation was created and held its first meetings at the ministerial level in Ottawa in March 1981 and in Algiers in April 1982. The pace of ministerial visits and of trade missions accelerated. Prime Minister Trudeau, accompanied by some 20 Canadian business leaders, visited Algiers in May 1981. His talks with Algeria's president and prime minister dwelt not only on the bilateral agenda, but also on

Louis A. Delvoie

his efforts to help launch the process of "global negotiations" on economic issues as a contribution to fostering a North-South dialogue in international relations. The visit represented, among other things, an explicit recognition on the part of Prime Minister Trudeau that Algeria was one of the "key developing countries" and "major nations" whose views would have to be taken into account if the process of global negotiations were to be launched with any prospect of success.

These were the terms used by Prime Minister Trudeau in a statement to the House of Commons on June 6, 1981.[4]

The "global negotiations" project never came to fruition, of course, not least because of the conditions laid down by some of the "hard line" developing countries, among them Algeria. However, marked differences of views between the two governments on this issue had no discernible impact on the conduct of the Canada-Algeria bilateral relationship.

Increasing numbers of visitors at times severely stretched the resources of my relatively small mission (twelve Canadian and fifteen local staff), but I welcomed it nonetheless. Visits by intelligent, interested and charming political leaders such as Prime Minister Trudeau, House of Commons Speaker Jeanne Sauvé and Treasury Board President Donald Johnson were invaluable in advancing our economic interests in Algeria. They not only opened new doors into the Algerian political and economic hierarchy, but also underlined the importance which Canada attached to the relationship, something to which many Algerian leaders were highly susceptible. And these visits helped to raise the Canadian profile among Algerian decision-makers at all levels by virtue of the coverage they were given by the government-controlled press, radio, and television.

Other visitors made their mark in equally useful ways. The highly professional heads of government agencies such as the Export Development Corporation, the Canadian Wheat Board, and the Canadian Dairy Commission established solid relationships with their counterparts in Algerian banks and state corporations. So too did the ever increasing number of senior executives of private sector Canadian companies who made their way to Algeria. But in all instances the success of these visits depended on a lot of time and effort invested by my staff and myself. We prepared programmes, secured appointments, provided political and commercial briefings, and often accompanied visitors on their calls. The complex nature of the Algerian bureaucracy and the vicissitudes of the Algerian phone system turned every visit into a challenge.

Needless to say, this steady increase in the traffic between Canada and Algeria was not an unmixed blessing. The president of one Canadian corporation did our reputation no good by promising his Algerian partners a wide array of technology and services which his small company could not deliver. And one particularly obnoxious and arrogant junior minister (who shall remain nameless) managed in three days to alienate half a dozen Algerian ministers by his habit of lecturing them on how they should be tackling their jobs. In each instance, my staff and I had to spend considerable time in trying to mend fences. But these were exceptions to a trend which greatly helped to establish Canada's place in Algeria and in the Algerian market place.

Concluding Thoughts

Trade was obviously not my sole preoccupation as ambassador to Algeria. I was required to make démarches and report on Algeria's involvement in a number of political and economic questions, including the North-South Dialogue, the Arab-Israeli conflict, and the Western Sahara dispute. I was responsible for the management of a CIDA programme of economic and technical assistance, valued variously between $5 to 10 million per year. And, even though the resident Canadian community of three hundred was relatively small, it presented the usual variety of consular problems ranging from rape to arbitrary imprisonment of Canadians. And, perhaps most mundane of all, I had to devote considerable time and energy to keeping the embassy afloat administratively and to sustaining staff morale in a difficult and occasionally hostile environment. But in a country in which the political and the economic were so totally intertwined, it was on the commercial front that I found my most interesting and rewarding challenges as an ambassador, and the ones that provided the greatest long-term benefits to Canada and Canadians.

By the time I left Algeria in 1982, the annual value of our exports had risen to nearly $500 million, as compared to $27 million when I first arrived in the country in 1971. And the diversification of our exports had gone on apace to include not only food and raw materials but also pre-fabricated buildings, industrial machinery, oil drilling equipment, and construction vehicles. By 1982, Algeria ranked as our largest export market in Africa and the Middle East, and our thirteenth largest market in the world. Not bad going for a country with which we had had only the most cursory of relations only a dozen years earlier.[5]

Louis A. Delvoie

Beyond the statistics, there are also the intangibles which serve to measure success in the building of a bilateral relationship. I became convinced that we were on the right track when in late 1981, the Algerian authorities decided to entrust to a Canadian company a prestigious project invested with a great deal of national pride. This was the construction of a monument to mark the twentieth anniversary of Algeria's independence. Rising two hundred feet high on a hill above Algiers, the monument was to incorporate not only an observatory, but also radio and television transmission facilities. Five hundred Canadian construction workers, housed in a cruise ship anchored in Algiers harbour and working round the clock, completed the project in less than six months and in time for the anniversary celebrations. For the Algerians, the monument was dedicated to the memory of the hundreds of thousands of their compatriots who had lost their lives in the war of independence. For me, it also stood as a symbol of a new economic partnership between Canada and Algeria.

1 To the best of my knowledge, there is only one published article that deals at any length with Canada's relations with Algeria. See L.A. Delvoie, "Bilateralism in Foreign Policy: Canada and the Maghreb Countries," *Canadian Foreign Policy*, Vol. IV, No. 2, 1996, pp. 55-69.

2 *Department of External Affairs (DEA), Statements and Speeches, No. 81/2 (Ottawa, 1981), p. 5.*

3 *Ibid.,* p. 2.

4 DEA, *Statements and Speeches,* No. 17/81 (Ottawa, 1981), p. 9.

5 DEA, *Communiqués,* No. 60/82 (Ottawa, 1982) and No. 154/83 (Ottawa, 1983).

GHANA, SOUTH AFRICA, AND CUBA: SOME SELECTED MEMORIES

by R. M. Middleton

These are my recollections of the eight or so years that I was High Commissioner or Ambassador to Ghana, South Africa and Cuba. They focus on what I and my colleagues in these three successive posts did to carry out government policy and what our advice was to Ottawa in the process. For various reasons my postings to South Africa and Cuba have provided me with rather more material than Ghana to illustrate the thesis that a head of post has some scope in initiatives to advance and protect Canadian interests abroad, but this may be primarily a function of memory. I should warn the reader that I am not John Diefenbaker. I once heard him say in 1969 at the Embassy in Washington that he did not need to consult the files in writing his own memoirs as he had a photographic memory. Any day, month, or year could be mentioned and he could cite the events that had occurred and the decisions he had made from them. I am sorry to say that I do not possess this capacity. This deficiency on my part may lead me (unlike Mr. Diefenbaker, I am sure) to wander a little into historical revisionism. I hope, though, that these notes will not turn into the summary of activities which all heads of posts were required to submit every year to Ottawa. In them, senior officials recast the material and used it to document in the annual appraisal exercise how their colleagues in the field occasionally walked on water in carrying out their heavy responsibilities.

Some of my contemporaries in the Department recounted how they came entirely by chance to write the examination for the Foreign Service. Not I. I am embarrassed to admit that at the age of fourteen the prospect of becoming an ambassador (whatever he did) had occurred to me. I did entertain other career possibilities in my teens, but on the whole headed fairly single-mindedly for UBC in 1949, took a degree in economics and international studies, performed very badly in the interview for the Department in 1954, and to my astonishment was invited to enter it the following year.

My introductory experience as a head of post came very early. In 1963 in Rio I ended up as chargé for seven months between ambassadors. I enjoyed it all and even became a little nonchalant over whether the fortnightly diplomatic bag was as full as it might be. I liked being held responsible for the running of an Embassy at the age of thirty-two, including the right to sign, years before the normal time in the Department of External Affairs, my own telegrams and dispatches. Such an experience early in one's career is invaluable. I concluded that the job of a head of mission in a medium sized post in the 1960s was not – dare I say it – as difficult as all that. I then set out to repeat the experience on a more permanent basis. I was given my first chance in 1976 when, after service in United Nations work, security and intelligence, the European bureau and the Embassy in Washington, I was appointed High Commissioner to Ghana.

Ghana, South Africa, and Cuba could not have been more diverse when it came to Canada's interests and our relations with them. We gave aid to the first, but hardly any to the other two for different reasons. With Ghana we enjoyed easy and close relations: with South Africa and Cuba we had major differences on political and human rights issues. In Ghana and Cuba markets for our exports were limited; in South Africa the potential market was very large but because of government policy we could not exploit it. The Canadian community in Ghana was small and largely confined to aid workers and missionaries; in Cuba it consisted of a couple of dozen people, while in South Africa it was probably very large but not very visible. Ghana had very few Canadian tourists, South Africa a few thousand, and Cuba well over 100,000. In Ghana and South Africa I had multiple accreditations in six neighbouring countries, in most of which we had respectable aid programmes. In Havana I was only accredited to Cuba. Political freedoms were curtailed or nonexistent in all three – in South Africa on the grounds of race alone.

Accra was a delightful post. Since Ghana became independent we had seen eye to eye on most issues. All Canadian High Commissioners were warmly welcomed and I was no exception. It was our largest aid recipient in Commonwealth Africa and much of the relationship between Ghana and Canada was conducted at the official level by my two colleagues from the Canadian International Development Agency (CIDA). We also had three senior Canadian officers involved in the training of the Ghanaian armed forces. We kept a close eye on the increasingly depressing economic scene. Ghana was slipping further down the slope from the halcyon days of the sixties when its first president squandered his country's patrimony in domestic

High Commissioner Middelton at Terra Harbour near Accra unveiling a plaque marking the foundation of a school project financed by Canadian aid

and foreign initiatives that it could ill afford. We witnessed one general removing another as chief of state with little improvement in the governance of the country. We in the High Commission watched the shop and took all the steps to assess the implications of these trends and events for the stake we had in the country through our development cooperation programme.

In late 1978 I was asked to go to Pretoria as ambassador when the post unexpectedly became vacant. There was some urgency about it as progress was expected in the negotiations for the independence of Namibia and Canada was a member of the international Contact Group. After two and a half years in black Africa, a posting to South Africa had little visceral appeal and I tried to telephone Ottawa with words of regret. I failed to get through, thought about it for another day and concluded that my grounds for refusing were weak. I sent a telegram of acceptance and spent the next few weeks disengaging from West Africa and undergoing briefings in Ottawa and New York. I arrived in January 1979.

South Africa turned out to be personally and professionally the most stimulating of my posts, although the first six months were depressing since there were reminders every day of the apartheid laws. Conversations about South African politics and policies were by definition conversations about race. Still, as the Canadian ambassador, I could take a good deal of satisfaction from the policies that Ottawa had developed over the past thirty years. I was meant to display some initiative and imagination in giving expression to them on the ground. Indeed in some respects our policy toward Pretoria then called for almost the reverse of the traditional ambassador's duties. I was not to promote friendly relations with the government to which I was accredited other than in a narrow legal sense, but rather to make clear that Canada sympathized with and supported the views of the opposition, both black and white. I was meant to expand contacts and relationships with the black, coloured, and Indian communities. I was to do this while remaining on reasonable terms with the government of the country whose attitudes we wanted to influence. In a formal sense it was not intended that the relationship should be warm and easy but on a daily basis the dialogue with Foreign Ministry officials was civilized and professional. They were readily accessible at all times. In accordance with the Vienna Convention on Diplomatic Privileges I was allowed to travel anywhere in South Africa I wished, although once there was an attempt to insist that I apply for a permit before visiting Soweto. I declined to do so and the Foreign Ministry relented.

Contact with South African ministers was more distant. Canada was not high on their list of preferred countries. My initial call on P.W. Botha, then Prime Minister, was a little cool as he defended forthrightly his policies. It perhaps did not help that I had come directly from a black African country so he could guess rightly my frame of mind. This previous posting served me well in periodic discussions with South Africans about the perceived shortcomings of black governments. I was able to deal with their arguments from the vantage point of firsthand experience. Pik Botha, the Foreign Minister, could also be fairly robust. With a somewhat bombastic manner he tended to harangue ambassadors of the Contact Group on Namibia whenever he saw them collectively or individually. Beneath this rather bold exterior he belonged in fact to the liberal wing of the Nationalist Party and was the first leading member thereof to say, years before it came about, that one day South Africa would and should have a black president.

Other ministers were approachable enough at receptions and other social occasions. They were not, however, very willing to accept offers of hospitality presumably to underscore their unhappiness with our criticism of their government. I was not much troubled by this reluctance: indeed it symbolically fitted my own understanding of where things stood between our two countries. Such constraints, though, did not apply to some of the younger, more "liberal," Nationalist MPs whom I saw and entertained on my information gathering "traplines." Some held senior posts in the coalition formed following Nelson Mandela's election in 1992.

As I considered it important to understand as fully as possible the pressures on the Nationalist government from many of its "volk" I had a long conversation with the MP of the riding where the Pretoria residence was located. He later joined other right-wingers to form, in opposition to the government, the Conservative party. He commented on the domestic scene and the personalities therein with a candor that at times left me speechless. He spoke bitterly about such liberal Afrikaaner backsliders as the then head of the Progressive Federal Party. He expressed dismay about the ill luck of the Nationalist Party which over the years would elect as their successive leaders respectable keepers of the faith only to see them, once in office, turn progressive and give into black demands. This was a point of view that had not occurred to me before, as I had never regarded John Vorster, P.W. Botha and others as subversives and threats to the established order.

I think that I took useful initiatives in expanding contacts with the black opposition and encouraged one of my officers to dedicate much time to this area. I sought out and saw from time to time such figures as Dr. Nthako Motlano, who played a particularly key role in Soweto, Archbishop Tutu, the charismatic churchman who carried a good deal of weight politically, Alan Boesak, then a very influential leader from the coloured community, and Chief Gatsha Buthelzi of the Zulus who was a thorn in the side of the African National Congress, the main part of the black community. The black trade union movement grew rapidly in importance and influence while I was there and I spent some time on a lengthy paper for Ottawa trying to describe its complex organization and conflicting objectives. I always found it instructive as head of post to occasionally do such research myself as a way of getting to the bottom of an important subject. It is this sort of political reporting which should help Ottawa get a grasp of developments in a country.

From the beginning I pressed hard for the establishment of a small Mission Administered Fund for the blacks in South Africa. I had to contend with initial reservations in CIDA about its ineligibility. The existing terms of reference required a host government's approval for the projects in question. The fund proposal made slow progress through the system, but it had at least reached the desk of Mark McGuigan when, as Secretary of State for External Affairs, he came from Canada to attend the funeral of Sir Seretse Khama, the well known President of Botswana. Pik Botha asked to meet McGuigan at the airport in Johannesburg before he returned home. The conversation did not go easily as each of them did not hesitate to frankly lay out their views. As Mr. McGuigan was about to mount the stairs to his aircraft he turned to me and said, "You will have that MAF or whatever you call it." It became a very useful facility. Not only (and most importantly) did it help black organizations and enterprises advance their work, but it also drew all of us as members of the embassy more directly into the lives of the blacks of South Africa. The fund began with $75,000 a year and before long its disbursements were several times this amount. Later involvement moved into the field of scholarships at Canadian universities.

Relations with the white liberal opposition were always easy and fruitful. There was obviously a wide area of agreement between them and us. The remarkable and charismatic Helen Suzman comes particularly to mind. She and her colleagues were often the source of very useful insights into the developments, politics, and institutions of South Africa. They also played an important role in using their parliamentary immunity to focus attention upon prisoners, detainees, and victims of police violence, and the English speaking press was a continuous thorn in the government's side. They tended to attract unjustified criticism from NGOs and some observers living abroad because they remained within the constitutional structure of South Africa, but Nelson Mandela understood the contribution they had made and paid full tribute to it in the foreword he wrote in 1993 to Helen Suzman's memoirs.

Aside from démarches on particular human rights developments and other means of complaining about them we were free to use our initiative to express Canadian misgivings in a number of other ways. Attendance at prominent funerals was one means of demonstrating Canadian sympathy and support; but more happily I was invited to the wedding of Archbishop Tutu's daughter. I drove through the streets of Soweto with the flag flying to participate in the large gathering.

I followed as closely as I could developments in the various churches, as they played a very significant role in the political and social life of all races in South Africa. Apartheid had really begun in the Dutch Reformed Church when in the 19th century the first blacks were barred from attending its services. At an early stage in my posting I called on Dr. Byers Naude. A few years earlier he had been the moderator of the church, a position equivalent in Afrikanerdom to a major cabinet post, but had resigned on concluding that apartheid had no biblical foundation and indeed was totally contrary to the teachings of Christ and the New Testament. His departure represented a major moral threat to the Nationalists and he was still under a modified form of house arrest when I saw him. What he stood for did, over time, have an effect on his church and gradually, even while I was there, clergy and laity who supported him began to win appointment to influential positions.

The Anglicans, Methodists, and Roman Catholics had always stood their ground against apartheid in all its emanations, even occasionally at some risk to themselves as institutions. We at the embassy kept particularly in touch with a couple of the churches in Soweto which were heavily engaged in aid work, education, and social leadership. In 1981 Archbishop Edward Scott, the Anglican primate of Canada and a prominent member of the World Council of churches, came to South Africa. I made it clear to him that I was prepared to give his visit as much prominence as he wished in terms of a reception for him, but respected his request to confine it to a large lunch attended by the heads of the principal "opposition" churches, including the Roman Catholic cardinal. Some ambassadors, including the Papal Nuncio, were also present. It was useful to the churchmen to meet one another informally. I seized another opportunity to underscore Canada's support for the work of the churches by bringing Archbishop Tutu and other South African church people together to meet the moderator of the United Church and other Canadian visitors with whom they had been in contact over the years.

I kept in touch informally with newspaper editors and gave the occasional interview. These required a certain balance in comment on the domestic scene, although I felt free to refresh a journalist's mind on Canadian policy if it were required. I also saw Canadian correspondents from time to time. I have always felt rather torn in dealing with the press. On the one hand I wanted to brief them as fully as possible but, on the other, I had some responsibility for my own sources and the need for confidentiality in my dealings with my host government. Once, however, I decided to give an off-the-record background interview to a senior Canadian journalist. It immediately appeared in the Canadian press with the quotes ascribed to "a diplomat in Capetown" where I was alone. Ottawa was not very happy with me nor I with the Press.

Opportunities to remind the South African authorities about apartheid presented themselves in various guises. I was delighted when one arrived on my doorstep, as it were. The son of a much-respected South African member of the embassy was one of the first blacks to want to secure a place as an undergraduate at the university in Capetown. The admittance of this 18-year-old required my personal approval. I consulted sympathetic people and worded the application form submitted in such a way as to make difficult any attempt by the authorities to divert him to a much inferior school. I also indirectly let the Foreign Ministry know how free I might be with the news, be it good or bad. It worked and he is now in command of his own firm of labour lawyers.

As mentioned before, I was asked to go to South Africa as soon as possible as there was reason to hope that some kind of a settlement on Namibia might be on the horizon. The background to this question and the work of the Contact Group of which Canada was a member were well set out by W.H. Barton in *Special Trust and Confidence*, a book of essays. When I arrived in South Africa a plan had been approved by the Security Council in September 1978 that would put an end to the guerrilla warfare on the Angolan border, reduce significantly the number of South African troops in the territory, provide for constitutional measures acceptable to all parties concerned, and ensure free and fair elections under UN supervision. The outlook seemed promising, but, while members of the Contact Group and the states neighbouring South Africa accepted it, Pretoria decided that it did not like some of the provisions. Amongst other things it tried to introduce a constitution not unlike the governments of the so-called independent homelands and argued that it had no confidence in the impartiality of the United Nations. The new Republican administration in Washington added a further complication by linking a settlement in Namibia with the withdrawal of Cuban troops from Angola.

Because of "linkage," "impartiality," and other obstacles that arose, the negotiations were effectively stalemated until South Africa had a change of heart in 1988. Nonetheless, discussions did go ahead in a rather desultory fashion on related issues, including formulations for the constitution and electoral arrangements. With my colleagues from the United States, Germany, Britain, and France, I met with the South Africans from time to time to convey the démarches worked out by our respective capitals and coordinated in New York. We five also met to compare notes on the South African position as it evolved and at times visited Namibia either independently or jointly to have a look at developments on the ground. This involved both myself and the counsellor, Ed Skrabec, who had a gift for encouraging his contacts in Windoek to speak quite openly to him.

In October1981, I went alone as the representative of the Contact Group to present to the different tribal and ethnic groups some modifications of the original constitutional proposals. These were designed to meet the concerns that they and the South Africans held about the power that SWAPO could wield as the party of the predominant Ovambo tribe. I reported back on the initial reactions. In due course we five ambassadors went to Windoek for two days of consultations with the dozen or more leaders of the very diverse collection of Namibia's tribal and linguistic communities. They appeared before us in turn. It was an interesting exercise in multilateral diplomacy and conflict resolution to which Canada made a useful contribution. Indeed, when the reputation of the Contact Group was at a low ebb because of the lack of progress, Canada's continued participation helped to give it credibility amongst key African states.

In my postings to Africa I was also responsible for six other neighbouring countries – Togo, Benin, and Liberia when I was in Ghana, and Botswana, Lesotho, and Swaziland in South Africa. In all except Liberia Canada had aid programmes of one size or another and we supervised them from Accra or Pretoria. I visited these countries about every four months (Liberia less frequently) to keep an eye on local developments, deal with any aid issues that needed my attention and meet Canadians living or working there. Most were missionaries and aid workers.

The supervision of CIDA projects in neighbouring countries is not easy and involves lengthy periods away from one's home. This burden was also carried by my colleagues and I have especially in mind the work done in Benin by Howard Strauss where the projects and the environment were a real challenge for someone on his first posting. I also remember that he and I tried to coordinate a brief visit to Cotonou by our minister responsible for francophone affairs. I am sure that our hosts meant well when it came to organization, but I would simply say that it is a splendid sight to see a Canadian ministerial aircraft taking off in the African sunset at the end of a long day.

The impact of Canadian missionaries, particularly the Roman Catholics in Lesotho and Ghana over the previous sixty years, had been enormous and their work in the fields of education and health was carried out at a fraction of the cost incurred years later by aid donors. I also had a high regard for our aid personnel and particularly the young volunteers CUSO and SUCO had sent out. They selected with such good judgment that virtually all of them performed outstandingly well in difficult circumstances. I went to many of the places where these Canadians worked and if possible organized functions for them by way of showing Ottawa's appreciation for the value of their work. July 1 parties were a particularly useful occasion.

On my return to Ottawa and UN work in 1982 I tried to persuade either the University of British Columbia or the University of Toronto to award honorary doctorates to Helen Suzman and Desmond Tutu. Even by then Mrs. Suzman had collected a bushel of honourary degrees from a large number of very distinguished universities in Britain and the United States, and Archbishop Bishop Tutu won the Nobel peace prize a few years later. Archbishop Scott and Colin Mackay, a former President of the University of New Brunswick, supported my approaches. Frankly, I thought that honouring such distinguished South Africans would be a credit to these two universities if they accepted but neither institution saw it that way and both declined. I was disappointed in this seeming lack of vision.

I had better luck a few years later with another initiative. I was head of the Africa Bureau, and as such I proposed in August 1987 that the then forthcoming Commonwealth Heads of Government Meeting in Vancouver should put together a committee of five foreign ministers to coordinate as much as possible commonwealth policy on South Africa between CHOGMs. It was to promote dialogue with Pretoria, maintain pressure on it, and encourage support for the Front Line States while keeping policy matters as much as possible in the hands of ministers. The proposal was approved in Vancouver with Britain, Nigeria, India and Australia as members and Canada in the chair. This gave us a key role in the committee's work. It met every six months over the following five years.

After seven years divided amongst UN and human rights work, the Africa bureau and a sabbatical, I arrived in Havana in September 1989. It looked as if I had come to take part in a political deathwatch as we waited for the end of Castro's Cuba in the wake of the collapse of the Soviet system. But expectation of the Cuban government's demise proved premature. In fact I arrived to watch not the end of the regime but its efforts to adjust its life to the apparent calamity that faced the country, and to cope with the realization that what it had stood for during the previous thirty years was very much at risk. It had to rearrange as best it could its trading patterns, sell its sugar in new markets, and somehow find the money to pay for its oil imports. It also had to address itself to the idea of private investment and seek to respond to growing demands from abroad that it improve the way it governed its own people and treated those who opposed it.

Our policy towards Cuba had two objectives: to as much as the Cubans were capable of buying while pointing out their shortcomings in the field of human rights. Regarding the second aim the embassy was, as in

South Africa, left with some scope in how it gave expression to Canadian human rights policy as reflected in our votes in the United Nations and the instructions we received on key issues. I got away to an early start over the issue of family reunification when the Cuban authorities refused to give exit visas to the dependents of Cuban fathers who in one way or another had got out of Cuba and had been accepted as refugees by Canada. Some of them had been held for years as an example to any other Cubans who might be contemplating unauthorized departures. There were five cases and the embassy had been protesting at appropriate times to the Cuban Foreign Ministry without much effect for several years.

When I presented credentials to him, Carlos Rodriquez, the Vice President, expressed considerable satisfaction with Cuba's relations with Canada. He did admit that the family reunification issue was a problem, but thought that it could be seen as an aberration from the general thrust of the relationship. It was after all part of a general Cuban policy and was not aimed solely at Canada. As he had given me an opportunity that I wanted I said that my government would want Cuban leaders to understand that the issue of family reunification was central to our relationship. The matter had particular poignancy as it touched on the welfare of children and their mothers. I like to think that these remarks at this high level helped to reinforce our position in the official Cuban mind. We made still further démarches and some adverse publicity began to build up in Canada on the issue. In any case six months later the Cubans opened a meeting in Havana with Louise Frechette, then assistant deputy minister for Latin America, by announcing that all of the dependents could go to Canada. Their aim in making this concession at the start of our discussions was to introduce the right note to our exchange of views on other bilateral matters. Cuba still uses detainees of one kind and another as pawns for its foreign policy goals. I occasionally think that Canada does not demand a sufficiently high price in this field for what we offer in return to Cuba.

The meeting between Louise Frechette and Cuban officials went sufficiently well that she was invited to call on Fidel Castro. I accompanied her. At this distance in time I cannot remember in detail what we discussed but I do recall that the meeting went on for about three hours late in the evening and that the President dominated the discussion as he outlined his views on a large number of subjects. His "prime minister" and other advisers said nothing, although Madame Frechette was asked some questions about Canada. She returned the following year to enlist Cuba's support or at least its neutrality over the question of the Iraqi invasion of Kuwait. Again the President wanted to see her at his palace and after a two or three-hour meeting he also asked if he could come and dine at the residence the following evening. We were only three Cubans and three Canadians around the table although I reckon that there were about thirty or more Cuban security guards lurking about in my garden. Once more he expressed his views on a large number of issues but he did not often seek information on other subjects. I was struck by the fact that he would have this much time to devote to such encounters. He may have seen it, though, as an opportunity simply to talk not to a deferential fellow Cuban but to an intelligent listener from abroad. Still, these nine hours with him provided me with some further insight into his personality even if he was careful not to give away very much.

Conversations with other embassies revealed a number of interesting aspects to the turbulence that Cuba was undergoing. Eastern European missions, instead of defending the Cubans, now told us tales of their difficulties in dealing with them. Cubans were often were slow to understand changing policies of governments no longer able to sustain former levels of economic and commercial support to Cuba. Yuri Petrov, the Soviet Ambassador seemed more concerned than impatient with Cuba and its future. A senior political appointee who was well liked by the Cubans, he rather sought me out as if to remind the Canadian government through me that it had a role to play economically in Cuba and that he very much hoped that it could be expanded. We had over time three or four small lunches at his or my residence to discuss Cuba and related issues. He came only with his translator and I with one of my colleagues. As if to underscore the line that he had been taking with me he saw to it that I was one of only four ambassadors invited to his farewell dinner given by the Cubans. He returned to Moscow to serve briefly as chief of cabinet to Boris Yeltsin.

Along with attending to the issue of family reunification, we did try to give a little hope to dissidents in Cuba. During my time in Havana we began to meet with some of them at the chancery and sometimes outside of it in circumstances that could not get them into trouble. We watched the cultural scene with care for signs of opposition to the regime. On one occasion I rather obviously went to see an exhibition of protest art in order to lend a little moral support to this work. Part of the purpose of such exhibitions was to draw international attention to the situation in Cuba. The authorities might have concluded that it was serving this purpose only too well. It was closed down a couple of days later.

We complained to the Foreign Ministry about the arrests of some opposition protesters, the sentences that some received, and other human rights abuses committed by the regime. Sometimes this was on instructions but on other occasions we found opportunities to register our concerns on our own initiative. The opposition in Cuba was small and divided – most had departed over the years to Florida – but I was pleased to learn several years after I departed that on one or two occasions the dissidents, with their own sources in the Foreign Ministry, had received first hand accounts about what I had said in my démarches.

With the increased economic deprivations came a rise in the number of Cubans desperate to leave Cuba. Many tried to get hold of a boat or raft of some kind and sail across the Straits of Florida to Key West. A few attempted to force their way into embassies in search of asylum and the rather misguided hope that this would lead to exit visas and life in a new country. In 1990, with these invasions taking place at the embassies of Czechoslovakia, Spain, Belgium, and Italy, we feared the day when we would be visited.

Our turn came on September 29, 1990 when a Cuban dissident, who had been imprisoned for his activities, had escaped his guards while on a visit to a doctor, climbed the high fence surrounding our chancery and asked for asylum. I received the news at the Foreign Ministry where I had gone to be briefed about the current state of Cuban relations with Eastern Europe. I returned immediately to the Embassy to consult my colleagues, noted that it was surrounded by about fifty police or soldiers, told Ottawa what we intended to do about it and asked for their advice on legal points. I went back to the Foreign Ministry to speak to the Assistant Minister for the Western Hemisphere, and confirmed what had happened. I said that we needed time to consult Ottawa, asked him for background information on our visitor, sought his assurances that our inviolability as an Embassy would be respected and that no attempt would be made on the part of the police to enter our premises in pursuit of their prisoner. I added that we would be particularly disappointed if, despite the police cordon around the Embassy, other would-be asylees succeeded in invading the chancery. This was a reference to the use by the authorities of agents provocateurs who had been sent into other embassies to harass and pressure the mission concerned to hand over the groups or individuals seeking asylum.

I also made clear that we expected to deal solely with Foreign Ministry officials. I made this point as the security authorities obviously played a large part in such incidents. Indeed, they once or twice unsuccessfully tried to open a dialogue directly with us that included a vaguely worded threat about the asylee.

It was apparent almost from the beginning that he would have to be turned over since Ottawa reminded us that, unless we feared for his life or health, it would not be a proper use of our diplomatic immunity to shelter a fugitive from the local authorities.

However, when I advised the Foreign Ministry of our intentions I decided to go one step further and not only ask for their assurances that he not be harmed but also request that we have access to him on his return to prison to see that he was properly treated. This was new ground as we were asking that a Canadian consul visit a Cuban citizen who had been sentenced by a Cuban court to spend some years in a Cuban jail. However, my request was accepted and after a couple of days we drove our guest to a nearby street and handed him over. The visits to the prison to see him continued for a number of months. Several years later he was released and now lives in Spain.

In this whole operation I was very fortunate to have the good judgment, cool head and unusual linguistic skills of Paul Willox, First Secretary. We were also lucky to have five military police from Ottawa as our security guards. Indeed their presence might have helped to discourage the security authorities from sending in other "asylees" to harass us. But what probably carried the day on this point was the wish on the part of Foreign Ministry officials to play down this incident and their belief that it would resolve itself easily so long as respect was paid to Canada's concerns over its handling.

In the field of trade, Canadian exports to Cuba were limited, but they covered a fairly wide range of products. It was beginning to expand while I was in Havana and two or three very senior executives came to Cuba to investigate major sales and investment possibilities. These included leading members of the Canadian nickel industry whose initial visit in 1990 has led to extensive involvement in Cuba.

I left Cuba in January 1992. I admit that I expected the regime to come to an end one way or another in the then foreseeable future. But it remains well in place despite the United States embargo, or perhaps because of it, as it does allow Fidel Castro, the father of his own revolution, to appear in the minds of the population as a victim of the situation and not the architect of it. Meanwhile Canadian Cuban relations are stronger than ever, with successive visits to Havana by both our foreign minister and prime minister.

I retired shortly thereafter and look back at my career contentedly enough. My instincts as a fourteen year old were not entirely out of place, and I certainly came to value the support, friendship, and patience of those with whom I worked over the years. The role of a head of post has changed since I first went to Ghana in 1976 and much of it for the better.

CHINA

by Fred Bild

Outset

> *How can I go to Beijing, and assume a four-year assignment there,*
> *knowing that scores of places and people will bring back to me the*
> *haunting pictures of this decade's televised political massacre?*

These are the thoughts of a Canadian diplomat beginning his five
months' course in Mandarin. He knows from several previous attempts that
a "crash" course may acquaint him with a foreign language; with much
devoted labour he may even achieve a measure of familiarity with the way
the other culture communicates. But he is also aware that there is no instant
access to the machinery of a foreign mind. Intense introductory courses do,
however, prove amazingly diverting for a brain far too inclined to political
machinations, and beset with atrophying rote-memory powers. The ingenuity of a simplified grammar, its wealth of codified expressions and its heavy
reliance on ancient poetry for style and content are thus all helpful in sub-
duing his political reflexes, at least for a time. Indeed, even during the first
meeting with a senior cadre in Beijing, he is compelled to concentrate more
on uttered words than on bloodstained hands.

One prepares in different ways for an important diplomatic assignment. In getting ready for a posting to Beijing, some would seek refuge in
files and plow through every report ever written by the mission; others
would consult, seeking out old hands, business people or officials in provincial and federal departments involved in Chinese affairs; yet others would
undertake "une lecture sérieuse" (fiction, non-fiction, classical, modern).
Those of us who use a mixed approach frequently end up being less thor-
ough and ill prepared in all fields.

> *A "language student" has to make some choices, neglect other inter-*
> *ests, keep his priorities in line with his training schedule. I say skip*
> *the files. Let the other government branches write to me in Beijing*
> *if they have business to discuss. Forget internal admin briefings, I'll*
> *find out soon enough where the skeletons are buried. Come back*
> *and visit the Vancouver, Calgary, Toronto, Montreal business com-*

munities after I've been in China a few months. Perhaps I'll have some answers for them by then, instead of just questions. I wonder what my chances are of obtaining a proper ambassador's letter of instructions before my departure? Probably very slim ... unless I draft it myself ... but then, why tell myself what I already know? Some would say it provides a contract, an objective reference on what THEY expect of one ... No such thing! Circumstances make the contract: if you don't rise to events, you've failed, regardless of whether any of it was covered in your mandate.

It is always an exciting event to arrive in a capital where one will spend several years getting ever more involved in internal developments. From that moment onwards neither the landing formalities, protocol, nor lack of a letter of instructions can lessen the expectations that start growing.

It would have been nice, though, to already have some sort of blue print around which to plan the architecture of our redefined programs. The Secretary of State for External Affairs (SSEA) June 30th, 1989 declaration will have to do. Reorient our programs to favour people-to-people relations, reorient the trade and CIDA programs in such a way as not to favour the coercive arms of the Chinese government, keep senior official contacts to a minimum. Surely this doesn't apply to me; do I refuse to present my letters of credence to the President? Do I fail to greet the Chinese Foreign Minister? Why even entertain such thoughts? Next week we're marking the twentieth anniversary of the establishment of diplomatic relations. I expect to be inviting Politburo members to the event, marking, not celebrating; here's a distinction that only experienced flea circus fans will appreciate!

October 13, 1990 is the 20th anniversary of the date on which Canada and the People's Republic of China agreed to establish embassies in each other's countries. The Canadian festivities in Beijing include the Chinese première of the film "Bethune: the Making of a Hero," the first Sino-Canadian film co-production. No Chinese minister attends, as no Canadian at that level would attend the reception given that same day at the Chinese embassy in Ottawa.

What an awkward time to start a new relationship. "Let's work together to make things as productive as possible," I say, "but let's not forget that there are differences between us which will require considerable effort on the Chinese side if they are to be set right. Countries should not interfere in each others' internal affairs, but flagrant violations against international human rights standards cannot be overlooked." Not much of a riposte from the senior Chinese guest. Whatever cloud has come over China-Canada relations is in no way China's fault, he says, let's work together to repair our friendship. He didn't stay to the end of the film though. Only at the very end of the two-hour screening did I figure out why. After the last frame – Donald Sutherland as Bethune being carried down a mountain to his burial – the screen goes black and the following Bethune quotation appears: China and the world we fight for will have peace and justice. It will be free from hunger and tyranny, hatred and privilege and the arrogant use of power. It will be finally free of all uniformed bullies beating, beheading or shooting unarmed civilians.

Despite the coolness of official bilateral relations, Canadian programs in trade and development assistance progress smoothly. As we move into 1991, trade figures look up after the disastrous lows of 1989-90; the mission's CIDA officers manage without difficulty to reorient projects to favour more grass-roots activities. The overall objective, however, remains a conundrum: how to continue a cooperative relationship without reverting to business as usual? How to introduce human rights questions into bilateral discussions when the other side is deliberately keeping them extremely polite and productive?

Human Rights

Here we go again; another mission which is beginning to work at cross purposes: my political staff are eager to track human rights violations while my trade officers argue for discretion, "Don't do anything," they say, "which might hamper trade promotion initiatives." Where does one find the happy mean? Tomorrow I'm to visit the minister of industry representing a Canadian company that feels aggrieved by facing foreign competition on an uneven playing field. Obviously, that's not the moment to bring up the forthcoming trial of a well-known dissident. Besides, I'll just get told to take my pleas to the Procuratorate, the least accessible office in Beijing and also the most close-mouthed. At any rate, on this subject everyone in town speaks "la langue de bois." That is how the administration works in China. It is a remarkably effective system for having every-one of the more than 5 million officials in positions of authority mouthing uniform formulae – within days of the word having been sent out – but such highly political representations are unlikely to get transmitted to those in charge, i.e. the Politburo and the elders behind them.

Meanwhile, the political section of the embassy keeps close track of the human rights situation as it unfolds. As the June 1989 dissidents one after another are brought to trial, representations are made at the Chinese foreign ministry and no opportunities are lost to impress upon various interlocutors the opprobrium China reaps through the harsh sentences being meted out.

During my first few visits to provinces outside Beijing it occurs to me that local potentates, invariably very courteous and hospitable, are probably more vulnerable to such representations. I've done it a few times now: sitting next to a governor or vice governor at a lav-ish banquet I whip out a list of names of political prisoners alleged-ly in his jails.

They are invariably startled by my bad form, but manage to give me standard replies: no one is in prison for his thoughts or beliefs, only for criminal acts. Yes, there are crimes against the state, but no one in this province has been imprisoned for such crimes. No, the governor's office cannot make enquiries about the names on our list since that would "infringe the independence of the judici-ary." Can I maintain this calculated incivility? It will no doubt soon result in my getting lower and lower access in the provinces unless I get some reinforcements. I'll raise it with my "like-minded" colleagues. If we all use the same approach, our provincial hosts would have to take notice. They couldn't ascribe it simply to a deranged, over-zealous Canadian; eventually they might even put pressure on the local Public Security Bureau to provide them with some soothing data to pass on to us. Or so I thought, until my more experienced fellow ambassadors disabused me of the idea. Local potentates, they tell me, would be delighted if they could be rid of these frequently importuning foreign envoys. At any rate, I get only muted promises from them, and only two subsequently report to me that they'd made similar representations on a recent visit. So much for joint action.

The more junior officers in the political section of the embassy had more luck in transferring the idea onto their circle. First and second secretaries from a number of western embassies took daily turns making very early morning visits to the ministry of justice, where the day's upcoming trials were posted on a telephone pole nearby. This was the only advance public information available. At the appointed time, one of them would then present himself or herself at the courthouse and ask permission to attend. This went on for several months, until the series of trials ended. Permission was refused every time.

We've been doing this for months now. Should I be more concerned with concrete results or with the consequences to our day-to-day work life? Actually, there isn't much on either front. The trials of dissidents are proceeding apace with not the slightest sign that foreign representations have had an effect. Our local contacts are invariably polite, although restrained in all their reactions to us. It's hard to cultivate real "chums" in this kind of atmosphere. I think I've succeeded, though, in having all my senior staff, the program managers, adopt a uniform approach on these hypersensitive topics. Their approach is not quite "more-in-sorrow-than-anger" but more in the spirit of friends who can speak frankly to one another. The question remains, though, where will all this lead? Chinese official-dom has its own agenda: to restore external relations to a pre-1989 level and convince the world that China's policy of reform and opening to the outside remains unchanged. Starting with its own neighbours, the PRC normalizes its relations with Indonesia and Singapore, establishes diplomatic relations with Brunei, the last ASEAN member with whom it had no official relations; it is now in a position to request becoming a dialogue partner of ASEAN. In the same period, China manoeuvres North Korea into accepting the Two Koreas solution for UN membership, resumes boundary talks with India, makes peace with Vietnam on its own terms, recognises South Korea and, as they come into being, its three newly sovereign neighbours in the west, Kazakhstan, Kirghiztan, and Tadjikistan. Increases in cross-border trading posts on its northern border also lead Foreign Minister Qian Qichen to confidently declare to foreign diplomats in June 1991, "China's policy of good neighbourliness has created harmony throughout Asia ... we are welcomed as friends in all the countries we visit." He is more than hinting that the time has come for the West to again receive high-level Chinese visitors.

Here we are in the middle of a quandary. We continue to make our views felt on the touchiest of issues. The hard-liners in our own camp are happy, though some of them still hanker for punishment, such as cuts to our CIDA program. Barbara McDougall, who seems to have made China-slamming her favourite pastime, is delighted with how the first Canadian ministerial visit since 1989 turns out. Bill McKnight, representing our considerable agricultural exports to China, is displayed on Canadian television in only one dimension: during the first five minutes of each meeting in Beijing he upbraids his host with human rights protestations! These "photo opportunities" usually come to a close before the hosts reply, thus giving the spellbound Canadian viewer the impression that a slugfest is about to ensue. Three friends phone me from Canada, wondering if I am being recalled; they had concluded that every moment of the visit had been devoted to berating Chinese leaders. Such is the focusing power of TV! Did any of our citizens ever ask themselves why the minister of agriculture had been chosen for this task? I guess I'll never know, nor does it really matter. Our Chinese contacts don't watch Canadian television; by and large they think the visit was quite successful. Even the ministers who were raked over the coals consider it a small price to pay for breaking the ban on high-level contacts. Chinese TV of course put an entirely different spin on all this.

As time goes on, Chinese officials and leaders seem to have fashioned a response to what for them has become a bothersome refrain. While they appreciate the less haranguing tone we use on human rights questions when compared to other countries' opinions, and cite only the United States and the United Kingdom when alleging interference in China's internal affairs, at no time do they give any indication that they are prepared to have a real discussion on the subject.

A frustrating process, all this, but not by any means unbearable – except in cases where it is complicated by three Canadian MPs attempting to script their own grandstanding while under the careful scrutiny of the Public Security Bureau. What a week that was! I found myself in what is generally believed to be the archetypal two-faced role of the diplomat: John Ciaccia is in town doing all the things a responsible provincial minister of international trade should. I give him whatever support I can under the circumstances, circumstances which have me spending most of the daylight hours at the Foreign Ministry pounding the table about the ungracious treatment meted out to our three-party parliamentary delegation (they were expelled manu militari). In the evenings, I don my smiling mask and drink toasts to the ever-flourishing Sino-Quebec economic relations – not quite out of an Ian Fleming novel, but getting there.

Propaganda

None of the foregoing, however, compares in magnitude to the challenge of reaching out to 1.14 billion people. The Government's activities will henceforth focus on people-to-people exchanges, said the statement of June 30. Canadian public relations and cultural activities had at best been modest in China; now funds were absurdly low. Officials holding purse strings back home had lost all enthusiasm for the land whose capital surrounded Tian'anmen Square. In this area, the Beijing mission concluded, the only resources one could count on were those at hand.

Wonderful! Henceforth we only favour projects that do not involve dealing with state officials; we're going to support those which put us more in touch with the "people," a collective noun the Communists prefer to "the masses." In China, one deals with the masses via "mass organizations" like the Communist Youth League, the Young Pioneers, or the All China Federation of Trade Unions. But short of arranging exchanges with some of their Canadian "counterparts" (??) there seems to be no access to these organizations for any sort of meaningful joint activity. The obvious way of reaching the masses, of course, would be through cultural exchanges; especially those that are telecast nation-wide. But the Canadian National Film Board no longer seems to be making an effort in markets like China.

Do they realize that the world's largest and hungriest market for their sort of products has been open here for some years now? The Canadian feature-film industry likewise has yet to discover China, and no one is willing to let us have any of their material – even old, out of date titles of little commercial value. In fact, the only vehicle we have for daily access to a wide cross-section of the Chinese population is Radio Canada International, through its daily broadcasts in Mandarin and its very popular program "Everyday English." All in all, we have a pretty meagre collection of tools. I'll have to gather my staff together for some brainstorming.

After surveying the array of programs operated by the Canadian Government in China, it seems there are more grass-roots cooperative ventures than one might expect. CIDA projects in areas such as forestry development, cattle breeding, management training, and a host of university linkages have helped to foster a varied and widespread network of functional relationships. The slowly growing Canadian business community and the few joint ventures in the Beijing area, while not providing much access to the local rank and file, give us some insight into working conditions and the daily constraints faced by the average urban employee.

By far the most promising program, however, would appear to be the twenty-one Canadian Studies centres set up throughout the country by a succession of resourceful and innovative cultural attachés, each contributing their skills during his or her two year assignment to the embassy on loan from a Canadian university. Some of these centres, on their own initiative and with minimal financial support, have undertaken the translation and publication of major Canadian authors, text books and reference works (e.g., the *Encyclopaedia Canadiana*). Others have organised scholarly conferences on various Canadian subjects. Much of their activity and even their dissemination of Canadian works seem to be confined to fairly exclusive circles, but at least here is the beginning of a well spread-out network on which to build a healthy propaganda effort.

What a shame the word propaganda has only negative connotations in the Western world ... we have to disguise these perfectly legitimate activities with such euphemisms as "information work" or "public affairs." I'm sure Pope Gregory had no such hang-ups when he launched his 1622 propaganda fide committee of cardinals to be in charge of foreign missions. Does anyone really imagine that by calling it something other than what it is, we are actually projecting a truer, more all-encompassing picture of Canada, warts and all? On the contrary, the euphemisms reinforce the idea that what we are disseminating is publicity material. The Chinese see slick magazine images boasting about happy, multicultural Canadians joyfully going about their everyday activities under conditions of full employment, enjoying carefree harmony within the world's most splendidly preserved environment, whether it be in our spectacular wilderness, our lush farms or the confines of our thriving city cores. Chinese audiences must often be quite puzzled by material distributed in our literature and films. It will be some time yet, I imagine, before the PRC gives its embassies abroad films to show about the conditions inside their reform schools – such as the one Canada submitted last week for a Beijing short-films festival. Nor will we be witnessing the Chinese Ministry of Culture commissioning the translation into French of the Chinese equivalent of Michel Tremblay's "Les Belles Soeurs." Surely, as long as we keep some sort of realistic balance in the selection that we feed into the propaganda machine, our message will become more credible and thus more memorable.

Still, that doesn't quite solve my problem of access to the masses.

The mission's policy committee adopts a two-pronged approach. First, members of the embassy travelling outside Beijing should make sure to get in touch with one more of the Canadian Studies centres and organize some sort of social or academic activity there. Canadian students and teachers in many of these out-of-the-way places are eager to assist. Each centre is to be encouraged to specialize in a broad sector (for example, Canadian literature, economics, history, law). They are also to be asked to help in the dissemination of information on scholarships and research grants available in Canada.

Amazing what a little reflection, aided by a shortage of funds will produce. In less than an hour we've created a whole slew of mostly honorary mini-consulates. The 21-storey Management Training Centre established in Chengdu with CIDA funds, now almost ten years old, is certainly more imposing than any official mission we have so far in China.

Second, the mission will scrape together whatever it can find in the way of not too dated film or video material, get it translated into Mandarin and/or Cantonese, and peddle it directly to local TV stations. The priority for the interim is to update the image of Canada by whatever information is at hand.

Strange how an emergency atmosphere can arise spontaneously. Everyone seems to feel it springs from the fact that Joe Clark's statement on "people-to-people," almost two years old, has not yet been implemented. In fact, I think everyone is still under the shock of the recently resurrected 1988 public opinion survey.

In 1988, Professor Claude-Yves Charron of L'UQAM, then serving at the embassy as head of cultural and public affairs, directed a survey into Chinese perceptions of Canada. It revealed that most Chinese texts and audiovisual material given general circulation were extremely dated. Political commentary was limited to the head tax levied on Chinese immigrants at the beginning of the century.

> *Among Chinese, the most widespread perception of Canada is one of a vast, underpopulated, agricultural land, devoid of modern technology and with pronounced racist tendencies. This opinion is a far cry from our own image of a pluralistic, urban society with state-of-the-art know-how in every field.*

The results of the survey provided an important boost to efforts to bring information work into line with Canada's trade and economic objectives.

The inescapable conclusion, however, was that an information program in China would be successful only if it was based on a fair idea of China's rapidly transforming consumer tastes and expectations. The mission had neither the resources to commission the sort of survey this would require, nor the means to consult the rapidly expanding media industry. Yet the cultural section of the mission, headed from 1989 to 1991 by Professor Ruth Hayhoe of OISE, Toronto, managed to cultivate a number of provincial television networks and to place more recent material with them.

> *Pulling oneself up by one's own bootstraps is all well and good, but can it really lead anywhere? In Ottawa the June 1989 policy is being interpreted as "send China to Coventry ... no money for the likes of them." The business community, fortunately, still has enough clout to keep some export credit assistance alive. The CIDA crowd, through bureaucratic momentum, is managing to keep most of their program moving along, although not at the previous rate. In the arts and culture area, China might as well have been wiped off the map. No matter what sort of program we come up with (more publications, orchestral tours, literary exchanges) we'll not be able to finance any of it.*

In the summer of 1992, the embassy organizes a Sino-Canadian conference on film, video and TV. With virtually no assistance from headquarters, various directors, distributors, and a dozen or so producers are gathered together with their Chinese counterparts under the auspices of the Chinese Film Academy. A week's discussion serves to give the Canadians at least an inkling of the market opportunities opening in China in their area of work. On the Chinese side the seeds are planted for greater receptivity to Canadian film and TV products. Indeed, eighteen months later, these represent 13 per cent of China's imports in the sector.

Bull Market Returns

How could I have been spending that much time on public affairs activities? Ever since May 1992 I've been involved in commercial matters almost full-time. The number of Canadian business visitors seems to be doubling by the week – is this how trends affect policy? One deals with public relations only when nothing more immediate is at hand? And yet public relations do have an effect on commercial activities – but oh, how incalculably! Perhaps the most useful part of it all is that it kept us busy through the post-Tian'anmen doldrums. In the commercial area trends appear so much more clearly. After all, what was the impetus that brought the Canadian business community back to this side of the Pacific? Hardly the speeches I made to their Chambers of Commerce in Hong Kong and across Canada. No, it was the 88-year-old Deng Xiaoping's "Nan Xun," his grand tour of Guangdong and Shanghai, that did it. Not only did business start up again immediately, but his visit and subsequent manoeuvres also managed to get a slew of promotions for reform-minded officials at the Party Congress that fall. Now that's knowing how to stage a media event! Future historians will tell us what happened during the six weeks before the People's Daily could publish the event. The battles at the apex of the hierarchy must have been epic. There's no question, however – once the official imprimatur was given, business took off at a bewildering pace.

The Canadian embassy in Beijing in 1988 boasted a total of eleven commercial officers, the largest such complement in the world; after June 1989 they were reduced to six, and would not grow again, except briefly before the "Team Canada" exercise in November 1994. In mid-1992, they were assailed by an exponentially growing number of representatives of large, medium, and even small firms. The heavyweights of Canadian industry had stayed the course throughout the period of retrenchment and cooling down; many had made good use of the time to readjust strategies, mend fences, and strengthen official contacts that were to become very precious to them when the investment drive resumed and competition became fiercer. But other companies, for the most part, took much longer before they resumed their efforts.

All sections of the mission were affected. The number of Chinese business delegations going to Canada climbed, totalling over 12,000 visitors per year. The immigration section reorganised its services to be able to service their requests more rapidly. The public affairs section launched a trimestrial review focussed on Canada's industrial and technological capacities. It was headed by Professor Charles Burton of Brock University and augmented by the services of the inestimable Mark Rowswell, a Canadian student known throughout China because of his unprecedented linguistic performances on Chinese TV. A well thought-out report on the subject was submitted promptly to the state council.

> *Wouldn't you just know it! It never rains but it comes down in vats full of crocodiles. Just as we enter our most hectic state of affairs, we begin to realize a fourteen-year-old dream: our new embassy, in construction through six costly and frustrating years, is about to open. Two of my predecessors had been led to believe that they would actually get to live and work there. For my part, I'd pretty well given up on the idea. I figured it had probably been cursed by bad Feng Shui right from the outset.*

With a dedication and enthusiasm that did them credit, the entire community of some fifty Canadian employees, sixty-five Chinese and some twenty expats made the move from old to new premises without a single one of the mission's activities being neglected. The new embassy turned out to be a much-needed asset (even though its tremendous cost overrun could never be justified). After some weeks of running-in time, daily tasks are accomplished with more dispatch and the new reception areas are immediately put to good use in expanding contacts.

> *The SSEA insists, "No Celebratory Opening Ceremony!" What are we to do? In China the idea of not having an extravagant inauguration for a new building, let alone one as prestigious as an embassy, is unheard of. I'll have to invent facetious pretexts: the outrageous construction costs (for which the Chinese Diplomatic Services Bureau was at least 50 percent responsible), have left us without any representational funds; or simply "it's not a Canadian custom"; "we usually organize such celebrations to coincide with the first*

*major event to take place within the new premises, such as the visit
of our Foreign Minister – hah, ça lui apprendra!" When all is said
and done, I suspect the inexplicable lack of ceremony is making the
building even more mysterious to a number of our important contacts. We certainly seem to have no difficulty attracting them to all
and sundry functions. Perhaps the more discreet access and layout
of the premises also have something to do with it. After so many
years of waiting and budgetary extravagance it was time Canada
derived some unexpected benefits from the place! How convenient
too that all this should coincide with the new approach we are
developing on human rights and democratic development.*

Public Diplomacy and Democratic Development

As Canadian VIP visits become more frequent, the repeated litany of
Chinese human rights deficiencies simply creates glazed stares and blocked
ears. Quite coincidentally, in early 1993, some of the mission's university
acquaintances suggest joint research projects in areas of institutional reform,
perhaps with special emphasis on institutions relevant to democratic development. The idea elicits cautious support both in Ottawa and, it appears,
in inner councils in Beijing. Before long, five eminent scholars are chosen
to leave for a six-week study trip of Canadian democratic institutions and
practices. They meet political scientists, constitutional lawyers, provincial
and federal politicians, as well as administrative experts. Upon their return,
they reveal that what had made the greatest impression on them was the
Canadian system of redistribution of fiscal revenues and that a well thought
out report on the subject would shortly be submitted to the state Council.

> *Is one being manipulated or are the gleanings from cocktail parties
> sometimes revealing? Three times in succession now I've been accost-
> ed over a glass of Beijing's ubiquitous Dynasty by a senior official
> intent on telling me that serious work is being done on restructur-
> ing China's taxation system and that the Canadian "experience" is
> furnishing food for thought. "What about the other aspects of our
> democratic institutions, those dearer to the average Canadian?" I
> feel like asking, but dare not.*

Meanwhile the ambassador himself continues a speaking program
established several months earlier. My lectures in various Chinese forums on
"Public Diplomacy" highlight the functioning of Canadian institutions. The

high point comes when I am invited to address the Party School; the title of my talk, "Market Capitalism with Canadian Characteristics," produces no more than a few smiles. However, the theme and the setting allow for a full demonstration of the underpinnings of Canadian democracy: the rule of law, independence of the judiciary and a national consensus on social justice.

> *Who would have thought that a two-hour talk in front of a hundred or so senior cadres would clear the way for similar appearances at a series of other venues and finally on CCTV? Was it my tone, the fact that my jabs at Chinese deficiencies were all indirect, or was it my oversimplification of some points? There certainly was a gasp of disbelief in the hall of the Party School when I recounted the few times in recent Canadian history when a member of the cabinet ended his political career with a single telephone call to a judge presiding over a case in which the member had some interest. (I pointed out that a cabinet minister was "not at all like a Chinese Minister, but more like a member of the State Council or the Politburo.") Wasn't it the vice president of the school who exclaimed subsequently "it will take much more development before that sort of thing can happen in China after just one phone call." I guess I won't hold my breath, but I'd sure like to be able to wait and see.*

The New Policy

A few weeks later the Royal Society of Canada is invited to send a number of scholars to China to discuss the "transition from feudalism to the rule of law." CIDA, seeing such projects as fitting in with its democratic development mandate, provides some funds to encourage what has the makings of an extremely promising new program.

> *In the last few months all those connected with these new ventures behave as though they're walking on eggs. Despite this, no objection has been raised to the idea that current Chinese judicial structures and practices, as well as the modus operandi of the administrative apparatus all need to be made more transparent, predictable, and equitable. Quite to the contrary, whenever we approach themes such as these in a constructive and forward-looking way, we are rewarded by reasonable reactions and genuine understanding. Can this really lead to constructive exchanges, or will it simply provide already worldly scholars with greater opportunities for foreign trav-*

el? Even if a report harbouring a useful Canadian idea makes its way to the innermost sanctum at the apex of the power structure, how can we expect to influence any decisions taken on such a report? My skepticism is justified, but I suspect that some of my wiser academic contacts would point out that it's at that point that friendly advice turns into imperialism. We can help with research and with all phases of the thinking process, so long as we don't try to impose our solutions.

Canadian proposals to have Chinese judges take training programs in Canada or to have Ministry of Justice officials briefed on Canadian approaches to questions of human rights are all greeted with quiet approval. The mission extends its efforts in this direction and even envisages media briefings on the subject. Here is where the Chinese contacts started demurring. Publicity, in their view, can only hinder progress. Public discussion is thus limited to brief statements in varied contexts, but never in such a way as to encourage persistent follow-up on progress. Nonetheless, in background briefings, the mission starts explaining the reasoning behind the new approach on human rights questions, the need for a longer term outlook, and the potential for playing a genuine developmental role in this crucial aspect of China's modernization.

When all is said and done, the big issues in diplomacy have to do with weighing the interests of the long-term against those of the nearer future – and with the timing of moves. Had the change of government in Ottawa happened earlier, this new policy would probably not have been ready, it would certainly not have been tested to the extent it was, and therefore not as easily absorbed by our new masters. On the other hand, had they come to power a year later, the policy would have been tarred with the brush of the previous régime. How far would we have been able to take it? Timing? Perhaps. Yet it's hard to believe that any Canadian government, of whatever stripe, would not have seen the wisdom of this longer term, more constructive policy.

By the time of the first visit of André Ouellet, Minister of Foreign Affairs of the Chrétien government, the Chinese authorities were already well aware of the new PM's statement made several months earlier in March 1994 to the *Globe and Mail.* He said that it was unrealistic to expect him to tell the Chinese government how to behave when he couldn't even make his own provincial governments toe the line. Ouellet thus had a ready-made platform for explaining the "new" approach to human rights questions: individual cases and particular problems would continue to be dealt with directly but privately. He would neither confirm nor deny whether during his visit he had raised the plight of particular dissidents. In a wider context in May 1994, Canada's human rights objectives were enshrined in a new statement, "Foreign Policy on China: a Four Pillar Partnership," by the minister of foreign affairs in a speech to the Canadian Institute for International Affairs. Human rights were to be advanced through cooperative constructive projects seeking to develop good government and the rule of law. A few Canadian commentators took note; no one on the Chinese side made any comment.

> *Our Canadian media reps seemed almost relieved upon hearing this clearer version of the new approach. Was it that they would now no longer be obliged to lead with the same obvious question at every Canadian press conference in China? Of course, if they were really serious about following up these questions, they should now be concentrating on us defenceless officials. After all, the ball is now in our court. We're now doing structural changes together with our Chinese partners, scheming how to re-engineer China's institutions and lecturing future leaders about how to make their practices more transparent. The media should be beating down our doors demanding to know what came of the latest meeting between the Procuratorate's chief counsel and Canada's foremost expert on criminal law procedures. They don't. I guess there's no demand for that sort of news on prime-time TV. Tant pis, mais je ne m'en plaint guère!*

Four months later, Canadian Prime Minister Jean Chrétien will take this dialogue somewhat further in his meetings with Premier Li Peng. In the meantime, the embassy proceeds with its "public diplomacy" and its academic consultations.

Grassroots Democracy

> *Do we really know enough about how the Chinese system works to be able to make useful comments on potential changes? Perhaps the "Grassroots Democracy Program" being tried in a number of provinces will give us some hints. My wife and I have been invited to Shandong, the third most populous province (83 million). After almost four years in China, having visited twenty-two of thirty*

provinces and territories, it's quite embarrassing to have to admit we'd not managed to fit Shandong into our travel plans before now. After all, for many, Shandong – Qufu, to be more precise, whence sprang Confucius – is the home of Han culture. Now that Confucianism is back in vogue, with backing from the Chinese Communist Party, such dilatoriness is surely politically incorrect. What's more interesting about this visit is that for the first time we are travelling not in connection with our aid programme, or in support of some trade project, but to observe a political development – and, moreover, at the invitation of the ministry of civil affairs.

Governors, vice-governors, mayors, deputy mayors, and other dignitaries receive us with uncharacteristic diffidence. Normally they wax eloquent about the economic prospects of their respective regions, and are always so eager to load you down with facts and figures demonstrating the unequalled investment opportunities they offer. Now they seem at a loss for a script to describe the open election process in effect in some of their villages and smaller towns. They are not, as a rule, expected to guide foreigners through the inner workings of the political process. Oddly enough, they seem more comfortable railing against the corrupt practices of "many officials" than in talking about the CCP (Chinese Communist Party) and electoral practices. This is a fascinating beginning to something entirely different in diplomatic travel in the Middle Kingdom.

At the lowest level of local government, that of the more than one million villages in China, the village committee normally acted as the executant of the next higher level, the county. Its election was organized by the CCP. Voting was done from a single list of party members equal in number to the positions being filled. Since 1987 a new law was in effect encouraging villages to choose leaders and village committees freely from the local citizenry, regardless of party affiliation. Voters could write in any name they wished on their ballots. The results were now and then quite surprising, the elected officials turning out to be individuals respected for their abilities rather than for their party credentials. Thereafter, if they turned out to be effective intermediaries between the village and the local bureaucracy, they usually were re-elected.

Touring from one Shandong village to another, my small delegation and I are introduced to election organizers: past and present mayors, committee members, and in one case a whole village assembly.

It seems considerable persuasion is sometimes required to get local leaders to abandon previous practices. From what we can gather, the elections do seem to function without much outside intervention but the practice still appears far from universal, either in Shandong or throughout the country. It is clear, though, that the Civil Affairs officials guiding us are thoroughly committed to propagating the practice as widely and rapidly as possible. The Party, whose membership in the past ten years has sunk to extremely low levels in rural China, apparently feels it can thus reinvigorate itself at the grass roots by co-opting these more popular leaders. What, I ask, will happen when they extend this electoral option to the county level? Some counties have populations of small European countries.

It is obviously too early to judge how far the grassroots democracy experiment will go and whether it will ever be feasible to wrench it entirely out of the hands of the CCP. It is, notably, the only attempt at political reform since 1989 that is being brought to the attention of outsiders. There is probably no significance in the fact that Canadians were among the first foreign officials to be invited to inspect this initiative, but it would be wise for the Canadian Government to keep some involvement in this very primary phase of institutional development.

Is there room for some sort of cooperative project here? Funding for an institute on modern electoral practices? My hosts start to beam. It will obviously take closer investigation before we can determine what to make of it.

Prosperity is evolving at a rate far ahead of any institutional changes. This does not seem to worry people as much as the extreme inequality of the growth they see on all sides.

"Mao did not give us liberty," said one vice-mayor to me, "but he did give us equality and some fraternity. These last two revolutionary benefits will be hard for some people to forget."

Reform

The economic pitfalls ahead worry many, but optimism seems to be the general tone. Unstoppable economic reform produces social transformation, becoming more tangible every day. The "craze" that has everyone in its thrall is called "xia hai", to throw oneself into the sea, meaning to cut all links with one's lifelong work unit, the iron rice bowl that went with it, and launch oneself into the world of small independent entrepreneurs. The Chinese equivalents of Horatio Alger stories are popular but the ever-growing millions in the "floating" population are gradually casting a dark shadow over the general picture. Some make modest progress and start small, relatively secure businesses, but a much larger number end up unemployed (and without insurance) and adrift for a long time before they land some little job or a black market activity somewhere.

> *"Where is all this leading?" Canadian visitors keep asking for prognoses on the stupefyingly fast transformation of Chinese society, as if simply by living here and talking to people I can predict the future. My business visitors don't like it when I express uncertainty – what they want to hear is that their investments will be protected against the unpredictable. I list possible scenarios ranging from catastrophe to utterly smooth sailing à perte de vue. Most of my inquirers are left dissatisfied. Raising the spectre of corruption leading to massive unrest makes them uncomfortable and yet corruption is coming to be the leitmotif around which all sectors of Chinese society can – and do – express dissatisfaction.*

It is recognized today that criminal activities began to appear even at the beginning of the economic reform process. Indeed, the sudden appearance of a two-price system for many commodities was bound to lead to illegal transfers from one to the other with no value added. For the most part, however, corruption was then composed of meagre peculations, bribery of minor officials, or the traditional sort of nepotism. The scale and variety has now reached entirely different proportions. There are black-markets for everything from train tickets to electricity and even heavy industrial equipment, railway rolling stock, and locomotives. In some areas, gambling and prostitution are said to have taken on industrial proportions. The "sleaze" factor has invaded business deals of every size and sort. Perhaps most significant is the fact that a subject of daily conversation in all circles is the extent to which many profit-making enterprises are in the hands of "princelings," the offspring of senior leaders.

> *In Shandong, as in Fujian a few months ago, one hears tales of mayors and their deputies who sit on the boards of important joint ventures, as if that were a prerequisite for the smooth functioning of a foreign investment. Had I known it was going to develop at such a rate, I would have spent the last forty-eight months chroni-*

cling this phenomenon. Who knows, I might have turned it into a better exposé than "Beijing Jeep." What's most striking about the priority accorded this subject these days is that only a few years ago it would have had the effect of destroying the last remaining shred of the ruling clique's legitimacy. The regime's credibility, so badly undermined by the jettisoning of the remnants of Marxist egalitarianism and probity, might thus have been dealt a fatal blow. But today, the anti-corruption banner, emblazoned with a resurrected Confucian motif, can be brandished from the highest parapet of the CCP edifice and not provoke a snicker in a single passerby.

Among observers in Beijing there is a consensus that as long as a significant proportion of new job seekers find some sort of employment in the expanding industrial markets, the situation will not deteriorate to dangerous levels. The authorities understand this to mean that they cannot too quickly dismantle the social services provided by the numerous money-losing state enterprises. The government claims to be in search of a revenue-sharing formula with the prosperous provinces and, once assured of sufficient resources, will install a national social safety net. There is no evidence so far, however, that any serious preparations are being made for such a formidable project. Indeed, some technocrats have openly expressed skepticism about its feasibility, since it could turn out to be even more onerous than the deficits now caused by state enterprise support. Under the circumstances, some argue that it is safer to leave the present system in place and allow the free market sector to develop its own social security arrangements with private insurance companies. This possibility emerges in a conversation with officials of the State Commission for Restructuring the Economy in April 1994. For the time being, the major hope lies with continued growth, thus allowing for a proportional shrinkage of the state sector budget.

The government keeps announcing that it is on the verge of yet another valiant effort to modernize the state-owned enterprises. But it's obvious that short of driving millions of people into bankruptcy and creating destitute masses, they can only continue to try to force profitability upon these jurassic vestiges of the command economy. They are coercive through reorganization schemes, dismemberment, injections of joint venture capital, even through privatization in some cases. But how far can the regime go in this direction? The days of blind faith in an unregulated market are coming to an end. The hard-liners at the top (there are still some) resent the prospect of losing control over the essentials of the economy. They also claim that "privatization" of state assets lends itself to flagrant abuse and corruption to the benefit of former or existing senior bureaucrats. And yet their offspring (apparently with nary an exception) were the first to be thereby endowed with newly profitable organizations.

Whatever additional reforms are undertaken, it is most likely the planners will proceed, as in the past, through a three-stage process. They will begin with a few pilot projects in select locations, extend similar experiments more widely and adjust them to take into account operational requirements and local particularities, and then apply them region-wide. Only thereafter will any thought be given to a nation-wide policy. In effect, that is the formula currently applied to significant parts of the service sector. Before large foreign retailers like the Hudson's Bay Company or Wal-Mart are allowed to penetrate the Chinese market, they are given licences for no more than two or three centres; only after the results of such operations have been evaluated will permission for longer chains be considered.

The number of young people going abroad to pursue their studies is growing daily and so is the variety of disciplines they're engaged in. The same could be said of the number and types of foreign consultants and experts landing in China. Will this bring about radical occidentalization or some form of backlash? Those who are disgusted by the proliferation of Karaoke bars, the sale of the worst products of Western consumerism and the frenzied pursuit of the Renminbi are anxious about the unforeseeable social effects of it all. Some fear the leadership will find pretexts therein to put the brakes on economic and other reforms when it suits them. Others can even see it leading to public protests like those of May 1919, this time against the invasion of unhealthy foreign practices. It is easy to imagine how this could be exploited by the powers that be.

When I recently raised these fears with a Shanghai professor of sociology not known for his dissident views, he admitted that such scenarios could not be excluded. To my surprise, he attributed most of the blame to the weak image of the group in power and its inability to overcome public disenchantment with the entire leadership. "The day when the Centre has reason to fear serious protests or a breakdown in public order it will not hesitate to reverse engines, at least in those areas where decentralization has gone too far." Any Counter-Reformation of this sort, he added, would only be to enable

*the state to take some of the economic and administrative levers back
in hand and not to bring economic modernization to a halt.*

Public resentment is becoming quite palpable in the countryside.
There, income disparities with the city are widening, and in some of the
larger towns unemployment is reaching dangerous proportions. Nonetheless, the new nationalism that is emerging and being encouraged is neither
anti-modernist, nor, so far, particularly xenophobic. On the contrary, it is
founded on the progress of the last few years and fed by the prospect of
China's finally being able to attain its objectives of modernization and to be
able to take its rightful place among the world's big powers.

> *I'm sure that when I leave this assignment and reflect on my time
> here, I'll confirm the conclusion I have so far reached, however
> tentatively: China's current evolution and the frightening pace of
> change are by far the most interesting aspects of our stay here. The
> classical bilateral to-ing and fro-ing and even the spectacular suc-
> cess of Team Canada led by Prime Minister Chrétien, still don't
> match with the visible effect of the invasion of satellite dishes on the
> outlook of the general population. The amazing growth statistics
> don't truly reflect the impact of live rock music on the younger gen-
> eration in a country where rock is banned, or the glee with which
> the majority of civil service school graduates hurl themselves into the
> sea of private enterprise. All these are real history in the making
> and will shape the future of China. When I see colourful fashions
> taking the place of the old blue uniform, ads for Canadian Club
> replacing billboard quotations from Mao, and yuppies opening
> Cultural Revolution nostalgia cafés, my heart fills with joy at the
> thought of Mao spinning furiously in his marble vault. But, as
> always, China's on a roller coaster that's going to take some time
> before it reaches a level track. Many ups and downs and sharp
> curves are yet to come. They'll all bear watching if we want to be
> able to have a meaningful and productive relationship through
> what may be China's most crucial phase of modernization.*

Canada's Role in Chinese Reforms

When the present Canadian Government published the presumably still
current policy on China in 1994, it described its four pillars as economic

partnership, sustainable development, human rights, good governance and the rule of law, and peace and security.

No one in his right mind could take exception to these eminently reasonable, respectable, indeed laudable parameters. Elaborating on this policy, the embassy at the time sought to ensure that, as its masters were adopting the policy, they understood that each of the pillars would be vitally affected by the multitude of changes occurring in China. Indeed, the first three implied our taking these changes materially into account as we developed the relationship.

The sale of two Candu reactors is a good example, some would say, of the application of all four pillars, since there is no question that such an agreement would substantially enhance our economic ties, and make an important contribution to sustainable development, one of the reactor's strongest features; it would also reinforce legal foundations, since the long-term contractual relationship on such a sizeable project would require reliable legal underpinnings as well as sound safeguards to guarantee its peaceful use. That may well be, especially since the scale of the project and its many high-tech features would ensure a long-term mutual undertaking involving many far-reaching aspects of infrastructure and development. Even the controversial Three Gorges Dam, provided one could be relatively certain about its environmental safety, might provide an opportunity for Canadian political influence. It would involve Canada even more in helping the Chinese develop strategies on fundamental questions such as population resettlement, the sustainability of projects and the building of fair and reliable juridical frameworks around the entire enterprise.

Both of these examples serve to illustrate the kinds of engagement Canada could undertake in China, but sustainable development and democratic development are probably the two considerations which will continue to challenge Canadian policy makers the most in years to come, since they imply a direct involvement in the very process of China's transformation. The CIDA program has been at the forefront of this involvement for some time. Indeed, the Chinese have repeatedly recognized the sound contributions Canada's assistance projects have made to the modernization and development of China's capacities. The agency's involvement in environmental policy, through the China Council on the Environment is similarly commendable. CIDA is, however, only one arm of Canadian foreign policy. Every one of these four widely encompassing areas of the bilateral relationship will require that all the players get involved.

For some years those motivated by desires of punishment or coercion have demanded policies that link trade and human rights. All those who have worked in China, especially in the period 1989-93 when both approaches (coercion and engagement) were tried, have seen quite clearly how counter-productive the punitive approach can be. That is not to say that the business community must be ruled out of involvement in anything other than strictly commercial considerations. Canada's trade and investment in China does constitute by far its largest presence in China and the one through which it is involved most intimately in the ongoing changes.

Far from seeking to limit that involvement, the government knows that it must encourage the expansion of economic ties in every conceivable way. Within the next ten years China could well become Canada's most important market for capital goods and agricultural products. The business community then would become an ever-larger component of Chinese society and play a more deliberate role in that society's modernization. Its part in human rights development could most effectively take place within Canadian partnerships in industrial enterprises – for example, by instituting minimum standards of pay and working conditions. Similarly, Canadian industry's contribution to the rule of law in China will be substantial if there is proper insistence not only on the enforcement of contracts, but also on transparency in the legal process and on non-participation in doubtful arrangements.

Even more obvious is the part our business community will have to play in sustainable development. It will find its hand strengthened every time it takes a detour, even at some cost, to introduce more environmentally sound methods or technology. Indeed, the Canadian government may, before too long, find itself insisting on such contributions from industry. This would forestall future Chinese administrations from the inevitable call to the first world to help clean up the environmental disasters caused by its increasingly rapid development, from which foreign industrialists benefit so well. One could extend this to every major aspect of social change: education, health, housing, and, perhaps most significantly, the development of cooperative and democratic practices within industrial organizations.

For all these reasons, Canada's representatives in China will likely be paying ever more attention to the dizzily changing scene around them. Rampant corruption, the mood of the floating population, the increasing proportion of the male birthrate, the growing gaps between rural and urban revenues: all these will be among the factors influencing the orientation of the four-pillar policy.

The fourth pillar, though it would appear to be the most "traditional" of foreign policy themes (multilateralism, regional security, nuclear non-proliferation and test bans) is one that would break the last of post-Tian'anmen restrictions – military cooperation. While it is unlikely Canada will ever be involved in significant arms sales to China, it became clear as I left China that some sort of rapport with the Chinese military establishment was long overdue. This was especially so because the People's Liberation Army was emerging as a major economic player, a dominant partner in certain foreign policy issues, and the ultimate arbiter of internal political stability.

Looking Back

Mid-1989 to the beginning of 1992

Canadian policy towards China proceeded in stages once it got over the considerable shock of the Tian'anmen crackdown. Although Canada was prepared to back G-7 sanctions, from the outset it was concerned with avoiding the vexation of China and looking for opportunities to engage in meaningful dialogue. With Chinese leaders reeling from the after-effects of June 4th, Canada refrained from linking any but a marginal part of its trade to the deliberate cooling down of operations. Nor did we seriously interrupt the operation of export development loans, even the soft loan portion. The end beneficiaries of some project contracts, however, were scrutinized more closely. The same applied to the CIDA development assistance programme. None of it could go in support of the coercive components of the state apparatus. The "sanction" that the Chinese Government resented the most was the blanket authorization given all Chinese students to remain in Canada.

I've hardly been here two weeks and, apart from a couple of sorrowful references to the absence of official visitors, the only remnant of the Tian'anmen aftermath that I hear about is the large number of "non-returnees" among the students and scholars who'd been sent to Canada. I keep assuring my interlocutors that as soon as it becomes apparent to these young people that they have nothing to fear in coming back, and that there are genuine career prospects for them here, they will return in larger numbers. In the same breath I tell all and sundry how pleased I am that we have by now resumed fairly regular consultations at the level of vice-ministers, but that I'm not too anxious to have politicians visiting, since they require much more careful preparation of the terrain, a stage we have not yet reached.

Early 1992 to Early 1993

Even though a ministerial visit happened as early as October 1991 (Minister of Agriculture McKnight, ironically), the post-1989 suspensions did not really start to dissipate until after the expulsion of the three MPs in January 1992. The Canadian public and media reaction was so negative to the behaviour of the three parliamentarians that the Government realized its policy of increasing trade ties while maintaining a cold shoulder would not be viable for much longer. The visit in April 1992 of Minister for Industry, Science and Technology and International Trade, Michael Wilson, makes this clear. "We wish to put that matter behind us," he says, referring to the expulsion. The relationship starts to fill out. It is the time of the Canada-China film conference, the beginning of the embassy's Public Diplomacy campaign and the search for a more constructive policy of engagement on the human rights front.

> *Meanwhile, trade is flourishing. In 1990 it adds up to over $3 billion twoways, with capital goods making up more than 50 percent of Canadian exports. By 1992 it is up to 4.6 billion. I keep trotting out these facts, as well as those of our exemplary cooperation on CIDA-financed development projects. When my Chinese interlocutors complain about the lack of high-level contacts, I ask them why look for symbolic shenanigans, when materially everything is looking up. It produces embarrassed smiles and no more. The sort of cooperation we now receive on all fronts could not be better even if our relations were, as the Chinese keep saying, "normalized." If it keeps on this way, I'll have to apply for more foot soldiers. I know there aren't any reserves in the barracks, but my trade people, as well as those doing public affairs, and the consular and immigration staff are all showing signs of serious overwork.*

The Remainder of 1993

Vice-Premier Zhu Rongji visits Canada and establishes a very warm rapport with the Canadian business community. His message: Canadian entrepreneurs are not aggressive enough in Chinese markets and are losing out to other foreign competitors who are sometimes less qualified. Whether this visit was a catalyst or not, the growth of Canadian exports of high technology products and value-added goods reflect a much greater diversity of companies crossing the Pacific. From here on, Canada-China economic ties move into high gear and pull the bilateral relationship with them.

At the same time, Canada takes initiatives to extend China's involvement in multilateral affairs. The embassy pursues a dialogue at the highest levels of the foreign ministry on nuclear non-proliferation questions, regional security, restraints on the export of missile technology, as well as on the nature of China's participation in Asia-Pacific Economic Cooperation. CIDA renews a number of cooperation agreements with China, adding a special emphasis on democratic and sustainable development. Having helped set up the China Council on the Environment, a body of international and Chinese environmental experts to advise Chinese authorities, CIDA now takes on active participation as vice chairman.

This period is one of fast moving and extremely practical cooperation, despite the lack of formal normalization.

> *If only we could contract long-term loans of personnel from other missions. I sure could use some of the thirty-five people in Hong Kong who do nothing but issue visas. Once again, though, unacceptable pressures produce useful ideas. We've completed a data bank of all Chinese who have been trainees with CIDA. We'll talk to them and see what comes of it.*

There are more than three thousand form letters sent out asking the recipients whether they would be prepared to establish contact with Canadian business people visiting their areas. The idea is greeted with enthusiasm by over 80 percent, who are delighted at last to have some form of regular relationship with Canadians. For most, Canada is the only foreign place they've visited.

1994 to 1995

This period is the one where all the aspects of the renewed relationship come together, not only in practice, but also ceremonially with the unequalled visit of Prime Minister Chrétien and "Team Canada." The scope and size of this event leaves no one in doubt as to the seriousness with which Canada seeks to intensify its relations with China at all levels and in as many areas as possible. The special relationship of yesteryear is no longer invoked. Canada's trail-blazing initiative on the recognition of the PRC is now more than 25 years old and the memory of Norman Bethune is gradually being pushed into the background along with so much other memorabilia from the Maoist past. The newly mature relationship has given rise to a strong recognition in China that Canada is indeed a country of modern technology and considerable economic strength, and the potential to be a partner with staying power.

Canada still doesn't have the public profile in China it should, but we've made some progress since the 1980s when we were seen as an enormous agricultural backwater with a tiny racist population. The increasing number of leaders, senior officials, and ordinary Chinese who have been to Canada know that Toronto is the largest Chinese city outside of Asia; they've seen Vancouver and the Rockies and they now know of the sizeable number of Chinese technicians in our electronics and telecommunications firms. They'll never understand our politics nor our internal unity problems, but they admire Canadian candour and the pluralism of our cities. This may not add up to much when it comes to protecting really vital interests in China, but the foundations are laid for something that could blossom into genuine understanding and mutual confidence, the kind of relationship that the Chinese have with far too few countries.

When Canada-China relations started to accelerate in 1984, with Premier Zhao Ziyang's visit and his address to Parliament, no one could have predicted the tragedy five years later that would cause the relationship to regress so far. Nor could one have predicted in 1989 that five years later the prime minister of Canada, accompanied by nine of the ten provincial premiers (itself a unprecedented event, no Canadian PM had ever been accompanied on an official visit abroad), two territorial leaders and close to 500 business people, would fill the Great Hall of the People. A total of 1600 people including ten provincial governors, eighteen mayors of major cities and hundreds of directors of various Chinese enterprises with their Chinese guests, played host to the premier of the PRC. The event was the gala dinner of the Canada-China Business Council, which had planned its annual general meeting in Beijing to coincide with the Canadian visit.

This was more than an overdose of symbolism. It was the consummation of a year that had witnessed the negotiation of a nuclear cooperation agreement and six new CIDA agreements, including one on the training of senior Chinese judges. Visits were made by the newly appointed Canadian secretary of state for Asia Pacific, the foreign minister, the minister of International Trade, the governor general, as well as at least ten important provincial visits.

Finally, during the PM's visit, he and Team Canada were present in one ceremony at the signing of sixty-five separate transactions (letters of intent, MOU – memoranda of understanding, and final contracts) totalling $8.6 billion. Of the total, $2.4 billion were for firm contracts and $3.5 billion were the MOU for the sale of two Candu reactors. One year later, in October 1995, Premier Li Peng returned the visit and came to Montreal to celebrate the twenty-fifth anniversary of the establishment of diplomatic relations. The two government leaders were able to conclude that the content of virtually all of the sixty-five agreements signed 11 months earlier were developing as they should. Thirty-three were now firm contracts, and more contracts had been signed worth another $850 million. Li Peng's visit itself generated another $1 billion worth.

While the Chinese like to say that there is now not a single cloud in the firmament of their relations with Canada, in fact both sides know that problems will continue to exist. Certainly the vast gap between the two systems of government and human rights violations in China will continue to be bones of contention. In substance, nothing very much has changed on that score, except that both sides now have a number of ways of addressing these problems: in private, in public, and through constructive cooperation in the crisis of transformation besetting China.

Nor will everything always go smoothly on the other fronts. As the PRC enters a much more sophisticated phase of its economic reforms and Canadian investors and suppliers become more diverse, the economic relationship will grow in complexity and encounter ever more challenging difficulties. The same can be expected in all the other major areas where we try to work together with China, be it in consular affairs, legal relations, cultural or educational exchanges. That is to be expected as Canada carves out for itself an ever greater stake in the next century's largest economy. Canada's assets for facing these challenges lie in our experiences so far, and our history of cooperation with China in numerous agreements. Most valuable of all will be the straightforward approaches we've developed for handling differences in a spirit of mutual respect. The relationship has indeed matured.

HOW WE BECAME "A NATION OF THE AMERICAS": REFLECTIONS OF A PERMANENT OBSERVER

by Ken Williamson

On January 1, 1990, Canada became the thirty-third member of the Organization of American States (OAS). The decision made in the previous year to seek membership had stimulated some critical media observations but had not aroused much public interest.

The decision itself followed a much longer period of intermittent reflection on whether Canada should be a member. From 1948, when the OAS was founded and Canada was considered eligible for membership, until 1989 when we decided to join, the attitudes of successive governments could be summed up as follows. At first, in spite of limited interest among some political leaders, the answer to the question of membership was a well-considered negative one. This was followed by a hesitant "maybe, but not necessarily," then by "in principle, perhaps," and finally by "yes, we should have done so long ago."

In September 1997, at a conference on Canadian defence and foreign policy, I listened to a panelist describe the decision to join the OAS as an "odd" one. The speaker was an academic specialist in hemispheric affairs. The comment stimulated reflections on my part as to *how* "odd" it was, not least because I had been involved in policy discussions of the question at various stages in a foreign service career.

The scope of this essay does not permit a detailed review of the evaluations of interest, objectives, risks or obligations which went on in Ottawa whenever the question of full involvement with the OAS arose. The history of that evaluation has been fairly well covered in material already published. These reflections concern attitudes towards a basic question of whether we could really belong to the successor organization of the Pan American

Union. The Union embodied specifically Latin American perceptions of common interest, along with concepts held on global and hemispheric interests and power by its dominant member, the United States. Put another way, Latin Americans have asked me, not unreasonably, "Are you a nation of the Americas?"

Santiago, 1959

In 1959, thirty years before the Canadian government made its decision about the OAS, I was the acting head of mission, or chargé d'affaires, in the embassy in Santiago, Chile. In one of the intermittent rounds of discussion between the Department of External Affairs, its posts abroad, and other interested parties, I tried to bring together the various considerations of national interest relevant to our relations with the OAS In a dispatch dated November 3, 1959, I came to a negative conclusion about membership:

The Organization of American States has two fundamental purposes: the advancement of the common interests of the Latin American states, and the negotiation of certain types of business between Latin America and its closest neighbour and greatest problem, the United States. Neither purpose warrants the membership of Canada.

To the extent that this point of view was representative of the then current negative thinking, one might have supposed that the permanent answer on membership would be "in principle, never." Disinclination to consider full institutional involvement at that stage, however, was only part of the picture to be taken into consideration with regard to our relations with Latin America. (Relations with the Commonwealth Caribbean involved a different set of interests and assumptions.) In that same dispatch, I pointed out that Soviet representatives followed developments in the Economic Commission for Latin America (a United Nations agency with headquarters in Santiago) more closely than we were able to do, and that the British embassy had five times as many officers as we had. Surely it was more important to look to the advancement of our own interests in Latin America in a number of quite tangible ways, as the Europeans did, than to be too concerned with whether we really "belonged" to a vast hemispheric community in an old Bolivarean, Pan-American sense.

There was another perspective on these policy questions, however, and it was relevant to the "nation of the Americas" question. At the time when I wrote the dispatch mentioned above, I had been in Chile for over three years. Looking back, I recall now an important change that took place in my own political and cultural horizons. In my first few months in Santiago, in 1956, I remained more interested in the affairs of the Northern Hemisphere, East-West relations, the Soviet invasion of Hungary, and the Suez crisis, than in the political context of my daily work as first secretary. Slowly, all of that interest, with its own background for Canadians of two world wars, Empire, Commonwealth, and great pre-occupation with Europe, moved appreciably back over the northern horizon. New thinking at the Economic Commission for Latin America and the development of the Christian Democratic Party in Chile as a social democratic alternative to both Marxist socialism and to traditional conservatism became matters of considerable interest. There was both a "new world" political contest for me, and, in a more fundamental sense, a "New World" of which Canada also was a part.

Ottawa, 1969

Ten years after commenting on the OAS membership question from Santiago, and after being thoroughly immersed again in Northern hemisphere affairs in West Berlin and in Ottawa, I became involved in the organization of seminars bringing officials, academics, and representatives of trading interests together to consider foreign policy in various sectors. This was part of the "Third Option" initiative of Prime Minister Trudeau to find counter-balances to what he and others saw as excessive interdependence with, or dependence upon, the United States.

One such sector was "Canada and Latin America." In 1970, a booklet under this title was published, one of a series called "Foreign Policy for Canadians." Citizens were to be informed of the results of the review, and of some new directions in policy. At this point, on the specific question of OAS membership and the half-mystical issue of our identity as a "nation of the Americas," we were passing from what I defined at the beginning of this essay as a firmly negative attitude to the one defined as "maybe, but not necessarily." This latter policy formula certainly resembled one adopted by another prime minister on war-time conscription: "if necessary, but not necessarily."

What were the new directions of policy? As the booklet pointed out, the choice, for the immediate future at any rate, was to "broaden and deepen relations with Latin America" and to draw "closer to the Inter-American System and some of its organizations without actually becoming a member of the OAS" The advantages and disadvantages of membership were briefly sketched. In considering the fundamental question of the extent to which, politically speaking, we would be a suitable candidate for the hemispheric club, it was noted, significantly, that "if Canada had been a member of the OAS in 1964, it would have been called upon to sever diplomatic, commercial and transportation links with Cuba." Since Canadian Governments, with apparently strong public support, were firmly committed to a policy of not severing relations with Cuba, this was indeed a difficulty worth thinking about. The booklet noted, with cautious understatement, that "Canada's direct interest in the political affairs of the hemisphere is real but still somewhat limited."

In order to encourage citizens to respond, the booklet on Latin America offered various options for consideration. It stated, for example, that "A decision to seek membership in the OAS *could* be based upon the recognition that there is a certain trend toward regionalism in the world as a whole." In that event also, the decision "*would*" offer "unmistakable proof of Canada's desire to throw in its lot with the other countries of the hemisphere." The decision "*could* flow from a straightforward belief that it is Canada's duty to participate in collective hemispheric deliberations on defence" (my emphasis in all cases).

Any reasonably attentive citizen reading the booklet would have concluded that, whatever the initial inclinations of the Government in policy reappraisal, it would resist, for some time to come, any temptation to demonstrate "unmistakable proof," "straightforward belief," or "recognition" of the importance of regionalism in a final acceptance of Canada's hemispheric identity and roots.

The booklet ended with a survey of future prospects. The government decided "to follow the middle course." It would "prepare for a better-informed and more useful Canadian participation as a full member of the OAS should Canada, at some future date, opt for full participation." In the meantime, Canada would establish "a formal link between Canada and the OAS countries ... at a suitable level." As this policy review period ended with a public report in 1970, I was in the embassy in Washington, much more concerned with the American position in Vietnam and our involvement in the Truce Commission than with the OAS and Latin America. I had, however, as a result of the 1969/1970 policy review concluded that progressive and selective entries into the Inter-American system did make sense. We did join the Inter-American Development Bank, the Pan-American Health Organization and the Inter-American Institute for Cooperation in Agriculture. For Canadians, which organizations provided better evidence of the values of regional functionalism than ones concerned with money, health, and agriculture? We were taking our own cautious steps both into a "new world" and, in the broader sense, into the New World.

Two years later, in 1972, a senior diplomat arrived at OAS headquarters, designated as "Ambassador and Permanent Observer" of Canada to the Organization. He did not, of course, occupy the fine, carved Chair awaiting the Dominion of the North. Ambassador or not, Permanent or not, that would have been presumptuous. He did set up a small mission in our embassy to the United States. and embarked on the task of ensuring that the government would be "better-informed" when, and if, it had to face the challenge of a decision as to whether or not it really belonged in the organization.

A student of diplomatic history who felt that he, or she, was reasonably well informed as to the function of an ambassador, might still be puzzled about the role of a permanent observer. I will leave comments on that point for the following section. I was third in the series of permanent observers. This brings us into the next decade, when I turned up in the Hall of the Americas in the summer of 1980, ready to face the decision: "go in" or "stay out."

Washington, 1980-1983

From the summer of 1980 to the end of 1983, when I went to Cuba as ambassador and listened to Cubans telling me that the OAS member states were "lackeys" of the United States, I carried out the duties of a permanent observer. I attended meetings of the Permanent Council of the organization, annual General Assemblies, special meetings of foreign ministers, meetings of councils dealing with economic, social and cultural matters, and any other meetings which seemed useful to observe in relation to the basic mandate of the position. My attendance was intended, of course, to keep the Canadian Government informed of debates, decisions and operations of the OAS which seemed relevant to Canadian assessments of developments in Inter-American affairs, including the question of our own relations with the organization. We (another foreign service officer and I) dealt with a variety of matters arising out of our full membership in several specialized agencies of the OAS and received representations from those who wanted us to join their organizations. We went to conferences in various parts of Latin America for these general purposes. We had to do some lobbying in support of a Canadian application to join an agency dealing with Inter-American telecommunications.

Ambassador Ken Williamson (left) signing a debt agreement in 1985 with Ricardo Alarcón, a Deputy Secretary-General of the Cuban Foreign Ministry

My views of the effectiveness of the OAS, in terms of its own stated objectives, were mixed indeed. At the first General Assembly that I attended, I was favourably impressed by a scathing attack delivered by a member of the Inter-American Commission on Human Rights on the human rights record of the military regime in Argentina. The report referred to the "dirty war," the period of "los desaparecidos" (opponents of the regime who simply vanished). The assembly received that report and the reply of the foreign minister of Argentina, but passed no judgment on what was considered to be a domestic political matter. A comparable position was taken with respect to the Pinochet Government in Chile. As civil wars in Nicaragua, El Salvador and Guatemala went on, member Governments gave little indication of any intention to act through the organization to seek solutions. A Latin American journalist stationed in Washington summed up the situation: "the Permanent Council fiddled with the pension plans of the Secretariat while Central America burned." This was in the period before the launching of the Contadora peace initiative by Latin American governments, and the initiative of President Arias of Costa Rica.

Argentina claimed sovereignty over and seized the Malvinas islands (known to the British as the Falklands). Although Latin American governments gave no significant military aid to Argentina and took a variety of ambiguous positions about a resort to force, there was a strong and emotionally expressed denunciation of the British military response and support for the Argentine claim. The denunciation extended to NATO allies charged with helping Britain. When the United States secretary of state, Alexander Haig, entered the special assembly he was roundly booed by Latin American secretariat members, even by some delegates.

If Canada had been a member of the organization would our secretary of state for External Affairs have received similar treatment? Canada was mentioned once or twice in speeches about the NATO culprits. I maintained an inconspicuous position in the space allocated to observers. Delegates of the Commonwealth Caribbean took cautiously neutral positions on, or opposed, a resolution passed at the assembly. Under those circumstances, and in view of what I thought was a scandalously partisan performance on the floor of the assembly, I reverted to the "certainly not" judgment about membership expressed in 1959.

On the other side of the ledger, so far as Canadian perceptions of the effectiveness of the OAS were concerned, the Secretariat carried out some good programmes in economic, social and cultural development. The Inter-American Commission on Human Rights made honest judgments on what was happening in the hemisphere. I believe that their well-publicized reports helped to stimulate a return to civilian and democratic government in both Argentina and Chile. The establishment of both a research institute and a court in the same field strengthened their role.

In 1981, another policy review of relations with Latin America, comparable to the one undertaken in 1969-70 was begun in Ottawa. A sub-committee of the Standing Committee on External Affairs and Defence of the House of Commons was given the responsibility of conducting a review and of submitting a report to the standing committee which could, if accepted, then be proposed to the Liberal Government of Pierre Trudeau. The question of OAS membership, was, needless to say, on their agenda. The sub-committee, composed of representatives of all the parties in the House, came to Washington. The most useful task performed by our very small observer mission during the period in which I was there was to give the parliamentarians as comprehensive and balanced an assessment as possible of the factors to be kept in mind in this particular issue. I met with the subcommittee subsequently in Ottawa, at their request, before they prepared their report.

On November 23, 1982, the sub-committee submitted its Final Report to the standing committee, recommending that "Canada seek full membership in the Organization of American States and sign the Bogota Charter." It recommended that Canada should "not sign the Inter-American Treaty of Reciprocal Assistance, until a full review of the security obligations and implications is completed by the government." In the sub-committee, a minority of four members opposed the recommendation. In the standing committee, a minority of ten members opposed it. The majority argued that "it is time to recognize that Canada is a nation of the Americas" and that Canada should participate "with other nations of the Americas in trying to build a more effective OAS."

The report and its recommendations (which covered a number of aspects of Canada's relations with Latin America and the Caribbean) went forward to the House for the government's consideration.

The recommendation was put forward with considerable care. The report also stated that the "present effectiveness of the organization is not sufficient by itself to justify membership." Nevertheless, "Canada can make a contribution to improving its effectiveness" and should do so. The majority conclusion was reached, obviously, in light of consultations in a number of foreign capitals and in consideration of foreign policy objectives generally. The recommendation about OAS membership was the fifth on the list. The first was that the government should give "a much higher priority than it has in the past to Canada's relations with Latin America and the Caribbean. The central objective of Canadian policy in these regions should be the promotion of stability."

Positive assessments were made of specialized agencies. The Inter-American Commission on Human Rights was a "well-established organization with an excellent reputation." The Pan-American Health Organization and OAS technical assistance programs did benefit the poorest societies and provided "another bridge between North and South." "For all its weaknesses," the OAS was "the regional political organization of the Americas." It had resolved some disputes. With the United Nations "overloaded," increased use might be made of regional organizations. Canada should not have any illusions about reforming the OAS single-handedly, but we could make a significant contribution. The majority of subcommittee, and then of committee members, did not think that our participation would have a negative impact on our relations with the United States.

Those opposing membership stated that it was "based on the speculative comment about the possibility of reviving that institution. We do not believe that Canada's entry alone can bring about this revival." Furthermore, "a number of important Latin American States have indicated little interest in the OAS or its revival ... Canada's activities would be shaped and directed by old structures rather than by new directions." The second major basis for dissent was the traditional one. "Membership ... would inevitably, in the course of time, (we need only think of the Falklands crisis) put Canada in unresolvable conflicts of interest." Some issues could set "some (or all) Latin American countries (on the one hand) and the U.S.A. – and possibly the Caribbean States – (on the other) at cross-purposes." The dissenters, not surprisingly, avoided contesting assertions about our identity as a "nation of the Americas" or conjectures about the need for, or ultimate destiny of the OAS itself, regardless of Canadian membership. Their conclusions about membership came much closer to the earlier "certainly not" than to any of the cautious and conditional assessments beginning in the 1970s. They did support the need to work for stability in the region, to expand bilateral relations and to make the most of our membership in specialized agencies.

In the year I had spent at the OAS, I had changed my own 1959 negative view about full membership to a conditional one which might be summed up as "in principle, *if*." The "if" which I suggested to the sub-committee was that there should be, at cabinet level, a strong consensus first of all about the need to develop our relations with Latin America substantially across the board, bilaterally, politically, culturally, and commercially. On the basis of such a consensus, full membership in the OAS would offer *one* useful means of pursuing our objectives. It would provide, at the very least, a significant symbolic indication of the increased importance we were attaching to our relations with Latin America and of our hope to work more closely with Latin American and other hemispheric states to deal with the most difficult problems of the region. That point seemed an essential one to make to the sub-committee, since some members seemed to think that simply "joining the Club" would rapidly produce benefits to us, for example in our export trade. Presumably the sub-committee received similar advice elsewhere, since, as noted above, their first recommendation was to give "a much higher priority ... to Canada's relations with Latin America and the

Caribbean." Other recommendations, apart from OAS membership, followed the same line of thought.

The Liberal government of that period (1980 to 1984) was not, in the end, persuaded to seek OAS membership. That it might be getting closer to some kind of agreement "in principle" seemed evident from tentative indications given by members of the government to the media and in other circles as debate continued around the recommendations of the standing committee. One such indication, which I believe was accurate, had estimated that Prime Minister Pierre Trudeau was 70 percent persuaded that the time had come to join, with the secretary of state for External Affairs, Mark McGuigan, following closely behind at 60 percent. Nevertheless, in the end, the successor to McGuigan, Allan MacEachen, made it clear in one published comment that he saw no decisive advantages in joining. That ended the debate for the government of the day. The doubts of the standing committee dissenters had carried more weight than the advocacy of the majority.

While the debate proceeded in Canada, I tried to explain the complexity of Canadian attitudes to people in OAS circles. Those who hoped that we were going to join had been impressed by the report of the standing committee. I recall, however, some quite sharp comments after I gave a lecture at the Inter-American Defence College. I had tried to put Canadian foreign policy priorities into a historical and political context of Empire and Commonwealth, la Francophonie, two wars in Europe, commitment to the United Nations and then to NATO. I hoped to support assurances that relations with Latin America were increasingly important, but still relatively new, on our international horizons. I was approached by a member of the secretariat who summed up my remarks as, "in other words, no time for us." On other occasions, rather sarcastic references to the permanency of our permanent observer status were made. These occasional comments pointed to problems about our image that we could not ignore.

It was all very well to debate the possible symbolic value to us of membership. This was imagined at some hypothetical point in the future, in support of our particular national interests, as if that value (some indefinable gratitude on the part of Latin Americans) would be available for us at any time when we "had time for them." We could not lose sight of another possibility, and that was, as one Canadian academic observer pointed out, that we would acquire the image of a "hemispheric dilettante" if we went on debating membership, and declining it for the time being. For some Latin

Americans, Canadians seemed willing to be engaged at various improbable spots around the globe and yet decline any direct political involvement in impending disasters nearer to home in the Caribbean or Central Americas. To them, it suggested that we just didn't want to be more closely involved with the Latin Americans.

While such a possibility was a small warning cloud on the horizon, Latin American attitudes at the OAS were generally friendly, particularly among delegates who were not that enthusiastic about the current state of their organization, and maybe, behind the scenes, were amused with our conscientious agonizing about our identity and role. As for our most immediate American neighbours, I was pretty sure that, behind the expression of friendly hopes that we would join, the assessment was twofold:

(1) as members, we could be potential nuisances/on matters such as Cuba (which *would not* go down well in Congress) and

(2) if we joined, their budgetary quota would be reduced (which *would* go down well in the same place).

So, it seemed there was no reason to push us hard in either direction.

In March 1983, I was invited to speak to political science students at McGill University about Canada and the OAS. Since the government's decision about the recommendation of the standing committee was still pending, I had to be careful to observe the limitations on comments by a public servant. I had been told, quite informally, that some members of sub-committee thought I had been unduly negative about membership in briefings in Washington and in Ottawa. (Presumably members of the majority, not the dissenters!) I had been having twinges of conscience about the possibility that I had been far too positive ("in principle, if"), given my actual experience at the OAS up to that point! I entitled my remarks "a matter of choice," tried to define the two options as clearly as possible, and suggested that, as Canadians, they should think through the logic of each position and decide for themselves.

The argument for *not* joining the OAS was quite easy to define. It would be quite in keeping with many of the directions we have actually chosen since 1945, and probably in keeping with what many Canadians felt, to continue with the existing position with regard to the Inter-American system. Would there be anything wrong with saying finally and firmly that, looking from Europe west, we are the last European nation and the first American one, but that, in the vast expanse of the "Americas" we would choose the definition of a "region" which suited us. "North Atlantic and

North America" would always come closer to our history and sense of identity than any grand Bolivarean concept of the Americas, from pole to pole, for the purposes of political and institutional association. We could continue our selective, pragmatic and bilateral approach to hemispheric affairs and our national interests, just as the Europeans did.

The other option was harder to define. The benefits, costs, and risks were conjectural. Nevertheless, we were possibly at the beginning of an era in hemispheric affairs in which the deep-rooted Canadian criteria for participation in the international system could be met with regard to the OAS. In many ways, the functionalist criteria had already been met, or were being applied. Four Latin American middle powers had decided to try to do something themselves about the potentially disastrous consequences of a NATO/Warsaw Pact confrontation in Central America. The Canadian government had given full support to what was known as the "Contadora Initiative"; how could we not do so?

The second option, that of membership, had to be creative, and determined, to make any sense, and a new direction could involve both anticipated, and unpredictable, problems. It would also require a certain sense of being "a nation of the Americas." Beyond being a platitude, or a vague sentiment, this phrase did have some substantial meaning by pointing to the need for a certain change in attitude on the part of Canadian political leaders with regard to the possibility of closer cooperation with the Latin American states.

With this kind of summing up, on my own part, I left the OAS assignment, went to Cuba, did some limited tasks related to Latin America in Ottawa and then retired from government service. In 1986 I embarked on academic study and research focused on questions of politics and religion in Latin America and elsewhere. Six years after leaving the position of permanent observer at the OAS and retiring, I was invited to take part in a seminar at Carleton University at which people from government departments and various circles outside the government were to debate, again, what to do about Latin America ... and, of course, the OAS.

Ottawa, 1989

At a summit meeting of heads of state and of governments in Costa Rica in October 1989, convened by the president of Costa Rica, Prime Minister Mulroney announced Canada's decision to seek full membership in the OAS. The time had come to occupy the vacant chair; we would "no longer stand apart." In spite of imperfections and failings in trying to deal with particular hemispheric problems, this was the one regional organization which brought all governments together to deal with multiple problems of democracy, debt, trade, and the drug menace.

In Canada the announcement was greeted in what might be called "attentive circles" with what I think was, in some cases, genuine surprise, in others strong criticism, and among those who had supported OAS membership for some years, pleasure that their case had eventually been recognized. A national newspaper thought membership was a "first class loser." Academic and other observers of government policies set to work to explain the internal political winds, international climate changes, or bureaucratic intrigues which might have produced a decision which they had not expected. Commentators seemed to be as divided as ever on the arguments for or against membership which were repeated with little new light. Did the prime minister seek personal and domestic partisan advantage from a summit policy announcement? I had great difficulty imagining how the government of the day would get much domestic political advantage on this issue.

In the first term of the Conservative government, 1984-88, there were no indications that the negative conclusion of the preceding government was being re-examined or reversed. In 1985, a published foreign policy review made almost no mention of the question. My occasional contacts with former colleagues certainly did not lead me to think that a pro-OAS lobby was germinating in the Department of External Affairs. An official statement at the Permanent Council of the OAS in 1988 suggested to me that friendly, but permanent, observership was considered to be Canada's particular vocation.

The conference at Carleton University in May of 1989 made it clear that a real policy review about Latin America and the Caribbean was going on, initiated by the minister concerned, Joe Clark. Although the membership question was on the agenda, it did not seem to me as a conference participant from outside government circles that the government of the day was much more likely to seek membership than its predecessor. Those who expressed surprise after the announcement did have some reason to do so. As they pointed out, the decision did not seem to emerge from any apparent reason, or need, in terms of existing priorities and directions of policy.

How was the decision justified? The secretary of state for External Affairs amplified the comments of the prime minister. The central issue, he said, was the need for expanding our relations with nations in the hemisphere and assuming our own proper place there. Joining the OAS was both the symbol and the "*consequence* of this larger strategy" (his emphasis). Realistic and pragmatic approaches to major problems were on the increase in Latin America and this trend was welcome in terms of Canadian criteria for effective functioning of international organizations.

There had been a psychological distance between Canada and the southern part of the hemisphere. The hemisphere had been, in a way, our house. We had to "make it our home." Canada did have major interests and real influence in the region. Those arguing against membership used a completely outdated argument about not getting involved in the "backyard of the U.S.A." They displayed a strange mixture of nationalism, colonialism and isolationism. Clark pointed to what he described as "vigorous and productive" encounters with members of the Rio of Latin American governments. He had met to discuss security issues, to exchange ideas about debt problems between the Group of Seven and Latin American countries, and to talk about Canadian participation in a peacekeeping mission in Central America. All of these new developments pointed to the logic of making full use of the institutional means available to pursue Canadian objectives. Richard Gorham, the last of the permanent observers, as well as being a roving ambassador for Latin America and the Caribbean, explained new approaches to a series of audiences across Canada. Canada was now seen, quite properly, as a "nation of the Americas ... not only geographically but politically, economically and culturally as well." These were realities "never fully acknowledged before."

It was certainly true that the political picture in Latin America had changed in a more hopeful direction, with increased Canadian involvement, between 1983 and 1989. The much more dramatic changes in the disintegration of the Soviet bloc did call for new assessments of foreign policy directions, even if it could hardly be argued that those changes pointed to OAS membership as an obvious, immediate, and logical consequence. The reasons given for joining in 1989 had, to a large extent, been outlined by the subcommittee seven years before or were available in the files of External Affairs. If OAS membership was the consequence, then what was the principal reason for the marked up-grading of attention to our relations with Latin America and the Caribbean? Joe Clark stated that increased attention would have to be paid to regional efforts through multilateral means to deal with major international and transnational problems.

This assessment, I thought, must have been a major element in the decision to join. Perhaps the role of contributor to United Nations peace-keeping in situations remote from our interests, or from our ability to exert influence in any other way, seemed to require some revision. Certainly our long-standing contribution to NATO for Cold War purposes had to be examined. Our aspirations towards global roles and influence, (derived, in my view, from an imperial and missionary past), needed some relative modification in the interest of becoming an increasingly effective middle power in a particular region.

Those are my speculations. Until Messrs Mulroney and Clark offer us their memoirs, or Foreign Affairs turns over all the relevant files to the public domain, we can only speculate about all the considerations that finally triggered the decision to join. Somewhere in comments sent to headquarters in the 1980s, I raised the question of whether we could really send the prime minister to a hemispheric summit at which he, or she, would announce that we were not sure that we were a nation of the Americas but we might rather like "to try it out" at some time. We could get away with "edging in backwards" through specialized agencies up to a point. At a summit, we might end up looking rather silly. Mr. Mulroney could scarcely have overlooked such a consideration at the 1989 San José Summit.

In the meantime, I return to the question of "*how* odd" with which the comment of a few months ago, and these reflections, began. The decision was odd, perhaps, as a real departure from the past already mentioned. A Liberal government in 1983 made a "conservative" decision; a Conservative government in 1989 made a "liberal" decision about trying something a little new. Could it be argued, more dramatically, that for the first time since we took over our own foreign policy, we made a decision which did *not* follow from traditional associations? The phrase, "nation of the Americas," and the analogy of "house to home" did serve the obvious purposes of political rationalization of a decision and of rhetorical sentiment appropriate to a situation. I am still sure that a real sense of a new horizon, and an interesting one, played a part in the minds of those making the decision. I can well understand that when I think of how Latin America did become a new horizon for me in 1956.

The decision might well have seemed odd in 1989. In the longer view of Canada's cautious development from colony to nation to international actor, it seems now to have been quite predictably Canadian in the way it was reached. It was also the right decision.

FOREIGN POLICY ON THE FRONTIERS: CANADA–BURMA RELATIONS

by John G. Hadwen

The issues presented for Canada-Burma relations from 1967 to 1971 originated in the colonial period and in the events of World War II. In the four years of my accreditation to Burma, I was conscious of the severe burdens the country had inherited, and of the pressures on Burmese society since its independence on January 4, 1948. Canadian policy was to assist in building a basis for the future economic and social development of the country. This development would then benefit Canadian interests, provide regional stability, and improve the welfare of the Burmese people. In this essay I describe how my family came to be involved, what we tried to do, whether we succeeded, and to offer my assessments of the future.

Burma is hard to place in Asian studies. In a region of changing and inexact geographical concepts, Burma defies precise location. It is certainly not part of South Asia and indeed its history long demonstrates the country's determination to remain independent of the British East India Empire. It is separate from a South Asia led by India and unique from a South East Asia led either by Vietnam or by a regional organization, as in the Association of Southeast Asian Nations (ASEAN). Burma was even to be considered apart from the non-aligned movement. Some have argued that ever since its independence in 1948 Burma was one of the few truly independent countries.

When I became involved in 1967, relations with Burma were at the periphery of Canadian interests. The contradictions in our relationship were evident, however. Canada has never had its own embassy in Rangoon, yet quite consistently over the years, Burma has maintained an embassy in Ottawa. At Expo67 Burma established a significant presence with an attractive and original pavilion. It is an interesting phenomenon that Burma would do this in the face of relatively consistent Canadian unwillingness to reciprocate.

The Burma Appointment

At the post in Kuala Lumpur, Malaysia, a dispute developed over the need to purchase an official residence. For a number of years we had made do with a relatively small house for our head of mission, which was rented and had a number of disadvantages. A search for alternatives had begun when the existing head of mission settled on a site in the center of town. The property was so large and the house so big that the Treasury Board and the other authorities in Ottawa refused to consider it. The head of post eventually threatened to resign if the department was unable to purchase this property. This kind of issue seldom came before our minister, Mr. Martin senior. There was no alternative when both sides of the dispute stuck to their positions, and in fact, the head of post did indeed resign. I was involved in the handling of the communications on this matter but took no part in the discussions. When the decision was finally taken that the post would become vacant, I applied for it. Eventually a memorandum came up to Mr. Martin that listed my name opposite Kuala Lumpur. There were also about fifteen other proposed appointments to various embassies.

The procedure at that time was that once the department had made its recommendations, it was up to Mr. Martin to take the list up to the Prime Minister and obtain his approval. Mr. Pearson was very careful to respect Mr. Martin's position. He seldom made unilateral changes to Mr. Martin's recommendations and, although there were tensions between the two men, they in fact got along very well. In this case, Mr. Martin seemed to refuse to approach Mr. Pearson. He used to say that he wasn't going to recommend any of us if it meant that I would leave his office. The result was that the memorandum rose to the top of his "in" basket for discussion with Mr. Pearson and then fell to the bottom. I would bring it forward and, in response to the undersecretary's request, urge him to take it to the Prime Minister, which he refused to do. The situation was beginning to have adverse effects on the department's plans to service its relations with a number of governments. Soon after that Mr. Martin got approval for our list, confirming that I would be leaving his office and going to Kuala Lumpur.

There was no time for much in the way of preparations but I began to think of the responsibilities I would have from my base in Kuala Lumpur for relations with Malaysia, Singapore, and Burma. I began some scattered conversations with officials in the department who knew something of the assignment, and started to get our family ready to move sometime in the fall of 1967.

Washington

Released from Mr. Martin's office, I managed to get agreement that I should visit Washington and have an exchange with the State Department on the subject of Vietnam. We had spent most of our time from 1964 to 1967 on one element or the other of the Vietnam situation and there was concern for the consequences of the war – the "domino possibilities" – for the countries around Vietnam. There was a good deal of interest in the techniques that the British and Malaysians were employing to fight communist insurgency and how these related to the changes in American policy regarding the conduct of the war in Vietnam. I went together with an embassy official to call on Mr. George Bundy. I listened and had little to propose myself, but I had been closely involved in all our efforts to promote peace in Vietnam and had accompanied Mr. Pearson on his famous visit to Camp David for exchanges with President Johnson. I also called on the International Bank for Reconstruction and Development (IBRD) at a senior level to discuss Burma. I had learned that the Burmese, fearful of damaging their fiercely protected independence, had effectively allowed their membership in the World Bank to lapse, and that by 1967 there was no ongoing World Bank program. I asked World Bank officials if they thought there was any chance of a change in mind amongst the Burmese and if so would the World Bank respond? I was told that the Burmese under General Ne Win were reluctant to have any international economic relations. Indeed, about this time Burma withdrew from the non-aligned movement. The Bank would, however, welcome a change in the Burmese position. I undertook to see what could be done to promote such a change and said that I would report to Ottawa if I saw it as a prospect.

A Brief History of Burmese-Canadian Relations

Scattered Burmese-Canadian connections existed before the Japanese invasion of Burma in 1942, but I think it would be fair to describe them as of marginal importance. As a result of the Japanese invasion and of the battles from 1942 to the end of the war, however, a substantial Canadian association developed because of the many Canadians in the allied air forces. The role of Canadians in the Royal Air Force from 1942 onwards in Asia has been documented in detail by the late John R.W. Gwynne-Timothy, in his two-volume study *"Burma Liberators."* This history was quite recently recalled when the remains of an aircraft were found in the Burmese jungle, and a Canadian team visited Burma to investigate. In the course of the investigation and recovery the Burmese and Canadian authorities worked closely and harmoniously together. The incident culminated in a special RCAF flight from Canada to Rangoon and back in February/March 1997 during which next of kin and Canadian veterans took part in the ceremonies.

Some relations also were created by the development of the Colombo Plan fellowship and scholarship programme under which Burmese studied and worked in Canada. Very few Burmese stayed in Canada as a result of their studies because draconian Burmese regulations heavily penalized individuals and their families if students did not return to Burma at the end of their time abroad. The Burmese, however, in general seemed more committed than other Asian groups to return to their country at the end of their courses. A significant Burmese community has not developed in Canada, in comparison with many other countries whose students benefited under the Colombo Plan.

Canada's decision to enter into relations with Burma only after independence did not seem to affect our standing with nearby countries. Even though we were associated with Britain, India, Pakistan and Burma seemed very quick to understand the Canadian position as one of friendly and close relations with Britain while, at the same time, these countries were moving towards a position of ever increasing independence. Neither in Burma nor anywhere else in the former British Empire in Asia was Canada in any way politically involved. The story becomes more complicated as the history of British colonial possession proceeds, especially in Africa, but as far as South Asia is concerned, Canada began relations with Burma and, of course, with India and Pakistan and other South Asian countries, with a fresh slate free of British associations. This was not always an advantage, although Canadian speakers sometimes talked as if it were. What it did mean was that we had very little or no knowledge of countries with which we were coming in contact and few Canadians spoke the languages. As a result we had to accumulate much background information before we could move with ease in these societies.

There has never been a Canadian embassy in Rangoon. As there was no direct channel of communication, correspondence was handled through the British embassy in Rangoon as part of its Commonwealth burden. The Burmese seemed satisfied with this kind of relationship, which was similar to the work that British authorities undertook on behalf of other Commonwealth countries elsewhere in the world in the period after the

Second World War. It was not possible, of course, for this system to continue indefinitely.

It seems likely that the first Canadian officially sent to Rangoon was Miss K. Griner who arrived there in July 1957 and came out in 1958. She had been cross-posted from Singapore. The British Embassy was glad to provide her with space, and she functioned as a member there to whom any work connected with Canada was passed, mainly the processing of Colombo Plan fellows and scholars. In 1958 and until 1960 Miss Grace Stowe succeeded her. Edith Jarvis was there from 1960-62, and she, in turn, was followed by Marie Hyndman, who was in Rangoon from 1962-64.

It was clear that the Burmese valued even the minor contacts they had with Canadians. When I visited first in 1967 there was still a very small number of elderly Canadian nuns serving their church in educational institutions in Burma and particularly Rangoon. My wife and I followed the example of our trade representative, Phil Stuchen, who brought food and comforts to these worthy people. The Burmese government had over the years taken a firm position against conversions by foreign religious orders and had also decided that such people could stay but that they could not be replaced. Accordingly, these Canadians had decided that their duty was to remain in Rangoon as long as they physically could do so. I suppose that, as in other places in Asia, they were tolerated as long as they did not conduct aggressive outreach practices.

I should note that some of my predecessors, especially Arthur Menzies, left their mark. There had also been a few Canadian Colombo Plan experts in Burma. A woman by the name of Jane Goodall had set up cancer treatment clinics with Canadian cobalt beam therapy units in Rangoon and in Mandalay, and had been very popular with the nurses and the medical community in Burma. There were others who had similarly made their name, particularly representatives of a Western Canadian firm who had worked on the Thaketa Bridge. The challenging technical problems of this bridge included the need for it to have a raised center so that ships could pass under it. The problems of construction on silt and delta foundations were forbidding. One of its foundation pillars had leaned several degrees out of kilter. This raised the serious and difficult question of how to get the foundations for the bridge back into line. Despite rumours to the contrary, nothing fell down at this bridge and the difficulties with the foundations were overcome. I visited the bridge in 1994 and it was still operable, and clearly a major transportation link.

Not all views of Canada were benign, however. During my time as the accredited Canadian representative to Burma, a newspaper item appeared which suggested that Canadian funds were being channeled through a company in New York to support the programmes abroad of U Nu. General Ne Win had displaced U Nu as prime minister of Burma in 1962 and the latter had left Burma for overseas from where he tried to conduct a Government in exile, sometimes from Thailand. After informing Ottawa, I was able to convince the Burmese in fact there was no Canadian Government connection with the funds which were being received from New York and that, however U Nu was being financed, he was not getting assistance from the Canadian Government. I believe the Burmese accepted my assurances and I heard nothing further of this incident. There is no doubt that the Burmese authorities were hypersensitive about the possibility that the CIA was conducting operations against their national interest inside Burma. Some American authorities, including the CIA, had apparently encouraged the nationalist Chinese contingents that had installed themselves in the border areas of Burma towards the end of the civil war in China. These nationalist Chinese units supported and conducted major drug producing ventures that have been hard to eradicate.

There has even been, in recent years, a revival of claims – first made soon after independence – that the British secret services were involved in the assassination of Aung San and of part of his cabinet. It now appears to be generally accepted that British military officers had taken part in efforts to provide arms to the dissidents in Burma in 1946 and 1947. There were some unexplained departures from Rangoon of British officials accused of taking part in subversion. However, over the years the Burmese authorities have accepted the fact these efforts were not a consistent policy by the British Government. The fact that Canada does not have an offensive clandestine overseas intelligence service has certainly worked to our advantage in countries like Burma.

A similar advantage from which Canadian policies and interests benefitted was the nature of our involvement in the Vietnam War. The Burmese were, of course, very uneasy about the war and did everything they could to remain distant from it. Americans in Rangoon were constantly comparing Burma and Thailand and described Thailand as enjoying a boom brought about by American investment and the presence of American troops. Burma, on the other hand, was in economic difficulties. However, the Burmese looked at the situation completely differently. They considered that the Thais were selling their civilization for money and that they would eventually regret having done so. The Burmese took pride in not participating in the Vietnam War and its commercial benefits. Indeed, it was in this period that the Burmese refused to accept aid to preserve the historical monuments of their great cultural center of Pagan. At various times, American interests were willing to "rebuild Pagan" but the Burmese have consistently refused their offer. They maintained responsibility for whatever preservation is possible of the ancient monuments in which Burma abounds.

The Burmese attitude is perhaps best illustrated by a story I recall being told when I was confronted with the motto of those days, "The Burmese Way to Socialism." My diplomatic colleagues explained to me that whatever the Burmese policies might be, they did not constitute a "way," since the extreme nationalism of the commercial and economic development policies of Burma had produced nothing of advantage to its economy. I was also told that the type of socialism evident in Burma in the 1960s was unlike anything known elsewhere in the world. The USSR ambassador in Rangoon even said to me one day in exasperation: "Why are the Burmese on chapter 1 of *Das Kapital* when we are on chapter 40?" However, it was also apparent to me and, indeed, to any observer of the Burmese scene, that there was a true word in this motto of the Burmese Government and it was the word "Burmese." Burma displayed, certainly in 1967 and in the years until we left in 1971, an extreme form of nationalism.

Although we gave no encouragement to the extreme forms of Burmese nationalism, it is a fact that the Burmese sympathized with the force of Canadian nationalism in any of its forms. I am of the opinion that their Canadian embassy and connections with Canada helped them to understand developments in the United States. Generally speaking, the Burmese have used their representatives in Canada to help staff their delegations to the United Nations. In the same way, I have argued, it is possible to understand developments in Thailand, China, and even in India from the vantage point of Rangoon. The Burmese experience in relatively successfully negotiating its borders with China, in conducting relations with Thailand (satisfactory regardless of some of the difficulties arising from the border areas) and in maintaining relations with India (wary, and also affected by the fact that the border with Bangladesh is one which is subject to refugee movements in either direction), can be instructive to outside observers.

It is also true that Canada's continuing Commonwealth membership interests Burma. Burma itself had left the Commonwealth at the time of its independence. The history of Commonwealth membership is a long and complex one and I suppose that it is theoretically possible that there could be closer associations for Burma with the Commonwealth than there have been since they left in 1947.

In summary, when I was appointed as Canadian ambassador to Burma the background to our mutual relationship was that both countries had only minor interests in each other. This was, of course, a fact reflected in my assignment. My main responsibilities were to develop Canadian-Malaysian relations. I was also expected to do anything possible to improve Canadian-Singapore relations. For both Malaysia and Singapore there were major commercial objectives and a full and complex range of Canadian national interests to pursue. Burma represented a challenge and an interesting secondary area of operations.

When I arrived in Kuala Lumpur in 1967 I was faced with the probability that there would be no major development in Canadian-Burmese relations. This was a reflection of the policies that were in vogue in Ottawa and which resulted from parliamentary committee reports that recommended a concentration of Canadian aid in countries where it could have an obvious and useful impact. I resisted this policy from the beginning, arguing not only for the interests of our relations with Singapore and Burma, but also that it was not wise to commit ourselves only to those large countries where it was thought we should concentrate our efforts. The problem is that in the large countries like Indonesia, India, Pakistan, and even Malaysia, there are many other interests involved. No matter how important our aid programme might seem to us, it would still be only of marginal interest to such large recipients. Furthermore, in the smaller countries – and I would include Nepal, Sri Lanka, Bangladesh, Afghanistan, and Burma – there is more potential to make a significant proportionate contribution and develop political relations with the local governments.

One senior CIDA official in this period said to me "there will be no Canadian aid programme for Burma." I challenged this and said to him and to others at CIDA that I was not prepared to agree with such a position when I was about to embark on general discussions on many subjects with the Burmese government. It was decided that CIDA would at least consider my recommendations and it was on that basis that I set off for Kuala Lumpur.

Beginning the Assignment

Our preparations to leave Ottawa were made somewhat more difficult by the delay in the appointment being confirmed, in the agreement to it being requested from Malaysia, Singapore, and Burma, and then in making all the other arrangements to rent our house, sell the car, and look after the interests of our children.

The only unique element in these preparations may have been the health precautions. We were advised that we should take every inoculation that there was to be had. We recall that we had fourteen inoculations each before we left. We had the plague shots in Rangoon. The children found this quite a burden but we eventually became quite inured to it then and throughout the years.

Two instances proved to us that we had been wise to take the recommended medical precautions. We were paying a visit to a forestry center in middle Burma called Pyinmana. One evening, one of the senior local officials arranged a dinner for us at the official rest-house where we were staying. It had no kitchen facilities, so each of their wives brought a dish for the dinner so that we ate a combination of delicacies. My wife was seated beside the medical doctor for the region and during dinner she asked him what the main medical problems were. He replied that one of the chief difficulties was the spread of disease by the rats. (Just before we had arrived there had been a major rat extermination drive which resulted in the killing of 635 of the rodents.) He went on to say that there were many diseases that were relatively uncommon elsewhere, noting that bubonic plague was still extant in a number of Burmese centers including this one, and that there was also diphtheria, small pox, measles, typhoid, polio, tetanus, tuberculosis, and all forms of dysentery.

The second occasion was in Pagan where we were at a government rest house when there was an influx of European doctors. This specially chosen group had been sent to Burma to study one of the last remaining areas of the world in which bubonic plague was active. In the mornings we said goodbye to this group who went off with their box lunches, and in the evening listened to them as they told us of their adventures. (Malaria was also very prevalent and we took throughout our time in Burma anti-malarial drugs about which there was even then considerable debate.) This also perhaps explained why we did not take any of the children with us to Burma, a fact that in some respects they resent to this day.

A Colombo Plan Conference

In the fall of 1967 we flew to Bangkok, spent a day in consultation with our embassy there and then flew directly to Rangoon for the annual meeting of the Colombo Plan, at which I had been designated to lead the Canadian delegation. (We travelled in tourist class and on arrival there was great confusion until the welcoming party at the first class exit was re-assembled for us.)

The Colombo Plan was a most important organization to the Burmese. They attached a great deal of significance to the meetings because they gave Burma a formal association with the United Kingdom, the United States, and other countries of South and South East Asia. In these forums they could operate freely and as an equal member. However, as the years went by and bilateral programmes took over the administration of development cooperation plans, Burma and other smaller Asian countries found that the Colombo Plan had less and less importance. It is possible that, as the Colombo Plan declined in importance, Burma came to realize its interests lay in joining ASEAN. For many years Burma was the most isolated of Asian countries. It never became as closely involved with the policies of the non-aligned movement. It is perhaps hard to understand how strongly and how consistently nationalist the Burmese were and are. (In 1997, Burma did not suffer from dislocation in the same way many other Asian countries did since it did not have anything like the same degree of foreign investment or foreign capital involved with its currency.) The problem and the challenge for the Burmese of course is, as always, how to draw the benefits from international cooperation without at the same time placing their national objectives in jeopardy.

On arrival in Burma I had many calls to make and in due course met the President General Ne Win. These calls for the presentation of credentials were not expected to be substantive in any way, however when I met General Ne Win I asked him if I could make one point when the formal ceremony was over and he agreed. I told him that before arriving in Rangoon I had been able to determine that if the Burmese authorities gave a sign of any kind, the World Bank would be willing to re-open the question of Burmese membership. General Ne Win seemed somewhat surprised by this suggestion but instructed his officials to look into the matter. Subsequently I repeated this point to officials in the foreign ministry and I was later told that in fact contacts had been renewed with the World Bank. A substantial World Bank programme in Burma began to develop soon after and continued until the troubles of 1988. Of course, I kept in touch with the UN office in Rangoon and tried to monitor and keep up to date on its various programs. We were closely involved in the joint program with WHO (World Health Organization) and the Netherlands on malaria eradication and there were a number of Canadian doctors going to and from Rangoon in this connection.

Almost immediately after our arrival in Rangoon we began to work as a delegation on the Colombo Plan meeting and this pre-occupied us for about two weeks. We were all quartered in the Inya Lake Hotel, a large building constructed with Russian assistance on the banks of one of the lakes that form part of Rangoon. It was a vast and unwelcoming building but there was a little used piano in the entrance hall. My wife began to play and there developed a pattern of informal sing-songs around the piano at the end of the day's business. These became rather notable occasions. The Ceylon delegation contained an official who had a remarkable memory for the songs of the forties and fifties and led us regularly. We were conscious that the hotel was very likely to have been equipped by its Russian builders with listening devices but of course our work on Colombo Plan matters was not likely to have been of much interest to any outside listeners and we were careful.

We made a special effort to get to know the Burmese delegation and with their help I began a comprehensive tour of the Burmese Ministries to discuss possible Canadian projects. I was not, of course, in a position to discuss any amounts of aid or any possible areas of concentration. I made all this perfectly clear to the Burmese authorities but I did say that I thought it was worthwhile for us both to examine the possibilities for Canadian-Burmese cooperation in economic development. I tried to keep in mind throughout our discussions the possibilities that might exist for the sale of Canadian goods and services, but it was not likely, in view of Burma's lack of foreign exchange, that any projects would be possible beyond those under the aid programme.

I was provided with detailed information on possible projects in forestry and in the general area of mining. There were also suggestions, which I agreed to follow up, for further cooperation in the medical field, particularly for hospitals and for the malaria eradication programme. I also made it clear Canada could well support programmes to reduce drug production. The Burmese authorities appeared very anxious to proceed on the drug front, but it was clear that until peaceful conditions could be established in the north, particularly on the Chinese border, there was little

Ambassador and Mrs. Hadwen receiving guests at an official reception for international officials and Canadian aid workers in Rangoon

prospect of rapid progress. On our return to Kuala Lumpur I sent an extensive series of reports to CIDA giving details on a number of good possible joint projects for further discussion with the Burmese.

Eventually a number of projects were implemented to the satisfaction of the both the Burmese and the Canadian authorities. They included the establishment of a forestry machinery maintenance workshop at the town of Pyinmana on the railroad from Rangoon to Mandalay. There were also a number of mineral projects. One included a survey of a lead and zinc deposit, which the Burmese hoped would make large-scale developments possible. After a good deal of effort financed by CIDA including inspections on the ground, it was finally decided that the deposits were too widely scattered and in general, insufficient to justify large-scale development. When I reviewed the aid programme on subsequent visits with the Burmese authorities we agreed that this study had, in fact, been successful because otherwise the Burmese government might have made large scale expenditures in trying to develop a mining area which would not have been justified in the long run.

The Military Regime

One area of Canada-Burma relations which I did not pursue was cooperation between the Burmese and Canadian military authorities. I avoided discussions and any possible projects in this area because the Canadian authorities were wary of relationships with what many regarded as a military dictatorship. Also, there was no established programme for Canadian cooperation in the defence sector except with allied and Commonwealth countries.

Of course, the majority of the ministers and senior officials I dealt with in Burma 1967 to 1971 were very able officers from the defence services, but I had no conversations with the military leadership on armed services matters. I learned, however, that the Burmese armed forces were a well disciplined, well trained and experienced force that had been on a war footing since 1947. They had battled several communist insurgencies and faced continual regional and ethnic rebellions. They regarded themselves as the custodians of Aung San's efforts to maintain a viable central government. They campaigned vigorously against dissidents of whatever kind who threatened national unity.

As the years have gone by, ethnic separatism has to a considerable extent given way in negotiated settlements with the central government. Unrest on the Thai border and in the far north has been reduced in hard fought battles. The army remains the overriding force in Burmese politics. Any new constitution (and drafting continues) will, no doubt, have to provide for some political role for the armed forces. Many other Asian countries face similar problems. Any solutions for Burma will be pursued on a long term basis. Burmese officials have always pointed to the experience of other countries where the withdrawal from political power by the military has led to disorder and in some case disaster.

The Burmese military has two other somewhat unexpected qualities. In the first place, they are very careful to respect and, where possible, to co-opt the religious beliefs of the general public. Burmese Buddhism is itself a unique and pervasive force in society. The military has taken care not to create a situation in which the religion's influence becomes a kind of political opposition. Secondly, it seemed strange to a Canadian to find that the Burmese military paid deference to socialist economic policies. Some of these ideas appeared to go back to the Fabian socialism of a J.S. Furnivail from Britain who had exerted a great influence on early Burmese nationalists. This socialism is fading somewhat in 1999, but religion is still a potent and ever present factor in Burmese affairs.

Travels in Burma

Our visits to Burma in the period 1967-71 were necessarily limited in number and in duration in view of our responsibilities for Malaysia and Singapore. Nevertheless, looking back, it is surprising that we were able to cover as much territory as we did.

There were rather severe restrictions on travel outside Rangoon. In the north, conditions of unrest included active fighting between the central government and various tribal and local armed forces. There was no extensive or reliable bus service and the railway facilities were very limited. Even the train from Rangoon to Mandalay was insecure at times. Therefore, almost all travel had to be by private vehicle. We relied extensively on the British Embassy to provide us with Land Rovers when they could.

The local diplomatic community felt itself rather confined to Rangoon as a result of security factors and general transportation difficulties. When we came to Rangoon we decided to make appropriate calls on a few local missions, but not to try to cover the whole diplomatic community. We concentrated on whatever contacts we could make with the central government and on the possibilities that should be explored in order to develop a Canadian aid programme. This latter factor gave us some leverage. I can recall using the argument with the Burmese foreign office that I could not recommend projects which might involve visits or residence by Canadian families, if my wife and I could not visit the area concerned. As a result, we were able to make reasonably frequent visits outside Rangoon. Rangoon itself is fascinating but it did not seem profitable in the overall Canadian interest to spend any more time there than necessary.

Mandalay: Our Song

We made several visits by air and road from Rangoon to Mandalay. Mandalay is the second largest major city in Burma and was the ancient capital. It was very badly damaged during the Second World War. A huge walled compound was completely burnt to the ground, including constructions of wonderfully carved wood. Much of the damage took place as the allied forces reconquered Burma in the later stages of the war and there was always dispute as to which of the many shellings resulted in the destruction of the ancient buildings. At one point we visited a monastery which we were told was the only truly original Burmese wooden structure still standing in Mandalay. The local administration was later headed by a Burmese friend whom we had met repeatedly on Colombo Plan business. I asked him at one point to obtain for me a Burmese ceremonial gong made at the very famous Mahamunni Pagoda. Eventually, a large gong was made for our embassy in Kuala Lumpur and sent down to the British Embassy for me. It was too big and heavy to be accommodated anywhere except the lobby of our embassy building, and I was told that it attracted very great interest as it waited for our arrival in Rangoon. When we eventually got it I wondered how it could possibly be taken back to Kuala Lumpur. Fortunately, there was such interest in it as an important object that Burma and Thai airways seemed delighted to make special arrangements at no cost to ensure that this object was given special treatment all the way back to Kuala Lumpur. We certainly tried our best to make whatever contacts we could that would be useful to Canadian aid programmes in the future.

In the process we once fell in with a group of British tourists, led by an exuberant Scotsman, who decided that they wanted to see the "Dawn Come Up Like Thunder out of China Across the Way," this being a phrase from Kipling's poem "On the Road to Mandalay." We joined them by getting up at 2 o'clock in the morning and then climbing the relatively high Mandalay hill. As was the case with most Burmese religious sites, this was in the middle of the town. There was a route to the top for pilgrims that went through a series of pagodas all the way up to the summit. It was a long and complex climb because the temples had in them sleeping Burmese priests and also various precious shrines. Our feet were bare because the hill was sacred, andwe had forgotten flashlights. However, eventually we reached the summit in the dark and were able to watch the sun rise over the distant hills. We could not, of course, see China, but we certainly did see a beautiful sunrise over hills which eventually would have led to China. I suppose Kipling was entitled to poetic license but we certainly felt that morning in close touch with the pilgrim trail and with Mandalay's history.

Maymyo

From Mandalay it was relatively easy to get up to Maymyo. This typical British hill station was developed in colonial days to provide a refuge from the heat in the plains for British officials and their families. Although the facilities were in decline by the time of our visit in the late sixties, there were still the remains of a golf course and a series of cottages or villas with decaying gardens which had been used in British days for official purposes. There are descriptions still available of the life as it was lived in Maymyo, which must have been very similar to life in the hill stations of India, Pakistan, and Malaysia and other areas in South Asia which we visited. Maymyo was also a staging post for visits further inland. In particular, it was close to some of the areas in which the Burmese hoped to obtain Canadian aid to develop of their mineral deposits. Thus on one occasion we set off from Maymyo to visit the possible site for a mining survey where, in fact, Canadians were eventually stationed.

We were also able to make some visits to the border areas of Burma adjacent to Bangladesh, although we could not go to the area in which there had been the decisive battles of the Second World War with the Japanese near Imphal and Kohima, in Assam, India. However, we did get to Kalewa and Shwebo. These were more areas in which there were major mineral deposits and I believe there has continued to be interest by Canadian mining companies in cooperating with the Burmese in developing various sites. I think that our visits in a sense opened up these mining areas in such a way that it was possible for Canadian interests to lay the groundwork for future exploration.

We visited the oil fields of Yenangyaung – a most disturbing sight to anyone who has been to the oil fields of Alberta. Yenangyaung had been in the 1930s a thriving and extensive oilfield. When we saw it, it was a vast plain covered with derelict oil pumps and destroyed oil installations. In 1942, when the British retreated, they methodically destroyed the oil fields and then regularly bombed them once the Japanese took control. The oil fields were a major prize for the invading Japanese, and the British, understanding their great importance, made sure the destruction was comprehensive. When the Japanese turn came at the end of the Second World War they then carefully destroyed the whole area a second time. I don't believe it will ever be possible for this area to recover and I was told the pipeline which had gone to Rangoon was beyond repair. Canadian oil companies have long been interested in the possibilities of petroleum development in Burma but partly because of the wartime destruction most current efforts have been directed at exploring offshore. I believe there have been some successes but Burma has not yet developed major petroleum resources. In our time, we were not able to do more than lay the groundwork for possible future Canadian interests. There was seldom any Canadian official aid available for promoting petroleum activity, it being assumed that the private sector was fully capable of conducting its own exploration and development. In the same period (1967-71) the Burmese were also extremely cautious about entering into any foreign commercial relationships in petroleum development or in any other area requiring international cooperation.

We visited Meiktala, which had been an important junction during the Second World War, and also some parts of the Shan states, in particular Taunggyi and Kalaw. This trip also brought us to Inle Lake, a large lake famous in Burma for what would be called its leg rowers. Here Burmese fishermen had developed a kind of paddle around which they wound one of their legs. It was an extraordinary sight to see many small boats being paddled using this unique method. The Shan states had been the site of some of the most difficult insurgencies faced by the Burmese Government. It was not possible for us to visit or for any Canadian aid programmes to be conducted there. Except in the most travelled areas, we were almost always accompanied by a truckload of Burmese soldiers. As a Canadian veteran of the Second World War, it was a surprise to me to see throughout Burma quite large numbers of Canadian trucks. During the war Canada had made trucks for the allied armies, and many of these had found their way to Burma during the war. These vehicles, declared surplus in 1945, were in regular use by the Burmese authorities 25 years later in even the remotest sections of Burma.

Pagan from the Irrawaddy

Pagan, south of Mandalay, is a vast area filled with religious monuments. It remains one of the great marvels of Asia, rivalling Angkor Wat in Cambodia and similar areas in India. We were taken to some of the major attractions. On one occasion we were told that it was necessary to see Pagan with all its spires from the river. Without understanding what was involved, we said that yes, we would like to do this. Subsequently we were told to be available in the middle of the night and off we went to see Pagan at sunrise. It turned out that the officials we were with had requisitioned a large ferry to take only the two of us out into the middle of the river, where, over breakfast, we were to watch the sun come up. The only difficulty on this particular occasion was that as soon as any lights on the ferry went on, thousands and thousands of insects invaded the boat and our time was spent trying to avoid their attacks. Nevertheless, we did see the sun rise over Pagan and expressed our appreciation.

Tourism Possibilities

We remember the beauty of the beaches of Sandoway on the west coast of Burma. No doubt, sooner or later these beaches will be developed as they have been in Thailand. When we visited, most of their facilities had been left over from British colonial days. It was clear that in Burma, as in Thailand and Malaysia, there are extraordinary possibilities for tourism. Although Canadian companies have undertaken joint ventures in other parts of Asia, I don't think Canadian interests have yet been involved in tourism development in the area.

We did not spend much time in the delta, the enormous areas of rice cultivation south of Rangoon. When I went after retirement as a lecturer on a cruise ship making its first visit up the Irrawaddy to Rangoon I was summoned to the bridge one day and asked to give a running commentary on the sights as we went up the river. This was a difficult task because there are no sights. On both sides there were miles and miles of totally featureless rice land. I was able to describe the battles that had occurred in these areas between the Burmese army and Russian and Chinese supported communists in the 1950s, and I recalled as much as I could of what I had read, but there were no flying fishes to see and only the occasionally modest pagoda. At one point the crew came excitedly up to me to ask me to describe the Shwedagon Pagoda which they said they could see from the boat. I was sure this was not the Shwedagon Pagoda, large though it was, since we were miles from Rangoon, and indeed it turned out that this was yet another pagoda of the same general design in a small town. A long and difficult afternoon was spent trying to manufacture a running commentary on a practically featureless landscape.

We did make one visit to Moulmein, another important Burmese centre, and we were able to get down the Tenassarim Coast to Mergui which is at the bottom of a strip of Burma which runs down parallel to the border with Thailand. We stayed in an ancient British guesthouse and were surprised in the evenings to find we were left completely alone. We had no supporting service and no watchman. Later we learned that the house was reliably reported to be haunted and that no Burmese would stay in it overnight. We saw or heard no ghosts ourselves.

Security

On our visits outside Rangoon we never experienced security threats of any kind and I have been told that there have been no incidents affecting Canadian aid workers, some of whom have lived in remote and isolated areas. The Burmese are very tolerant of foreigners and certainly the traditions of Burmese kindness were obvious wherever we went. I was able to recommend and support various proposals for aid programmes outside

Rangoon; provided one followed the advice of the Burmese authorities in respect of areas that were still disturbed, there was no special danger. I have been told also that there has been a steady improvement in the security situation in Burma as agreements have gradually been negotiated with the dissident armies. Indeed in 1997 and 1998 western Canadian mining interests have travelled all over Burma investigating possible projects without any difficulty whatsoever.

The Counterbalance of NGO Hostility

Canadian non-governmental organizations (NGOs) have, in recent years, focused on Burma mainly in the context of human rights. In 1988, hundreds of lives were lost when the Burmese army put down a public uprising. General elections returned a number of parties each with a majority of seats in the proposed parliament. This political grouping was more or less led by Daw Aung San Suu Kyi, the daughter of independent Burma's first political leader Aung San. She has managed to continue as an opposition leader for the last eleven years, resisting the continuing military government. A series of political confrontations led to Daw Aung San Suu Kyi being given a Nobel Peace Prize. In various periods, her presence in Burma might have been the catalyst of another uprising but, on balance, the Burmese have avoided repeating the crisis of 1988.

Canadian NGOs have become quite active in supporting dissident Burmese on the border with Thailand. There, and in other parts of Burma since the Second World War, the Burmese army has mounted a series of successful campaigns in the course of which it has defeated many of the separatist forces that remained. At one time, there were two Communist armies operated in the Rangoon delta. In Northern Burma, also, there has been a group of nationalist Chinese who fled after the Communists took power in 1949. For a time they were a major and damaging drug related presence in the country. Various ethnic regional factions have resisted central authority in the north of Burma. On the whole, however, through military intervention and political negotiations, the Burmese authorities have gradually succeeded in establishing peaceful conditions throughout most of Burma. Indeed, formal agreements have been reached with many of the tribal units involved, and it is now possible for tourists to travel long distances in Burma into territory which was quite impossible for us to reach when I was accredited there from 1967 to 1971.

The hostility of the NGO movement in Canada to the military government in Burma has, however, produced organizations that campaign and raise funds against the Burmese government. To some extent these NGO groups have supported the Burmese government which in exile is headquartered in Washington, D.C., and some groups operate health and other facilities in the dissident areas along the Thai border. Canadian domestic political pressures have, therefore, resulted in current sanctions against new investment by Canadians in Burma. Thus, some favourable long-term factors affecting Canadian relations with Burma are currently balanced by adverse Canadian public responses to current human rights issues.

There was, naturally, a great decrease in all Canadian contacts with Burma after the events of 1988. In 1999 there is no possibility of any Canadian aid programme in Burma. It is, however, already clear that there is greatly increased foreign economic interest in the country following Burma's admission as a member of ASEAN. I think that it would be found that there is a good deal of Australian interest in mining development and there has certainly been substantial French activity in the petroleum sector.

Future Possibilities

It is still too early to envisage how Canadian relations with Burma will develop, but on the basis of the experience from 1967-71 there are a number of areas in which programmes could fairly quickly be established. For example, there is now a negotiation proceeding between the UN authorities and the Burmese about the possibility of major assistance from the World Bank and the UN for programmes designed to reduce the flow of drugs from South and South East Asia to the rest of the world. There will be an important drug control programme to be undertaken in parts of the north on the Chinese and Thai borders once security is improved. There is no doubt that the drug problems of North America can be alleviated with international cooperation involving these areas.

Another possible collaborative project between Canada and Burma relates to malaria control. The Burmese have long had major research programmes in this area, and it was one of the first and largest areas of Canadian cooperation with Burma in the time when we were associated with the country. Similarly, there have been long-term connections as a result of the establishment of cancer treatment facilities in Rangoon and Mandalay (previously mentioned), and we were able at one point to use the counterpart funds from the provision of agricultural aid to establish a children's hospital in Rangoon that still thrives as an institution. Of course, there are other possible projects in the forestry, agriculture, and transportation sectors.

Policy Contributions from the Field

My friend James Eayrs argued at one time that foreign service officers were by necessity hypocrites because they could not possibly believe at all times in all the policies that they were implementing. I have rejected this assessment both directly and in writing and I doubt if Mr. Eayrs maintains this posture today. Indeed, in the whole of a period of 37 years I did not find any of my fundamental beliefs or values threatened by my responsibilities as a Canadian public servant. This did not mean that I would always agree with everything I heard or said. There are a few examples from my period of responsibility for Burma which might usefully be described.

One of the different issues on which I tried to deflect my instructions concerns the making of lists. I think mainly because lists seem required constantly by the U.S. Congress that there were similar requests made in Canada which applied to Asia. We were often asked to prepare statements of the countries in Asia – which were democratic and which were undemocratic? The countries in Asia were also to be ranked in terms of their respect for human rights. In order to assess whether the countries of Asia measured up to "democratic standards," it would be necessary to establish precisely what those standards were. One of the factors was the extent to which these standards, whatever they were, were applied within Canada. Sometimes it was argued that foreign policy had nothing to do with domestic policy. But, the long and short of it is that there was no real distinction between foreign and domestic policy. Most if not all of Canada's domestic policies have a foreign affairs aspect and most, if not all foreign policy problems have a domestic element. Some have argued that we have not applied democratic standards to some issues within Canada such as relations with the native peoples or with Japanese Canadians during the Second World War. There are also times when events in Canada lead United Nations bodies to question whether Canada is measuring up to agreed international standards. To rank countries of the world in order of merit, as you sometimes must, as foreign service officers, is a meaningless exercise since the process is based on indefensible criteria.

We are inclined in a pragmatic way to use the word democratic as a moving phrase having different values at different times. Certainly during war time we were quite prepared to set aside some so-called democratic principles. In addition, however, we are inclined to consider different democratic principles in different ways depending on the political considerations. There have been times, for example, when one could argue that the Government of South Korea was not a democratic government. This became a complex situation on which to make firm judgment, particularly when Canada participated in the Korean War. We also have had a different view of a country's democratic condition over time. There were periods when it was possible to regard the government of Taiwan as undemocratic, but that has certainly not been our assessment in recent years. There have been periods when various governments in Asia had some form of dictatorship and we have often been reluctant to describe such governments as undemocratic and conclude that we should discontinue relations with them. In general we have followed the principle that our Canadian national interest was related to the peoples of such countries. This principle has enabled us to maintain contact with many governments whose structure could not be described as democratic.

In the final analysis the Canadian government has not been inclined to list countries that are either democratic or not or whether they observe human rights. I believe that this practice has helped us since the way you put a country on such a list invariably produces positions in bilateral relations that are hard to defend. When I was responsible for Burma, it was under the leadership of General Ne Win who led the country from 1962 at least to 1988. Although the regime has had military rulers of a different name since 1988 there are those who argue that even in very old age General Ne Win has a significant influence on the Burmese government. I did not have continuous personal contact with General Ne Win. I had a useful presentation of credentials, as already reported, and I used to at least shake hands and sometimes have conversations at the national day on the fourth of January. I was in any case conscious of his views and, from time to time, made proposals which I know went before him. In the period between 1967 and 1971 the style of the Burmese government was on the whole moderate. It certainly seemed to have the support of many Burmese, although there were, into the 1990s, serious insurgencies in many areas on the frontiers of Burma and the election of 1988 is still disputed. One of the reasons for changing the name of the country from Burma to Myanmar was that Burmans are the majority racial group within the country but there are other significant groupings with whom a balanced relationship must at all times be maintained. Over time most of these groups have modified some-what their armed struggle for independence, and there is certainly an improvement in the security situation in the country in 1999 which makes it very different from my period.

During my four years I think that on the whole the Canadian author-ities found it possible to maintain balanced relations with Burma and to conduct a significant aid programme. Indeed, the aid programme, which it could be said was revived in the period between 1967 and 1971, continued until 1988 when, following the large scale losses from civil disorder and the reimposition of martial law, Canadian relations with Burma were severely strained and all aid stopped. As I write this piece in 1999 there are some signs that the UN is prepared to lead some kind of dialogue with the Government of Myanmar which might result in substantial UN sponsored aid directed first of all at reducing the international drug problems and then at malaria eradication. It is too soon to tell whether in due course Canadian-Burma relations can return to some of the levels which applied to the period when I was responsible. However, in that period I was not required to certify that Burma was "democratic" or observed standards of human rights acceptable to us. I believe that the fact that Canada did not attempt to establish arbitrary standards which would apply rigidly to the world produced a flexible situation which was to our advantage. We will, I trust, be true to our convictions when we are sure what they are and when we have developed them "carefully" and with a degree of "humility" – both subjective words.

Opposing the Policy of Concentration

One policy issue forced me to differ openly and as forcefully as I could from my base in Kuala Lumpur. It had an immediate importance to the possibil-ity of Canada conducting development cooperation programmes. The issue applied from 1967 to 1971 to Burma and also to Singapore. In 1967, the British had recently implemented a policy of military withdrawal from South and Southeast Asia. Very large military bases in Singapore would close. It was not possible to predict the enormous economic success that Singapore has achieved since the British withdrawal. The future looked cloudy and uncertain. Singapore was a very small country and not a coun-try of "concentration." I argued, as strongly as I could, for some aid pro-grammes, particularly in the field of technical education. Eventually I was successful and we did undertake a number of programmes which I would like to think helped to create the industrial infrastructure which enabled Singapore to rapidly develop.

Similarly, Burma was not a country of "concentration" and one had to argue from the beginning of my assignment that it should be eligible for at least some forms of economic aid. As I have earlier described I began to make this argument as soon as I returned from Burma after the Colombo Plan Conference in the fall of 1967.

The policy of concentration emerged mainly from a series of parliamentary committees who were persuaded by witnesses that it was wise to provide our aid to a few countries and to work where it was easiest to operate with well-prepared and efficient local governments. These are superficial arguments since the result of adopting such principles would be for Canada to undertake programmes in only the large South and Southeast Asian countries and virtually ignore the needs of the smaller countries. In many respects the large countries were much better off by reason of their size and resources and more capable of attracting foreign investment. They had well established administrations, but in some cases this left much to be desired in the actual distribution of aid. For example, one could make a large investment of funds for social forestry (i.e. the provision of funds to local authorities for the planting of trees) and then find that the aid had passed from a central government with whom an agreement could be reached, down to the provincial and then to the local governments where there was much less supervision than needed and sometimes hardly any long-term control. It was not always the case that large scale projects undertaken in the large countries of Asia would have the best results in terms of the Canadian national interest. An additional problem was that many of the Asian countries in the 1950s, 1960s and 1970s followed patterns of economic development that were heavily centralized in nature. Industry was favored over agriculture, and corruption and incapacity significantly affected administrations.

While responsible for Burma, I sent a series of messages to Ottawa which flatly opposed the policy of concentration of aid. Indeed, I faced almost exactly the same problems, although often in a different policy context, when I was responsible in later years for Nepal in India and for Afghanistan from Pakistan. In each case there was reluctance to develop programmes in the smaller countries.

I did not favour large amounts of major capital aid for the smaller Colombo Plan countries, but I did recommend modest levels of technical assistance for trainees and for advisors, and some degree of development loan or grant aid for small projects. I agreed that we did not have the administrative capability in Burma to conduct a major programme, but I suggested that we could structure the programme so that it could be administered from Canada and be managed by my officer's visits from Kuala Lumpur. I argued that relatively modest amounts of aid would give us significant influence in Burma (and Singapore) and that this influence could help with democratization, human rights, and commercial efforts. I argued that the smaller countries were more vulnerable to economic fluctuations, particularly of raw material prices, and that any kind of assistance had a disproportionately significant result.

I also argued that in competitive terms we would be at a disadvantage against other countries, particularly those from Europe, who had significant aid programmes. Further, there was no evidence that multilateral aid (often proposed as an alternative to any Canadian aid at all) was more efficient or more effective than might be modest Canadian bilateral programmes. There should be, in the Canadian interest, a judicious mix of support for multilateral and bilateral aid.

Finally, I argued that sometimes important political and other international developments were influenced by countries on the margins of world affairs. While Canada was not a great world power it is possible from time to time to have a significant impact on events of direct and indirect Canadian national interest, even in Burma.

When and Where Did the Colombo Plan Die?

It could be argued, and may well be generally accepted as truth in 1999, that the Colombo Plan has virtually disappeared. There were obvious trends in that direction during 1967 through 1971 while I was much involved in Colombo Plan affairs. When aid programmes began in the late 1940s, the Colombo Plan was virtually the only international effort in the field. The British initiated the plan itself, but Canadians played a significant role in its creation on broad international humanitarian grounds. To the British in 1947, it was essential that there should be some forum to promote the economic development in South and Southeast Asia for the countries which were struggling with independence and with the effects of the Second World War. These goals were to be pursued without draining down the sterling balances too precipitously. The United States was just beginning its overseas development aid programme and the meetings of the Colombo Plan each year were important events. It was obvious at the Rangoon Colombo Plan meeting of 1967 that aid patterns in South and Southeast Asia were changing. Most major donors by 1967 had developed substantial bilateral programmes. The United States had a very large programme involving every possible kind of development cooperation and it had become much more significant and widespread than, of course, it was in the 1940s. The same development had occurred with Canada. Our aid administration, after several re-organizations, was large and complex. As a result there was no particular need for a structure like that of the Colombo Plan. To the large aid donors the Colombo Plan constituted a long commitment of time and effort – sometimes six weeks – when working groups and drafting bodies met, followed by meetings of officials and then by ministers meetings. The Colombo Plan meetings also involved the preparation of an annual report. At the beginning this annual report served as a valuable document. It provided a record of the programmes and objectives of the so-called donor countries and of the economic plans of the receiving countries, involving a good deal of statistical material. The recipients were expected each year to produce an analysis of their economic situation and account for the use they were making of their aid. For some of the smaller receiving countries this was quite a burden. Sometimes the Canadian delegation privately assisted them to do an annual economic document. The problem for the donor countries was that they had their own reporting schedules to follow for parliamentary bodies and, in addition, they had to prepare material for other aid organizations including the UN, the Development Assistance Committee (DAC) of the OECD (Organization for Economic and Cultural Development), the Economic Commission for Asia and the Far East, the IBRD and the IMF (International Monetary Fund). There was a reluctance to put too much additional work into Colombo Plan material. The pattern for aid development was firmly of a bilateral nature and the Colombo Plan, never really a multilateral organization, began to fall into disuse. It had no or very modest funds to distribute. The level of attendance at Colombo Plan meetings declined with the result that medium level officials and sometimes, as in the case of Canada, ambassadors attended the ministerial meeting on behalf of their countries.

Around 1967 an annual negotiation would begin and follow a predictable course. The American or the British administration would begin by questioning the value of the Colombo Plan meetings and raising the possibility that the organization might be changed, downgraded, or even eliminated. These suggestions which were privately conveyed would get very little

Canadian response although Canada had already begun to favour different procedures and different channels than the Colombo Plan. Approaches might then be made to the large countries of the region, particularly India and Pakistan. These two countries, although sensitive to the position of each other, would generally have no particular position on whether or not the Colombo Plan should be supported. They were large enough and had sufficiently developed administrative machinery to make them relatively independent of the Colombo Plan structure. Australia tended to favour some change in the Colombo Plan itself, but because it was going through a period in which there was emphasis on Australia's membership in Asian affairs, Australia would be sensitive to the reactions of the regional Colombo Plan members. Ceylon would favour maintenance of the Colombo Plan (perhaps partly because it was born in Colombo) and would react negatively to any suggestion that it be altered or seriously changed. Word of these discussions would eventually reach the smaller countries of the Colombo Plan, and Burma, Nepal, Bhutan, and sometimes Afghanistan and other smaller Colombo Plan countries would react negatively to any change in the Plan. As a consequence, India and Pakistan would then be sensitive to the smaller countries, Australia would draw back, and then Canada, the United Kingdom and the United States would decide that they were not prepared to press the issue. The Colombo Plan annual meeting would go ahead more or less as scheduled. This atmosphere continued for a number of years. In 1968 the meetings were held in Seoul, Korea. (Conference room 4, as I remember, was complete with slot machines because the meeting was held at the infamous Walker Hill resort). Again, because the meeting was held in one of the smaller countries, there was little or no querying of the Colombo Plan machinery.

In 1969 it had been decided that the meeting would be held in Canada and I was asked to come back from Kuala Lumpur and take charge of the meeting as its Secretary General. When I returned, my first action was to write a memorandum to the senior Ottawa officials and ask them what our objectives might be during the meeting. I said that as the host country Canada was in a position to have some influence over the conduct of the meetings. There was no permanent secretariat of the Colombo Plan and each host country was free to organize the meetings as it wished, in accordance with past practice. There was a Bureau for Technical Cooperation in Colombo and sometimes that bureau could assist member governments if they were unsure how the Colombo Plan meeting was to be organized. The meetings produced substantial records each year which provided the host country with a lot of useful material.

My submission was that we could, if we began negotiations early enough, substantially address the future of the Colombo Plan and quite possibly lay the groundwork for its termination. However, the political reactions as described above would be the consequences. Therefore, if we decided on general grounds not to formally propose the termination of the Colombo Plan, which might be the course of wisdom, we could try to restructure it so that it might have a better chance for the future. I was told to go ahead and reorganize as best I could. This is what happened at the Victoria, B.C. meeting.

It is possible that over time the major donor countries, the United States and the United Kingdom in particular, found the Colombo Plan procedure cumbersome. There was a strong tradition of equality among all Colombo Plan members. Every country was expected to report in more or less the same way. Indeed, at the Rangoon meetings Canada was asked to assist with French translations in order to make possible the participation of the Indochina countries (Laos, Cambodia and Vietnam). I suppose that as the procedures of the World Bank and the IMF evolved, in which there was no question of the authority and voting rights of the major donor countries, the Colombo Plan began to slip in priority.

This decline may also have been due to the fact that there were no financial decisions taken at Colombo Plan meetings. Discussions at the meetings had an indirect effect on a number of government policies. Some donors found that the conduct of their aid programmes came under criticism at Colombo Plan meetings. Debates developed over the extent to which deficit financing was appropriate in developing countries and over the ways in which counterpart funds were established and used. The major donor countries and the major recipients came to the conclusion, however, that their objectives for the conduct of aid were met mainly in bilateral discussions. While at the UN there could be private bilateral exchanges in the corridors, both donors and recipients preferred that any difficulties be discussed privately at national capitals rather than at Colombo Plan meetings. The discussions at the Colombo Plan meetings and the documents prepared for them became less and less important.

It is also true that as the years went by the work of the Colombo Plan was in every respect overtaken by the expanding programmes of the IBRD and the IMF. Indeed, there was no point in discussing international financial flows or international financial stability at the Colombo Plan meetings since these two areas were the responsibilities of other international organizations. Even overall aid coordination and the study of particular regional problems were transferred gradually to the Economic Commission for Asia and the Far East located in Bangkok, and to the Asian Development Bank in Manila. The Colombo Plan was superseded by other international structures. Even the Commonwealth as an institution developed a substantial aid programme and undertook programs that in the 1940s and 50s might easily have been initiated within the Colombo Plan. However, international organizations, which are relatively easy to establish, are hard to stop and the Colombo Plan withered very slowly. Sometimes at its meetings the decline was imperceptible. The changes at Victoria were, in retrospect, a kind of final effort at recovery.

The Rise and Fall of Technical Assistance

The provision of technical assistance was the last of the Colombo Plan's structures to be downgraded. The reason was that at the Colombo Plan meetings administrative procedures were worked out under which individuals from Asia went to the so-called donor countries for undergraduate and postgraduate study. In the same way, the sending of experts from the so-called advanced countries to the Third World was regulated and controlled by Colombo Plan processes. Many receiving countries liked these procedures because they had been worked out by an organization in which they had full control. One of our initiatives at the Rangoon and subsequent meetings was to replace the word "expert," which had pejorative connotations, with the word "advisor," which had much better psychological associations in the Third World. Another factor affecting the fellowship and scholarship programmes was that it was soon discovered that many of the participants remained behind in the developed countries at the conclusion of their studies rather than returning to their home countries. The so-called brain drain was discussed repeatedly at Colombo Plan meetings. During my time in Southeast Asia I was once asked to go to Laos, Cambodia, and Vietnam and explain to them that Canada had outstanding francophone educational institutions. The three Indochinese countries had been offered Canadian fellowships and scholarships since the plan began, but had put all their effort into sending their students to France. I was able in the course of a two month period, equipped with the calendars of most of Canada's major francophone institutions, to make it clear to the governments of the three countries that there would indeed be some advantage to using some of our offers. Soon after my arrival in the three countries, I called on the French mission and explained that we were not attempting to compete in any way with France but that since the requirements of the three governments were so large it would no doubt be possible for some reasonable programme to be developed which would make use of Canadian aid. Generally speaking I had a favourable response from the French authorities who, of course, still enjoyed a major influence over these local governments. Following my visit in the autumn of 1955, fairly significant numbers of Laotians, Cambodians and Vietnamese went to Canada. Very few of them returned to their home countries and almost invariably they applied for permanent residence in Canada. This is perhaps not very surprising given the turmoil in Indochina. I remember that when, much later, I headed a task force that supervised our departure from Saigon in 1974 I found echoes of this Colombo Plan experience. We were assisting our post in its withdrawal from Saigon and from the Indochinese community which had Canadian connections. The stage has now been reached in 1999 when it could be said the Colombo plan had withered away. This has not been done as a result of a formal decision so much as a result of a gradual decline of interest and support. Some Colombo Plan programmes continued in some form or another. For a long time the United States financed a drug education programme which was operated out of Colombo and there was a Colombo Plan college which performed a useful role for some years. Aid programmes which were described as "Colombo Plan programmes" gradually stopped being described as such and were overtaken by increasingly complex bilateral development programmes or new multilateral aid programmes. Even the Burmese shifted their priorities to ASEAN.

A Canadian Initiative – "A Reverse Aid Flow"

Soon after I became high commissioner to Malaysia and to Singapore, and ambassador to Burma, I developed a proposal for a new form of international aid. I made this suggestion to Ottawa, and in November of 1967 I was authorized by telegram to make a "reverse aid proposal" in general terms at the Rangoon meetings of the Colombo Plan. I did so at a meeting of the technical cooperation committee of the Colombo Plan and on the whole it received a broadly favourable response. The report of that committee contained the following paragraph:

The idea of the regional member countries of the Colombo Plan offering fellowships in technical and economic fields to the non-regional countries was raised. The committee considered the proposal favourably and felt that the Council for Technical Cooperation in Colombo might consider pursuing it with the member countries.

This was all that was necessary to get the idea carried to a further stage. We later circulated a document describing it in greater detail as an idea designed to broaden the nature of the cooperation between the countries of the South and Southeast Asia and the so-called donor countries on a mutually advantageous basis.

Even the smallest of the recipient countries in South and Southeast Asia had educational facilities which would be of interest to relatively small numbers of individuals from developed countries. There would always be students in the United Kingdom, the United States, Canada, Australia, and New Zealand who would wish to study and work in South and Southeast Asia. The governments of that region were also proud of their various centres of excellence. Aid under the Colombo Plan did not have to be a one-way street.

When the proposal was first made, there were a number of obvious administrative and practical difficulties, not all of which I tried to meet. In the documents which were eventually distributed at the Council for Technical Cooperation in Colombo, the more obvious issues were briefly considered. Of course, the concept was not totally new. There had always been a few individuals coming to South and Southeast Asia for study. These individuals came more or less on their own. It seemed possible that if the Colombo Plan encouraged this kind of activity, these individuals might be in a better position when a general framework governed their work. It seemed also that if the governments of the region considered the matter there might be a number of situations not previously identified in which individuals could come to institutions in their countries. Under the Colombo Plan a framework had been developed to enable students to go from South and Southeast Asia to the donor countries. These arrangements provided for the selection and preparation of the students and for the terms and conditions under which they were supported in their programs abroad. It would not be too difficult, I thought, to work out similar arrangements to cover individuals coming the other way. In the case of Canada, for example, a considerable administrative framework had been established in

Ottawa to manage Colombo Plan fellowships and scholarships. There had also been a surprising number of organizations established across Canada to assist individuals from South and Southeast Asia coming to study at Canadian institutions.

In early 1968 Allan Strachan, then Director of the Colombo Plan Bureau, took the initiative in negotiating the reverse aid flow initiative with governments in and out of the region. In one of his papers the advantages of a so-called reverse flow were listed. One key advantage was to create and maintain potential experts who would have first-hand experience in their own specialized fields following courses of study in the countries of South and Southeast Asia. A British delegate noted that following the colonial period there were a number of individuals in his country with long experience in South and Southeast Asia. However, in the nature of things, this body of expertise would be reduced and there would be advantages in encouraging expertise familiar with advanced centres of training in South and Southeast Asia. There had been a number of institutions in the non-regional areas established which would benefit from programmes of study abroad. In addition there were institutions in South and Southeast Asia of high quality which could certainly provide experience and training that would help in developing educational and commercial exchanges between the two regions. The programme would add to the background and experience of these centres in the region. The last advantage listed was that the programme would promote "goodwill and understanding as in all other technical assistance programmes." A series of practical comments followed on how to get the programme started which would involve activity by the Council for Technical Cooperation in Colombo in obtaining ideas from the regional countries of areas in which they would be willing to accept students from abroad. It was emphasized that there was no expectation that there would be a large number of places available since the objective of the Colombo Plan was the promotion of economic development in the region and this was a more generally and mutually advantageous programme. It was suggested, for example, that there might only be a few positions offered from each of the countries in the region open to the non-regional countries, and that the positions would be for periods of research and for post-graduate work and advanced studies, since there was no intention of adding to the strain that was already obvious on the under-graduate facilities in South and Southeast Asia. It was also realized that the foreign exchange costs would have to be provided from outside the region but that local costs in each case might well be provided on agreed levels by the recipient countries of the region.

From Kuala Lumpur I reported on this programme to all the Canadian missions in the Colombo Plan area. The Bureau in Colombo's survey of past experience with this kind of assignment also identified the areas in which opportunities could be expected. They included such fields as tropical medicine, tropical agriculture, tropical forestry, rubber cultivation and research, rice cultivation and research, tea cultivation and research, geology and mining. These were areas in which considerable expertise was accumulated in the regional countries of the Colombo Plan and advanced research and study fields established.

During 1968 it became clear that the idea was beginning to attract attention in the region and, when I was appointed as the Canadian representative to the 1968 conference to be held in Seoul in the fall, I went there expecting that the concept could be further pursued. I heard nothing from Ottawa of any further development of our own position but when the officials from Ottawa arrived in Korea and we had our first delegation meetings I was told that CIDA was unable to support further exploration of the idea. After study of the concept in Ottawa, it had been determined that Colombo Plan funds authorized by parliament could not be used to finance travel or study by Canadians going overseas to the regional countries of the Colombo Plan. This was a position which I thought could, with effort, be dealt with, that is, it might be possible to get agreement in Ottawa for the possibility of minor expenses to provide the international travel costs with the other expenses being assumed by the countries of the region. I suppose officials in Ottawa might have been concerned that there would be a good deal of administration involved in selecting Canadians to go abroad and in negotiating the conditions of their assignments. Of course there was no intention of stimulating anything comparable to the Colombo Plan programme for students to Canada. However, it was clear that there would have to be further effort provided in Ottawa to enable Canada to play its part in a new programme under the Colombo Plan. Thus, while I was not instructed to withdraw our initiative I was not able to support it at the meetings in Korea and in the absence of a defender the programme did not develop. So far as I know little further action was taken in the Council for Technical Cooperation and no other country picked up the concept.

However, in this as in other policy matters it is possible that the suggestions we made in 1968 fell on fertile ground in a number of unexpected ways. For example, I have been told that the idea stimulated discussions which began in New Delhi in 1968 and which led to the establishment of the Shastri Indo-Canadian Institute. This was (and is) an important programme to promote cultural and educational exchanges between Canada and India. That programme has grown from strength to strength. Under it large numbers of Canadian fellows and scholars have gone to India and worked at Indian institutions. The flow has been mainly (as we had proposed in Rangoon) of senior Canadians doing post-graduate work at Indian institutions, although there are groups of undergraduates who have gone for short periods of exposure to India and its educational institutions. There have also been a substantial number of Indian scholars coming to Canada for work at Canadian institutions and there have certainly been many joint exchanges both ways between Canadian and Indian universities. Book exchanges have developed and other related programmes.

It is also my assessment, although I have not of course been able to follow this up in detail, that many institutions in South and Southeast Asia have made available places for individuals from outside the region with mutually beneficial results. Our reverse aid proposal may have encouraged authorities in the South and Southeast Asian countries to believe that their institutions had international value. Exchanges between the countries of the region were also encouraged on a significant scale.

Ottawa made a decision in later years that technical assistance would be offered when it was a supplement to a large capital aid programme, but not as a completely separate and ongoing general programme. The result was that the number of Asian students at Canadian institutions declined. In the fullness of time a foreign students programme had to be re-invented largely at the initiative of educational institutions in Canada. They discovered the important market open to them if they were able to offer facilities for which the countries of South and Southeast Asia seemed glad and able to pay. However, for students going the other way there has not been any organized encouragement. There should be joint public and private support for this activity. The French have realized they have fallen behind and have started a major effort.

A Canadian Security Defence Technical Assistance Programme

By May of 1968 I also put forward from Kuala Lumpur a proposal that consideration be given to a Canadian security defence technical assistance programme. I suggested that "Canada should consider offering security defence technical assistance to selected countries of South and Southeast Asia in a form that would be comparable, but smaller to our economic technical assistance programmes."

I had been a soldier in the Second World War and came from an environment in Toronto and Ottawa in which relationships with the defence services were an integral part of foreign policy efforts. My External Affairs service beginning in 1950 in Ottawa included substantial contacts in the intelligence area with the Canadian armed services and my associations in my first posting as head of mission to Kuala Lumpur and Singapore included responsibility for relating to their defence communities.

Malaysia had succeeded in turning back a major subversive threat from communist guerilla forces. Indeed, one of the dispatches to which I devoted considerable effort after arrival in Kuala Lumpur was an analysis of why the British authorities had been successful in containing communist subversion in Malaysia when the American forces had faced such difficulties in Vietnam. This led me to oppose any support for the so-called domino theory, which was used to justify western intervention in Vietnam. It was relatively obvious from the contacts I made on arrival in Malaysia and also in Burma that in those two countries strong domestic nationalist forces were capable of resisting communist subversion. It was clear, although the fight went on for years, that the Burmese armed forces were having success combatting Red flag and White flag insurgency in Burma; and it was also clear that the Malaysian authorities were gradually eliminating the threat of subversion in the jungles along the Thai border. Similarly apparent in Singapore was the fact that nationalism had produced a strong reaction against communist subversion in the trade union movement and the armed forces. The security authorities in Singapore had made considerable progress in combatting any form of communist subversion. No dominoes were falling in my three countries of accreditation.

The Canadian defence forces had few direct connections with the countries of Southeast Asia. There had been some navy visits to Singapore and to Malaysia but no contacts of any kind with the armed forces of Burma. We did have some prospects for the sale of aircraft in all three countries.

However, with respect to Burma it was not feasible to consider any direct relationships between the Canadian and the Burmese military authorities. In Singapore and Malaysia some connections were possible partly because those two countries were Commonwealth members. Long standing British associations with Burma in the defence field, arising from the extensive military campaigns in the Second World War, meant that for the British some connections did continue afterwards. However, my experience in Malaysia and Singapore did lead me to conclude that Canada was at a disadvantage in our relations with these two countries because there was so little content in our overall foreign policy which reflected the record and experience of the Canadian armed forces.

In all these countries other governments operated what could be described as an integrated foreign policy to which their defence forces made a consistent contribution. In Kuala Lumpur for example, there were active military officers attached to the British, Australian, and New Zealand missions who contributed greatly to the overall successful functioning of their embassies. The same was true of the American embassy and for a large number of other embassies who regularly had military or defence staff. In my service period, there were no Canadian military attachés resident in Malaysia or Singapore. RCMP officers paid regular visits to Kuala Lumpur and Singapore from Hong Kong essentially on immigration-security business, but I came to consider that we were losing out in comparison to other governments for lack of a contribution from the Canadian defence services.

It was not possible to envisage any kind of formal defence relationship or treaty between Canada and Malaysia and Singapore and therefore the only possibility it seemed to me was some form of technical cooperation. I should note that Canada did provide a Canadian air force officer, Brigadier General Keith Greenaway, who came out as an advisor to the Chief of Staff of the Royal Malaysian air force during my time. This assignment had been worked out bilaterally as the result of a Malaysian initiative and was an outstanding success. General Greenaway was not a member of the Canadian High Commission in Kuala Lumpur and his responsibilities were entirely to the chief of staff of the Royal Malaysian Air Force. Nevertheless he was a member of the Canadian community and he turned out to be a great help to me in developing my modest golfing capabilities. We played regularly on the Royal Selangor Golf Club Courses. He made a significant contribution to the development of the Royal Malaysian Air Force.

The proposal which I eventually made in May 1968 was drafted with broad relevance to Canadian foreign policy. It envisaged the training in Canada of small numbers of the armed services of the Third World in Canada at military training facilities. These facilities were based on our needs for large armed services after the Second World War in response to pressures from NATO, from the war in Korea, and from peacekeeping. Nevertheless there were possibilities for using these facilities for a broader training programme than that required directly by the Canadian Armed Services. Other countries drew benefits from training programmes for foreign nationals at their defence establishment chiefly in terms of defence sales. Canada has never been a significant exporter of military hardware but there are a number of fields particularly in respect of dual use aircraft and civilian items required for foreign armed forces where Canadian capabilities have advantages. For example, the military attaché in Islamabad in my time (1972 to 1974) managed to secure a major contract for footwear in Iran during his period of responsibility for the Middle East. Canada has certainly been the source of a good deal of expertise in the development of arctic cold weather gear, and there are many other possibilities that could benefit the Canadian economy.

There are as many benefits to Canada from having been involved in the training of foreign officials in the fields of defence as there are in the fields of finance. There are many countries of the world in which the defence services have important and continuing responsibility in the government. If by definition you have no relationship with those defence services, then a Canadian representative is at a big disadvantage in developing a serious relationship with that country. You cannot be selective in deciding which elements of a government you should connect with if you expect to have full overall cooperation with that government. I have argued that the relationships between Canada and many foreign countries are as dependent on administrative and technical capacity in the military field as they are in the economic field. Similarly, we have favored regional cooperation where in many parts of the world that cooperation requires extensive military relationships. We are unable to participate actively unless we have some kind of defence related capability.

Canadians are uniquely positioned to encourage defence relationships with other countries partly because our services would be regarded as non-threatening and as defensive in nature, in keeping with our overall defence policies. Thus in sensitive areas there is a willingness to consider Canadian expertise as an alternative to the provision of such expertise from more threatening countries. There have been a number of cases where governments have sought Canadian help in areas of financial and administrative control and in services management techniques.

Conclusion: Some Modest Progress Here and There

It is not easy to review the recommendations I made from abroad and to assess our success or failure in the four years involved. I should emphasize that I tried at all times to operate a consolidated and cooperative mission and depended heavily on the staff members assigned to my post. Therefore, I do not represent the successes or failures as being the result of my efforts, especially since there were many outstanding officers who worked with me in this period.

To take one of the major policy issues with which I was faced – the policy of concentration – I believe we made a significant impact from Kuala Lumpur. As the years went by, the phrase "policy of concentration" gradually fell into disuse and was succeeded by a series of policy directions which were applied to all Canadian aid programmes irrespective of their size. This process was helped by the fact that as our aid resources shrank we became less and less able to undertake and less and less interested in major capital infrastructure programmes. I think there is also recognition that, perhaps because we came to depend on the NGOs more, we should continue to be involved in the programmes of the smaller countries.

When I left Kuala Lumpur in 1971 we had a significant programme in Burma, a useful one in Singapore, and a major programme of development cooperation in Malaysia. It could be said that, insofar as development cooperation was concerned, the pressures we reflected from Kuala Lumpur were by and large accepted in Ottawa. I believe Harold Innis would have approved the fact that policies initiated on the frontiers were sometimes of importance to the central authorities in Canada.

I also believe we contributed to reducing Burma's isolation. Of course, it used to be a form of humour among diplomats in Rangoon to argue that there were "signs of change in Burma's policies" when in fact there were no really important changes at all in the period 1967 through 1971. However, Burma did cautiously begin to have relations with the IBRD and the IMF and with the Asian Development Bank; and perhaps these contacts contributed to Burma's subsequent willingness to become associated with ASEAN which has made a major contribution to recent Burmese contacts with other countries. In a general political sense I think Canadian connections with Burma did support a gradual awareness in Rangoon that rigid socialism – or what was described as the London School of Economics model – was not working to Burma's advantage and that a more varied and complicated set of economic policies involving at least some kind of private sector were required. Although

Burma's isolation remains greater than for many other countries in 1999, there is a different atmosphere, if only one of degree, than there was for the policies I encountered on arrival in Rangoon in 1967. I think we may also have played our part in enabling the Burmese to thread their way through the confusions of the non-aligned period; we may have in a small way encouraged Burma to protect its independence from the USSR and China. I think also that in the fullness of time we came to understand the Burmese unwillingness to be associated in any way with the war in Indochina.

One of the fundamentals that affected the way we conducted ourselves in Burma, Malaysia, and Singapore was the concern for the promotion of Canadian national unity. Certainly in my period all missions abroad were expected to do whatever they could to promote this objective. This meant that we took great care to ensure that we were as bilingual as we could be and that we treated all businesses equally wherever their roots in Canada might be. We also took care to avoid any statements or contacts which would call into question our support for national unity abroad in any countries with whom we were associated. In dealing with the press we had constantly in mind the need to avoid any comment which would exacerbate the national unity debate at home. I do not suggest that this is any less of a priority in 1999 than it was in 1967, but I should emphasize that the importance of national unity was very much before us at all times in our dealings with Malaysia, Singapore, and Burma. Indeed all three countries during our period had significant national unity issues with some of which we were able to provide modest low key assistance. Furthermore, they never created any problems for us, so perhaps we explained ourselves well enough.

Although it seems a little strange to describe this policy in 1999 we were also conscious in the period of a need to oppose in any way the spread of communism. I continued to believe that some of our allies underestimated the strength of national movements. This was true in the cases of Malaysia, Singapore, and Burma but there were times when, by example or by public statement, we were able to support the resistance of the societies in which we were working to any communist threat.

There was also, of course, the problem of dealing with geographic distance. It is a fact that Canada's relations with the countries of South and Southeast Asia are greatly affected, indeed governed, by the distance separating Canada and the countries of this region. Even British Columbia interests were somewhat slow to take advantage of opportunities in Malaysia, Singapore, and Burma. I well recall, for example, writing directly to all the

Canadian Banks in this period and drawing their attention to the importance of opening branches in Malaysia and Singapore. I did not make exactly the same recommendations in respect of Burma but gradually the Canadian Banks did move from Hong Kong and Tokyo, where they were long established, to Malaysia and Singapore and at least they took account of the possibility of further developments in Burma. It has remained important that Canadian missions abroad make special efforts to help any Canadian interests showing a willingness to enter into commercial discussions in Malaysia, Singapore, and Burma. The costs of air travel alone, however, were prohibitive for smaller businesses and even the major Canadian multinationals found it hard to maintain offices or to conduct significant operations at such a long distance from Canada.

Later discussion about how Canada was accredited in its representation to Burma continued with many of the same arguments used when the subject was raised in 1967. For a time, the responsibility for representation to Rangoon was transferred from Kuala Lumpur to Bangladesh and then later from Bangladesh to Bangkok. I don't suppose it makes much difference to the Burmese whether our official representation comes from Bangladesh or from Bangkok. There is a tendency to favour whatever decision the Canadians take in this respect with some emphasis on the reputation of the particular person involved. At the present time the Burmese seem very happy with the effort put into Myanmar-Canadian relations by our Ambassador in Bangkok.

One change has been the transfer of ongoing Canadian representation in Rangoon from the British Embassy to the Australian Embassy. I am not familiar with the specific reasons for this decision but it seems to have been taken largely for general reasons within the context of Canada's representation in South and Southeast Asia. It reflected to some extent the desire to economize in our overall costs for representation in Asia. It may be also that the British in one way or another asked to be relieved of any burden we may have been putting on them. I don't think the Burmese would have found a change necessary since, with all the difficulties of the past taken fully into account, Burmese-British relations have always remained at a significant level. One factor that might be considered is that Australia is in fact one of our main potential competitors in Myanmar. There are Australian mining interests and petroleum interests in direct competition with any conceivable Canadian interests in these fields. In agricultural commodities, particularly wheat, and other areas even including aircraft production, we are in direct competition with the Australians in Myanmar. The Australians also have a somewhat more aggressive international foreign policy and of a somewhat different style than that of Canada.

Predicting, with Hesitancy, the Future

My own experience from 1967 to 1971 suggests that there are reasons for which we should take some care in the maintenance of our relations with Burma. One of these is that the Burmese have so far been consistent in their decision to maintain representation in Ottawa, and the other is that sooner or later Myanmar will become of commercial and economic interest to the Canadian economy. As in all diplomacy, you maintain channels which might be important in the future even though their present value may be hard to see.

One general factor will be constant regardless of future economic and political developments in the region. It is the unique, and to most objective observers, the attractive features of Burmese society. Although violence and prejudice have been evident at times in Burma (as in their past relations with the Indian and the Chinese communities), fundamentally the Burmese are and have been circumspect in their international relations. They have been slow to condemn, and are rigorously independent and nationalist in their views. This has given them a standing in international affairs, which resulted, for example, in the decision to appoint U Thant as Secretary General of the United Nations.

The Burmese are also a devout community. Their religion is an everyday factor in people's lives and, except for some periods in the U Nu regime, religion is regarded as independent of political processes. The way in which Burmese pagodas have been maintained over the centuries is per-haps the most striking evidence of this commitment to Buddhism. The Shwedagon Pagoda in Rangoon must be considered one of the small number of truly great ancient religious monuments. It is certainly compa-rable in its importance to its own society and in its uniqueness, beauty and historical importance to St. Paul's Cathedral, London, for example. There are other religious monuments of antiquity and importance in Burma which are carefully protected.

There is a tradition of respect for education in Burmese society, includ-ing in the countryside, with the result that Burma has one of the highest adult literacy levels of any country in Asia. It is also quite striking that women have played an important role in Burmese history and still play an important and recognized role in Burmese affairs.

There are other special features of Burmese society. They include a unique form of ritual dancing, extraordinary woven fabrics, impressive carving, distinctive pottery and indeed religious and cultural artifacts of all kinds. The Burmese have a particular gift for the use of lights and the presidential buildings and the grounds are lit in an unusually attractive manner at the time of the national day. There is a rich cultural heritage of all kinds which is very attractive and interesting to those from outside.

Forget, Ignore, or Constructively Engage

There are a number of at least theoretical options for the future of Burma-Canadian relations. One of these is to ignore Burma as too far away and too peripheral to Canadian interests. I found it impossible to support this posture when I was accredited to Burma and I believe there are very few who would take this position even in 1999. Such a position did not work well in respect of the PRC and, as somebody who participated in developing a Canadian posture for our relations with the People's Republic of China, I find such attitudes arid and contrary to the Canadian national interest.

There is another option, which is to adopt a minimalist approach and to act when necessary but not necessarily act. This is perhaps the easiest policy in relation to Burma, but it will be seen in the foregoing analysis that I did not follow such a policy and that by and large I was supported, although seldom explicitly, by the policy infrastructure in Ottawa. I think that the extent of our relationships with Burma in the future will depend on the efforts of the individuals involved who will have to decide when to propose or support modest initiatives of one kind or another in Canada-Burma relations. The American position will also be a determinant.

One recent assessment of the situation in Burma is that it is "a train wreck about to happen." The reference was to the apparent standoff in negotiations between Aung San Suu Kyi and the military government. In assessing the likely course of international events nothing ever turns out exactly as expected, but based on my experience, and on discussions about Burma with members of the Britain-Burma society in England, it is my belief that the situation in Rangoon will not come to resemble a disastrous train wreck. In the first place, Aung San's daughter has demonstrated great skill and endurance in her campaign to secure concessions from the government and she is not likely to risk a formal confrontation and a breakdown of negotiations which might well bring large-scale casualties to her followers. At the same time, although there are not many constraints on the government of Burma, the fact is that they have also demonstrated that they wish to avoid a major confrontation which would have adverse consequences for their government and for the future of their country. It is likely, therefore, that the confrontation will continue in one form or the other. It is not possible to use the phrase "almost indefinitely" since there can be miscalculations on either side, but it is also unlikely that outside forces would attempt to intervene in this situation in such a way as to provoke a conflict. Again, there have been, in many situations around the world, times when outside forces have promoted or exaggerated internal domestic conflicts in individual regimes. However, Burma is somewhat isolated and it seems unlikely that any of Burma's neighbors would attempt a direct intervention. This would certainly not be in the tradition of Thai or Bangladesh international politics, and it does not fit the pattern of recent PRC international politics. It is even hard to imagine, given Burma's political remoteness, that there would be great power intervention from outside the region. None of the countries of ASEAN, given their own internal problems and the absence in many cases of interventionist capability, would be inclined to play such a role. Thus it seems likely that future developments in Burma would depend on domestic political factors over which there is not very much outside influence. This has indeed been the course of developments in Burma since independence in 1948.

It is a sad fact that some uprisings in post World War II have been ill timed. Even during the Second World War the revolt of the Polish forces in Warsaw just before the end was ill timed and resulted in heavy and almost pointless casualties when the revolt was put down by the German forces. There have been successful uprisings in Iran but there have been many failures. Given the strength and the discipline of the Burmese armed forces it would be a brave interpreter who thinks that they are likely to lose their determination and cohesion.

An interesting new development is the possibility of some role for the United Nations. These authorities, in the spring of 1999, began a substantial development project focusing on the control of the drug traffic in Burma's frontier regions. Any concerned observer of the scene can only wish the participants the best of luck. Presumably, most governments concerned will try to avoid any statements or actions that would create difficulties for whatever possibilities of success the discussions may have. Thus, although the phrase may have many meanings, there would seem to be a requirement for the kind of "constructive engagement" which I was able to encourage from 1967 to 1971 and which still seems to offer the best chance for stability and prosperity for the people of Myanmar.

1 John R.W. Gwynne-Timothy, *Burma Liberators – RCAF in SEAC*, Toronto: Next Level Press, 1991. Gwynne-Timothy records the achievements of about 7,500 Canadians of all ranks. It is perhaps surprising that such a large Canadian contingent in the RAF had participated during the campaign to recover Burma, but there is no doubt that this particular piece of war history had its impact on relationships between the two countries.